MY WEREWOLF SYSTEM

JKSMANGA

Podium

To my wife, Wandong Chen.

After we met, my writing journey began. None of this would have been possible without you buying me a new laptop when we had just met.

Cover design by Podium Publishing

ISBN: 978-1-0394-1795-3

Published in 2023 by Podium Publishing, ULC
www.podiumaudio.com

Podium

CHAPTER 1

AN OBSESSION

"Hey, Gary, get your butt over here and check out the highlights from yesterday's Altered fight!" a boy yelled from his seat.

The sound of the school bell rang out through the halls, signaling that it was time for lunch. Immediately opening the drawer under his desk, the boy pulled out an object. However, it wasn't a packed lunch like one would expect; instead, the boy took out a tablet and put it on the table, propping it up, tilting it so he could comfortably watch the video.

The immediate destination: PouTube, the number one video-sharing platform. Soon there was a crowd of classmates around him, all with their eyes glued to the screen.

"If you're not here in five seconds, I'm starting the video without you," Tom warned. But Gary was focused on playing with something under his desk, moving his knees up and down, and he had made sure to cover his actions from the eyes of others. Tom was starting to think his friend was doing something that could get him in serious trouble.

Bro, we're in the middle of class, come on! At least go to the bathroom if you're that desperate, Tom thought.

"Just give me a sec, okay?" Gary shouted back. "Can't you see I'm in the middle of something?" Underneath his own desk, Gary was staring at his phone. He had received a message and wasn't sure how to reply. It was already the fifth time he had typed out his response but ended up deleting it because it seemed insignificant.

Be there this evening at 6, the message read.

Duuuuun nun, dun, dun na na!

With the sound of the opening theme song playing, Gary understood they had really started without him. He had given up coming up with a proper response, and in his haste, he wrote one letter. K.

"K? . . . K? Who does this kid think he is?" a man shouted in frustration as he received the message on his end.

Meanwhile, Gary had gotten over to the others by shoving his way through the crowd, allowing him to stand directly behind his friend Tom. Just in time, for the fight was about to begin.

Two men stood opposite each other in nothing but tight shorts. Their muscles were on full display. They were proud of all the hard work they had put in for the fight this day.

In one corner, weighing in at 200 pounds, undefeated for thirteen fights in a row, stood Kirk Summerfield, a man with a small goatee and black spiked-up hair that was short on the sides.

His opponent, weighing in at 190 pounds, with a record of ten straight wins, was Sam Dillpickle. He was a shorter, bald-headed man with a creepy smile.

"Hey, don't you think these two look a bit like Tom and Gary?" one of the students suddenly mentioned.

"Holy crap, you are right! They totally look like those two!"

The students in the crowd laughed together at this discovery. Everyone but Tom and Gary themselves. Unfortunately, it was hard to deny the similarities between the two friends and the fighters.

Although Gary didn't have facial hair, even though he was sixteen, he never could grow a single hair on his face, torso, chest, or legs. He was hairless.

It was the genes that some women wished they had. Although he did have hair in one area, he promised, and made sure everyone knew that.

It was an incident many of his male classmates wished to forget. Having been teased so much about it, he decided to show everyone proof. Of course, flashing your fellow classmates wasn't the best way to prove it, and it had cost him a week's worth of detention.

At least he made sure it was during the boys' PE class; otherwise, it could have been worse.

Still, he did have the same hairstyle as Kirk, only his hair was green. It wasn't his natural hair color but a decision he had made over the summer. Everyone was initially surprised when he had come to class looking like that, but at the same time, it wasn't that strange for Gary to do something like that. He already had a reputation for doing absurd things.

As for Gary's best friend, Tom, he looked like the spitting image of the other man in the video. He wasn't exactly bald, but he always got a number one when going to the barber.

When Gary asked him about his hairstyle choice, Tom explained that it was low maintenance to keep it so short. That was pretty much his goal in life. He liked things like computers, games, TV shows, and books. Things that couldn't talk back to him.

Tom hated interacting with people so much that he refused to go to anything but the self-service scanner at supermarkets. The idea that someone would try to make conversation with him about something he didn't like was enough to send shivers down his spine.

Given their complete differences in character, it was odd that these two boys had become friends in the first place, but it had somehow worked out.

While their classmates were all busy laughing away, the fight had started.

As soon as the bell had rung, the appearance of both men in the ring had started to change slightly.

"Ladies and gentlemen, it looks like our Altereds are starting at full throttle right off the bat!" the announcer said, hyping up the crowd.

The most notable changes in Kirk were his grown-out nails as well as his skin color, which had slightly yellowed. Black spots started to appear up and down his arm, and small patches of fur showed up on his face.

On the other side, Sam's cheeks had puffed up, and his legs appeared to be slightly webbed after his change.

"As you can see, Kirk is an Altered based on a cheetah-like beast, while his opponent Sam is based on a frog type. It's going to be an interesting matchup if I do say so myself!" the announcer shouted.

The transformations took less than a second, and the first one to make a move was Sam. He whipped out his toadlike tongue and grabbed onto Kirk's forearm.

The look on Kirk's face just screamed *DISGUSTING!* He tensed up his arm, making his huge biceps grow even larger. The veins were visible, practically bulging out, and with a single slash of his claws, he managed to cut off the tongue of his opponent.

"Yes!" Gary shouted. "Come on, Kirk!"

Sam had leapt up, jumping higher than any normal person could thanks to his frog-powered legs. Alas, he just wasn't quick enough. Kirk managed to grab him by the leg before he slammed his opponent to the ground.

It didn't take long for the referee to declare Kirk the winner of this match and also the winner of this Altered fighters' rookie tournament.

What everyone was watching was known as an Altered match. It was currently the most popular combat sport globally, mostly because it featured a new breed of humans called the Altered, although some argued whether they could even be called humans anymore.

Humans had discovered fossils of the ancient beasts that used to roam the earth. They were undoubtedly the progenitors of today's animals, only fiercer, larger, and more powerful.

In the end, a scientist had made a major breakthrough and discovered a way to alter humans by injecting a fossil's DNA into a human, thereby creating what people now knew as an Altered.

These "special humans" possessed the ability to shift their appearance, changing parts of their body to mimic the beasts they had been infused with. They were stronger and faster and even aged slower than normal humans. If one was ever struck with a disease, it could change its human composition to the point where it felt like it had a new body, ridding itself of such a thing.

But not everyone could become an Altered. The fossils discovered were limited in number, and although new fossils would be unearthed every so often until science found a way to re-create them artificially, they were valued at absurd prices. Only the rich and powerful could afford to turn themselves into Altereds.

Even the contestants they were watching right now had only received this opportunity because they were sponsored by big corporations.

Nearly every boy looked up to the Altered. In a way, they were like real-life superheroes. But the two biggest fans in the room were undoubtedly Tom and Gary. They were the ones who had gotten everyone hooked on the sport in the first place.

It was normal for people to wish to one day become an Altered, and it was the same for these two. Only the reasons for them wanting to become one differed greatly.

"A big round of applause for our winner, Kirk Summerfield!" the announcer called out at the end of the show.

When a beautiful woman came onto the stage to deliver the oversized check for ten million dollars, Gary's eyes practically turned into dollar signs. The young boy was obsessed with money, and watching the Altered fight, especially the large check, he couldn't think of an easier way to quickly become rich and famous.

Ironically, this obsession with money would soon take him down a dark path. A path from which he wouldn't be able to turn back.

CHAPTER 2

THE GAME OF RUGBY

A loud, piercing whistle served as a reminder to everyone out on the school field that it was time for their daily warm-up, meaning they had to run two big laps around the school field.

School lessons might have ended, but that didn't mean it was the end of the school day.

Staring off into the distance, Gary watched the large clock on the front of the school building. He was squinting hard, trying to make out where the two hands were on the dial, not because the clock was too small but because his eyesight had gotten terrible.

Still, Gary had always refused to wear glasses. He felt like if he did, it was only admitting to himself that he had bad eyesight. He was afraid that it would only deteriorate quicker if he gave in, and it would prove that he had bad genes. Something Altered did not have.

After placing his hands on the sides of his head, he pulled slightly, narrowing his field of vision, allowing him to focus—a technique he had learned when trying to see the screen at the back of the class.

"Three thirty, I still have a lot of time left."

"Get a move on, broccoli head, unless you want my size-twelve shoe in your backside!" Mr. Root shouted. He was a large man who towered over not only the students but also all the other adults.

His last name was very fitting. If Gary didn't know any better, he would have sworn that his teacher's genes must have been mixed in with some giant ancient tree. He was that large and sturdy.

Not wanting to anger his teacher further, he joined the rest of the students trotting along at the back of the pack. There he ran side by side with his friend Tom, who was huffing and panting away.

"Why . . . do . . . they . . . want . . . to . . . kill . . . me?" Each time Tom uttered a word, he had to take a deep breath before being able to say the next.

"Did you know that it's easier to breathe if you don't speak and run at the same time?" Gary pointed out. He was doing just fine and could have passed his friend, yet he still chose to stay at the back.

It was the same every day, and this didn't go unnoticed by Tom. He was aware that Gary was staying behind because of him.

In the end, Tom decided to give up keeping up with the rest of the class and started to slow down his pace. "That's better. According to the internet, when you're jogging, you should jog at a pace where you can still talk."

"Yeah . . . but I don't think they meant this." The two of them were now moving so slowly that they were practically walking. Trying to make their loss of tempo less obvious, they were swinging their arms backward and forward, imitating those running in front of them.

Unfortunately, this didn't get past Mr. Root, and the rest of the students were now busy waiting for them.

"Just get over here, you vegetables!" he commanded.

Once the students were all lined up, Mr. Root placed a rugby ball on the ground right in front of him. Out of the lineup, he selected the largest student, a boy named Blake.

He was the pride of their class, the type who was too good to be true and usually only appeared in movies as the main character. However, this wasn't a movie, and he was right in front of his fellow students.

Blake had golden tanned skin with wavy brown hair that had just the right amount of curls. To top it off, his body was that of a naturally lean muscle builder, seemingly designed to excel in sports.

"You know, they say ten percent of the boys match with ninety percent of the girls," Tom whispered to Gary while looking at Blake. "On Binder, I mean. Not that I've used that app myself. Seriously, what's the point when I know nobody would swipe for me. That's why I go on the app, just to swipe the other direction. That way, I've rejected all of them before they could ever reject me."

"I thought you just said you didn't use the app?"

Looking at his buddy and then looking at himself, Gary was a little disheartened. It wasn't because someone like Blake must have girls lining up to be his girlfriend. No, it was because people like Blake were the perfect candidates to be chosen to become an Altered. As long as there were people like Blake in the world, how would he ever get selected?

"I won't mince words. We all know that Blake here is the best on our team. Too bad for you all that there are hundreds of Blakes out there on other teams as well," Mr. Root said, giving a very "motivating" pep talk. "What this team lacks is a good line of defense. People who can tackle. We're here to find our tacklers."

The aim of today's training was to try to either (a) get the ball off Blake while he was running toward you, stopping him from reaching the white try line, or (b) tackle him to the ground.

After everyone watched the first few students attempt and fail, it became clear that it was an impossible task. Eventually, it was time for Gary to have his go at it.

Mr. Root clearly didn't really have any high hopes for Gary, but everyone deserved an equal chance according to school regulations. He blew the whistle, and Blake started bulldozing his way toward Gary, gripping the ball tightly as if it were a newborn baby.

Hey, hey, can't you go easy on me? Gary thought. *My weak little hands aren't ever going to be able to rip the ball off him. The only thing I can do is go for a tackle.*

Charging forward, Gary summoned the will to face Blake. If there was one strong point making Gary stand out from the rest, it would be his lack of fear, something even Mr. Root had to admire.

When they were closing in on each other, Gary bent his knees slightly to get into a lower position. Although it might have looked like he wasn't paying attention to the others, Gary had picked up on multiple details and habits.

Whenever Blake feints, he does so with his right foot first. You can see his extra weight shifting to that side. The field is soft today, and his feet are sinking deeper than usual. That helps him push himself forward, spinning his body over to the right side.

Knowing all of this, Gary went along with his feint, aiming to go in for the tackle, but stopped at the last second and went to his own right. Just like he had predicted, Blake's plan was to spin around to avoid the tackle, but Gary knew where he would end up.

Going low, he saw Blake's legs and was ready . . . only to see Blake's colossal knee slam toward his face and whack him right on the nose, followed by a loud crack that even the onlookers probably heard.

Blood started to pour down in an instant, and Gary lay there on the cold grass field.

Shit. So what if I figured out where he would go? It's not like I have the body to do anything about it.

From his years of watching Altered fights, Gary was great at seeing how people's bodies moved before they did. He could see patterns that maybe even the person themself didn't realize they had.

Alas, it was all useless.

"Hey, man, I'm so sorry. Are you all right? Let me take you to the doctor," Blake said as he helped Gary off the ground to see if his nose was okay.

As Gary touched his nose lightly, blood started to gush down even more. "I think it's broken," Gary said, more to himself.

"Oh, man, I'm so sorry. Let me take you to my family's clinic. I'm gonna tell them what happened so that they won't charge you."

The worst thing about Blake in Gary and Tom's collective minds was that despite being so popular and seemingly having been handed everything in life, he was actually a nice guy. At least in movies or TV shows, someone who was this perfect would have a bad side and act arrogant, probably even bullying the geek in class, but in real life, that wasn't the case at all.

No one hated Blake; everyone loved his gentle, soft side. Including Gary and Tom, who were merely jealous.

"Don't worry about it. It wasn't your fault," Gary muttered under his breath as he walked off toward Tom on the sideline. "It was my fault for trying anyway."

Blake heard Gary's words. Out of everyone who had tried to tackle him today, Gary was the only one who had managed to predict where he would be going. This classmate of his obviously had talent, and Blake wanted to tell him that, but he had already gone off with Tom, who was accompanying him to the nurse's office.

"You should have seen your head fly back!" Tom teased, all excited. "You know, when I first saw you after the summer break, with your hair all dyed green and that, I thought you had changed, but it turns out you're just the same idiot as always."

Usually, the two would laugh about something like this, but it seemed like today, Gary wasn't in the mood to be joking around. He didn't respond.

"Why do they even make us do this sport, anyway? Oh, that's right, because our country has an obesity crisis. So they made it mandatory for every student to take part in a sports club every day, so we don't turn into pigs like most of the adults who came up with that stupid idea," Tom continued, yet this didn't get a response out of Gary either.

"Hey, so how's your sister doing?" Tom asked, trying to change the subject.

"You can't date her," Gary replied instantly, still holding pieces of tissue up his nose.

"What? I didn't mean it like that. Although truth be told, she is growing up to be quite the beauty. I can already picture it; in a couple of years, she'll be embarrassed to be hanging around her big brother. She won't be like she is now. You should treasure these days."

A picture started to form in Tom's mind, of a slim-waisted but curvy girl with short brown hair and perfectly shaped large eyes. Only his vision was slightly altered in a particular area. Instead of mere melons, they were the size of watermelons.

"I know." Gary sighed in defeat, aware that soon enough he might have to fight off his sister's suitors.

After he arrived at the nurse's office to have his nose looked at, she told him what he had already guessed himself. His nose was indeed broken. The nurse recommended that he visit the hospital if he didn't want it to remain crooked. It was possible to do surgery to fix it later on, but it would be easier to do it before it healed crookedly.

That was when he noticed the time, and Gary rushed out of the room.

"Thank you, I'll promise to have it looked at!" he called back.

But he wasn't rushing off to the hospital. Instead, he was running back home.

Leaving school, he rushed outside the gate. It was a small town, so it was quicker for him to run than to take the bus. Not to mention, there was another reason why he wanted to avoid using the bus. He didn't really want to spend any money, especially since he could be back home within ten minutes if he hurried.

Litter filled the streets of his neighborhood, and there were patches of graffiti near the apartment buildings. He was aware that their area wasn't the greatest compared to others.

It was by no means the worst place to live, but it certainly wasn't the best either. Eventually, he reached his own apartment building. The buzzer lock attached to the side of the door had been broken a long time ago and had never been fixed, allowing anyone to come in as they pleased.

The only thing left was the grueling task of walking up five flights of stairs. The building had no elevator, and Gary's family was "lucky" enough to live on the top floor.

When he finally made it to the top, he felt like someone was reaching into his stomach and trying to pull out all his organs. He was huffing and puffing louder than Tom had been out on the field.

He waited a minute to catch his breath before entering apartment 604.

"Welcome back, darling. You're just in time for dinner, although I'm gonna need a couple of minutes. Do you want me to leave it out for you tonight as well?" his mom shouted from the kitchen.

"Yes, Mom. I'll be going out with Tom tonight too," he shouted back, rushing into his bedroom.

Their apartment was relatively small, consisting of only two bedrooms and a kitchen that was simultaneously the dining area and the living room when not in use. It was all his family could afford, and since there were only two bedrooms, it meant . . .

"Gary, what the hell happened to your nose?" His sister, who had been lying on her bed, was still in her school uniform and listening to music on her phone. Just moments ago, she had been singing away until a certain someone had bulldozed into the room.

"Amy, don't worry about it; I've got to go," Gary replied as he quickly changed out of his school uniform. "And please don't tell Mom."

That was right; the two of them shared a room, even though he was sixteen and she was fifteen, only a year younger. Of course, both of them kept this a secret from their friends. If people found out, they might spread rumors about them being in some sort of a freakish family who got up to some strange things.

But it wasn't like they had much choice. Their family situation wasn't the best, and they both knew that. They had never once complained about their situation to their mother, since the poor woman was raising her teenage children to the best of her ability while working multiple jobs.

After changing clothes, Gary left the apartment. Along his way, he constantly looked at his phone to check the time, and it was now almost five thirty.

I made it, with time to spare.

He had arrived outside a well-known nightclub. Above him a sign read *Basement*. It was in the town center, and he wasn't here to meet Tom. He had lied about that part.

I promise I will make our lives better, Gary thought as he walked through the doors.

Inside, a group of men in suits greeted him. Sitting on one of the sofas was a man with a cigar in his hand. Two more men stood close to him, obviously acting as his personal bodyguards.

"I've been waiting for you, kid," the man said with a smile as he let out a puff of smoke.

Gary had a deep, dark secret that he had been hiding from everybody. Not just his family, but his closest friends too. There was a reason for the sudden change in his appearance over the summer.

Unbeknownst to them all, he had joined a gang.

CHAPTER 3

THE UNDERDOGS

The summer break had been an eventful time for Gary. It was not just because he had chosen to dye his hair and get a new look, but because he had decided to join a gang. He had kept it hidden from his friend, his mother, and even his sister.

"Had you been late, I was thinking of chopping one of your toes off, so you wouldn't forget," the seated man told him.

It was only five thirty, so the nightclub had a few hours before it would officially open. However, the club itself was actually just a front, run and used by the gang known as the Underdogs. The smoking man who was talking to Gary was the leader of the Underdogs, Damion Hawk.

The gang members mostly wore suits, making each one look like an average businessman or someone who worked for the Secret Service. This included their leader, although even a student could tell he wasn't a businessman. He had a look about him that was just too wild for someone who supposedly sat in a cubicle all day. He had a black Mohawk and a hoop earring in his right ear.

Yet the man's most prominent feature was his eyes. They were the eyes of a madman. Usually, Gary was fearless for someone his age. If he hadn't been, he would have never gathered the courage to join a gang in the first place . . . But these people scared him.

Gary gulped a little, not saying a word. The palms of his hands were starting to sweat a little.

"Hey, I'm just kidding." Damion laughed. "Why don't you head to the back while the grown-ups do a bit of talking? I'll get someone to fetch you when we need you."

As Gary went back, he was shaking a little. It was hard to tell whether Damion had actually been joking about this sort of punishment. There had been times when he had been forced to watch the leader actually cut off one of his own men's limbs.

Before joining this gang, Gary had decided to do some research into gangs. Unfortunately, he had only ended up reading a few comics and manga books here and there, and to be honest, this had led him to the conclusion that it wouldn't be too much trouble. Even his internet searches and movies had romanticized gangs.

Alas, being in a real gang had turned out to be nothing like in those comics and manga books. The members of the Underdogs did anything to make a profit. They didn't shy away from selling drugs, killing, stealing, or extorting others. There were many times when Gary had wished he could just leave, but there were two things keeping him there.

One of them was the fear of leaving the place. Would they even let him? After everything he had seen and heard? It was a question he didn't dare ask out loud.

Come on, Gary, you can do this! Just think of the money, man, come on!

And that was the second reason.

Pushing the door open, Gary entered the back of the nightclub, where there was a large staff room. Inside were some other teens who were not too far apart in age from him, sitting on a sofa. He sat down beside them, but not a single one spoke a word.

Gary had seen them a few times before, but from what he could tell, none of them went to his school. He wondered about their reasons for being here. Not why they were here today, he knew that, but why they had decided to join a gang. Most people his age only joined out of necessity.

The world was a tough place to live in at the moment. The economy had been greatly affected ever since the introduction of autonomous machinery. It had created new jobs but at the same time gotten rid of many old jobs. Gary's own family had suffered the aftermath.

His mother had lost her job as a factory worker sorting out parts, but she wasn't the only one. Mass unemployment had ruined many families.

The government's solution to all of this had been to offer retraining in the new skills and departments that the world now required: cybersecurity, programming, engineering, mechanics, and so on. But it had proven to be too hard for her to go through any type of training with the little time she had, since she was stuck doing odd jobs.

All of this had created a tiering system within the towns and cities, making the divide between the rich and poor even more evident. Tier 5 was the lowest, while Tier 1 was the highest. These tiers were based on how high their monthly productivity was. Quality of life, technology, medical care, all of these things were better the more cash a town or city generated.

However, one sector had started to boom because of this, and that was organized crime. It was highly profitable for them, as they fed on the truly desperate, who were clinging onto anything they could in the Tier 5 cities while also serving the very top people in the higher tiers. Gangs existed in all of the tiered cities and often worked together as middlemen.

The Underdogs were one such group. They weren't a huge gang, being in a small town, but they were widely known and feared there. Gary was aware of the bad things they had done, but he had chosen to ignore them.

The town was a Tier 3, so the quality of life was okay, but Gary's family had to make sacrifices to stay here, forced to live in a small,

run-down place with little room. Still, they were barely hanging on, and both children knew that, despite their mother's best attempts at hiding it from them.

Gary had seen the bills that came in the mail. If this carried on, it would just be a matter of time until they would have to move to a lower-tier city. The education would be worse, and crime rates would be higher.

He wasn't going to let this happen. Their life had already turned to crap as it was, and he didn't want it to deteriorate. No, he wanted a better future for his mother and his little sister . . . even if he had to pay the price for it.

He was the older sibling, the only man of the house, and he wished to return the favor to his mother, who had been looking after them even when times had been tough. He did not wish to run like that man!

Suddenly the double doors opened again. When Gary saw who it was, his eyes lit up with excitement.

"Hey, kiddo, you're here again." The man greeted him with a smirk.

"Kirk, I just saw your fight this morning! Congratulations," Gary said, jumping up from the sofa.

Most Altered worked for some type of organization, and Kirk was no different. He worked for the Underdogs as well. They were his sponsor, or at least they owned the corporation that Kirk was part of. Gary didn't know many details about the relationship between them. Still, he couldn't imagine how much money the Underdogs must have put into Kirk for him to become the Altered semi-superstar he was today.

"When the frog man jumped up like that, and you used your raw power to smash him to the ground, it all seemed too easy for you," Gary said excitedly.

"It might have looked easy, but most of the things I did today, I only managed because I was an Altered. Don't go around trying to do things like that yourself; otherwise, you will just end up hurting yourself," Kirk cautioned his overeager fanboy.

"I know," Gary replied, a little depressed as he thought about how different his life would be if he could be an Altered himself.

As Kirk saw the strange look on Gary's face and noticed something else about him, a lightbulb lit up above Kirk's head.

"I know, you should have some time before you have to do your thing, right? Come with me," Kirk ordered. "And don't worry, if Damion calls for you, I'll say you were with me."

Gary didn't know what was going on, but he trusted Kirk and decided to follow him. Ever since he had joined the gang, everyone had seemed a bit scary to him, rough around the edges, all but Kirk. With the Altered, everything just seemed to click.

The good thing was, Kirk was treated as a valuable asset to the group, so he could get away with things the others couldn't. If Kirk said he wouldn't get in trouble, then he should be safe.

The two of them left the staff room and went over to one of the empty clubrooms. It was quite a large club, with three rooms that featured different music types. Right now, they were in what was known as the cheese room. It usually featured favorite hits from the time Gary's mother had been his age.

Still, during the day, it looked completely different. The lights were on, so there were no fancy colored lights, and the disco ball above looked less than special.

"What are we doing here?" Gary asked. "You're not going to ask me to dance, are you?"

Kirk started to laugh; Gary seemed to have a talent for making him laugh.

"No, you idiot. I'm going to teach you how to fight."

"How to fight? Why would I need to learn that?"

Kirk pointed to his own nose, and that was when Gary remembered that his nose was broken from rugby practice.

Huh, wait, I think he has the wrong idea. Does he think I'm getting bullied or something?

"No, wait, this is—"

"You don't have to explain yourself. I'm sure the other guy looks even worse. Anyway, it will be good just to show you a few basic things. With the line of work you're doing, who knows when it will come in handy," Kirk said.

Gary didn't say anything else. He decided it would be stupid to try to clear up this misunderstanding. Besides, since one of his idols had offered to give him a personal lesson, he would be silly to try to get out of it.

Kirk started by showing him a basic punch, a jab in boxing. Punching the air, he demonstrated it a few times. The major point that Gary took from this was that Kirk's right hand was always covering the side of his face, even when throwing out the punch.

His left foot would twist slightly while he was throwing the punch outward; at the same time, his hip would move in as well. Rather than a push, the punch was more of a snap.

Next it was Gary's turn, and he repeated all the steps in his head. He punched a few times, and it looked good and felt right.

"It looks like I have a talent for this. Maybe I should join a boxing club instead; what do you think?" Gary asked, but turning his head he saw the look of disappointment on Kirk's face.

"Sorry," Kirk said, rubbing the back of his head. "Your punch is good, the movements are perfect, and you did everything right . . ."

Gary had a feeling a huge *but* was coming.

"But . . . your punch is so slow. Is that as fast and hard as you can go?" Kirk asked.

Gary would have loved to tell him it wasn't, but unfortunately, that would be a lie. He had been trying his hardest without holding back. Things always seemed to end up this way for him. He understood the theory, understood how things worked, yet for some reason, it was impossible to perform the way he pictured it in his head.

The doors to the cheese room opened, interrupting their training session. One of the men in suits walked in. "There you are. The boss has been looking for you."

When Gary returned to the first clubroom, he saw Damion still sitting on the sofa. Opposite him were five kids, including Gary, all standing up straight and waiting for orders. On the table were five metal briefcases, each one locked with a unique combination.

"Time for you guys to get to work," Damion said.

This was Gary's job in the organization. He worked as a transporter, and tonight his job would be to deliver whatever was in one of these briefcases.

While Damion explained the job details, something caught Gary's eye. It was just for a brief moment, so he was unsure if his eyes might have played a trick on him, but he felt he had seen something very odd . . .

Did that briefcase just move?

CHAPTER 4

THE SYSTEM

Damion continued his explanation of today's special task. There were five briefcases in front of five people. Each person was to deliver the briefcase in front of them to the correct location, safely; naturally, they had all been given different locations.

Damion was describing some other details, but Gary was not paying much attention, still focused on the briefcase in front of him, waiting for it to move again. Gary was smart enough to figure out the reason for there being five briefcases. A few had to be dummies, mixed in to confuse whoever might plan to steal them.

If his intuition was right, the one in front of him was the real one. That and the fact that he could have sworn he saw it move, although ever since he had started staring at it, it had behaved like a normal briefcase.

Am I imagining things? Gary started to doubt himself.

He looked at the suited man who was closest to the case. The two of them made eye contact for a brief second before Gary looked away. If he kept up eye contact for any longer, he was worried he was going to get hit.

"All right, are there any questions?" Damion asked.

One of the students raised his hand. He was a tall, weak-looking boy with curly hair. He hadn't been in the organization for long, and Gary had only seen him a couple of times.

"What's in the package?" the boy asked.

Immediately Gary clenched his fist and looked down at the floor, as he knew what was coming next. Just as expected, a few seconds later, he heard a whack and saw the student tumble from the corner of his eye.

The man looked like he was about to hit him again, but Damion interrupted him. "Stop. The boy is still new, so I'll forgive him." Damion then looked at the others before stopping at Gary. "Greeny, tell him the rules of being a transporter."

"Yes, boss," Gary answered, turning to look down the line of people. "Never take the package, never ask what's in the package, and never look inside the package!"

"Excellent," Damion replied with a slow clap. "Break one of these rules and . . . let's just say you don't want to break these rules. I can proudly tell you that we never had anyone break the rules twice. Make of that what you will."

He clicked his fingers, and one of the suited men handed each of them a small wad of cash wrapped in an elastic band. It wasn't thick like in the movies, but judging by the size and weight, this job was the highest-paying job Gary had ever been on.

Each of them had been given five hundred dollars, which was half of the payment up front. They would get the other half when they returned upon completing the job. Seeing the amount of money in his hand, Gary gulped. A thousand dollars was a lot of money to him—especially for someone who was sixteen—and best of all, it would go a long way to help out his family.

He was already doing calculations in his head. They could pay the electric and gas bills, and with what would be left, he could buy a new phone for his sister. This money was nothing for the gangsters, and simply put, they were taking advantage of the students; both sides were aware of that, but the students didn't have another choice.

Where would they get a job at their age, not to mention such a high-paying one? All the supermarket and fast-food jobs had been replaced by computer screens and machinery. The construction sites were already full of manual laborers. Only technology whiz kids might get a job helping another corporation be the next new thing, and Gary wasn't one of those people.

That type of stuff was more suited to his friend Tom.

Each of them was given a location, and the job had officially started. When he picked up the metal briefcase, it had some weight to it, but it was hard to tell if anything was inside.

Jiggling it, he tried to guess what it was, and once again, another man gave him a stare.

"Right, don't ask what's in the case."

They left the nightclub and went their separate ways, including the tall, curly-haired boy who now had a bloody nose.

"Stay safe, guys," Gary said quietly, more to himself than the others, as each of them went off. During all of this, there was one big worry at the back of Gary's mind. This was the highest-paying job they had ever received. The gangsters wouldn't just hand out money willy-nilly, so this also meant it was the most dangerous job that he had ever been given.

There had been no problems so far on all of his runs. It was why the Underdogs were using students in the first place. They didn't look suspicious, and their faces were unknown. There was less of a chance for the students to rat them out to another gang, and they would be too scared to do something like that anyway.

Still, with every job, there was risk, and it didn't get easier. On the contrary, with each successful mission, it felt that at some point his luck would run out.

It was safe to say that Gary stood out a bit. He was running around with a metal briefcase that looked too fancy for the clothes he was wearing. Usually he did his drop-offs on foot, so he was still in his sneakers and his favorite black and red tracksuit.

He didn't care about the gawking eyes that were looking at him, and he just hurried on. When he eventually reached the location, it turned out to be a construction site. The workers had already left and gone home for the day. The foundation for an apartment building had already been built, but there were no walls or roofs yet.

Gary was to give the briefcase to a person who would meet him there. He waited in the center of the foundation, where there was nothing but the ground and a few bags of cement here and there.

Gary nervously tapped his foot as he continued to look around. When he pulled out his phone, it was 8:05 p.m., already past the meeting time.

"Hello!" Gary shouted, "I'm here." His voice echoed slightly, but there was no reply.

Am I in the wrong place? After double-checking that he was in the right place, he sent a text to Damion.

No one here, what should I do?

It was the first time something like this had happened.

Tired of waiting, Gary started to walk around, checking to see if he could spot the person.

Then he saw it. He discovered a dark red liquid on the floor, coming from behind one of the building's support pillars.

Please tell me that's just paint, Gary silently prayed.

This wasn't a movie, and Gary wasn't dumb enough to go around the pillar when he was already sure there would be a dead person behind it.

Ding. His phone went off.

He pulled the phone out of his pocket, and there were only two words.

Run back!

Lifting his head, he saw a four-inch blade coming right toward him. Out of instinct, the only thing he could do was lift the metal briefcase up, and thankfully he heard a clanging sound as the briefcase clashed with the knife, protecting his face.

He saw the man who had thrown the knife for only a brief second, because, before he knew it, Gary was running for his life. He didn't know where he was running; he just knew he had to get away from that psycho. He could feel his heart beating so loudly that he thought it would jump out of his chest. He also noticed that his underwear was feeling uncomfortably warm as he had released his bladder.

I'm going to die! I'm going to die! That was a real gangster, and he just tried to stab me!

Running toward where he had come from, he saw a few more men wearing suits at the gate. As soon as they saw him, they charged.

There's more! What the hell do I do?

Dashing to the side, he left the apartment building and headed to the more gritty area of the construction site, where there were several mounds of dirt, diggers, and more. The problem was there were only two entrances to the construction site, the one that he had entered from and the other on the opposite end.

One was stationed in the north, the other south, yet in his panic, he had run west. A wall topped with barbed wire surrounded the area. Even if he didn't care about hurting himself, scaling something like that would be impossible.

Eventually, the adrenaline in Gary's body had lessened, and he was feeling incredibly weak after the rush. His hands and legs were shaking, and he knew he couldn't run away for much longer. Diving in between objects, he eventually decided to hide behind a mound of dirt to catch his breath.

Peeking out, he saw three men, each with a blade in his hand.

At this point, Gary wondered if he should call the police, but if he did, then it would just be his own gang after his life.

Suddenly, the briefcase started to move about again, jiggling Gary's hand slightly. It definitely felt like there was something alive inside.

What the hell is in there? But that wasn't important right now.

He peeked around the corner again, planning his next move. He saw one person on his far left and the other on his far right, searching for him.

Wait, where's the third person?

Suddenly a sharp shooting pain spread in Gary's lower back. It throbbed and felt warm.

Gritting his teeth, Gary turned and slung the briefcase around. The corner managed to smash the top of his assaulter's head, causing Gary to let go of the briefcase, which fell to the ground. The man appeared hurt and dizzy momentarily, but he wasn't knocked out. More notably, Gary saw blood on the man's hands.

Touching his back, he felt blood there as well. He had been stabbed.

"Damn it, I'm just a kid in high school," Gary blurted out.

The man looked stunned by the words for a second, as Gary's weaving body was about to fall over from the shock and the tension of everything that was happening. As he fell toward the man, he thought about his sister's smile and his mother's crying face if he were to leave them now.

Before hitting the ground, he fought through the pain and placed his left foot out, stabilizing himself. He twisted his hip and back foot, and with his right hand he threw the strongest punch he could, hitting the man right on the chin. It wasn't a jab but another punch that he had seen Kirk do. Learning the principles of the jab had set him up for this perfect punch. A straight right.

On contact, he felt it connect cleanly, with a surge through his arm.

The man fell to the ground, knocked out, as Gary fell down at the same time.

Despite his accomplishment, he felt tired and weak and just wanted to close his eyes. The only thing he could see in front of him was the briefcase. It was moving more than ever, so much so that it looked to be jumping up and down.

"I don't want to die," Gary whispered, with barely enough energy to speak.

Click.

He heard the briefcase opening up. The next moment his vision had gone to black. His senses were still slightly there, and he felt an even more immense pain now digging into his wrist. It was far worse than the stab wound, but he was too tired even to react or shout out.

Then, even with his eyes closed and his vision gone, something appeared in front of him.

Congratulations, you have been granted the Werewolf System!

CHAPTER 5

WHAT AM I?

Gary's eyes fluttered open slowly as he regained consciousness. The first thing he saw was some very tall trees above him. The sky was gray, making it hard to tell if it was just about to turn to night or whether it would soon be day again. As he lifted his body, he heard a rustling sound, which turned out to come from the many leaves underneath him.

Am I in the woods? He looked around and saw nothing but trees, no sign of a pathway or road. *Why did I come here? Wasn't I jus—*

"Argh!" His head started to ring with pain. When he lifted it up, he could see that his sleeves were partially torn. He tried to remember the last thing that had happened, but all that came to mind was the throbbing pain in his back.

That guy . . . he stabbed me! Lifting his shirt, he peeked over his shoulder but found nothing, not even after running his fingers over the supposed wound. For a second, he questioned himself. *Could all of this be just a bad dream?*

Alas, he quickly noticed something that made him think all of it had been real. Running down his trousers were signs of dried blood; they appeared to have dripped from his own wound. Something had definitely happened earlier.

He should have been in pain. There should have been a wound, yet there was nothing! In fact, his body felt far better than it had ever felt before.

Just what the hell happened after I got stabbed? How the hell did I get here? Shit, where the hell is "here" in the first place?

He had no memory whatsoever of what had happened from the construction site to where he was now, and in all his thinking, he had ignored something obvious. His vision had slightly been altered, and in more ways than one.

Even though it was quite dark now, he could make out details in the night he shouldn't have been able to see. The leaves on the trees a distance away, the ants crawling up their trunks, passing food to each other, and then there was the moon. It was still out, suggesting that it was still the middle of the night after all.

Hang on . . . are those ants? Eventually, Gary noticed the discrepancy about his eyes. *How is that possible? Could it be because of all those carrots Mom has been cooking lately? They say carrots improve your eyesight . . . Or is that just another myth? I bet Tom would know.*

In the middle of his crazy thoughts, he registered something in the top left corner of his vision. It reminded him of a notification from an email or a game. He moved his head, trying to get rid of it, but wherever he looked, it stayed there.

Then he started to touch his face to see if he was wearing anything, but there was nothing. The notification appeared to be glued onto his vision.

How the hell do I get rid of this thing? As he was thinking about the notification itself, it suddenly opened, and a screen appeared in front of him, hovering in midair.

Your bloodlust has been lowered
You are no longer enraged
State has been updated to Normal

Is that . . . a system?

Gary had played a few games in the past with a similar interface. However, he wasn't quite the gamer himself. He seldom had time for them, as he was always busy trying to come up with ways to make money. His buddy Tom would have been perfect for this, but with his limited knowledge, Gary still knew how to navigate it a bit.

The notifications looked like they could be deleted, and it looked like there were more options on the general interface. The annoying thing was it was all blocking his field of vision. Still, he couldn't deny it was kind of cool. Like he had been turned into some futuristic robot.

Nevertheless, he didn't like what he was reading. The word *bloodlust* did not sound good at all. What exactly had happened? Had he been turned into some type of vampire, now required to feed on blood? It would at least explain the wounds healing on his body. He had read supernatural stories about such things before.

Quickly touching his teeth, he felt nothing, and they appeared to be the same as they had always been.

Then there was the second half of the message: that his blood-lust had "been lowered." Reading it again, he gulped and tried to look at himself. There wasn't a huge amount of blood on him apart from that on his trousers. Somehow he'd managed to escape from that construction site alive while three men were chasing him; he started to consider the worst-case scenario.

No, nothing happened, stop being paranoid! Gary thought, trying to convince himself. *Surely I would have remembered something like that . . . But would I really? . . . I still have no clue how I got in the woods in the first place.*

Unfortunately, with his tendency to forget even menial tasks like emptying the washing machine when his mother asked him to, he was unable to rely on his memory.

After deleting the notifications, Gary decided to study the system a little. The first thing he saw was his own image looking back at him and his name on the side with a few stats.

Name: Gary Dem
Level 1
Exp: 0/100

Health: 100/100
Energy: 100/100
Heart rate: 42 BPM
State: Normal

He tried to figure out what this information meant. He was unable to open any sort of description, and there wasn't really anything that told him what was going on.

"Health" seemed to be pretty self-explanatory, but "Energy"? The best he could come up with was that it might be something similar to stamina. As for "heart rate," he considered that a very strange thing to appear. What worried him was that his resting heart rate had never been that low. That was a heart rate that athletes were able to achieve, and although Gary wasn't unfit, he was far from being an athlete.

As for "State," he could only relate it to the message he had gotten previously about his bloodlust decreasing, which he chose to ignore for now. What interested him more than anything was the level by his name. It reminded him of the RPGs that had been introduced to him.

He didn't know why, but his favorite part of those games had never been the completion of quests or the exploration of the world, but simply the grind. He would spend hours just killing creatures, watching that bar increase. Tom always complained about his playing style, stating that it wasn't the fastest way to level up. After all, he was a "noob" in Tom's eyes.

On the screen itself, at the top, the tab read *Status*, but right next to that was another little tab labeled *Quests*. It had a little red dot, which would usually indicate that there was something new that he hadn't seen before. At least that would be the case if it worked like his phone notifications.

When he clicked on that, a few more screens popped up in front of him again.

New Quest received
Get the perfect body

You can now do amazing things you could never have done before, but you're limited by your former weaker self. You need to get into top shape to display your full potential! Do you even lift? No? Then start lifting! Diet is crucial to this task. You will soon see improvements beyond your wildest dreams! The most important thing is to stay consistent!

Daily tasks (Monday)

Push day: Get to the gym and start pushing. Instructions will appear once you get there.

Diet: Eat 2 kilograms of meat per day. Get that sweet protein!

Quest reward: That sweet Exp you need and love

Two kilograms of meat? Is the system crazy? What does it think I am, a tiger or something? How is it even possible to eat that much?

Apart from that, the system messages seemed enthusiastic to say the least. Whoever had designed it must have been a very strange person. As he scrolled up, there seemed to be one more quest that he had received before that one.

New Quest received

Your first turning

14 days until the next full moon

Survive!

As he read this carefully, his thoughts reached a certain conclusion. He could think of only one supernatural creature in books and movies that had any relation to the full moon. Heading back to the notifications, he scrolled up and checked the first one he had received. It wasn't a new one he had missed before, but now he remembered seeing something before the blackout.

He read the words multiple times, the first system message that had ever appeared.

I'm not a vampire . . . Well, it seems like I won't have a problem with body hair anytime soon.

CHAPTER 6

WEREWOLF

Werewolf.

Gary had seen the concept of the mythological creature being used in books and movies, but he had never really been the type to pay too close attention to these things. As he remembered the few films he had watched with such beings, a thought came to his mind.

Am I now an Altered?

It sounded a bit strange, because from what Gary knew, becoming an Altered should be a long and difficult process. Maybe the thing inside the briefcase was been a new product from some company that had discovered a way to speed up the process.

He looked around him; the briefcase itself was long gone, probably left behind at the construction site.

Maybe it just says Werewolf *because it has made me into an Altered based on a wolf-type beast? Who knows, maybe all Altered have such a system and have just kept it a secret, or maybe it's something new that was in the briefcase? Either way, if I am an Altered, then my body should have changed!*

His vision had suddenly improved, so why not other things?

When a human became an Altered, one of the big changes was acquiring superhuman strength. To test his theory, Gary walked up to one of the trees, looked at it for a few seconds, and then started to shake his whole arm.

He was confident; all the signs were telling him he had become an Altered. With no doubt in his mind, he threw out his fist and hit the tree with great force.

For a few seconds, there was nothing, and then Gary let out an almighty scream that traveled throughout the forest.

"Ahhhh!" The tree was completely fine, but the same could not be said about Gary's knuckles; they were grazed and slightly bleeding, and the skin was starting to peel off. It was apparent he hadn't held back at all when throwing the punch.

You have been injured
–2 HP
98/100 HP

Minus 2 HP for that? I'm not sure if I should complain about this being a lot or be happy about it not doing more damage to me . . . Also, what happens when I hit 0 HP? Will I just instantly die? Well, I suppose hitting it forty-nine more times at full strength would eventually break my fists and lead to severe blood loss . . . Maybe.

It was clear that the system itself was quite complicated.

Your heart rate has increased
50 BPM

It seemed kind of useless to Gary that the system showed his heart rate. He didn't see any need, as it didn't seem to affect anything else.

After the pain had subsided, Gary wanted to run a few more tests. He planned to check if he was now faster or could transform parts of his body. Unfortunately, being in the middle of a forest, he lacked any equipment to measure his speed, and just running felt the same as always. Gary also had no idea how to change parts of his body.

He tried concentrating on his arm, wishing for it to turn into something else, but nothing happened. It didn't make any difference when he tried to do the same with his legs, nose, ears, eyes, or any other parts. Eventually, he sighed and gave up for the time being.

He was interested in the quests, but it was already late, so he couldn't go to the gym to see if there would be any improvements. The food quest was theoretically the easiest to complete, but it would be a tough one given his family situation. Meat was expensive, and eating two kilograms a day would be near impossible. There was half the payment up front, but if he could, he would have still liked to help his mother with that.

Finally, there was the other quest that would take place in fourteen days. He had an idea of what would happen on that day, but he couldn't believe it. So far, there had been no signs of his body drastically being altered other than what the system was telling him.

At least he had fourteen days to figure out what to do about it. It was dark out, and if he stayed out any later, his mother would probably worry about him, so he decided to exit the woods.

It didn't take long as he could clearly see a pathway with his improved vision, and when he was out of the woods, he knew exactly where he was. From there, he started to jog.

He had become quite the good runner, working as a transporter and being cheap with his money. The journey from where he was would take around twenty minutes.

Finally he arrived back home, and he could hear his sister singing from outside the door. When he went to open it, he noticed something. His breathing.

I just ran for twenty minutes, and I'm not even tired. Maybe I am an Altered after all!

This thought excited Gary more than anything. Checking his heart rate, he found that it had also dropped to 45 BPM.

After entering the house, he headed to the room he shared with his sister and started to take off his clothes. They had been torn to rags, and some had signs of blood on them. Amy was a little surprised that her brother was just stripping in front of her. She immediately closed her eyes and turned around.

"What the hell? Gary, hurry up and put some clothes on!" Amy shouted.

He quickly stuffed his clothes into a school sports bag and shoved it in the corner before throwing the rest of his belongings on his bed and finally changing into something new.

"Oh, you're back, Gary! The food is ready for you whenever you need it; just warm it up in the microwave!" his mother shouted.

"Thanks, but I'm not hungry," Gary replied. "Feel free to have seconds if you want."

"That's strange; you usually come back starving. Did you eat at Tom's?" she asked with some motherly worry.

"Err, yeah!" Gary shouted back.

It certainly was strange; every time he came back from his work Gary was hungry, and he hadn't eaten before leaving. The last meal he'd had was lunch, but he didn't feel hungry at all.

He began rummaging through multiple drawers, looking for first-aid supplies. Without noticing, he eventually found himself searching Amy's side of the room.

"What the—? A diary?" he murmured to himself, picking it up.

"Hey, stay away from my things!" She snatched the diary away. "Just tell me what you're looking for."

"Bandages, gauze, or something for my han—" He looked at his hand and saw that it had completely healed.

When did that happen?

100/100 HP

99/100 Energy

Eat more meat to restore your Energy. When idle, Energy points will be used to restore HP.

It looked like super healing could be added to the list of abilities he might possess.

"Did you go to the doctor? Your nose looks better," Amy pointed out, noticing it wasn't crooked anymore.

"Err, yeah," Gary replied, which seemed to be his go-to response today. It was hard for him to process everything that was going on around him.

Ding. Ding. Ding.

Multiple notification sounds were coming in one after the other. When Amy turned around, she noticed that they were coming from her brother's phone. Since she was closer to it, she passed it to him, but not before sneaking a peek at the messages.

Bastard, I'll kill you!!! was the preview message. The rest of it was cut off.

"Gary, are you in trouble?" she asked while handing over the phone.

He snatched it away and left the room in a hurry. "It's nothing; it must be Tom playing a prank on me. Don't worry about it." Before his sister could ask any questions, he had already locked himself in the bathroom.

Sitting down, he started to read the messages coming through one by one, and his hands couldn't stop shaking.

Where are you?
Answer now!!!
The item is missing! You know the rules!!!
You have until the end of today to return with the item!!!
If you're not here, you can say goodbye to your family.

"Oh *shit!*" Gary was unsure what exactly had happened to the item, but he could come up with a few guesses. The item was currently with him, or, more accurately speaking, it had combined with him.

After a person became an Altered it was impossible to reverse the process.

If he returned to the gang and tried to explain to them what had happened, he would be killed for sure. That or they would enslave him and make him work as an Altered, although he first would have to prove to be one, which ironically he was unable to do.

Alternatively, the real item might still be in the briefcase, but if so, it must have long since been taken by the other group. However, that would mean that his current situation was unrelated, which seemed unlikely.

Either way, he had failed his job, and that meant that his end wouldn't be a pretty one.

It was the first time this had ever happened to Gary, yet he had seen what had happened to others in the gang who had failed the Underdogs. Going back would be suicide.

It's a good thing I gave them a fake address. They don't know where my real home is, but what do I do if they find out? What will happen to Amy and Mom?

CHAPTER 7

WHITE ROSE

"Sir, the police have arrived, so we had to stop our investigation," one of the suited men reported on the phone.

"Damn it! Do you have any idea how important that thing inside the briefcase was? 'Course you don't! Screw this, just bring that kid here and find out who the hell betrayed us!"

It was early morning and the sun had barely risen, causing a dull gray sky. That day, at a construction site, when the workers were about to start work, they came across three gruesome bodies.

In fact, it was hard to call them bodies. Each one appeared to have been mauled beyond recognition, with huge scratches across the faces and large pieces of flesh torn off. Blood was splattered all over the construction site.

The first thing the workers did was call the police, who promptly closed off the site as a crime scene.

"What do you think, boss?" a young police officer asked his superior, whose most prominent features were his brown overcoat and his scruffy beard. Anton Millstun was this small town's chief of police.

They were used to little scuffles happening here or there, but nothing on this sort of scale.

Kneeling down, he looked at the blood.

"Did you take DNA samples of all the blood you could find?" Anton asked.

"Yup, they're already testing it and should come up with a few things soon. Hopefully, we already have them on file."

"If my guess is right, it looks like we have a little gang war going on. Someone transporting certain goods, a trade gone wrong, and an empty briefcase. In that case, chances are good we already have their prints in the system." And yet there was one thing Anton had no answer for yet. Why had the transporter left behind the briefcase?

"You mean these three corpses were the attackers, boss?"

"Transporters usually travel alone since it's easier to blend in that way. From what we know, the gangs mostly use teenagers and young adults, none of whom would dress as flashy as the victims. Still, this makes it even more bizarre that a transporter could kill three armed thugs."

"Unless, of course, the one transporting goods was something they didn't expect. An Altered," a female voice said.

Turning around, the two of them saw a middle-aged woman and man walk underneath the yellow tape. Neither one was dressed like the police. They were in uniform, although their clothing looked a little fancy to be wearing out in the open.

The uniforms were gray, with gold around the edges where the trim would be. They were tight-fitting while still allowing for free movement, expandable, and, most important, breathable. What stood out most, though, was the crest on the left chest: a silver rose with a sword going down the middle, clearly showing who they were and where they had come from.

"Damn it, what are you guys doing here? It's too early to say for sure that this is an Altered case!" Anton stood up to complain.

The handsome middle-aged man with the strange uniform, whose name tag read *Frank Hue*, had short black hair and a serious look to him. When Anton looked at him, he felt a slight shiver go down his spine; there were no emotions emanating from this man. Despite the gruesome state of the victims, he didn't even blink an eye.

At least his partner, Sadie Nimper, displayed an arrogant air of importance. Unfortunately, she seemed not to be shy about it either.

"Look, Millstun, even a toddler could tell you at first glance that this crime scene could only have been caused by an Altered," she told him. "The two of us will take over this investigation. I expect you to support us, as is your duty."

Without waiting for a reply, Sadie was off to talk to the others about the evidence that had been found so far.

"Sir, are they really members of White Rose?" the young police officer whispered, so as not to attract the attention of the scary-looking woman.

"Yes, and unfortunately, that means they're in charge," Anton replied, clenching his fist and walking away. He had never liked their attitude and how they behaved as if they were above the police force.

He wasn't upset because they outranked him. No, it was because they genuinely behaved as if they were superior beings. "Heed my advice, boy, never fight with them. I'm sure you know this already, but both of them are Altered."

With the introduction of Altered, it was, unfortunately, a sad reality that certain people would try to use these special abilities and powers for no good. As the police's simple guns wouldn't do much when faced with an Altered, the government decided to combat fire with fire.

The Altered Investigation Force was established, more commonly known as White Rose.

When Gary's alarm woke him up, he instinctively hit the big snooze button to turn it off. He felt horrible, and his head was pounding with a strange pain.

Seems like I fell asleep after all.

He had hardly gotten a wink of sleep. Less because of all that had happened to him ever since yesterday's cursed transporter job and more because he had been too scared imagining what Damion would do to him . . . or to his family.

I have to make sure they never find out about this place.

His thoughts were suddenly interrupted by a strange scent.

Like a dog, he sniffed the air unconsciously and followed the origin of the scent. That was when he noticed his belly rumbling. He was extremely hungry after last night.

Eventually, he arrived in front of the fridge. Opening it, he found a fresh uncooked steak sitting in a small puddle of myoglobin.

Before he knew it, he had already reached out and grabbed the piece of meat. He lifted the whole thing up, about to place it in his mouth.

"Ewww!" Amy shouted. "What are you doing? That's still raw!"

Hearing his sister's voice, Gary snapped out of it, realizing he had been about to eat a raw piece of meat. Caught in the act, he quickly placed it back in the fridge.

"Now we'll have to eat steak tonight with all your germs over it! Did you even wash your hands? Look, they're covered in blood," Amy complained. "Mom was saving that to treat us tonight! You should know how seldom it is that we get to eat something so nice!"

To make matters worse, his mother entered the room, drawn in by the commotion.

"What are you two arguing about so early in the morning?" she asked with bags under her eyes.

"This doofus just tried to eat a raw steak!" Amy shouted, pointing at him.

Gary's hands were shaking. Everything was kind of getting to him, and now he couldn't even control his body . . .

"I'm sorry," Gary said as he ran past the two of them and headed to the bathroom. "I'll buy a new one, I promise."

When he entered the bathroom, he looked at himself in the mirror, half expecting to see someone else, but from the looks of it, he was still the same. The only thing "wrong" with him was his fast-beating heart, and the system was there to tell him.

Then he noticed something else: his bloody hands that had touched the steak were in his mouth. He pulled them out quickly, but it was already too late. by the time he checked the system, he had licked them clean, and he could still taste it. Even worse, he enjoyed the aftertaste.

After spending some time regaining his composure, Gary finally left the bathroom to join the others for breakfast. The TV was on while they ate. Amy refused to talk to him and just gave him the cold shoulder.

Similarly, his mother also stayed quiet. Gary was unsure whether it was because she was mad at him or just too sleepy.

In front of him was a sliced ham sandwich. It didn't take long for him to finish it, and afterward, he decided to check the status of one of his quests.

28/2,000 g of meat consumed

The single slice of ham only weighed twenty-eight grams. If possible, he would like to test whether completing the quest would give him the promised Exp and if he could eventually level up just like in those games.

Unfortunately, there was a large barrier. Meat was expensive. He still had the five hundred dollars of up-front payment in his pocket, but that much money could help his family a lot.

The TV interrupted his thoughts. "In recent news, it looks like the Altered Hunters have struck again, this time killing an Altered in his own home. Just as in previous cases, their calling card had been left in the victim's residence."

Altered Hunters, huh? If he really was an Altered, they might be something he needed to worry about in the future.

Not everyone liked the idea of Altered existence. Altered Hunters seemed to believe that either everyone or no one should have access to this kind of power.

"In other Altered-related news, three mutilated corpses have been found at a construction site in the small town of Slough. The extent of their wounds suggests that an Altered was involved, in what the police currently assume to be a gang trade gone wrong.

"Upon examination of the evidence, all three of the deceased have been identified as members of a certain gang. Although the blood of a fourth person was found at the crime scene, the police have been unable to find that person, currently believed to be the killer Altered.

"The police have offered a reward for any hints leading to . . ."

Gary had stopped listening to all the words after the news.

Great, now the police are after me as well . . .

CHAPTER 8

FIGHT BACK!

Gary walked to school a lot slower than he usually would. He looked around constantly, checking to see if anyone was following him. He had recognized the three deceased gang members on TV as the same ones who had been after him at the construction site.

The Underdogs must have tried to get their package back. Whatever was inside must have been important enough for them to have killed the gang members! If they killed them that easily, then what are they going to do to me? The unknown blood, it has to be mine from the stab wound. Gary thought back to the system and the news report, about how it was an Altered's doing.

He stopped in the middle of the pathway and gulped.

At least I hope it was the Underdogs, it couldn't be . . . could it? I would have remembered something like that.

Shaking the horrible thought from his head, he decided that he'd better hurry to school. It was about the only thing that was normal at the moment for him.

Suddenly there was a loud, piercing shriek. Looking around, Gary discovered that it had originated from an alleyway close by. The poor girl was surrounded by four guys who had brought her there, with one of them currently pinning her up against the wall. The neighborhood wasn't exactly the best, but for something like this to happen in broad daylight so early in the morning . . .

Really, is it just that kind of day?

Gary's initial reaction was to just walk away. He didn't want to get involved, especially since there was nothing he could realistically do against four adult men. After all, he was no hero but merely a teenager. Besides, if they were about to commit such an atrocity, who was to say that they were unarmed? Maybe they would do more than just beat him up if he tried to interfere . . .

The men continued to push the girl down the alleyway, out of sight from the main road, around the back of one of the apartments. At this point, when the girl turned the corner, Gary's sharp eyes spotted something on her uniform.

It was his school's crest. She went to the same school as him.

Damn it; my own ass is already on the line. Should I try to bluff, telling them I'm part of the Underdogs? No, that won't work; given my age, it's clear that I'm merely a transporter. And using their gang name might not be the best idea. Shit, why did it have to be a girl?

In all honesty, if their victim had been a guy, then Gary wouldn't have dithered so much. People were struggling all over the world and having bad things done to them. He himself had even joined a gang in hopes of a better future.

However, when he saw a girl being abducted, especially in his own neighborhood, not too far from where he lived, he couldn't help but imagine the men doing the same thing to his sister. Who knew whether she had a brother who would blame himself for the rest of his life that he hadn't been there? Even if she was an only child, what about her parents?

Gary considered creating a ruckus. But there weren't many others around who would help, and if he explained the situation, he knew that no one would for fear that the men belonged to one of the gangs. It was easier just to hide their heads in the sand, pretending not to have noticed the situation, telling themselves there was nothing they could do . . .

Alternatively, he could try to call the police, but one of the things he had learned in the Underdogs was that the police reacted slowly to such cases, not only because they were understaffed but also because those higher up had been paid off, to make sure the response time was delayed. By the time they actually got here, whatever those guys were planning would have already happened.

Looks like I've got to figure this one out myself.

As soon as he had made the decision to act, a notification screen appeared in front of him.

New Quest received

Save the girl!

You have determined that there are no other options, and you're the only one she can rely on; are you really going to turn your back on her now? It's time for you to show off your new skills!

New skills? That's right; I'm an Altered now! . . . well, at least I think I am. I have super healing and . . . and . . . good eyesight? Hey, system, how the hell am I supposed to beat them with those things? Do you want me to act as their punching bag?

"Get away!" The girl screamed again, but it was quickly muffled.

He knew he didn't have time to think about what to do next. If there was one thing he was known for, it was his tendency just to act. Right now was no different; his legs had started moving and he was already heading down the alleyway. When he took the turn, he could see one of the guys with his hands over the girl's mouth.

The men turned their heads, and they didn't look like the friendliest bunch, that was for sure. Most of them were wearing similar clothing. Baggy trousers with a black top of some kind.

A color gang? Damn it; I should have noticed sooner!

No wonder they were able to act so brazenly in broad daylight. Color gangs usually were college students or high school students; some of them worked under one of the large main gangs, and the black color gang was affiliated with the Underdogs, which meant that fighting them would pose a risk.

"Kid, we're feeling nice, so why don't you just get out of here and head back to school." One of the men at the back waved him off after recognizing him as just a stupid brat.

Gary looked at the school uniform, confirming that he and the girl did indeed go to the same school. He was looking for an excuse to avoid the situation, but then he saw the fear in the girl's eyes again. She had a similar hairstyle to his sister's, only her hair was black. Seeing this just built up the rage inside him.

Four of them, I'm going to get hit a few times, but it can't hurt more than getting stabbed, right? Gary mused, trying to convince himself. Committing himself to the situation, he went into a boxing stance as Kirk had shown him.

The men started to break out in laughter.

"Oh, looks like we have a knight in shining armor. All right, let's see what you got, boy, maybe we'll give you a little invitation," one of the men said, walking forward.

Gary waited, focusing on the man's toes. He thought back to when he had landed a punch on the gangster the night before and to everything Kirk had taught him.

Not yet; he's still not close enough.

Then, when the man was finally in range, Gary threw out a perfect jab that even Kirk would have praised him for. However, the punch ended up hitting nothing but air. The man had moved to the side and grabbed his fist.

"Do you have any idea how obvious that punch was? Seriously, if we allowed ourselves to be hit by amateurs like you, we wouldn't be doing what we're doing in the first place!"

The man pulled Gary forward by the wrist and punched him right in the head, flinging his body backward. Yet the man didn't let go; he pulled him forward again, this time kneeing him in the stomach.

The blow knocked the wind out of Gary, who was finding it hard to breathe.

I was wrong! This pain feels a lot worse than getting stabbed.

While the men were distracted watching the beating, the girl saw this as her opportunity to escape. She pulled down the hand that had been covering her mouth and bit down as hard as she could. When the man let go of her, she followed it up with a kick toward his crown jewels before running out of the alleyway at the other end.

"Now look what you've done!" one of the men shouted. "You let her get away; now it's going to be ten times harder to catch her again! Kid, how are you going to pay us back for this?"

Gary was on his knees, still hurting from the blow to his stomach when a notification screen appeared in front of him.

Quest completed
40 Exp received

She really got away, huh? But what's the point in Exp if I'm not going to live to see another day?

The man had recovered from being hit in his sensitive area and was walking toward Gary heavy-footed. The others went up against the wall, not getting in his way as he suddenly threw out a kick, hitting Gary right in the head and sending him to the ground.

"Hey, don't you think you're going too far? You could kill him," one of his companions cautioned, but another one stopped him.

"Don't try stopping Raph now, or he will just take it out on you instead."

"Answer me!" Raph shouted at Gary.

Do people like this really deserve to live? I'm already beaten.

The next kick landed in his stomach.

If I weren't the one getting hit right now, would they have done this to the girl?

As these thoughts filled his head, his temper was rising, and so was something else.

BPM is rising
85 BPM

Another kick, again aimed at his stomach, and blood started to dribble out of Gary's mouth.

These scum, would they have done this to Amy as well?

120 BPM
125 BPM

Raph went for another kick.

"Bring that bitch back now!" he shouted, but this time, his leg stopped and, looking down, he saw that Gary was holding it.

The girl was running back as fast as she could, and two policemen were following her. As soon as she was set free, she had gone looking for help and had eventually found some police who were in the area.

"It's down here; we have to hur—"

She paused as she looked down the alleyway and saw four men on the ground. Some of them were knocked out, others were rolling about in pain, and the leg of one of them had been bent to an unnatural degree.

What happened here? Did that boy from before do this?

CHAPTER 9

MY HEARTBEAT

When Gary opened the door to his classroom, he was surprised to see that not everyone was there yet. He peeked at the school clock and saw that there was still a good fifteen minutes before class started.

What, how? I was walking so slowly and then I got caught up in that . . . incident.

His hands were still slightly shaking; he still didn't understand what he had done or what had happened. He'd sprinted toward the school to get away from the scene.

Which made up for any time that he'd lost on the way.

Still, I shouldn't have arrived this early . . . just how fast was I running?

He went to his seat and placed his bag down, and his friend Tom was there as usual to greet him.

"What's wrong with you? You look like . . . I don't even know how to describe you. You just don't look like your usual self."

"Thanks for the concern," Gary replied. In truth, he just wished things could go back to normal. School was the one place where he didn't have to worry about his second life as a gang member.

However, now with his whole body going through these weird changes, it was hard to keep everything separate.

"Actually, I have a question for you. You're into games, books, and all that stuff, so what do you know about . . . werewolves?" Gary asked.

Tom had a little smirk on his face. "Oh, I thought you weren't interested in these types of things. Don't tell me, you're going to ask me the age-old question: 'Which one is stronger?' or 'Which would you rather be, a vampire or a werewolf?'"

"Vampires? No, I just wanted to talk about werewolves; I'm just curious about what they do. Is there anything to look out for? You know I'm terrible at looking these things up on the internet."

It was strange that Gary had a sudden interest in these things, but at the same time, Gary was always obsessed with the next thing he was watching or reading. At one point, he was reading a comic about tennis and tried to become a professional tennis player.

The next time, Tom saw Gary playing chess after watching a TV series, and before summer, he had been fanboying stories about gangs. So Tom didn't think much of this, besides it just being Gary's latest obsession, so he decided to humor him.

"Well, it's hard to say. There are so many different types of lore out there, depending on where you get your information or what you're reading. Silver bullets, magical plants, bites, and more, but they all have one thing in common: at the full moon, that's when a werewolf is at its strongest, and in some stories, that's also when they go out of control and eat their closest friends," Tom explained, acting like a wolf in an attempt to scare Gary.

However, Gary didn't flinch, nor was he laughing. Instead, he had a very deeply concerned look, and his palms felt incredibly sweaty.

"Are you sure you're okay?" Tom asked.

Gary contemplated whether he should tell Tom. He was still unsure if he was an Altered. It was easy to explain his symptoms by just telling him he was one; the problem was that then Gary would have to tell Tom everything.

How he had come across the strange briefcase, informing him that he had joined a gang . . . one that was hunting him. He couldn't do that to Tom.

There was also a high chance that telling Tom anything would involve him in all of this as well. This was Gary's problem, and he was going to solve it.

The door opened once again and, seeing that it was the teacher, the kids got into their seats and stopped their chatter. Their teacher, Mr. Grey, was a skinny man who wore glasses. Although he had a reputation for being very strict, everyone still respected him greatly; he just knew the right way to deal with kids.

When Mr. Grey entered the room, a student that none of them had seen before followed behind him. The color of her long, flowing ash-gray hair stood out nearly as much as Gary's. Her bangs fell just down to her eyebrows, making her big eyes and small symmetrical face stand out.

The moment Gary saw this girl . . .

Something strange started to happen; his heart beat faster, but not just a little. It was pounding in his chest as if it wanted to escape. He could hear it clearly, banging and banging, overpowering the sound of everything else around him.

BPM is rising
140 BPM
145 BPM

While staring at the girl, he heard a slight creak coming from below. His tight grip around the desk had caused it to break a little; what was worse, his thumbnail had grown and had pierced the top layer of the wood.

Oh no, it's happening again, that strange feeling from before—but this *didn't happen!* Gary started to panic, and it was only raising his heart rate even higher.

150 BPM

These system messages are really starting to piss me off!

And his anger only raised his heart rate even more.

155 BPM

Gary did the only thing he could to calm himself down: he closed his eyes and took deep breaths. Trying to think about nothing.

Like a monk, think of nothing . . . nothing . . . he repeated inside his head.

"Hello, everyone." The girl's sweet voice greeted the class. "My name is Xin Clove; it's nice to meet you all. I recently moved into this town, so I don't know anyone, and I'm a little nervous, but the school looks like a good place to be, and I look forward to getting along with you all."

"Clove?" a student mumbled. "Isn't that the new mayor's name as well?"

"Oh yeah, you're right; he was the person who wanted to take the town and raise this place from a Tier 3 to a Tier 2 town, right?"

"Yeah, everyone has high hopes for him."

Hearing all these things, Xin took a little step back, and that was when they noticed that her face had gone a little red.

"Wait, don't tell me, you're the mayor's daughter!"

The revelation had caused quite a commotion, and everyone was excited to see someone of importance in their class.

"Can we have some respect in the room, please!" Mr. Grey said in a firm voice, and the students quieted down. "No matter who Xin is, I expect everyone to treat her just like any other student."

Xin was given a seat by the window, away from everyone else, and it was quite noticeable that she had gained a lot of attention not just because she was related to the mayor but because the boys considered her a beauty as well.

Throughout class, for some reason, Gary couldn't help but stare in Xin's direction, and every time he did, his heartbeat sped up and he had to look away. The one thing it was helping him with was controlling his heart rate by finding the best method to get in a meditative state to calm down.

Seriously, every time something gets me excited or gets my heart beating, am I going to have this problem?

"You horny dog!" Tom commented, punching him on the shoulder. He had been watching Gary for a while now and noticed that he kept staring at Xin.

"Tom!" Mr. Grey shouted. "Are you really interrupting my class again? I know, once school ends, why don't you take Miss Clove and show her around before heading to your club."

Damn it, he's in one of those moods today, Tom thought.

At the end of the school day, there was thirty minutes until they had to go to their compulsory club lessons after school.

"Hey, so do you want to come with me and take the new girl around the school for a bit? Maybe you two can get to know each other," Tom suggested, giving Gary a nudge while he packed his things.

"I'm sorry, but there's something else I need to do, and I'm in a bit of a rush," Gary said, and before Tom could say anything else, he left.

Gary couldn't control his heart rate just looking at the girl, so he couldn't imagine what talking to her would do; however, this wasn't the only reason he had refused. He was worried about the gang on his back and them finding out where he lived, and he needed to tie up any loose ends.

And there was a really big loose end. There was one person in school he needed to speak to: Kai, a fellow student and also the person who had introduced him to the Underdog gang in the first place.

Seeing his friend storm out of the room, Tom couldn't help but think Gary was acting weird. When he turned to look at the desk where Gary had been sitting, he noticed something.

From both ends of the desk, the wood had been destroyed. It looked like someone had done it with their bare hands. But that wasn't possible, for a human at least.

CHAPTER 10

HOW TO MAKE MONEY (PART 1)

Given that whatever had been in the briefcase had been able to change Gary into an Altered, or at least an Altered-like being, the Underdogs should be desperately looking for him by now. However, judging by the fact that Gary didn't see any of the gang's members waiting for him by the school entrance, he could only assume Kai hadn't informed them yet, for whatever reason.

It was the end of the day, so Gary knew where Kai would be. Everyone at their school was required to attend extracurricular activity clubs. Since it was impossible to circumvent this requirement, Kai had somehow talked the teachers into letting him create an astrology club. Unsurprisingly, he was the club's only member, but since he actually stayed at school for that period of time, the teachers let him be.

Opening the doors that led to the roof, Gary saw Kai standing against the surrounding outer fence, looking down at the school field. His bleached-blond hair blew in the wind along with the dangly earring on his left ear.

It was as if Kai were posing for a K-pop photo shoot. It didn't hurt that he totally had the looks to go with it. Gary didn't swing that way, but he could easily imagine how a girl would swoon over Kai after seeing the picturesque scene in front of him.

"Kai," Gary called out as he carefully strolled over to him, making sure to pay attention to his surroundings. He was ready to sprint away in case this turned out to be some sort of elaborate trap. "I need to speak with you."

Watching Gary act so paranoid, Kai tried to stifle his laughter but failed, to Gary's surprise.

"Don't worry; the Underdogs don't know that you're here," Kai informed him as he wiped away a tear from all of his laughter. "I was sure you would come to me, and you're right on time."

Looks like they already did contact him. Just how much does he know, and why hasn't he reported me yet? Did he want to make sure I wouldn't try to run away first?

"You've really caused quite a commotion. I knew you were desperate for money, but I thought the Underdogs were paying you well. From what I've heard, you're actually regarded as quite the capable and reliable transporter, so just how much did the other side pay you to bring them the package?" Kai asked. His face didn't change, making it hard for Gary to judge whether this was a trick question or just pure curiosity.

"That's not what happened!" Gary protested vehemently. He would have loved to explain what had really happened; alas, it was impossible. The situation was just too crazy to be regarded as anything but some bad excuse from a teenager. What's worse, if someone were actually to believe him, Gary had the feeling that the consequences for him might be far worse.

"Yeah, you're right; you've never struck me as the double-crossing type. You care too much about your family to try something like that. Correct me if I'm wrong, but the whole reason you wanted me to introduce you was for the sake of your sister Amy and your mother, right?"

Gary's heart started to thump louder and faster.

The situation at Gary's home had taken a turn for the worse a few months ago. He had noticed that more and more bills were coming through the door, and he was beginning to suspect that his mom was hiding great pain behind the smile she gave him every day.

Desperate to help out, Gary needed to find a way to make money, but being only sixteen years old prevented him from doing any official work. The only thing he could do was a paper route, although that paid peanuts, and you were competing with around a hundred twelve-year-old boys who wanted to do the same thing.

While thinking hard about the best thing to do, he walked past a student in the hallway: Kai Hamper. His designer black-and-gold watch shining brightly as he swung his arms. His limited-edition sneakers cost more than the wardrobe of Gary's entire family put together. And at Gary's eye level, he wore a unique thick gold chain that Gary was sure was made out of twenty-four-karat gold.

Kai was a student who just screamed wealth. It was strange, as being in a Tier 3 city meant there weren't many wealthy people. Still, it wasn't impossible. There were a couple of reasons for wealthy people to live in a lower-tier city. The most common one was having a company based in that city, or if they had decided that trading guaranteed safety for the chance to live like a king instead of a commoner would be worth it.

After all, house and apartment prices rose to ridiculous levels as you went up the city's tiers. A mansion in a Tier 3 city could only get you a small apartment in Tier 1.

Whatever the case, ultimately, this kid who was barely older than Gary had access to a *lot* of money. Plucking up his courage and concerned about his family's situation, Gary went to pay him a visit one day. It was lunch break, and Gary was surprised to see Kai sitting alone at the back of the lunchroom, staring out the window.

He wasn't eating anything, nor was anyone paying him any attention or bothering him. Pulling up one of the empty seats, Gary sat next to him at his table.

"Do you mind?" Gary asked.

What Gary didn't realize at the time was that other people avoided Kai at school. He never really paid any attention to those things, but Kai often got into fights, and there were rumors about where he had gotten his money. But even if Gary had known about these rumors, it still wouldn't have stopped him.

"I came here to ask you, how do I make money?"

CHAPTER 11

HOW TO MAKE MONEY (PART 2)

"I know I don't know who you are or what you do. You might just be some kid who has a rich parent, but whatever it takes, if you want me to be your lackey, bring you food in the morning, I don't care, I just need the money."

Even when Gary had propped himself on Kai's table, he still seemed uninterested, and it wasn't until Gary spoke that Kai turned his head and smiled.

This kid, his eyes, his determination to do whatever it takes— huh, well let's see how long he lasts, Kai thought.

After that day, Gary had learned how Kai made his money, and Kai had become Gary's "in" to joining the gang.

"Relax, I haven't told them anything," Kai informed Gary, who had gone silent. "Still, you're not wrong to be cautious. They seem to be very keen to find you. I don't know what exactly you took from them, whether it was important, or rare, or something like that, but it's already too late to simply return it. Right now, it's just the principle of the matter. You stole from them, so they need to punish you for what you have done. It's been quite a while since someone last dared to cross the Underdogs, so they likely have something grue-some in store for you. You know, to send a message to others."

Of course, Gary already knew everything Kai had said. Still, hearing it from someone else just made matters worse.

"Fortunately for you, I don't plan to tell the Underdogs about you," Kai told him with a giant grin on his face.

Huh, he won't? Why would he be looking out for me? We're not friends or anything like that, barely acquaintances. There has to be something . . . something he wants from me. Gary became wary about Kai's generosity.

"Ooh, you seem to catch on rather quickly. Indeed, I don't plan to simply help you out," Kai admitted. "I want to ask you for a favor that will benefit both of us. You see, for a while now, I've planned to leave the Underdogs. However, if that were so easy, you wouldn't be in your current situation; now think about how much worse it is for me, who knows so much more about their gang.

"Still, it's not impossible. What do you think we would need to do to protect ourselves from a gang like the Underdogs?" Kai asked with a mischievous grin.

Gary wasn't sure if Kai actually wanted him to answer the ques-tion, but in case he did, Gary had no clue what the right answer would be; otherwise, he wouldn't be in his current predicament. All of this seemed to be some sort of spiel from Kai to get Gary's help. The strange thing was that as far as he knew, Gary didn't have any-thing to offer Kai.

No longer waiting for Gary to come up with an answer, Kai en-lightened his classmate. "It's actually quite simple; we would have to be part of a bigger gang. Of course, just joining another one is out of the question. The Underdogs could simply pay them off to rat us out. So our only choice is to create our own gang that's bigger and more powerful than the Underdogs. That's where you come in. You will be my little dog in all this. You will help me grow our gang!"

Gary gritted his teeth, annoyed that Kai was calling him a dog, but he had to put his emotions aside. What Kai was suggesting was crazy for more reasons than one. The problem was that Kai could report him at any time. He held all the cards while Gary had none.

Gary was smart enough to understand that threatening to reveal Kai's wish to leave the gang wouldn't help him in any way. Going against Kai would risk getting his family involved, not to mention that he could simply deny Gary's accusation.

If it came down to it, who would the gang believe? The boy they assumed had stolen from them, or the boy who had worked with them for a long time who also happened to have told them where to find Gary?

"How would that even be possible? The other gangs won't follow someone in high school. They already have a base of strong people, and those in college are already in different color gangs. It's impossible to form a gang!" Gary argued, trying to put some reasoning behind his plan.

Lifting his hands, Kai did a little spin.

"Where are we right now? Did you forget? Aren't there plenty of people right in this school? Why do the gangs use us as transporters? It's because people underestimate high school students! There are plenty of us who are strong and love to fight, and I have my ways to persuade them.

"The gangs think of us as nothing but kids, but soon enough, we will be adults. We'll start off small, but eventually we can create something greater than all of them. Now tell me, Gary, are you with me or not?" Kai asked, holding out his hand as he looked into Gary's eyes.

This person is crazy . . . but what choice do I have? Gary thought as he shook Kai's hand. "Fine, but you have to promise, not a single word to anyone in the Underdogs or the other gangs about my family or me!"

"Of course, you have my word."

At that moment, a notification screen appeared.

A spoken deal has been made, would you like to mark Kai Hamper?

There was no other information about what a mark was or what it did. Gary tried to ask the system, but by the time he did, Kai had let go, and the message had disappeared. Whatever it was, it was too late to implement now.

Kai waved Gary off as he walked back to look down on the school field. Gary began walking away to prepare for his own club activities. Turning around, he briefly saw Kai grin at him.

"So, Marie, are you really sure he was the one who defeated the members of that color gang that was chasing after you today?" Kai asked.

From behind the roof's storage room, a girl with black hair stepped forward. "No doubt about it. I don't know how he did it, but all of those guys were rolling over by the time I returned with the police."

Kai's grin got even wider. "It sounds like this is going to be an exciting year."

CHAPTER 12

THE GIRL OF YOUR DREAMS

After the conversation with Kai, Gary was stomping his foot on the ground, twisting it about in the grass. The whole conversation with Kai had put him in a sour mood.

"Hey, are you okay, bro?" Tom whispered to his buddy. "I don't know where you went, but I think it's best you calm down before you get called up."

At the moment, both of them were taking part in their mandatory extracurricular club activity, rugby. It would be an understatement to say that Gary wasn't really in the mood for it. The two boys sat on the bench along with the rest while Mr. Root gave his typical lecture.

The gist of it was that they were going to try the same thing today that they had done last time, as they had shown enough talent to be selected for the team, not that Gary was paying much attention to what the coach was saying anyway. He was more preoccupied with the agreement he had just made.

He didn't know when, but during their conversation on the roof, Kai had somehow managed to slip Gary a burner phone. Often used by gangs, they weren't digital like smartphones and instead just had physical buttons and a poor screen display.

I don't even know when he slipped it over to me.

He only realized it when in the middle of his walk, something started to vibrate in his pocket. On the screen was a message.

This is your new phone. Don't give this number to anyone. Whenever I need to contact you, I will do so here, so remember to keep it charged ;-)

So, he really is going to treat me like his loyal dog to do his bidding. Hmm.

Before his anger could get the better of him, he reminded himself just why he had joined a gang in the first place.

For the sake of his family.

No matter what he needed to do, his priority was to keep his family safe from the Underdogs. If that meant he had to become Kai's personal dog for a while, then so be it. Personally, he found it a lot more annoying to be ordered around by someone so close to his own age, but that was something he would have to swallow.

"What is wrong with you kids?" Mr. Root shouted in his deep booming voice. Apparently, Gary wasn't the only one who hadn't been paying attention to Mr. Root. Even Tom seemingly considered picking his nose to be a more fruitful activity.

"It seems you guys need some motivation! Luckily for you, I know just the thing that would have rattled my behind when I was your age." Mr. Root blew his whistle to cue in their surprise.

At that moment, a group of girls who were still in their school uniforms walked onto the field. A couple of boys who looked to be a few years ahead of them were carrying a couple of benches with them and placed them on the field for the girls.

Immediately, Gary noticed that the new girl, Xin, was among the spectators.

"Hey, calm down, buddy, or your little soldier might pop out," Tom teased.

Gary looked down at the ground and started taking deep breaths. Tom might have only been jesting, but a teenage boy's hormones truly were no joke. Just thinking about the possibility elicited a reaction in his pants.

"You know, Xin's a cool girl. You should have come with us; she actually likes playing video games, and I'm not talking about those cheap-ass phone games. Also, she seems to be into martial arts. I believe she might even practice some kind herself. Oh, and get this, the best thing about her . . . she friggin' loves Altered fights! She's like the perfect girl; something's got to be wrong with her, right?" Tom nudged Gary, expecting some type of reaction.

"Hey," Gary said, taking in a deep breath.

Gary, first you scare me by saying weird things and doing strange things. You would tell me if there was something wrong with you, yeah, bro? Tom thought, but he was too afraid to say it out loud.

Tom was afraid of rejection and he didn't want to seem pushy, especially since Gary was his only friend.

"I think I'm feeling better now," Gary said, lifting his head, his face slightly red.

Tom sighed and wiped his forehead. Normally he would have had another snarky reply, but something was clearly off about Gary today.

"Now that we have an audience, some of you might actually start to take things seriously. I bet some of you will be looking to impress these sweet young ladies," Mr. Root said. "And if you aren't able to do that, then you should feel embarrassed for wasting their time, making them watch such a pathetic display of sports!" he screamed.

Just like last time, Blake carried the ball, and the coach called groups of three people from the bench to try to take the ball away from him. Unsurprisingly, nothing really changed now that the girls were watching them.

Eventually, after everyone else had failed, Gary, Tom, and Harry were called up to be the defenders. Gary dragged his feet across the ground and didn't look up once, too afraid of what might happen if he caught a glimpse of Xin again. If he were to transform with all eyes on him, the situation would be . . . *disastrous* didn't even cover it.

"Hey, what the hell is wrong with him? Why is he walking so strangely?" one of the girls whispered from the sideline.

"I think he might have crapped his pants," another one snickered in a hushed tone.

"Why is his hair so green? Does he want us to mistake him for grass?" a third one said.

Even though they were a fair distance away from the girls, Gary could hear it all. He could hear his heartbeat, the boys, and all the girls talking about the boys, including him. Naturally, everyone had nothing but good things to say about Blake, but then something interesting caused Gary's ears to twitch.

"Hey, Xin, as the new girl, who do you have your eyes on?" one of the girls surrounding her asked. With Xin being the mayor's daughter, there were plenty of girls who wanted to befriend her.

"It has to be Blake, right? All these other boys are a bit immature and strange, if you ask me. Like, can you believe it, they get far too obsessed with those Altered fights. Why would you find two people hitting each other fun, I just don't understand it," another girl commented.

"Oh," Xin replied in surprise. "I actually like those Altered fights a bit myself. As for the boys . . . hmm, I agree that Blake has potential. His muscles are built solidly, and his lean body frame allows for fast movements. His reflexes so far have been amazing as well.

"However, if you mean romantically, then I'm not interested in any of them. Maybe if one of these boys could beat me in a fight, then I would be impressed."

Her words stunned the other girls, and they didn't really know what to say.

"Erggh, right. I guess those Altered fights are a little cool." The one who had just made fun of the sport quickly changed her tune.

What a bunch of fakes, Xin thought, but outwardly she kept her friendly appearance. *This is exactly why I told Dad that I didn't want to transfer here or at least wanted to use a fake name.*

Gary had heard it all from the field, and specifically, he was repeating in his head the last thing Xin had said: that if someone could beat her in a fight, she might show a bit of interest. He smiled.

If I beat Blake, won't it show her that I'm strong? Maybe that will get her interested in me!

New Quest received
Woo the girl of your dreams
At your age, boys only care about two things: money and girls. So, act as if your life depended on it and show her who the alpha is!
Task: Retrieve the ball from the opponent!
Quest reward: 10 Exp

Gary was a little bit distracted by the new quest popping up right in front of him, but the piercing sound of the whistle quickly snapped him back into action. Blake was running toward them, gripping the ball tightly. Passing Tom was easy enough, as his best friend just stood there like a plant.

"Tom!" Mr. Root shouted, enraged. "I'm going to . . . I'm going to . . . just get off the field, you disgrace!" He kicked a patch of grass.

Harry attempted to get the ball, but as usual, Blake easily avoided the grab, leaving only Gary, who was now intentionally hyping himself up.

130 BPM
135 BPM
140 BPM

His pulse didn't stop rising, and Gary wasn't trying to control it. A large piece of mud and grass flew into the air as Gary shot off like a rocket toward his schoolmate.

Blake didn't even have time to react, and the only thing he could do was go for a spin.

I'm faster! I'm faster than before! I can do it! Gary thought triumphantly.

When Blake had finished his spin, Gary was right there in front of him. The two of them collided, shoulder to shoulder.

Defying everyone's expectations, the one to fly through the air with the ball still in his hand was none other than Blake, despite his larger size. Not letting his eye off the ball, Gary followed up with a great leap that would even make some professional basketball players jealous.

When they landed on the ground, Gary was the first one to get up, with the ball in his hand.

"I got it; I got the freaking ball!" Gary shouted with joy, holding a deflated ball that his thumb had managed to pierce through.

"Excellent!" Mr. Root shouted. "Now that's what I call a tackle. Congratulations, you're officially off the bench!"

Out of the corner of his eye, Gary peeked toward the girls. Most of them were saying horrible things about him for hurting the school's superstar, but he didn't care about their opinion. He was only interested to know what Xin thought about him.

"What a crazy good jump," the girl muttered to herself. Although this was in no way a direct compliment, it was nevertheless enough for Gary . . . for now.

Maybe this werewolf thing isn't so bad after all. I will just have to learn to control it.

13 days until the next full moon

. . . the sooner, the better . . .

CHAPTER 13

THE GYM

Quest completed
10 Exp received

"Amazing performance! Did you all see that?" Mr. Root seemed ec-static at Gary's performance. "Last week, he was sitting on his ass, and today he put Blake on his backside instead."

Honestly, even Gary was impressed with his own performance; something like that would have been impossible for him before. Al-though he was able to follow Blake's movements, he had always lacked the strength or speed to act on it, so this was a huge improvement.

"You're on the team and will be playing in the first match, broc-coli head!" Mr. Root shouted as the field was being cleared up. It was the end of practice for the day.

Gary, having briefly forgotten about what had happened to him, suddenly noticed that Blake was still on the ground, and he went over to offer him a helping hand.

"I'm sorry about that! You're not hurt or anything, are you?" Gary asked, worried that he might have scratched him or broken a few bones. He had yet to find out just how strong he was in comparison to a human, something that he had not taken into account in all his excitement.

"Don't worry; I'm a lot better than you were yesterday," Blake answered jokingly as he accepted Gary's hand. He could see that

Gary wasn't paying attention to him directly; his eyes were aimed right past him, toward the girls who were leaving the field.

Seems like Coach's method really got you motivated, Blake thought with a smile.

The others got to work clearing the rest of the field, putting away the cones and the balls that they used for practice. Tom was one of these helpers, and he was also the one to have stumbled upon the very ball that Gary had taken out of Blake's hand.

It was completely deflated; he turned it around and saw several large punctures. One could have been a coincidence, but the football had five, as if someone had pierced it with their fingers.

First the desk in class and now the ball? Gary, what the hell did you do? No, this isn't a movie or a book. I'm sure there has to be a perfectly normal explanation for this . . . but then why did you ask me all those questions about werewolves earlier? Tom was feeling more distant from his friend than ever as the whole rugby team congratulated him on his performance and welcomed him onto the team.

Walking back home, Gary had a huge smile on his face. It had been one horrible day followed by one of the best days of his life, he mused, but soon he was reminded of the troubles he still had to face.

It looks like the faster my heartbeat gets, the more it affects my transformation. Shit, doesn't that mean if I get too excited, I might fully turn? How the hell would I explain suddenly growing fur or becoming larger? And what was that thing with the mark when I shook Kai's hand earlier?

Thinking about this, he opened up the system screen, and information about the mark was displayed.

Bond Mark

A Bond Mark is a type of marking you can leave when you have made a sincere promise with another party. Those who are marked are given a unique scent, allowing you to track down the Bond Mark at any point in time. If the promise is broken, the marking will break as well.

Those with a Broken Mark automatically become hunting targets. Additional stats will be awarded if you manage to successfully hunt your target down!

Gary grabbed the side of his head, cursing himself for not having taken advantage of the opportunity to mark Kai.

Wait, is the mark invisible, or at least something only I can see? Wouldn't that raise a ton of questions otherwise? Then he gulped as he thought about the second part. *Successfully hunt down a target . . . so does the system want me to kill them?*

Trying to forget about the negative side, Gary thought back to practice, when he had snatched the ball from Blake.

The quest gave me 10 Exp just for that alone, coupled with the 40 Exp I got for defeating those guys earlier, that means I'm halfway to leveling up! Just what will happen once I reach 100 Exp? Will I just get stronger, or will I gain an ability or a skill?

Thinking about this reminded Gary that he still had to try to complete the other quests. One of them was eating two kilograms of meat a day, and the other required him to join the gym. With the prepayment from his old gang job, he still had a wad of cash on him to go for the latter.

I guess it wouldn't hurt to try it.

He headed to a downtown gym and paid them the one-day trial fee. He was ready to work out. A few people inside the gym looked at him as he entered wearing his school clothes, making it clear to everybody inside that he was an amateur.

Where am I supposed to even start? Did the system just expect me to come in here and start lifting? With a confused look on his face, it wasn't long until a gym employee approached him, smiling as he rubbed his hands together.

"This looks like your first time here. I'm a personal trainer, so if you need any help, I will give you the first lesson for free."

"It's okay, I—"

"No need to be so cautious; as I said, the first lesson is completely free! Here, let me guide you on how to use the equipment. You won't believe how many gym users injure themselves because they do things wrong. So first of all, let's weigh you and then we'll look at your body fat percentage. With that data, I'll create a personal plan just for you."

Not even letting Gary get a word in, the trainer hustled him off to the scale; he had Gary just where he wanted him.

These personal trainers . . . they're worse than car salesmen! I just wanted to try to do my own thing and get out of here! What am I supposed to do now? Then again, the guy had said the first lesson was free.

After some measurements, the trainer took him over to the bench press. He was quite buff, nearly as muscular as Mr. Root. He put weight after weight on either end, and soon the trainer was pressing away while describing all the correct moves.

Is this guy really trying to teach me, or does he just want to show off in front of a newbie?

Finally, the trainer stopped and allowed Gary to try while he went around the back of the rack to help him in case anything went wrong.

I've never even been to the gym before; how much weight can I lift?

The trainer was looking at the weights on the bar, with his hands ready. He hadn't even removed any of the weight he had originally put on the bar.

This kid, I can see he wasn't impressed by my bulging hard muscles. I guess he's never been to the gym before, so he doesn't know how hard this is. When he tries to lift the weight off the bar he'll understand, and I'll be there to pick the weight off him when he does, the trainer thought.

Although it didn't look like Gary had paid close attention, he remembered each of the points the trainer had made and was now copying his starting position, arching his back slightly. He copied the trainer to the point where he almost looked like a replica.

Oh, this kid's form is pretty good. The trainer was surprised, wondering if Gary was just pretending to be new to this.

When he tried to lift the weight off the rack, Gary could feel it budge only slightly. He held his breath and began pushing and pushing.

It's no use.
100 BPM
110 BPM
120 BPM
Your Strength is increasing

Soon Gary had lifted the bar off the rack and lowered it to his chest. He then lifted it again and placed it perfectly back, completing one full rep.

Wiping the sweat from his head, Gary got off the bench.

"Did I do a good job?" Gary asked.

The trainer stood there stunned and started to look around to see if anyone else had seen what he had just witnessed.

This is a joke, right? One of those PouTube videos, surely. He laughed to himself, but when he tried to lift the bar, the weight was still there; no one had tampered with it.

The weight's at least a hundred kilograms; how was he able to press that much in one go?

You've had your first taste of working out!
I'll let you off for now and allow you to complete the quest, but remember to work out daily to get a body fit for a werewolf!
Daily Quest complete
10 Exp received

"Ah, this is great! I thought I would have to stay here at least a few hours. I'll come back tomorrow." Gary was elated and ran off, leaving his stunned trainer there.

Knowing that the system was giving him Exp for completing all these quests, Gary decided to stop off at the supermarket. There he bought two kilograms of meat, and now it was time for him to complete the second Daily Quest.

While walking out of the supermarket, though, he suddenly stopped.

No, I can't just bring this back! If I cook all of this and eat it in front of Mom, she'll ask where I got the money to buy it, and she'll think I'm a monster for scarfing down so much meat!

Gary pulled the meat he had just bought out of the plastic bag and looked at it through the cellophane: the red juice dripping off the raw steak, the white marbled areas. He'd never found raw meat appetizing before, but for some reason, he was just drooling at the sight of it.

He made sure no one was looking and then stepped into an alleyway. He used his fingernail to pierce the plastic, and the scent immediately hit his nose.

There was no second-guessing himself; as if he were being controlled by something, he grabbed the raw meat and tore a big chunk out of it. Soon he found himself wolfing it all down, easily ripping through it with his teeth.

When all the meat was gone, once again the message popped up.

Daily Quest complete
10 Exp received

He wiped his mouth with the sleeve of his shirt, which was now covered in meat juice.

What the hell am I? No regular Altered ever said that their instincts got the better of them. Oh God, I really am a monster! Gary lamented having accepted the job that day.

On the walk home, Gary grew depressed as his head filled with negative thoughts, but when he entered his bad neighborhood, he was soon reminded of why he was doing what he was doing.

If this system is really like a game, then when I level up I should get stronger! Those quests were daily, so I should get them again tomorrow as well, he thought. *The problem is, meat isn't cheap, but neither is joining the gym, and I still want to help Mom and Amy. To do all this, I'm still going to need money and lots of it, yet I can't go back to my old part-time job.*

Racking his brain, trying to think of anything he could do, he regretfully decided to text one person.

I can't go back to the Underdogs, but I really need some cash ASAP! Do you have a way for me to make more? Maybe I can help you with something?

Even though they had both belonged to the same gang, he had never seen Kai work as a transporter, not to mention that he was clearly a lot better off than Gary was, so Gary was willing to bet Kai was doing something else for the gang.

No problem. Meet me at the school gate tonight; just make sure to come alone!

CHAPTER 14

CURIOUS TOM

Once school was over, Tom had headed directly home, only today it had been without his best friend by his side. Honestly, after how weirdly Gary had behaved the whole day, Tom was convinced that something was going on with him.

The broken desk, suddenly being able to send Blake flying, the pierced rugby ball . . . could Gary really be a . . . He gulped before allowing his mind to finish his thought. *A werewolf?*

Just one day ago, he would have immediately refused to believe such lunacy. Unfortunately, it was an answer that would completely and perfectly explain all the strange occurrences today. If Gary hadn't brought it up earlier, it might have never even crossed his mind.

As always, Tom was the first one to arrive home. His parents were both scientists working for an important company a few hours' drive away in a Tier 2 city and were therefore gone for most of the day. He was happy that their income allowed them to live comfortably in this middle-class house, in their middle-class city, although he wouldn't have minded seeing them more often. By the time they came home, they were completely tired out, and working overtime and on weekends was unfortunately the norm than the exception.

Tom worked extra hard at school to avoid ending up like his parents. His dream was to one day own a huge mansion in a Tier 1 city, surrounded by beautiful maids who would cater to his every wish. Just like Gary, he saw becoming an Altered as a surefire way to end up living such a cozy life.

However, unlike his best friend, he was also interested in the technical side surrounding the Altered. Tom had clearly inherited his parents' curiosity, so he kept up to date on everything in that regard as well, be it new fossils that were unearthed or any developments that might allow humanity to gain more Altered.

Tom entered his room, which was filled with computers that he had built himself: multiple towers and multiple screens with multiple tabs open. He sat down at his desk, and his hands were slightly shaking as his fingers hovered over the keyboard.

If Gary really is a werewolf, and it's like in those movies and books, then at the full moon this could get very dangerous. He could end up hurting people, including his mother, his sister, or even me.

With this in mind, Tom knew what to search for, and he started typing away.

How to kill a werewolf

As usual, the internet was full of contradicting information. Some sites claimed that werewolves didn't exist, while others made them out to be just supernatural beings, most likely dog-type Altered, which could be killed similarly to humans; it would just take a little bit more effort.

However, this wasn't what Tom was looking for. He just wanted to find an easy method to verify whether Gary was one. The most common answer that came up was to use silver, which was supposed to hurt these creatures to varying degrees depending on the source.

He opened his drawer and pulled out a snake-shaped silver pendant his parents had given him on his last birthday. He had never worn it at school because he thought jewelry was a little tacky and didn't really fit his style.

Of course it's a snake, Tom thought as he looked around the room. During his childhood, he had a phase when he had been fascinated by the cold-blooded reptiles, and he had made the mistake of telling his parents exactly that. From that day on, all of his relatives, including his parents, bought him presents pertaining to those creatures, be it snake posters, snake toys, or snake movies. Unsurprisingly, he had long since grown to hate them. Still, for once, he was glad as he held the silver pendant in his hand. However, it wasn't enough for him; Tom wanted something else.

After a couple of hours of research, he found something else that might work, though opinions on it were split. The hypothesis was that since chocolate was toxic to both dogs and wolves, the same was likely true for werewolves. As dumb as he found the idea to be, it was the best thing he could actually test for.

Tom rushed down to the cupboard, only to be disappointed when he opened it.

I better go out and get some, then.

It was late at night, and he had heard his parents come home, today of all days. They might be sleepy, but they wouldn't let him go out unless he had a very good reason for it. It didn't take a genius to figure out that "getting chocolate" wouldn't cut it.

This left him with no other choice but to sneak out his bedroom window. It wouldn't be his first time climbing down to leave the house without anyone finding out. Fortunately, there was a shop not too far away that should have some, so Tom wasn't too worried, but just to be safe, he still changed into a hoodie.

During the day, the city was largely peaceful, but everyone knew that it had many gangs. Once the sun had set, it wasn't uncommon to run into someone belonging to one of them. Covering his own head made him feel a little safer. It was just a short ten-minute walk to the nearest convenience store, so he gambled on his luck to not encounter any.

On the way, he passed through an empty park and then through a few back streets without a hitch. However, standing outside his destination were a few older-looking high school students, each wearing a black band around either an arm or a leg. They were smoking and drinking alcohol, with their bikes on the ground.

These lowlifes . . . is this really how they plan to live? Just hanging outside a shop all day smoking and drinking? Good luck getting into college! For a second, Tom made eye contact with one of them.

"What the hell are you looking at, man?" one of the students said. "You look at me like that again and I'll bust your lip!"

Tom didn't want any confrontation, so he quickly averted his gaze and practically rushed inside the shop. He purchased quite a few large chocolate bars, then left the shop and quickly walked away, ignoring the gang members.

I hope this is enough chocolate, Tom thought. *The question is, how do I get Gary to eat it without it seeming odd?*

Walking back home through the dark alleys, Tom was starting to feel nervous. There was no one else around.

Suddenly, he heard several people laughing derisively, and a few seconds later several bikes skidded out in front of him, blocking his path.

"I told you, no one looks at me that way and gets away with it!" the person in front told him, while the ones behind him were looking forward to a good show.

CHAPTER 15

TOP DOG

What a horrible situation, Tom thought. *This shitty neighborhood! I didn't even do anything to you! I may have thought you were scum, but it's not like I told you that to your face!*

There were four of them; the black bands showed their affiliation to a color gang. Tom was considering what to do, but he was afraid resisting or fighting back would just worsen his situation. And outrunning them on their bikes would be impossible.

Looks like there's no way around a beating. I just hope after a few punches he'll get bored, and they'll leave.

The one Tom had offended hopped off his bike, while the rest stayed on theirs, most likely to catch up to him if he tried to make a run for it. Tom had resigned himself to his fate, so he gritted his teeth, clenched his hands, and closed his eyes as he waited for the impact from the inevitable fist.

Instead, he heard a scream.

"My arm! You shithead, this had nothing to do with you! Who the hell are you?"

Opening his eyes, Tom saw the boy down on the floor, holding his elbow, which appeared to have been broken. He was addressing a man dressed in a large black trench coat who had suddenly appeared in front of Tom.

"Me? I'm just someone who happened to pass by. This world has enough dangers that we humans don't need to be fighting each other, yet here you are ganging up on a defenseless kid. You scum are the worst."

Since the man was in front of him, Tom could only see that he had long flowing hair and a solid body. Calling him tall would be an understatement; Tom estimated him to be well over eight feet. As he turned around, Tom got a good look at his face. His savior had a scruffy beard but overall good looks. It was as if he was staring at an older version of Blake.

The other students who hadn't gotten hurt got off their bikes and started to pull out weapons, and the one on the ground took out a pocketknife.

"Don't worry about me; I deal with things a lot worse than these small-time trash on a daily basis." The man smiled at Tom as he ran toward one of the students, who held an iron bike chain.

The boy panicked and lashed it out, but stepping away, the man avoided it and grabbed it. He then ripped the chain out of the attacker's hands and swung it at his legs. Tom found it a bit ironic that the man seemed to have better mastery over the boy's weapon.

The man easily dispatched the others one by one. Without breaking a sweat, he simply knocked the pocketknife from the first boy's hand before kneeing him in the face.

Tom had to pinch himself to make sure he wasn't dreaming. He even looked around to check for hidden cameras, but of course, there were none. There was no one else to witness the six of them. It didn't take long, and the man had taken out all four of them carefully.

"Go home, kid, there are a lot more dangerous things out and about in the middle of the night, and you won't always be lucky enough to have a Good Samaritan to help you out," the man advised as he walked away.

Who was that? Tom wondered.

There was one more person who had snuck out of his house, only in Gary's case, it was a lot harder to do so. At least it should have been; however, this time he found it a lot easier to escape their apartment on the top floor. There was a lot more strength in his fingers as he grabbed onto the window ledges and slowly went down until he reached the bottom. Even landing on the ground didn't result in any pain in his feet or knees.

Gary smirked. *Maybe this whole werewolf thing does have more perks than I initially thought.*

The meeting place set by Kai was in front of the school. Gary would have usually changed into his normal black-and-red tracksuit, but that was also the uniform given to him by his gang. There was no reason to run around with a target on his back; instead, Gary had grabbed some plain clothing, just a white top and black pants.

When Gary arrived, Kai was standing there, staring off into the distance just as he had done on the rooftop. The only thing missing was the wind to make his hair flutter. From a distance, Gary could tell that Kai was still wearing his black-and-gold Bolex watch, which just annoyed him even more but also reminded him why he was here.

"I'm here just like you asked, so what's the job?" Gary asked, getting straight to the point.

Kai looked Gary up and down and scoffed a little at what he was wearing.

"You got here a lot faster than I expected, seeing as I only texted you a short while ago. Did you already happen to be in the area?" Kai asked in return, and Gary just scratched his head nervously and nodded. "Well, it seems to be a good thing, considering your current outfit. There's no way in hell I'm letting you go like that. Here!"

Kai threw a sports bag over to Gary.

"What's this?" Gary asked. Opening it up, he found some clothing inside waiting for him. He was surprised to see that it was just his size, even though he had never told Kai that information.

"Have you already forgotten what I told you? We'll be making a new gang, and today you'll be the one to represent us. I don't want us to be one of those poor gangs who wear hoodies and tracksuits and harass people. The first impression counts, and since this will be our debut, you'll need to make yourself look sharp."

Gary looked around for somewhere to change, but the school was already closed, and there was nowhere else. Seeing him hesitate, Kai crossed his arms expectantly.

"It's nearly the middle of the night, so there's nobody to see you anyway." Kai tapped his foot impatiently.

Gary wanted to argue that Kai was there, but his gaze made it clear that he was starting to get irritated. Unfortunately for Gary, he was depending on Kai and couldn't risk pissing him off. Although he didn't want to, Gary reluctantly got changed in front of the school into the new clothes that Kai had brought for him.

Gary now wore a small jacket over his white top, without a hood, yet with a collar that popped outward. The trousers were quite tight-fitting, but in a material that expanded, and he had a matching pair of boots. In fact, even though the clothes looked uncomfortable, the material was very flexible, making it feel quite nice on his skin.

However, there was one thing he didn't like: the colors, which made him wonder whether it was his fashion sense that was off or Kai's.

"Perfect, you actually look half-decent now. Don't look at me like that; you should know that every gang has something that symbolizes which gang they're from," Kai explained. "Before, you wore red and black, and now you'll be black and gold. Trust me, with how many gangs there are, this was the best available color combo!"

Now that Kai had pointed it out, Gary noticed that he was already dressed that way. The main color of his clothes was black, with the trim, the outline, and the small details golden.

"Unfortunately, your hairstyle still sticks out like a sore thumb, but we don't have the time to do anything about it. It's something we'll have to solve another time," Kai stated with a smirk as he jokingly made a cutting gesture. At least Gary hoped that it was just a joke.

The two of them did not move inside, since the actual meeting place wasn't at the school. No matter how many times Gary asked where they were going, after telling him it would be a surprise the first time, Kai ignored his questions.

Eventually, they reached a parking ramp. It was a bit away from the main shopping street, and it also looked a little run-down, but it appeared to be quite lively inside. There were people hanging around outside acting as bouncers. The most surprising thing was that they looked to be high school students no older than eighteen.

Finally he and Kai entered an elevator and went to the top floor. Once the elevator doors opened, Gary was hit with a wave of cheers and screams as if he had come to a rave party.

What the hell is going on? Gary thought.

They were all high school students, some even still in their school uniforms, and they were all cheering at a fight happening in the center of the room.

"This is an illegal fighting event, for high school students only," Kai explained, with a nasty smile. "This is where the strongest students meet up and duke it out among themselves to decide who the top dog is!"

CHAPTER 16

GREEN FANG

"It's pretty impressive for just high school students, right? And this isn't the only one. This is one of the many underground fighting clubs spread through the whole country. Although this is just a small one," Kai told Gary, who was still a bit taken aback at the idea that people his age would gather to watch teenagers fight for amusement.

If this is considered "small," just how large is big?

Gary found it hard to comprehend, since he guessed that at least five hundred people were present. On closer inspection, he noticed that the teens and tweens seemed to be gathered in groups, each wearing their own sort of uniform. It looked like a club meeting, with students from all sorts of different schools.

Kai, having a keen eye, noticed what Gary was looking at.

"Remember what I said about many people from different school groups being here? Those school gangs take this quite seriously. They dress the way they do so they can make a name for themselves. Just like with the gangs, the idea is for you to see their clothing and instantly know who they belong to. It might sound impressive for a bunch of students to organize all of this . . . it's because the ones responsible are the gangs."

"Gangs?" Gary gulped, looking around to see if he could see any well-known ones among them. "Do you mean like the Underdogs?"

Kai couldn't help but chuckle, seeing Gary acting so nervous.

"Do you think the Underdogs would come down here personally? This here is the *very* minor leagues, basically just a gathering of a bunch of no-name schools, or what we refer to as 'loners' attempting to join one of the other gangs, proving their strength.

"Still, this is technically a recruitment field, and there are scouts from gangs here, but they would be like D Tier gangs. They either absorb one of these smaller gangs into their own or look at who they can snatch up to join their gang in the future. You know, since guns are now nonexistent, knowing how to use your fists or a weapon is a big deal. At the bigger events, there are even those that are Altered."

What Kai was referring to was the No Lethal Weapons Pact, which had come into play a little after they were born. With how fast and how badly the world had been deteriorating, countries were worried that World War Three could start at any moment and humanity would just end up destroying the planet.

So every single country in the world had agreed to a pact to get rid of nuclear weapons, missiles, tanks, and anything of mass destruction. With technology, it was nearly impossible to hide anything from other countries, so they couldn't even build things in secret.

This just accelerated the development of Altered between countries, as they strived to create the perfect human being.

What shocked Gary was that there were apparently things like this going on all over the place that he hadn't known about. The underworld was certainly another side that people didn't see unless they were involved in it . . . and, more importantly, invited.

"So what are we doing here?" Gary asked as the two of them pushed through the crowd until they eventually reached the outer edge. The onlookers had formed a large ring so as to not interfere with the fighters. The fight was also being livestreamed, so others could watch it on their phones and devices.

"Well, remember what I said about loners not belonging to a gang? It's easy to see who is part of one and who isn't by their colors, or more accurately the lack thereof," Kai pointed out.

Gary saw quite a few people who weren't wearing any obvious colors, like the ones currently in the ring.

"Wait, what are you saying?"

"I'm saying we can't create a gang with just the two of us! We need more people, and can you think of a more perfect place than this?"

Gary suddenly understood why Kai had more than one set of clothing in the bag he had handed him earlier. He intended to give it to new recruits on the spot!

Gary watched the two as they fought, wanting to get an idea of just how skilled these fighters were. Both looked the same age as him, about fifteen or sixteen years old.

One was a Black boy with short spiky blond hair who wore a sleeveless shirt; his muscles showed quite well, and he had a couple of scars on his shoulders.

His opponent was a larger boy who was nearly twice as big. It wasn't that the first boy was small; it was just that this one was incredibly large.

The two of them exchanged a few blows, and a few punches from the Black boy hit the larger one in the stomach, but he just laughed it off as if it were nothing.

"Who will win, Innu the Warrior or Spike the Blob? Last chance to place your bets, everyone!" one of the students announced, walking around with a board showing the odds, which were currently in favor of the Blob.

"Interested in placing a bet? If I'm not mistaken, you should have received a nice down payment. Although knowing you, you probably didn't bring any cash along, so want me to lend you some?" Kai offered with a wide grin.

Watching the two fighters gave Gary a good idea who he thought would win, but placing a bet was out of the question for him—although he was sure anything could happen in a fight, especially one like this, without any clear rules. He came here to win money, not risk losing it all, and he had a premonition that borrowing from Kai would just be placing a leash on himself.

"Is this what you meant when you said we could make money?" Gary asked.

"Nah, as I said, this is just for fun. I'm merely curious to know, who do you think will win? Remember, I haven't finished testing out how useful you are to me yet."

So far, none of the attacks from Innu the Warrior had proven effective, and it looked like Spike the Blob would soon tire him out and beat him. Just then, Innu took a stance where he bent his knees slightly and raised his hands above his head.

It looked similar to a boxing stance, but Gary knew straightaway that it wasn't.

"I don't gamble, but if I had to place a bet, I would place it on Innu," Gary said, making sure to emphasize his no-gambling policy. However, Kai was no longer listening. He brought out a wad of cash and waved the person over to register his bet.

"All of this on Innu!" Kai demanded as he put down what Gary estimated to be at least one thousand dollars.

"Wait! I told you I don't want to borrow any of your money!"

"Who says it's for you? Don't worry, this is my own bet."

The fight continued, and this time the Blob got into a downward position similar to one in football. He then readied himself and charged forward at a great speed that no one had seen before in the fight.

Those who had bet on the Blob cheered. Before, they had thought it likely that he would win, but seeing this display of his talent, they were sure of it. Even the scouts from the gangs seemed to consider giving him an offer after this round.

At that moment, though, Innu used his knee to strike the Blob in the face, using his own force against him. Blood splattered as his nose was broken; the fighter himself was thrown through the air and landed in a daze. Innu the Warrior didn't stop there; he leapt off the Blob's thigh and struck down with his elbow at the top of his opponent's head. Innu did this three times in a row and then gripped the Blob's head with both of his thighs.

As they fell to the ground, Innu never let go, and once the Blob's body hit the floor, Innu finally rolled over and there was a clear winner.

The crowd erupted in cheers despite some of them having lost their money, as people always loved seeing a turnaround, and Innu had given them quite the spectacle.

After collecting his own fight money, Innu went to rest, and Spike the Blob was carried off to the side.

"Just a lucky guess?" Kai asked as he gleefully counted his winnings—which Gary couldn't stop eyeing, wishing he had made the bet.

"His stance; although it looked like boxing, he's actually a Muay Thai fighter. They focus on using their knees and elbows. One had fighting experience and was calm throughout the match, never looking worried, while the other was just a street fighter, in other words, your average bully," Gary answered.

Kai let out an appreciative whistle, realizing that Gary was more special than he had thought. He brought out his phone and started to type away, and without looking up, he asked Gary a question. "So, have you thought about an alter ego name for today? Given that the Underdogs still want your hide, using your real name or the fake one you've given them isn't advisable. What would you want as a stage name?"

"A stage name?" Gary thought about it for a moment. Given his change, he would pick something werewolf-related. "Erghh, maybe something like Silver Fang, but wh—"

"Silver Fang won't do; your hair's green," Kai said, interrupting him as he finished typing and sent out his message.

"Next, we have a new fighter, fighting for the first time. He wishes to keep his name a secret, but he goes by the name Green Fang!"

the announcer shouted out to the crowd to hype them up while Gary had still been connecting the dots.

"You wanted to make some money, right? Don't worry, I will bet on you, and we can share the profits. This is the best way to get our name out here, so it's time for you to go make us some money, Green Fang." Kai said with a smile.

CHAPTER 17

ROUND 1

Before Gary had a chance to refuse to participate in the next fight, the crowd opened up a path for him, and with a not-so-gentle push, Kai forced him to enter the arena. The high school students were now looking at him from every direction. It felt as if they were seeing right through him, trying to analyze what type of person he was.

Was it a mistake to go to Kai? Gary was left wondering. As a fan of Altered fights, he had naturally dreamed about being on stage himself. Who would have thought he would get a chance . . . only that it would be at an underground fighting club?

The spectators did not seem to be too impressed with Gary, as he was pretty average in terms of height. Today had been the first time he had ever visited a gym, so his lean figure did not have any muscles for him to show off. Compared to the previous contestants, he just didn't look as if he would last long.

BPM is rising
90 BPM
95 BPM
99 BPM

Goddammit, Kai, why couldn't you have warned me at least? Shit, I have to calm down. With so many people watching, I can't dis-

play too much power! Gary worried as he looked around. His fight-or-flight response had kicked in, and he would definitely prefer the latter option until he got a better feel for his newfound powers.

Unfortunately for Gary, Kai was nowhere to be seen.

"Let's now give a big welcome to his opponent! With fifteen fights under his belt, he has won ten of them . . . Biiillllllyyyy Buuuuussssstttteeeeerrrrr!" the announcer called out, and the crowd erupted in cheers as a large bald man entered from the opposite side. Billy had his top off, displaying his six-pack of flabs, and in addition to a normal-looking pair of pants, he wore a pair of thick gloves.

"Oh, you gotta be kidding me! I thought this was high school students only? Why the hell is my opponent a middle-aged man?" Gary complained to the announcer, panicking far too much to realize that what he had just said could be heard by everyone, including his opponent.

"Your opponent might have been held back, but he is merely nineteen years old!" the announcer explained to Gary as well as some newcomers.

"Thanks for not making me feel bad about giving you a beating!" Billy said, approaching Gary as he punched his right fist into his open left hand, a large vein sticking out on his forehead because of his anger.

"Looks like both of our fighters are ready; let's get this show on the road!" the announcer shouted, and Gary's system apparently agreed with him as well.

New Quest received
Win your debut fight
The opponent in front of you is out for blood! Use whatever means necessary to defeat him!
Quest reward: 50 Exp

The quest this time didn't make Gary feel any better about the person he had to fight, and through the clear screen, he could see Billy charging right at him, swinging his right fist. The attack seemed sloppy to him, and Gary's improved eyesight allowed him almost to see the very wrinkles on his opponent's hand.

His natural instincts kicked in, and he ducked down, placing his hands over his face. Having dodged the attack, Gary didn't use the chance to attack in return. Instead . . . he started to run away from Billy.

After winning his fight, Innu had gone over to the bar counter and ordered himself a beer, one of the perks he had received for winning. As he had expected, several people quickly came over, attempting to recruit him over to their teams.

It was rare to see a loner who was quite talented and knew martial arts on top of that. Innu had listened to the various offers, but none of them had piqued his interest.

Kai had deliberately waited for all the hyenas to disappear, but rather than approaching Innu directly as all the others had done, he had ordered himself a fancy cocktail. Once he received it, he took a big swig and leaned against the counter to watch Gary's match for a bit.

So far Green Fang had managed to avoid Billy's wild but powerful swings a few times, and even had thrown a couple himself; unfortunately, they all had rebounded off Billy's large belly.

"Do you fancy yourself a betting man, Innu?" Kai said, addressing him for the first time.

Innu took a second to reply, as he had started to believe that Kai might have really just come over for a drink. He had noticed that Kai was dressed in the same colors as the fighter in the arena.

The strange thing about that was, although Kai had the looks of a pretty boy, he nevertheless appeared to have the physique of an experienced fighter—much more so than his buddy, whose only strength appeared to be dodging and running. Even under his clothes, his muscles were apparent, and Innu had a feeling that Kai was someone who would not shy away from a fight but might actively seek it.

However, most importantly to Innu, the one trait that stood out even more than the others . . . was that this eccentric boy next to him smelled of money! From the clothes he wore to the expensive watch on his wrist, all of it looked to be genuine brand-name items!

"If I weren't a betting man, then I wouldn't be here, and I bet with my life every time I fight," Innu eventually replied.

"Well, that makes two of us, then. Thanks to your performance in the last match, I've already earned a pretty penny," Kai said as he took out a wad of cash, which he then playfully tossed up. He noticed that Innu's eyes became bigger, seemingly trying to estimate how much it was worth, putting a mild smirk on Kai's face.

"I saw that you rejected the offers of the other guys, so how about a little wager to make things interesting? In a moment, I will go over to place a bet on Green Fang with the money I used for my earlier bet. If I turn out to be correct, you'll join our gang, and half the payout sum will be yours. We can call it a nice little advance payment for joining the crew. On the other hand, if he loses, all the money you see here will be yours."

CHAPTER 18

ROUND 2

This wasn't Innu's first underground fight. He had been to quite a few before, and each time he showed off his skills, people approached him. It was the first time he had been to a fight of this size, so he thought today would be the day he finally decided to join a gang.

To him, it was a stepping-stone. These small gangs would be recruited by bigger gangs in the future, or maybe if he stood out he would get on the fast track; but when this blond boy spoke, he did so with a confidence different from all the others—which made Innu want to know more about him.

Innu smiled, as this was less a bet and more of a win-win scenario for him. Either way, he would get a lot of cash, but he was intrigued.

He started paying a lot more attention to the ongoing fight. Innu recognized that Green Fang could see Billy's movements clearly, yet neither his punching nor his kicking showed any sign of him being a trained fighter.

Between the two of them, there was also another clear difference. Weight class. The weight class of one was too large of a gap to overcome. Of the few hits that Gary had landed on his opponent, none seemed to have had any effect, so his downfall would be whenever Billy managed to catch him. In the middle of the fight, he wouldn't suddenly grow in strength. Perhaps he might be able to tire out his opponent, but this arena had something that would combat that strategy to make things more interesting.

If fights took too long, the crowd would start to close in on the fighters, forcefully shrinking down the arena size. Eventually, there would not be enough room for fighters like Gary to evade, in which case it would take only a couple of hits from Billy for him to win.

"Why would I say no to free money?" Innu chuckled, holding out his hand, and Kai slapped it, confirming their deal. Although Innu believed there was a low chance of losing the bet, he also wouldn't mind. The way Kai treated money as just something he could throw around leisurely, Innu was sure that joining him wouldn't be entirely bad. Besides, his eyes gave off the impression that he knew what he was doing.

Now it's all up to you, Green Fang, Kai thought as he went over to place the bet.

In the middle of the match, Gary made a discovery. Looking at his stats, he noticed that his Energy had dropped by 2 points. His system had told him that Energy would be used to restore his HP when idle and that meat could be used to fill it up. Apart from that, he had been under the impression that it would function as a sort of a stamina gauge.

Despite all the running and wild swinging he had been doing, he still felt like he could go on for hours, so if it was that, then he had far more stamina than a normal human. He just had to take a look at Billy for that. The fighter was no longer in the best shape of his life, with sweat visibly dripping down his face. He was deeply huffing and panting, and his swings were getting slower as his arms felt heavier.

Should I just wait for him to run out of gas? Gary wondered, and just then a buzzer sounded. The next moment, everyone in the crowd took a single step forward. Suddenly the arena had gotten smaller.

Gary didn't know the rules of the event, but he could tell that something was about to change, and it was unlikely to be anything good. As Gary looked around in slight confusion, Billy saw his chance and went in for a grab. With no path of retreat, Gary did the only thing he could.

It should be something like this, right? He jumped toward his opponent and shoved his right knee forward. Billy's head had been slightly tilted, so Gary's knee connected with his face.

From the outside, it looked like an exact replica of what Innu had done. He nearly choked on his beer as he watched how Gary had copied his move after seeing it once.

Alas, unlike Innu, Gary lacked the experience to follow up. He had clearly heard and felt Billy's nose break and thought that would be the end of it. But Billy shook it off and, filled with rage, swung his right fist, for the first time managing to hit Gary.

He wasn't sure if he was imagining it or not, but Gary could have sworn he heard a few cracking sounds as he tumbled to the ground, holding his side.

The pain was intense, and with every breath he took, it seemed to hurt even more.

Does that blob have a sledgehammer hidden in those gloves?

You have incurred a grave injury
–17 HP
83/100 HP
The left side of your rib cage has been broken
Energy points will be used to perform emergency healing
–10 Energy
88/100 Energy

As soon as this message appeared, Gary could feel something escape his body. His Energy was sapped away, while at the same time, his breathing got better. A few breaths later and he was back to normal. It was as if he had never been hit in the first place. His broken bones had completely healed. However, his HP value said otherwise.

Whoa! Gary thought, tapping his hurt side slightly. *I healed, and so quickly. Is this what it means to be a werewolf?*

CHAPTER 19

BPM RISING

Gary had visibly suffered a large blow, yet he somehow managed to stand up as if it had been nothing more than a light tap. The crowd was flabbergasted, but not as much as Billy himself, who knew best how much power should have been behind his hit.

Billy's weight should be two times that of Green Fang, Innu mused, calmly analyzing the fight from the sidelines. *Unlike the rookie he should also know how to fight properly, so it's impossible for him to have gone easy on his opponent. I'm also pretty sure there's a reason behind him wearing those gloves . . .*

Innu had been certain that Billy was the clear favorite in this match. Although Gary hadn't been too bad in terms of dodging and evading Billy's attack, the rules of the arena were too much in favor of the veteran fighter. That one hit alone should have been the deciding factor.

"There's always a puncher's chance, as they say in boxing," Kai commented, looking on leisurely, as if everything were proceeding exactly according to his calculation. Nobody noticed that the cocktail glass he had put aside was on the brink of fracturing.

Gary was just as amazed at the extent of his resilience as everyone else, but since it was his body, he was simultaneously the first to realize that it sadly changed very little. If anything, it just meant that he would have to suffer longer as a punching bag.

As if on cue, Billy's experience helped him come to the same conclusion. Since Green Fang had not used this opportunity to fight back, it just meant that his opponent still lacked the means to defeat him. Why else would he have run around the whole time?

So Billy went in for another punch to Green Fang's head. Sensing the incoming threat, Gary braced himself and used his hands to block it, yet in the next moment, he felt a sharp pain from his sides once more.

"Closing your eyes in the middle of a match? You really are a greenhorn!" Billy shouted.

You have incurred a grave injury
–20 HP
63/100 HP
The left side of your rib cage has been broken
Energy points will be used to perform emergency healing
–15 Energy
73/100 Energy

Gary was unable to reply, too busy to grit through the pain. His opponent had fully intended to incapacitate him by striking at his supposedly injured side once more. Were it not for his newly attained healing factor, Gary was sure that the resulting injury would have put him out of commission for a few weeks in the best-case scenario.

I need more power to be able to do anything to that blob! Gary thought. *I just have to be careful to not let my heart rate rise too much!* He was not sure where exactly his limits were, but from the few times he had experienced them, Gary was aware that around 100–120 BPM he seemed to grow more powerful. Nevertheless, somewhere between 130–150 BPM he also started to transform and lose his sanity . . .

The pressure of having to dodge Billy's fists continuously, but more prominently the second buzzer sounding and the crowd closing in on them, making the fighting area even smaller than it was before, worked in his favor.

100 BPM
103 BPM
107 BPM

Unfortunately, although Gary's plan was working as intended, it was not doing so fast enough. Unless he got a power boost fast, he might end up losing this fight. His Energy was seemingly unable to heal his HP, and he was not looking forward to finding out what happened once it hit zero.

He thought back to earlier today and what had allowed him to get his boost. It was one person, the new girl, Xin. He imagined that she was somewhere in this crowd, watching his fight like she had done earlier today.

111 BPM
118 BPM
125 BPM
Your Strength is increasing

Gary could feel the strength rising in him, and seeing Billy's fist, he didn't evade it. This time he widely swung back, and both fists collided in midair. Some of those in the crowd squealed as they imagined the pain Gary must be experiencing at that moment. They were not wrong; he was in a lot of pain, convinced that the knuckles in his fist were broken, yet if they were, it didn't seem to be to a degree that his Energy healing kicked in.

"Ladies and gentlemen, this is the first time that Green Fang has not been pushed back by Billy Buster," the announcer gleefully commented. "Could this be the start of a comeback for our underdog?"

The crowd erupted in cheers as this fight finally started to resemble an actual brawl instead of a game of tag.

Gary couldn't care less about entertaining the crowd. Internally he was cursing because of the pain in his hand, begging the system to do to his hand what it had done to his ribs. Alas, it was to no avail. He had no choice but to continue to ignore it, yet the good thing was that Billy was suffering even more than he was.

Gary's fist had smashed into the metal plating that Billy had kept hidden. Using such devious tricks was not against the rules of the arena, merely frowned upon since the crowd was expecting to see a fair fight. Using brass knuckles was basically the equivalent of a fighter admitting that they didn't believe in their own skills.

How is that possible? How did that broccoli head's punch suddenly get so much stronger? Billy was left wondering as he stood there looking at Gary with his right hand throbbing. *Was he just pretending to be weak to play with me? No, that's impossible; he's obviously a greenhorn, so how?*

It was a strange sight to behold, but Green Fang suddenly seemed like an entirely different person. His eyes were dead set on the person in front of him, and Billy could feel a slight shiver run through his body.

It was midnight already, going into the next day, and the sky was quite clear; moonlight was shining down on all of them. Although Gary was unaware of all of this, he was just ready to go with his natural instincts.

I . . . I . . . need to calm down, Gary thought.

The pain in his hand, the adrenaline of the fight, and thoughts of Xin were all pushing his heart rate higher than ever.

150 BPM
155 BPM
160 BPM
What is happening to me?

CHAPTER 20

HE DID WHAT?

Gary could tell that he was slowly losing his mind, and all his thoughts focused on his desire to get rid of the person in front of him. He ran forward, ignoring the pain; he hoped that if he could win the fight fast enough and get out of the arena, he could try to calm down.

Or at least get far enough away from anyone he could end up hurting.

Billy, who had been too frightened to move up until now, finally snapped out of his daze, having convinced himself that Gary must be far worse off than he was after smashing his fist into the brass knuckles. At that moment, he saw his opponent leap through the air with his hands behind his back.

For the first time, Gary was the aggressor. He latched onto the surprised Billy with his legs under his armpits and his hands behind his neck. Billy managed to loosely grab Gary's hair and pull him forward; although it was not enough to free his arms, it allowed him to punch Green Fang's head.

After the first hit, almost possessed, Gary decided to dig his teeth right into Billy's right shoulder. His powerful jaws easily broke through the thick skin. His victim screamed in pain, wanting nothing more but to get his crazed opponent off, and let go. This prompted Gary to do the same, and he landed on the ground.

As Billy stumbled slightly backward, he worried about the throbbing wound. Unfortunately for him, Gary was not done yet. He leapt through the air once more, this time delivering a dropkick aimed right at Billy's head, which whipped to the side, and his whole body followed. Billy tumbled to the ground; he had taken quite a hit, and the spectators at the front felt the tremor as he landed. Unable to think straight, Gary was determined to finish Billy off. He climbed on top of him, pinning his arms under his knees, and started to strike his head with his open palms as if he were clawing at him, one blow after another.

"Gary, stop! Listen to me; the fight is over!" Kai shouted from the side. The smirk on his face was gone, replaced with a serious expression. He had seen many go through a fighter's high, but in Gary's case, it seemed that there was something more to it.

"Hey, announcer, are your eyes only for decoration? Even an amateur could tell you that Billy Buster is out cold. Announce the result!"

Innu, just like everyone else, couldn't believe his eyes. How was it possible for such a scrawny guy to have such strength and such wildness? In the end, his fighting style, if one wanted to call it that, seemed more like that of a wild animal, one that had been backed into a corner and forced to fight without any concern for self-preservation.

Fortunately, the call had reached Gary, who stopped, looking over toward Kai. He suddenly felt exhausted. His gaze seemed to ask Kai whether the fight was really over, and the next moment he felt as if he had run a marathon.

"Ah, yes. Everyone, as you've heard, Billy Buster seems to have passed out. Please give a big round of applause for our newcomer, GRRREEEENNNN FAAAANNNNNGGGG!!!" the announcer declared after it had become clear that the fight could not continue. Once he did, the system screen appeared in front of Gary to congratulate him.

Quest reward: 50 Exp
Congratulations, you have now reached: Level 2
A new skill has been unlocked
A stat point has been granted

Gary was quite interested in the new skill, but quite honestly, he felt like he was going to collapse at any second, and just when his eyes were about to close, he could see that Kai had hurried over with his hand held out.

"You did well, Green Fang. Come on; I'll take you home," Kai insisted.

Gary accepted his hand, and Kai helped him up and carried him out of the ring over his shoulder. Many people wanted to speak to them on the way out, but nobody dared to stop Kai as they made their way back.

Before leaving, Kai turned toward Innu. "Remember our deal; I'll contact you about where and when to meet tomorrow," Kai said as he continued to walk out, stopping briefly to collect his earnings.

"But how will I contact you?" Innu asked, with a big smile on his face.

"Check out your new uniform!"

Looking down into the bag that Kai had left next to him, Innu pulled out a uniform, and under the clothes was a little burner phone. It was old and had physical buttons, but programmed into the phone was Kai's number.

Looks like I found my gang, Innu thought.

A few minutes later, after Kai and Gary had left, Innu suddenly realized that Kai had yet to give him his money!

Unable to move, Billy had been taken off the stage and transported to the medical area. He had woken up around half an hour after he had been knocked out. The last thing he remembered was being bitten by Green Fang. Although he wasn't sure what had happened next, he just knew that there was no way in hell he would ever fight that crazy bastard again.

The medical staff present were mostly college students who were studying medicine. They were able to treat most things as long as they were not too serious. Billy's broken nose had not been a problem, and once he had woken up, they had informed him that he was mostly fine. The main thing they were concerned about was the bite mark on his shoulder.

"We tried our best to disinfect it, but if it still hurts or stings by tomorrow, it would be in your best interest to get it checked out at the hospital," the one in charge, an actual graduate who was already helping at his parents' medical office, advised him before he went to check on his other patients.

Standing up, Billy did indeed feel fine; only the wound on his shoulder continued to throb.

How the hell am I supposed to explain to them that I was bitten by a human, though?

CHAPTER 21

RABID DOG

After a while, Gary felt fine enough to be able to walk on his own, yet he didn't know how to tell Kai that. His schoolmate was still carrying him over his shoulder, and it would be strange for Gary to recover this fast. After the fight he'd had, he wouldn't be surprised if it took him a week to recover. Without any better ideas, Gary just continued to play the role of an exhausted fighter.

I really need to find a way to control this power. Whenever my heart rate rises, my whole body feels . . . different, and then soon after when it's all over, I get to a low point.

By *low*, Gary was referring to his Energy, which would deplete after a while; according to his status, he had used a lot of Energy points for healing as well, and that seemed to affect him.

Eventually, he and Kai arrived at their school.

"Are you going to be okay getting back on your own?" Kai asked. "I've noticed you're walking a lot better."

Gary hadn't even noticed that Kai had stopped helping him as soon as they got close to the school, and he was standing fine, meaning his cover was blown.

"Ehh, yeah, I'll be fine," Gary replied nervously, his face turning a shade redder for having been caught. Fortunately, with how late it was, Kai didn't notice . . . or at least pretended not to.

"Good." Kai nodded while retrieving a bundle of cash and placing it into Gary's hands. "Here's five hundred for tonight's fight."

Gary had to repeat the number in his head, and he instinctively counted the cash to make sure Kai wasn't joking. It was only a couple of days ago that he had received five hundred for doing the most dangerous job ever, and now he was receiving this much because of one fight.

"Is this how much I won for fighting?" Gary asked, still shocked, wondering why he had ever risked his life working as a transporter when he could have just become a fighter.

Actually, scratch that idea! What are you thinking, Gary, you would have lost every single fight before getting this system! his voice of reason reminded him.

"Not quite. This is a low-level event, after all. Normally, you would have received between one hundred and two hundred bucks, depending on how exciting your match was. As an incentive from the arenas, you get extra depending on how many bets were placed because of your fight.

"Most of that is due to the bets I had made on you. As a newcomer, your odds were naturally horrendous, so great job pulling through. Since this was your debut fight and you left quite an impression, it seemed kind of shabby, just giving you the minimum amount. Besides, I haven't forgotten that you came to me because you were in dire need of money.

"There's actually a lot more to it than that, but for now, the rest of today's earnings will be set aside as 'gang funds' for the future. I'll keep setting that money aside for a rainy day or when the gang needs expanding. Once our gang has grown into a respectable size, you'll have free rein over it," Kai explained casually, as if he had planned this all along.

"You'll let me have access to even more money than what I'm holding?" Gary asked. His brain was trying to process all this information. He had come out today just to earn some cash, yet his partner in crime apparently had already made plans far beyond that.

"Of course I will let you use the money. I'd advise you to discuss what to use it for with your future lieutenants, but as the leader of a gang your word will be law," Kai answered nonchalantly.

"Leader? Now hang on a moment. I know you said you wanted to form a gang and wanted me to work, but this is the first time I'm hearing anything about me being the leader of it! Why would you even do that? It's your gang," Gary complained.

"Look, I've already made up my mind after watching you fight today. A gang needs a certain type of leader, and I think you're perfect for that role. Me, I will be the brains behind the whole thing; I don't really like being in the limelight anyway. It's not my style," Kai argued.

However, Gary wasn't really convinced by that. In school, Kai stuck out like a sore thumb, not to mention that all of his fancy jewelry and expensive clothes practically screamed "Look at me!"

"Do you really think you have much of a choice, Mr. Loyal Dog?" Kai teased, after seeing the unwillingness in Gary's eyes. "Just think of it as being the public face of our gang. All you need to do for the time being is concentrate on getting stronger. For starters, you might want to pick up a proper style, otherwise 'Green Fang' might soon enough become infamous as 'Rabid Dog.'"

Afterward, they each went their separate ways. It had been a crazy evening, that was for sure, and it was hard for Gary to take everything in. Truth be told, he didn't take it all in. One event was just leading to another for him, but most of all, he just wanted to figure out this crazy system.

Level 2
Exp 20/200

Before, Gary had 70 points of Exp and needed 30 more points to level up. After defeating his opponent, he had gained 50 points of Exp, bringing his total to 120/100.

At least it looks like the Exp carries over, but the way quests come up is so random, the only one that is consistent is the workout one and eating food, since they're both Daily Quests.

However, with the level up there also seemed to be a few more changes. For one, he had received a stat point, which appeared as if it could be used in a number of different ways.

A stat point can be used to improve a user's basic stats or to increase one's Health or Energy. If used on Health or Energy, the stat will be increased by 10 points.

Wait, I have stats? I didn't see that before. What even are my stats? Another status screen appeared in front of him.

Strength 4
Dexterity 3
Endurance 8

Gary didn't really know how to gauge these numbers, but he knew, based on how high his Endurance was, that his Strength and Dexterity were extremely low.

I knew I was weak, but that weak?

So I have Health, which seems to go down as my body gets injured. Then there's Energy, which is used up just on a day-to-day basis, but if I start fighting more than it uses, it's similar to a stamina bar in a game. However, it can be used in an emergency to heal my body as well.

As for the normal stats, Strength has to mean how strong I am, right? Dexterity must be things like speed, agility, and reflexes. I'm pretty slow, so that makes sense, and then there's Endurance. I'm glad to know that the only thing my body is good at is taking a beating, but I'm guessing some of that has to do with me turning into a . . . I don't even want to say the word. It feels like bad luck or something.

Thinking about the fight that had just occurred, Gary wondered what the best way to use the stat point was. At first, he thought Dexterity would be most useful. He could become a counterhitter, using his opponents' strength against them, especially if he was going to participate in more underground tournament fights.

However, his mind started to wander, and he found himself thinking about the rugby match and how Xin thought he was kinda cool when he had tackled Blake.

Don't be stupid; your life is more important than getting some girl.

Your Energy has now increased to a maximum of 110

In the end, Gary opted for increasing his Energy. He wondered if the other basic stats would change by themselves if he continued to go to the gym. His stats were based on his body's current state, so he thought this was possible, but how would he increase his Energy or his Health without the system?

The Energy was important for him to fight for a long time, which would give him more time to come up with a way to defeat his opponents and also heal him up. This was a no-brainer.

One more message had appeared in the middle of the match, and that was that Gary had acquired a new skill.

Another screen appeared in front of him.

Current list of skills
Marks: 0/5
Charging Heart (new)

He had already seen what a mark was and what it was meant to do, but it was interesting that he could only have five of them active at one time.

Charging Heart
When activated, the user's heart rate will increase to 150 BPM
The skill will use 10 Energy points
When the user's heart rate is above 150 BPM, all physical stats will be doubled

Does that happen even if my heart rate rises that high on its own? That would explain where the sudden surge of strength came from, but if I'd had this in the last fight I wouldn't have had to start thinking about it . . . Anyway, this is good news; if only there were a skill that could lower it as well.

After reading all the notifications, Gary thought it was time for him to head home. He couldn't stop counting the money that had been given to him as he walked. With this amount, depending on how regularly he earned it, he would be able to help out his family.

He was still unsure how much he could rely on Kai, but it was working out for now. Using some of the money, Gary stopped by a twenty-four-hour convenience store and bought some raw steaks. They were expensive, but his Energy was low and he knew he had to replenish it; he needed to eat, plus it didn't hurt to treat himself once in a while.

It was the middle of the night, so no one was around, and this time it was a lot easier for him to eat. He dug into the meat so quickly that he didn't realize how much his body needed it.

Daily Quest complete
5 Exp received

The quest to consume two kilograms of meat had already been completed, and it was nearly one o'clock in the morning, but this time the Exp awarded was half as much as before.

Looks like I'll have to find other ways to gain Exp later. For now, I better head home, Gary thought as he ran through the empty streets to his bed.

The next day at sunrise, Tom was a little nervous. He had his silver pendant ready and his bag of chocolate.

Gary, I hope what I'm thinking isn't true.

CHAPTER 22

CHARGING HEART

After consuming the raw meat he had purchased from the convenience store, Gary's Energy quickly started to increase, and by the time he snuck back home, he already felt as good as he had before leaving for this nightly adventure.

When he woke up nearly five hours later, he felt completely fine. He was unsure whether this meant that he could use the raw protein as an energy drink substitute to keep on going for as long as he needed, but at least his need for sleep appeared to have lessened.

I feel so alive! Gary thought as he got ready for school. His mother and sister were not even awake yet. There was one thing he was thankful for, though: the fact that his sister was keeping everything a secret for him.

Gary was sure that she didn't know what he was doing, but since they shared a room, it had been impossible to hide the fact that he had disappeared. *Damn, I bet she's going to ask for some big favor later on*, Gary lamented as he scribbled a note for Amy to make sure she knew he had returned and hadn't gone missing.

Waking up before everyone else proved to be a blessing in disguise, especially since his acquired taste had changed. During his nightly trip to the convenience store, Gary had not only purchased meat for himself to consume. Right now, the Dem family fridge was fuller than it had been for weeks.

If Mom asks where I got it from, I'll just say it was a gift from one of the local stores. He had already done this a few times during his work as a transporter, so it shouldn't stand out too much. Anything to lighten his mother's load and reduce her stress.

With all this newfound Energy, Gary didn't waste time leaving before everyone else, yet on the way out, he noticed all the bills that had piled up on the kitchen counter.

A dozen more nights like last night should help us get out of this mess. The only question is, how can I help us without having to explain where I got all this money?

No normal sixteen-year-old should be able to get a job that paid this well, at least not legally, and Gary wasn't proficient in coming up with excuses. The fact that he was a miserable liar and his mother could instantly tell when he lied wasn't exactly in his favor. In fact, even his excuses about the convenience stores giving them food had been met with skepticism the first few times he had brought it up.

I guess I'll just have to ask Kai; I'm sure he will know a way. Gary bemoaned the fact that he was relying more and more on his schoolmate, but at least so far Kai had been keeping his promise, and it was undeniable that he knew how to make money.

This early in the morning, barely anyone was out and about, but Gary still kept his hood up on the way to school. He was afraid that any moment now, Damion and the Underdogs might pop up. He was sure that they had not given up their manhunt for him, and he was already dreading opening up his phone. In fact, he was planning to purchase a new one after school and throw this one into the river or perhaps bury it somewhere in the forest.

Just as Gary was daydreaming about how he could get rid of the phone without leaving a trail leading back to him, he suddenly spotted a particular girl up ahead.

She looks familiar . . . hang on, isn't she the same girl who got in trouble with that color gang from before? And then he realized who it was.

They were quite far away, but Gary was convinced. It was impossible for him not to recognize someone who'd indirectly forced him into playing the part of a hero. Despite the crest on her uniform telling him that they attended the same school, he had never actually seen her before he had rescued her, nor afterward, for that matter.

Admittedly, he had forgotten all about her because of the plethora of other problems in his life right now, but seeing her again made him wonder what exactly she had done to get into trouble with a color gang.

Didn't she learn her lesson last time? How can she walk this way all alone again? At this point, she's just asking for trouble. Gary shook his head in disbelief. He would have loved to just mind his own business, but seeing as the two of them were using the same route, he couldn't just not look out for her.

Eventually, Gary decided to catch up to her since there was no real reason for him to hide. He had followed her from a distance for a while and was happy that there had been no encounters; however, a few moments ago, the girl had abruptly quickened her pace. Gary had yet to realize that she had done so because she had felt that someone had been following her . . .

Let's see what I can do and how close I can get.

Skill activated: Charging Heart.
All stats have temporarily been doubled. –10 Energy

After activating the skill, he instantly felt great pain in his chest, to the point where he nearly fell over. His heart was beating as if he were sprinting even though he was just standing still. After the initial shock of impact was over, though, he was filled with Energy. He'd used 10 Energy points, and his heart was now above 150 BPM. With this new Energy, Gary started walking faster, but he knew he couldn't just get straight up behind her, so he thought maybe there would be a better way.

Going down one of the alleys behind a small apartment building, he looked at all the pipes and window ledges.

This is crazy, right? Am I really going to try this?

CHAPTER 23

THE TEST

Only a few days ago Gary couldn't do any type of physical activity, and now he was planning to scale the side of an apartment building. He jumped higher than he had ever before and grabbed onto one of the ledges. The only way to progress farther up was to leap up to the next windowsill or jump to the metal pipe and climb that.

After completing the first jump, he was full of confidence and swung his body over, but he hesitated at the last second, after his fingertips had left the windowsill.

"Aw, crap!" Gary shouted as he completely missed the metal pipe and fell onto the hard concrete.

"That freaking hurt," Gary said, attempting to get up slowly. His heart was still beating fast, though, and his Energy points were going down quicker than when he didn't use his new skill.

I guess even if this skill does make me stronger, it still doesn't change me; I need to get used to it. He flexed his fingertips a bit; the skin on them had slightly ripped, and his arms were now sore from holding on to the ledge, but the pain was going away quickly.

I guess double my current strength and stats isn't so impressive. If I can improve my whole body and increase my stats, that will make the skill more effective. I also have to be wary of my Energy points.

Using the skill itself takes up 10 Energy points, and it almost feels like an adrenaline shot, but then I have fewer points to heal myself.

Getting my heart rate up naturally won't use Energy points initially.

But other than thinking of that girl . . . I don't really have a good method of controlling my heart rate.

Gary had almost forgotten why he was trying to scale the wall in the first place. He thought if he got up high, then maybe he could start leaping across rooftops while following the girl.

It was a fantasy that was short-lived.

Canceling the skill was easy, and Gary stuck to what he was doing before as he exited the alleyway and attempted to catch up with the girl.

The good news was there didn't seem to be any sign of trouble. Gary wasn't sure if it was because it was so early in the morning or if something else was going on. Eventually, though, they reached the school and, at least knowing this place was safe, he could take off his hood, but he didn't stop following the strange girl.

Damn, I feel like a stalker; why am I still following her anyway? I was just going to protect her, right? Gary eventually found himself on the third floor, where the senior students would be. He'd never expected her to be a senior. Just as he was about to turn away, though, he saw the girl talking to someone else he knew, and it looked like the two of them were on good terms.

Is that Kai? Why would these two know each other? He thought that anyone who would know Kai would also be involved in the underworld like he was. The girl was also being attacked by the gang; could it have something to do with Kai?

Unfortunately, without getting any closer and being found out, Gary would just have to leave it at that, so he made his way back to his first class.

Just outside, though, he managed to bump into someone that he was actually pleased to see.

"Oh, Gary!" Tom said, holding a bag, and nearly stepped backward.

"What's the matter? You seem a little jumpy, is everything okay?" Gary asked as he walked past Tom and entered the classroom, putting his bag on the desk. He was happy to see Tom because Tom was the only normal thing he still had left of his ordinary life, and he was hoping talking to him would remind him of the time before all this craziness.

Tom touched the pendant in his pocket; he held it for a second and wondered how he would get Gary to wear it or touch it, or if it would do anything.

"Hey, do you mind if I show you a magic trick?" Tom asked. *If it starts hurting him, I'll take it off straightaway, and I'll know the truth.*

"Okay, but I didn't know you were into magic," Gary replied.

"Just keep your palm open and close your eyes for a second," Tom said.

That was when Gary heard it: something was definitely up with Tom. The two of them weren't far from each other, and he could hear Tom's heartbeat, beating faster and faster.

Is he that nervous that the magic trick is going to fail? Gary closed his eyes, opening the palm of his hand to give him more confidence.

Tom was about to place the silver chain and pendant in Gary's hand when he started to have second thoughts.

Why am I doing this? Shouldn't I just ask? Tom felt a little bad that he was tricking his longtime best friend.

Meanwhile, Gary was getting impatient. "Come on," he said, opening his eyes and grabbing the pendant. He looked at it and wondered what it was. Tom nearly shouted out, telling him to stop, but Gary seemed to have no reaction at all. So Tom smiled instead.

"Did I ruin the trick?" Gary asked.

"Umm, yeah, but don't worry, I need more practice anyway," Tom said as he took the pendant away and placed it back into his pocket. *What the hell was I thinking? Gary? A werewolf? Maybe I've been reading too many novels.*

"Hey, so what's in the bag?" Gary said.

"Oh, this?" he replied. He opened the bag, pulled out a large chocolate bar, and tossed it to Gary with no worries at all. "I had a craving in the middle of the night, but I can't eat all this on my own, so I decided to bring it to school." Tom smiled.

Class hadn't started yet. The students were still coming in; the teacher had arrived but wouldn't take attendance until the bell rang anyway. So Gary thought it wouldn't be bad to take a nice bite of chocolate; after all, everything he had been eating recently was a little strange.

He bit off nearly half of the chocolate bar as if he didn't have a care in the world. Suddenly he felt his throat swelling up. He grabbed at his throat as if he couldn't breathe.

"Gary, are you okay? What's wrong?" Tom asked.

But Gary's body was rejecting the chocolate, and he threw it up as the shocked students stepped away. "What is that? Is that bile? But why is it so . . . red?"

Tom started to panic. *He threw up . . . Why did he throw up? Don't tell me it was from the chocolate bar!*

CHAPTER 24

RED SICK

"Is that ... blood? Should we call him an ambulance or something?" The students started mumbling to each other, unsure how to react.

Gary could hear everyone around him whispering, but he was too busy throwing up. At least he started to feel a lot better after doing so, but his sense of balance was off, and he grabbed his chair to support himself.

You have come into contact with a substance that is poisonous to you
−20 HP
80/100 HP
Until your body has broken down the poison, you are unable to heal

What is happening to me? Gary struggled to understand what had just happened.

As if his luck weren't bad already, the next person to come into class turned out to be Xin. At first she was confused about what was going on, but as she looked where everyone was pointing, she quickly got the picture.

If he's ill, then why did he come to school in the first place? Xin wondered as she walked over and saw all the red vomit on the ground with chunks of meat that strangely enough looked to be raw. More students began to enter the classroom, and a group of girls screamed at the sight of the vomit. "What is that? Why is it so red? That's disgusting; someone get him out of here!"

Xin turned to look at them, only to recognize the ringleader as the one who had been so heavily interested in Blake when they were watching the rugby match. The girl had introduced herself as Tiffany, and she was the one that everyone seemed to follow.

"Tiffany's right, he could be infected with something, throwing up like that. He could pass some disease on to us! Get him out of here," a boy declared, quickly checking up on the class diva.

What have I done? Tom was still trying to make heads or tails of the devolving situation. *Shit, I never thought it could have such an effect on you. Gary, don't you die on me, man! I can't be responsible for killing you!*

While the rest of the class was busy ostracizing Gary, the first one to approach was none other than Xin.

"What's wrong with you all? Are you sure you're all high schoolers and not just a bunch of kindergartners? Have you never seen anyone get sick before? You act like he's got a deadly disease, when I bet the poor guy must have just drunk some tomato juice or something before coming here. Teacher, I'll take him to the nurse's office!"

She pulled his arm up onto her shoulder and was ready to take him away. When Gary turned his head, even though he was still feeling groggy, he recognized who it was.

"Are you an angel?" Gary blurted out, slurring his words like a drunken man.

"Easy there, Romeo, if you have the energy to spout such fluttery bullshit, then get a grip and help me take you to the nurse's office," Xin replied. If not for his miserable situation, she would have been convinced he was hitting on her.

"Wait, let me do it," Tom insisted, clenching his fist. After all, this entire situation was his fault. He had been so focused on wanting to find out the truth about his best friend that he had failed to consider the consequences of his actions.

"You probably don't know where the nurse's office is yet, and he's my best friend. Let me take him," Tom argued, ashamed that the new girl was the first and only one who had been willing to help Gary.

Xin was a bit surprised that Tom wanted to take over with such enthusiasm, but she saw no need to argue as long as someone helped the poor guy.

"Damn, Gary, can you please stop leaning on me so hard? You should know that the only muscles I have are in my fingers!" Tom complained in a hushed tone as soon as the two of them had exited the classroom.

With the two of them gone, Xin looked over the contents of the vomit one more time, and then she noticed something. Tom had placed his bag down on his table, and it was full of chocolate, while Gary's table had a half-eaten chocolate bar on it.

Is the green-haired guy allergic to chocolate? Shouldn't his "best friend" have known that?

Suddenly someone grabbed Xin's shoulder. Driven by instinct, she grabbed the offender's wrist and spun the person around. The next second she had dug her hip into them and flipped them onto the ground . . . right into the vomit.

Only after finishing her routine did Xin suddenly realize what she had done.

Oh no, why did we have to practice throws all day yesterday? Xin cursed as she looked at Tiffany, whose blond hair was now covered with red vomit.

"I'm sorry, let me help you up." Xin quickly apologized, offering her hand, but the other girl unsurprisingly slapped it away.

"You bitch!" Tiffany shouted in anger. "What the hell did you do that for? Thanks to you, I have puke all over me!"

Two of her friends suddenly appeared and were now standing behind Xin. One of them was a small girl with short purple hair, while the other was quite muscular with black pigtails.

"I swear, it was a complete accident! You startled me when you came upon me. What possible reason would I have to do this to you on purpose when I don't even really know you?" Xin said, trying to explain herself. She wasn't the least bit afraid of the two goons who had placed themselves between her and Tiffany as if to protect their queen bee; no, she was just unwilling to deal with the possible aftermath if this situation was left unresolved.

Her father had warned her not to use her fists. Even though he was the mayor, it wasn't like the past, when mayors had the highest authority. In reality, they had to comply with the many gangs that really ran the area, and if she angered the wrong people, not even he could help her.

The last thing she wanted to do was make her dad's stressful job even harder.

"You think a simple 'sorry' is going to cut it?" Tiffany bellowed at Xin, her eyes filled with anger and malice. She could easily just wash off the puke, but nothing could change the fact that everyone in the classroom had seen her make a fool of herself. It was practically a given that jokes would spread about her being a "puke girl."

The teacher cleared his throat, reminding everyone that he was still there, and the sudden tension seemed to relax as the two girls helped Tiffany up. The teacher wanted to say something as they walked out of the classroom, but with a glare from Tiffany, he quickly zipped his mouth shut.

Screw me. Judging by her eyes, there is no way she is just going to let things go. Xin sighed, wishing she could just turn back time a couple of minutes to avoid all of this drama.

Tom and Gary eventually made it to the nurse's office. Fortunately, Gary's metabolism was doing a good job of expelling the poison, allowing him to recover slightly. His system had even told him that he was no longer poisoned.

"Gary, you've been coming in here quite a lot." The nurse shook her head. "Well, I guess you can't really help it if you ate something bad. Just make sure to not eat whatever it was again, and for the time being, take this medicine; it should be able to help you. It might be for the best if you rest here for the first period, and we will see how you do after that. If you still feel unwell, I'm going to have to recommend you go to the hospital."

There is no way I can go to a hospital! If they find out what I am, who knows what they will do with me! Gary thought, but outwardly he just nodded weakly.

"I'll stay with him and make sure he takes the medicine!" Tom volunteered, and closed the curtain. The nurse had left a small round pill next to a white cup with water for Gary to take, but Tom wasn't sure that it would help. Since Gary had reacted so violently to the chocolate, which he had been able to eat without any issues in the past, who was to say how he would react to this pill?

So Tom placed the pill in his own mouth and drank the water, gulping it down.

"Tom, what the—? Why did you do that? Don't tell me you've become a . . . pill popper!" Gary exclaimed, worried for his friend.

"No, you idiot!" Tom whispered back in an angry voice. He pulled the curtain back to see if the nurse was still there, and though she was, she seemed completely focused on her phone call. Whatever it was, it seemed to have been important and urgent because soon after she hung up, she left the room, telling the boys she would be back in a few minutes.

"Good, she's gone; we can finally talk." Tom sighed out a breath of relief, but Gary was still confused about why Tom was acting so mysterious. His body might have recovered, but he still had trouble thinking clearly.

"Gary, do you even know what happened back there and why you got sick?" Tom asked.

"I have no idea; maybe it's the raw meat I've been eating," Gary blurted without thinking.

"Raw meat . . ." Tom repeated; his hands were shaking. He had to reassure himself that the boy before him was still good old harmless Gary and not the beast he had tested him to be.

"Gary . . . I've noticed you have been behaving super strange these last couple of days. I gave you the chocolate to test a hypothesis of mine, but I didn't want to hurt you. I never thought it would turn out this way; please, you gotta believe me. You know you can tell me anything, right? So I gotta ask . . . Gary, are you a werewolf?"

CHAPTER 25

THE TRUTH

As soon as he heard the question, Gary felt the palms of his hands getting sweaty and his heartbeat rising. These weren't good signs, especially if he was going to try to hide it from Tom. He placed his hand on his chest and bent over slightly, appearing to be in pain.

"What's wrong? Is the chocolate still hurting you?" Tom asked worriedly as he checked to see if his friend was okay. "Gary, you shouldn't deny it; being able to poison you is proof that I'm right!" He pointed at Gary, as if he were a famous detective who had just solved a case.

The sight of Tom acting so ridiculous was somehow enough to calm Gary's heart rate a little.

"Come on, don't you find it ridiculous? Chocolate being some sort of kryptonite for a werewolf? Next thing, you'll tell me you're a vampire or a dragon." Gary tried to make a joke, but the nervous smile on his face made him appear all the more guilty. He was struggling to decide whether it might be better to just admit it.

So far, he had tried to make sense of all of the changes to his body by himself, tried to learn all these new things on his own . . . he would actually welcome having someone to talk to about it. Sometimes he didn't know if he was doing the right thing, but he couldn't imagine trusting anyone more than he trusted Tom.

Since accusing Gary and trapping him into a corner didn't seem to have worked, Tom tried a different approach.

"Look, I know that the chocolate alone would be ridiculous, but then how do you explain suddenly being able to tackle Blake? Or the punctures on the rugby ball? You were the only one who held it yesterday. If you have some other explanation, then I'm all ears. I'm your best friend, right? I'm not here to hurt you, and I just want you to know that we can handle this together," Tom offered in a soft voice. And from the look on Gary's face, this approach worked far better.

Gary had already been on the verge of telling Tom, but with Tom pulling on his heartstrings, it was hard to remain silent. However, now the question was, how much should he tell Tom? Admitting it also meant he would have to come clean about his work as a member of the Underdogs, who had given him the metal briefcase that had that strange Werewolf System inside it. But if he told Tom, there was a big risk of dragging him into all of this mess.

"You know what?" Tom asked while Gary was still debating on how much to reveal. "I'm just going to take your silence as a yes. I mean, you aren't even denying it like you were just seconds ago. Now, I've done a lot of research into this matter because I know you're bad with all this fantasy mumbo-jumbo.

"I don't exactly know how much lore is true out there, but now that I have finally met a real werewolf and he's my friend, it's better to be safe than sorry. From all the stuff I have read on the internet, they all pretty much have one thing in common. All sources seem to agree that on the night of a full moon, a werewolf turns without being able to control it. That gives us only twelve days to think of a way to restrain you; otherwise, you might go on a rampage and kill everyone."

Tom looked directly at Gary as he spoke. Tom, his friend who never confronted anyone and was bad at all types of physical activity, looked powerful and reliable at this moment.

What worried Gary even more was that he already knew that something was going to happen on the night of the full moon. His system had given him a quest titled "Your first turning" that had a countdown for that day. Even more worrisome was the fact that his quest only specified that he would have to "survive."

Since Gary still wasn't saying anything, Tom sighed and started to leave the room. He had already done whatever he could; now he hoped that either he had been very wrong, something he seriously doubted after all the time he had put into thinking things over, or that Gary would eventually come to him on his own to confess.

"Wait!" Gary called out. "Fine, since you've already figured things out, you might as well know the whole thing. You're right . . . I'm a . . . I'm a werewolf," Gary admitted, his face going red saying the words out loud.

Tom closed the door, after making sure nobody else had heard, then turned toward Gary, a sparkle in his eyes.

"I knew I was right! Tell me, Gary, when did you become a freaking werewolf? How did this happen? Did you venture into the woods at night? Did an alpha wolf come, greet you, and turn you? What the hell happened?" Tom asked in a barrage of questions, unable to contain his excitement.

"Oh man, now my version sounds so boring in comparison. I just got turned by a briefcase." Gary smiled wryly as he explained. Since the whole werewolf situation was already a lot to take in, Gary decided to omit the fact that he had been a gang member and technically was now in another gang. Instead, he told Tom that he had taken a part-time delivery job.

Of course, since he was sixteen and still in school, all of this was illegal, which was why he had hidden the job from Tom. Technically all of it was true, so Gary's face didn't betray him for once. After that, he came mostly clean, sharing how he had been sent out, how other people had wanted to steal the package, and how the package had suddenly opened, turning him into a werewolf.

After saying everything he needed to say, he waited to see how Tom would react.

CHAPTER 26

A BOND

"All this from a simple package? I've never heard of such a thing," Tom said as he placed his hand on his chin. "It doesn't really help that you didn't even see what was in the package because you passed out."

This bit was partly true, only Gary had passed out after being stabbed.

I wonder how Tom would react if I told him the real story. I guess I can tell him once everything is cleared up. And I will also have to tell him about Kai eventually . . .

"We need to look into where that package actually came from; this could be a big deal! And if it's a big company, they might even send people after you to get their little experiment back. It's best if you keep this a secret," Tom said.

Gary gulped, surprised at how quickly his friend had grasped the situation, and what was more, the possibility that Tom was worried about what was happening. Fortunately, that at least meant Gary didn't have to tell him to keep this whole thing a secret either.

Tom continued, "Well, from what you told me, it really does seem that your heart rate might be connected to your transformation, so learning how to control it should be the first thing on the agenda. For the next few days, we should also observe your behavior. I haven't seen any huge signs yet, but you might start to get a little bit more moody the closer we are to the full moon. I would also advise you to quit the rugby team."

"Quit the rugby team? But then how am I supposed to impress Xin?" Gary blurted out.

"Really, Gary? Do you think now is the time to be worried about how to impress the new girl?" Tom facepalmed. "Part of you transformed when it was you against Blake. What will you do when it occurs in the middle of a match? You could hurt or even kill someone!"

"Come on, I'm not a monster!" Unfortunately, his first transformation was testimony that Tom did have a point. "Besides, don't you think if I put myself in more situations where I have to control my heart rate, that would help me get better at it?"

"Aargh, fine. It's not like I can force you to do it. You know your body better than me, after all." Tom was still worried, but he'd known Gary long enough to know how stubborn he could be. "Speaking of which, it's a shame, but it looks like I'm going to have to eat all that chocolate myself," Tom joked, and the two of them were soon well on their way to being friends once again.

Once the poison had worn off, Gary could use his Energy to heal his body once again, but the Energy didn't seem to recover, and as his Energy went down, he felt hungry. It was a small pain like a cramp, but he could bear it for now.

I have to keep my Energy up; when I'm fighting, it doesn't seem to bother me so much, but when I'm doing nothing, it hurts. Hopefully, it doesn't get worse once it falls lower; I can't exactly bring raw meat to school.

Since Gary was feeling better, the two of them walked down the hallway. They had decided to stay in the nurse's office until the bell rang, allowing them to skip the first two periods, and now they could go out on break with each other.

Students filled the hallways, and everyone was excited to get a breath of fresh air. Now that Tom and Gary had cleared the air a bit, they chatted away until they banged into what felt like a solid wall in front of them.

It was so sudden that Tom nearly fell to the floor, but Gary's quick reflexes allowed him to grab Tom by the hand and pull him back up.

"Looks like we got a little superhero over here," said a student who was towering over them.

Gary looked up and realized that there were actually two people, and he recognized them straightaway: Barry and Gil. Although they didn't share any classes, they were all part of the rugby club. These two were part of the scrum in rugby, the meaty players who fought each other as they locked together and pushed the other team forward.

They were essentially walls of muscle, explaining why it had felt like Tom and Gary had literally run into a wall, but one thing was for certain: the hallway was plenty wide for them all to pass each other.

"Did you bang into us on purpose?" Tom asked, a pissed-off look on his face.

"Watch it, scrub! You were the ones who weren't paying attention! I still haven't heard a single sorry from either of you!" Barry grabbed the scruff of Tom's neck. "We were just waiting here for a chance to talk to the onion head over there."

"Look, Gary, drop out of rugby; we all know that what you did to Blake was a fluke, and if you join us, it means one of us regulars will have to warm the bench and become your substitute," Gil said, but Gary wasn't looking at him at all. Instead, he was looking toward Barry, who was holding Tom by his neck.

Suddenly, Gary grabbed Barry's wrist.

"Let go of him now!" Gary demanded. Of course, Gil wasn't afraid of someone so small, but the same couldn't be said for Barry, who saw something in Gary's eyes.

Bloodlust has been detected
Forced Bond has been activated

No, those eyes, if I don't do something, Gary might just snap! Tom thought.

CHAPTER 27

FORCED BOND

A notification screen had appeared in front of Gary, one containing new, unfamiliar terms, but blinded with rage, he ignored it as he continued to hold Barry's wrist. His grip was slowly getting tighter and tighter.

Shit, my wrist is starting to feel a little numb. How much power does that onion head have? Barry thought.

"Hey, look, it's Mr. Root!" Tom suddenly exclaimed, making Barry let go of him.

Both Gil and Barry turned around, and at that moment, Tom grabbed Gary and quickly pulled him away, dragging him down the hallway and into one of the other classrooms. Since they were still on break, the room was empty.

"Are you all right now?" Tom asked as he felt his heart settling. "It looked like you were ready to jump that guy."

"I don't know, man. I just got so angry when that guy grabbed you. Who the hell do they think they are? It's one thing to go after me, but you have nothing to do with it!" Gary answered, clenching his fists again.

Tom knew that Gary tended to be hotheaded, but this seemed out of character even for him. He was normally a guy who would try to run away from a confrontation, but now he seemed to be actively seeking it, making Tom fear that Gary's werewolf self might have already started to influence him.

I'll need to keep an eye on him. This time his aggression might have been triggered because he wanted to protect me, but what if it becomes worse? Who knows what he'll do if there's nobody to stop him?

"Look, it's over. I'm fine, right? We both are. Those guys were just two assholes; heck, the world is full of people like that, but we can't just go around beating them all up. Even if you are stronger than them," Tom said, then added jokingly, "I mean, if you tried, you'd be busy 24/7, and then you wouldn't have time to impress a certain someone."

Gary started to calm down a little as he realized that Tom was right. The second part especially helped him get into a better mood, although his heartbeat was now rising slightly for a different reason.

If word got out about what Gary could actually do, then it wouldn't just be the Underdogs after him, but whoever had asked them to deliver the briefcase in the first place. Now that he had calmed down, Gary went to check the message from before.

Forced Bond has been activated

1/5 Marks have been assigned

A Forced Bond is put on a target when enough bloodlust is dedicated toward it, making it a hunting target.

Those who are marked are given a unique scent, allowing the user to track them down at any point in time.

Additional stats will be awarded if one manages to successfully hunt their target down!

Those who are marked because of a Forced Bond will be the first to be targeted during a full moon.

Gary's eyes widened as he read the screen and came to a few realizations. The Forced Bond seemed to be a different subtype of his marking skill. He had already encountered the Bond Mark, which allowed him to mark certain people based on agreements, whereas the Forced Bond seemed to be automatically assigned based on pure bloodlust.

Both types of bonds seemingly occupied one of Gary's five slots. He was unsure whether there was a maximum of any one type of bond, although he felt like it didn't matter how much he had of one or the other. The major difference seemed to be that a Forced Bond directly designated the other party as a hunting target, whereas the Bond Mark only did so in the case of a broken promise.

The most worrisome thing of all was that the message had warned him that those who had been marked would become his targets during a full moon.

Gary gulped as he thought of what might happen. *If I really do turn in twelve days, doesn't that mean I'm going to kill Barry if I don't learn how to control myself?*

He couldn't be too sure until it happened, but it was something he didn't want to risk. *Screw this; if I can assign these marks, then there has to be a way to get rid of them, right?*

Tom and Gary left the room, ready to head back to class and finally participate in their normal school day. Fortunately, they didn't run into any more trouble along the way. But Gary noticed a strange lingering redness in the air, and it wafted into his nose. It smelled like raw meat.

It was faint, and as he followed it, it took on a stronger shade of red. It looked like a strange floating red fog. He looked at Tom, who appeared blissfully unaware of what Gary was perceiving.

The red fog led to a classroom, and Gary looked through the window and saw where it was leading . . . right to Barry, who was sitting in his seat.

Is this what the marking does? Does it leave a trail so I can find them around the school? Maybe I should try to activate a Bond Mark on Kai after all. It would be handy to be able to find him whenever I need to, and I would also instantly know if he broke the promise.

Shit, but if he does, then that would make him another hunting target! Or maybe this thing only follows things that are meant to be hunted.

Still, in twelve days' time, if he didn't find a way to remove the marking, Barry might be in trouble.

CHAPTER 28

ETON HIGH

There wasn't much Gary could do for now with his powers. He was only a Level 2, after all. Although he might have the power to become superhuman at certain moments, he still wasn't the best when it came to fighting, as well as other things. Not to mention it was a secret in the first place, so it was best he stayed out of trouble.

Classes continued as normal, with a few people staying away from Gary. They were a little worried about the vomit from earlier, but it looked like it had been cleaned up while they were in the nurse's office. Xin was also in the classroom, but she was unable to concentrate properly with Tiffany staring daggers at her.

When the day finally came to an end, it was time for everyone to head to their club activities. When Tom and Gary arrived at the rugby field, both Barry and Gil were staring at them.

"Damn those guys; it looks like they didn't quite get the message, huh?" Gil said provocatively.

However, Barry stayed quiet. He looked down at his wrist, which had been bruised and was slightly red. His better judgment was telling him that it might be better not to get involved with Gary after all.

The rugby team had been together for a long time now, and it had been a while since anyone new had joined them. That was also why the duo had wanted to scare Gary away. Even if he were to tattle on them, Gary knew they wouldn't back down, so it was pointless to do so.

The training continued as usual, at least at the beginning. It was clear that during the practices, the regular members were doing everything they could to target Gary: covering him even when he didn't have the ball, tackling him when he didn't have the ball, and hitting him in the gut when they were in the middle of a scrum.

Each time, Tom had to be there to calm him down, but he could tell it was getting worse. Thankfully they made it through the whole training session without Gary retaliating. At the end of practice, Mr. Root had an announcement to make.

"All right, everyone, our first match is one week from Monday, and we will be going up against Eton High, so you better be on top of your game! As for you, Gary, remember you're part of the team now, so watch yourself!"

The players started to mumble and share odd looks as they talked about the upcoming team. Although he was a newbie, Gary knew why. Eton High's rugby team wasn't exactly the strongest, but that also wasn't Mr. Root's main worry.

Eton High had a reputation for being one of the roughest schools in the entire town. It was a place where gangs frequently recruited their next members upon graduation. There were even a few students who already belonged to different small-time gangs, some even from different cities.

There were rumors about how certain members of the opposing teams would often end up in "accidents" right before big games. This was why Mr. Root had cautioned him to be safe.

Everyone who lived in this city knew that the gangs were actually in charge, so the students of Eton High were certainly special.

"If Mr. Root is telling us to be careful, then it has to be true," one person said.

As everyone was leaving, someone approached Gary, and it wasn't someone he would have expected.

"Hey there, Gary, I see your nose is all better; sorry about that again," Blake said as he smiled, showing his beautiful teeth.

Damn it, I can't stay around this guy. If Xin sees me next to him, it's going to make me look like a frog next to a prince.

"Yeah, don't worry about it; it wasn't as bad as I thought," Gary replied, trying to cut the conversation short.

"Do you mind if the two of us walk home? There's something I want to talk to you about, and I think it might be better for you," Blake offered as he glanced at the corner, where the other club members, including Gil and Barry, were looking toward them.

Tom, who lived in the opposite direction, decided to head home. "Hey, Gary, you go ahead, and take your time to think about the stuff we talked about earlier. Just remember to give me a call tonight, okay?" Tom said, and ran off. He was still hoping that Gary would quit the rugby team like he had asked. It was the best choice in the end.

Gary didn't really want to walk with Blake, but it was obvious that his teammate was offering to shield him from the others. Out of all the players, Blake was the most reasonable and easiest to talk to.

"Sure, we can walk for a bit," Gary answered as he put on a fake smile, and the two of them headed off. They passed by the front gate, where Kai was standing with his eyes half-closed. When Gary walked past, he opened them and gave him a little wink.

Who could he be waiting for? A girlfriend perhaps? Gary wondered.

As he watched Gary and Blake walk off, Kai continued to wait at the gate until a student in a dark blue uniform, different from theirs, arrived. The boy's hands were bandaged up all the way to his knuckles.

"You wear those things, even in school? That must be uncomfortable," Kai commented with a smirk.

"You never know when you're going to need to fight. Not in this day and age. Anyway, I believe you still owe me the promised sum of money," Innu replied. As soon as he said it, a bundle of cash flew right toward him.

"Here you go. I always keep my word," Kai said as Innu happily counted the money.

"I did a little bit of research on you. Turns out you went to Eton High last year? Since you agreed to join our little gang, mind telling me what exactly happened that forced you to transfer to another school?" Kai asked as they walked off.

From the look on Innu's face, it wasn't a pretty story at all, and it was clear that it was bad news.

CHAPTER 29

SURROUNDED

There was a park not far away from the school. It had a playground with swings, benches, climbing frames, and all sorts of other things, making it a popular hangout spot for the younger kids, whereas the older ones usually played soccer once school was out.

"Um, isn't this a weird place to discuss things?" Innu asked as he looked at all the little kids and moms around. "Don't you guys have your own place? You know, a regular hideout spot like an abandoned warehouse or something?"

When Innu had followed after Kai, he'd expected to be led a place like that. Instead, they had gone to this park, and on their way, a girl had started tagging along. The gold and black outfit made it obvious that she was part of Kai's group, but so far she hadn't even said a word. Innu couldn't help but think she didn't belong in the underworld, except maybe as a damsel in distress.

"Nope, I don't have one of those yet," Kai replied matter-of-factly. "Come to think of it, I didn't really have time to fill you in last night. Oh well, no time like the present. Right now, there's just you, Green Fang who you've already met, and this here's Marie."

Kai acknowledged the girl's existence for the first time; in turn, she just bowed. Innu wasn't sure if she was just shy around him or if she might be mute. Innu's opened his mouth wide in disbelief, and he slapped his forehead.

I thought he knew what he was doing. Was I wrong? Is he just some rich kid who has too much of Daddy's money and decided to create a gang? Heck, can we even be called that? Right now, we seem more like a group of friends, if anything. And why did he exclude himself?

He sighed in defeat. Innu had never been the type to go back on his word. His academic performance might only qualify him for construction jobs, but at least he had integrity. The best way he knew how to make money was with his hands, knees, and elbows, which was why he had chosen to fight in the underground event in the first place.

"Don't worry," Kai said, smiling. "Every prominent gang started out just like us. I promise you that as long as you stay with us, you won't regret it. Our group will focus on quality over quantity, so you should be proud that you even qualified."

Kai's arrogant tone wasn't making Innu feel any better about his decision. Talk was cheap, but as long as the money continued to flow, he wouldn't complain.

Innu sighed. "So you wanted to know about my past with Eton High. What they're like and why I transferred, correct? Well, I'm sure you've heard the rumors. Let me tell you, it's worse than what they say. All the delinquents that the other schools deem incorrigible get sent to Eton High, and the school welcomes them happily. Calling it the garbage heap for the scum of society would be putting it mildly. The only reason it doesn't get shut down is that this makes it the perfect recruitment place for gangs. Heck, some even come from other cities!

"Other schools might have a top dog, one who at least instills a sort of order, but Eton High is more of a lawless zone. Not all of them behave like wild animals, but whatever factions there are seem to change regularly. The weak factions gang up on the stronger ones just to put them in their place. And they're not afraid to use weapons, either." Innu's fists tensed as he thought about what had happened to him before.

It wasn't hard for Kai to puzzle his past together with that much information. Anyone could see from the way he fought that Innu was capable of becoming the top dog. They must have ganged up on him so badly that he had to transfer.

"Anyway, why did you want to know about Eton High so much?" Innu finally asked.

At the same time, Gary and Blake were walking down the street, heading home. If Gary were to use one word to describe the current situation, it would be *awkward*.

That must have been the tenth time a girl has looked our way! Gary thought bitterly. The girls' faces would turn a shade redder when they peeked at Blake, only to turn sour upon seeing the boy walking beside him. What hurt Gary even more was that they didn't even try to hide it.

"I want to apologize, Gary." Blake's opening line surprised him. "I heard that Barry and Gil were bothering you during the break, and I've seen how the guys have been hazing you during training. I'm the captain, so it's my responsibility to make sure things like that don't happen."

Scratching the back of his head, Gary didn't really know what to say. Blake was the last person who should have to apologize to him. He seemed to really care about the rugby team, which made Gary feel bad since his primary reason for joining was to impress Xin.

Was it really okay for him to take another player's position just because of his infatuation?

"It's not your fault; I understand how they feel," Gary replied. "Besides, isn't that like an initiation ritual between guys?"

"No, it's not right. You're part of the team now. Instead of messing with you, they should get along with you and help you integrate with the team. Given your talent, you'll be a great asset. I'm going to have a word with them all tomorrow, so they don't pull that stupid crap on you again. If they cause you any more trouble, I want you to come to me!" Blake stopped walking and turned around, staring right at Gary, offering his hand.

How can someone be this nice in a Tier 3 town? Who the hell could hate him? Gary thought, looking at the hand in front of him. He was reluctant to shake it since he had already repaid Barry. He only had so much time to find a way to remove the Forced Bond from the poor guy to prevent him from ending up as the secret ingredient in a Barry Burger.

"I . . ." Just as Gary was about to make up an excuse, he noticed some people approaching. They were coming in fast, and one was holding an object, swinging it toward Blake.

"Duck!" Gary warned him. He was about to push Blake's head down, but surprisingly his classmate had instantly followed the instruction. Not expecting to grab at nothing but air, Gary helplessly watched as the wooden plank connected with his cheek. The attack had enough force behind it that he fell to the ground, leaving him with the taste of iron in his mouth.

"Gary!" Blake called out, seeing his classmate lying on the floor with blood dripping from his face. He quickly spun around, moving forward slightly, and heard something hitting the ground where he had just stood.

In total, there were four guys all wearing the Eton High school uniform. Two of them had wooden planks, while the others looked to be unarmed. However, it was just as possible that their weapons were concealed.

"Hey, looks like one of them is fast," the Eton High student who had just missed hitting Blake chuckled.

"He wouldn't be the ace of their team if he wasn't." The one with the plank who had just hit Gary joined in the laughter.

Up until now, Blake had only heard about this type of incident; Mr. Root had warned them about it earlier. Their PE teacher had once called him into his office, stressing to Blake that he was the most likely target. All the opponents Eton High had faced had lost their ace to some "accident" right before a match.

However, Blake had never expected them to be brazen enough to attack someone in the open like this. They were away from school, but the police shouldn't be too far away. The only reason the Eton High students could be so confident in attacking them here was if they had the backing of a gang of some sort; then it wouldn't matter if the police were informed.

These guys don't look like pushovers when it comes to fighting, either. Who knows when the police will come . . . or if they even will? Blake started to worry.

One of the unarmed students tried to punch Blake, but before he could reach him, Blake quickly kicked the student's thigh. His punch weakened slightly, but it was still coming toward Blake's head as the kid gritted his teeth. Pain alone didn't seem to stop him, or perhaps he was just pissed off enough to want revenge.

When the punch connected with Blake's forehead, the student's wrist bent awkwardly, and he cried out in pain.

When his buddy with the plank came over, Blake remained calm, pushing the student's wrist to knock him off balance, then kicking him in the back of his knee, allowing him to trip the other one.

"Looks like he can fight," the student with the damaged wrist snarled. The student on the ground with the wooden plank dropped his weapon and charged forward to tackle Blake. Although Blake tried to sidestep the charge, the Eton High student managed to grab him.

"Now!"

The other three Eton High students surrounded him. One had picked up the dropped plank, and the two who had planks were about to take a swing, while the third one made sure to cut off any way of escape.

I'm just going to have to take this hit! Blake thought as he decided between getting rid of the student holding him or protecting himself.

When the planks came down, they stopped dead, inches from his face. Blake saw Gary holding on to both. Blood was still dripping from his mouth, from a cut on the inside of his cheek.

"That freaking hurt!" Gary shouted as his heart rate started to increase.

"It never hurts knowing as much as you can about your enemy. From the sounds of it, you won't have any problem fighting against your former schoolmates. Eton High will be the first opponent in the underground tag team tournament next week," Kai said, answering Innu's question.

CHAPTER 30

HERE TO FIGHT!

The Eton High students who had come to the park were all members of the rugby team, which meant they were used to bashing into walls of muscle. Strength and speed were both key factors in taking down an opponent, but Gary had neither on his side.

So it was all the more surprising for Blake to see him holding both planks with a single hand. The two students from Eton High had their struggle written all over their faces as they attempted to yank their makeshift weapons free. But Gary merely tightened his grip until they all heard a snapping sound.

The two Eton High boys stumbled a few steps back, still holding the planks. They could see why their weapons suddenly felt that much lighter. One end of the planks had been broken off.

The next second, another student slammed a plank against the back of Gary's head, whipping it back and causing him to fall to his knees.

These Eton High guys are ruthless. How can they not even hesitate to hit him in the head? Aren't they afraid they might accidentally kill him? All of that for a stupid match? Blake thought as he tried to help Gary. Yet before he could even reach him, Gary had already recovered and thrown a punch back.

The student managed to block in time, raising his forearms, but the next second he found himself looking at the sky.

What the . . . ? Is this some sort of joke? Did Gary set this up somehow? How is he able to knock out a guy twice his size? Has he been holding back all this time? Or is he one of us as well? Still, Blake's main concern was the blood dripping down his classmate's head. He was surprised Gary was still standing after such a hit.

He might be okay for now while the adrenaline was pumping in his body, but once it was over, it would hurt like hell. They had to deal with these guys before that happened. Right now, Gary was dealing with the first two, leaving Blake with the other two.

He could easily deal with two of them. When one came rushing forward, pulling his arm back to throw a fist, Blake simply threw out a quick jab, hitting him right in the face and almost lifting his feet off the ground.

"If you charge forward like that, it's going to hurt a lot more when someone hits you!"

Now it was time to deal with the other one, but as Blake turned his head around, he only saw the student's back. He had actually run off, abandoning his comrade.

Guess they're not really a loyal bunch.

He turned around, ready to help Gary. His jaw dropped as he saw the other two already on the ground. Still, Gary didn't look good; he was huffing and panting, with a hunched back, his hands by his side, looking like some type of weird beast.

However, the other three students had been beaten, rolling around the floor in pain.

Damn, those guys' strength is similar to mine, even after I used Charging Heart, Gary thought. *I guess that shows how weak my original body is. Maybe I should have considered it some before putting my stat point into Energy after that level up. And I'm not the best fighter. It's one thing knowing what to do, but another knowing how to do it. I was getting hit too much, and now my Energy is low from having to heal all these wounds.*

"Hey, Gary, we need to get you checked out at a hospital!" Blake said, rushing over.

Emergency healing in progress
Energy will be consumed
Energy has been used up
Healing unable to complete
Eat more meat to restore Energy

During the fight, Gary had seen this alert a few times, and the system had been healing the rest of his wounds until it stopped. As long as he got some meat, he would definitely be fine after this fight, and he was worried the hospital could find something out.

"Don't worry about me; I'm tougher than I look," Gary shouted, already running off. "Just look after yourself. You're the ace of the team, not me!"

Blake wanted to give chase, but Gary was faster than he should be, even if it was still the adrenaline. Unsure where Gary lived, Blake decided to just check up on him tomorrow.

He looked around at the sorry state of the Eton High students.

He was able to take three giants like this down? He's a bit different. Blake smiled.

When his healing was complete, the first thing Gary did was head to a shop to purchase more meat. There were two reasons for this. The first was the fact that whenever possible, he wanted his Energy to be at 100 percent. He never knew when something like what had just happened would occur, and he needed to be at full strength if a fight broke out. The second reason was that he needed to complete his Daily Quests.

I need to get stronger as quickly as possible, and leveling up seems to be the easiest way. After replenishing his Energy, Gary headed to the gym once more.

Usually, after school Gary would head to the Underdogs to complete his transporter duties. His mother was used to him coming home a little late, so it was no problem. During his session at the gym, Gary was able to lift weights more easily than before; his muscles weren't sore either.

What Gary didn't know was that usually, beginners experience extreme muscle soreness for a few days after weight training, but Gary experienced no such thing. The muscle fibers in his body were breaking down and healing at an incredible rate—far faster than humanly possible, even if the person was taking enhancing supplements.

Congratulations! Your body is seeing the benefits of working out
Strength +1

So my stats can actually improve without needing me to level up! Looks like using that stat point on Energy might have been the right choice after all. My Strength was only at 4, which I'm guessing is still low. I wonder how long it will take me to gain the next point.

The best thing about Charging Heart was that it doubled all of his stats for a certain amount of time. So increasing his natural stats would be extremely beneficial.

Strength 5
Dexterity 3
Endurance 8

Gary wondered what he could do to improve his Dexterity since it was the lowest of the three. Perhaps asking professional fighters or someone who knew what they were doing would help. As for Endurance, he could only think of one thing for that: getting hit more. Which he wasn't looking forward to.

No matter what, though, he needed to improve all of these things, through leveling up or his natural strength, and he had come up with the best solution to do both at the same time.

I don't know when I'll be found by the Underdogs or have to fight in that underground fighting arena again, but if I want to live and protect my family, then I need to get stronger.

The next day Gary woke up and headed to school as he did every day. After he got home the night before, he hadn't received any texts from Kai. On the one hand, he was glad about not having to fight after the earlier scuffle; on the other hand, Kai was currently his only way to earn cash.

Hmm, should I just approach him instead? I don't really want to come off as needy . . . but then again, will it make any difference? He already has me by my balls . . .

When Gary arrived at school, Tom greeted him and asked him a hundred questions about how he was feeling. Of course, Gary replied that he was feeling fine and told him about the events of yesterday.

"They're seriously going that far just because of some stupid high school sports event? I really don't understand people," Tom said, shaking his head. "Anyway, that's two reasons why you should leave the rugby team now. Let's tell Mr. Root today during club practice. You can still play rugby, just not be part of the team."

"Don't worry; I won't be going to rugby practice today," Gary replied. "I need to go to another club instead."

Blake was out on the rugby field when school ended, looking for Gary, but he never turned up.

"Where is that damned little broccoli head? I've already told him that we have a game coming up soon! Does he want to set a record for fastest player to be kicked off the team?" Mr. Root shouted.

"Coach Root, me and Gary ran into some kids from Eton High yesterday," Blake reported. "They wanted to jump me, but he was unlucky enough to get involved. I assume he must still be recovering from that."

Looking at Blake's knuckles, Mr. Root didn't need any more proof. Despite his rough appearance and his tendency to yell at his students, he cared about their well-being. Unfortunately, he knew about the special status Eton High enjoyed, which meant that there was nothing he could do about it.

"All right, I'll let him off just this once, but tell him this is an exception. I don't need him getting a big head and thinking he'll get any special treatment. As for the rest of you, let this be a lesson! Although they went for Blake yesterday, they might go after one of you as well. Make sure to go home in pairs!" Mr. Root ordered.

"Hang on, so you bailed on rugby practice to come here? Be honest with me, has becoming a werewolf made you *lose your mind*? This might be even worse than rugby!" Tom whispered angrily, trying to appeal to his best friend as he followed him to the front of the school gym. They could already hear the chanting from outside.

Inside were around a dozen students in white robes, all performing a set of moves in sync.

Several students were seated off to the side; one of them was Xin. When the teacher noticed the newcomers, he asked: "Oh, are you guys interested in the karate club?"

Gary clenched his fist and shook his head. "I'm here to fight!"

CHAPTER 31

HONORABLE FIGHT!

In the beginning, Gary's Daily Quests had rewarded him with 10 Exp each. Unfortunately, now that his system classified him as Level 2, each quest was only paying out half that amount. With the requirement to reach the next level having already doubled, he didn't need to be a math genius to understand that it would take a long time for him to progress by only relying on this method to accrue Exp.

Nevertheless, Gary didn't intend to stop working out anytime soon. After all, right now it was the only reliable method for him to increase his Strength without any of the stat points he appeared to be getting to level up.

During his brief time with the system, Gary had actually gained the most Exp after fighting against others like the Eton High students. Although he had yet to confirm his suspicion, he strongly believed that it might also be an effective way to gain other stats like Endurance.

He was unwilling to go out and look for trouble in the streets, so his conjecture had eventually led him to challenge the martial arts clubs in his own school. The teacher of the karate club was an older man who folded his arms after hearing Gary's declaration.

"I like your spirit, kid, but things don't work like they do in the movies. This is a school club. I can't just let anyone barge in here and allow them to fight my students," the teacher explained calmly.

Tom was very pleased that this teacher seemed reasonable and hadn't just outright accepted Gary's crazy request. Now he would just have to pull Gary out of the gym. Unfortunately, just when he was about to grab his friend by the arm, Tom saw a strange look in Gary's eyes.

Wh-why does he have that look again? Tom was shaking; everything in his body was telling him that it was a bad idea to touch Gary right now. Unsure why, he listened to this feeling and took a step back.

Hearing the teacher's response, Gary smiled.

"I just wanted to know if karate was worth learning these days," Gary said. "These days Altered fights are being shown all over the internet and on TV. Everyone knows that the best fighters are those who don't just rely on their Altered forms but incorporate martial arts in their fighting style. However, despite being a huge fan, I have never seen a single one of the top Altered fighters use karate."

From Gary's experience, sports teachers, and even more so combat teachers, took great pride in the martial arts they had practiced for years. The teacher's black belt was proof that he must have spent countless hours honing his skills, and Gary couldn't imagine that he would just let it slide that he had basically called his craft "useless."

"And that made you think it might not be worth your time and effort? Very well. Steven, please help our enthusiastic friend find a gi in his size!" the teacher said.

Immediately, a student with a green belt stepped forward. Steven had short hair similar to Tom's, and he was a little larger than Tom and Gary, yet not as big as rugby players like Gil and Barry.

While Steven and Gary disappeared into the changing rooms, the other students quickly laid out mats on the floor, creating an impromptu arena for the two boys to fight in. Not long after, the two combatants came out.

Gary was now also in a white uniform just like everyone else. He and Steven both wore headgear as well as shin guards to protect their legs, and finally thick padding over their stomachs. This protective gear only made it harder for Gary to move, but even he understood that there was no way the teacher would let them fight without it.

I shouldn't be surprised; this isn't a street fight. Not everyone can heal as fast as me, so it's natural he wants to keep us safe. I just hope it still counts as a fight. Gary was worried as he took his position on his side of the ring.

Fortunately, the system promptly answered his desire.

New Quest received
Honorable fight!
You are complying with your werewolf instincts and have sought out a mighty opponent!
You have initiated a fight against a karateka (green belt)!
Win the match!
Quest reward: 120 Exp

This counts as complying with my werewolf instincts? When I fought the other guy before, I was scared, but this time I feel . . . a little excited.

This method appeared to work even better than Gary could have ever hoped. If he won this fight, he would gain exactly enough Exp to reach Level 3, allowing him to improve his stats even further.

"A hands-on demonstration should be the fastest way for you to get a feel for karate. Don't worry; Steven here should be capable enough to teach you a lesson without hurting you too badly.

"The fight will end when one of you gives up. If either one of you steps off the mats, stop what you're doing and restart at the center. Most importantly, this is a friendly spar, so neither one of you is to aim at your opponent's face or groin! Do you both understand?" the teacher asked.

The two of them nodded while the other students sat down around the mats, waiting for the match to begin. This was far more interesting than their usual training. As for Tom, he wasn't sure what to do. It seemed far too late to play everything off as a joke.

"Say, isn't your friend part of the rugby club? What is he doing here?" a voice asked.

When Tom turned around, he recognized the girl as Xin from their class.

"Umm . . . well, let's just say not everyone was too keen about Mr. Root's decision to let Gary join the rugby club. He's been harassed by them, so he planned to get better at fighting." Tom made up an explanation that wasn't too far from the truth.

"Okay, but it looks like your friend just exchanged one bully for another. If he had asked normally, I'm sure Mr. Haruki would have gladly taken him in, but now he's in for a beating. Steven used to be the strongest member in this club," Xin pointed out, just in time for Mr. Haruki to wave a flag, signaling the start of the match.

"I'm more afraid that Gary might not be able to hold back," Tom muttered to himself.

As soon as the match began, Gary activated his skill.

Skill activated: Charging Heart
All stats have temporarily been doubled
–10 Energy

All of his stats immediately doubled; his Strength rose to 10, while his Endurance was now at 16, but his Dexterity was still slow even though it was doubled to 6, making his slow speed regular.

Even at this level, he will probably be too fast for me, but he's a lot smaller than the guy I fought in the underground tournament. With all this gear on, I can probably afford to trade punches.

Once Gary entered into his range, Steven swung using the full strength of his body and hips to connect his roundhouse kick with the arrogant newcomer. As the bigger and more confident fighter, he expected Gary to fall, but as his foot connected, his opponent remained on the ground.

Thanks to the armor and his increased Endurance, the kick felt like just a light shove to Gary. Aware that he was unlikely to get a second opening, he made use of his opponent's momentary confusion by imitating his favorite fighter, Kirk. He started by bending slightly. With all his Strength, he sprang up to deliver a heavy punch, putting his weight behind the attack as his fist connected with the padding over his opponent's stomach.

Steven felt the wind get knocked out from him despite the protective gear. The force behind the attack was far stronger than someone Gary's size should have had. Before he could recover, Gary was already holding on to his opponent's shoulder, imitating Innu's actions by pulling Steven forward and kneeing him in the stomach.

As Gary stood above him, it was clear to everyone that Steven had lost the match.

Quest reward: 120 Exp
Congratulations, you have now reached: Level 3
A stat point has been granted

This guy, he isn't getting back up. I thought he would be like those Eton High kids. I guess he's not really used to taking a beating. Still, just because I can beat up someone my age doesn't mean I would fare well against those gangsters. And I know from watching those underground fights that there are people better than this.

Mr. Haruki rushed over to Steven, forgetting to declare the fight to be over, too worried about his student's well-being. It appeared that he had misjudged Gary. At first, he had believed him to just be a naive kid, but judging from his fighting style, although it was rough, Gary had fought before.

His own student had been at a complete disadvantage. Steven was used to fighting competitions; as a result he had stayed overly cautious about not losing any points, trying his best to show off his skills, while the only thing on Gary's mind had been winning the fight.

The students were murmuring among themselves. "He beat Steven, and it was only in two hits."

"It looked like he got winded from the first punch. Even with all the armor, that punch must have been strong."

"I think Steven was playing it too safe; he should have gone for a kick to the head."

What should I do with that kid? If he leaves now, he'll look down on karate, but I can't just face him myself. An adult beating up a kid would prove nothing to him, the karate teacher thought.

It was then that another student stood up.

"Mr. Haruki, I would like to fight him next."

"Wh-what are you doing?" Tom asked, wondering why Xin, who had been by his side mere seconds ago, had just volunteered to fight.

"Well, it would be pointless for your friend to fight someone weaker than Steven, wouldn't it? Who do you think pushed Steven down to being the second strongest in this club?" Xin asked Tom with a smirk.

CHAPTER 32

LOVER BOY

After defeating Steven, Gary was fully focused on one thing: his system. So much so that he remained blissfully unaware of what was going on around him at the moment, how the other contestants stared at him with a combination of admiration and hostility, and the mixed emotions on Mr. Haruki's face.

When he reached Level 2, he placed the free stat point into his Energy, increasing it by 10 points. Right now, he was carefully contemplating in which category to place the next point.

Putting it into Strength seems like a waste if I can just increase it by going to the gym. I still have to verify whether getting beat up is a viable method to increase Endurance, and I have no idea how to increase Dexterity manually yet. However, I'm sure there are ways. On the other hand, I doubt I can increase Energy or Health on my own, so which one should I choose?

Getting 10 more points in Health might not be a bad idea. Reaching 0 HP can't be good, so I should avoid it ever falling that low. Then again, Energy seems overly useful. Not only is it used for healing, but in the future, I'll most likely have access to more skills like Charging Heart. With a bigger pool, I could use them more often.

When Gary returned to the present, he noticed a girl standing opposite him wearing the same type of protective gear he wore. He had only taken a glance before he went back to his status screen, but he quickly lifted his head to look at the girl again.

"Wait a second, you—you—you're . . ." Gary mumbled like a fool, pointing at her with his finger yet unable to finish his sentence.

"You came here looking for a fight, right? Don't tell me that you already got your fill just from that match. You hardly did anything!" Xin said as she lifted her hand and gestured for Gary to come at her.

It was something that the spectators had only ever seen done in the movies. If they were to attempt such a thing, most would probably have died of embarrassment. However, for some reason, the way Xin spoke, the way she acted, was filled with confidence, giving her actions such a natural feel that nobody dared to point it out.

Gary started to look toward Mr. Haruki, hoping he would step in and at least tell her to back down from the fight. After all, he had just easily defeated Steven, though the teacher had been quite confident that he would lose. However, the teacher just stood to the side, taking care of Steven, who seemed to have recovered.

Is he really going to allow this fight to happen? But . . . she's a girl! Gary thought. It wasn't that he thought girls were weak, but despite Gary being on the smaller side, Xin had a more petite frame. What was more, he knew he carried an unfair advantage. When using Charging Heart, he had the strength of a person twice his size.

Most importantly, the last person Gary wanted to fight . . . was his crush.

Meanwhile, Tom was racking his brain to find a way out for his friend. *Damn it, I can't allow Gary to continue with this fight. If she gets him in any type of locking position and puts his head closer to her chest . . . the guy is guaranteed to turn on the spot!*

Gary said, "I'm sorry, I'm just worried that I might hurt you. I know this might sound a bit old-fashioned, but I really don't think I can hit you." He bowed his head—not out of respect, but to hide his face, which he feared to be beet red.

"Ha!" Mr. Haruki let out a loud laugh. "Boy, through this thick armor, you won't be hurting anyone. That's assuming you'll actually manage to hit Miss Clove. I can tell that you have fought a few times outside, but in martial arts, you should never discriminate against your opponent. You never know just how deadly someone with a weapon might be, even if that weapon happens to be one's own body."

Gary understood what Mr. Haruki was saying, and it was never his intention to discriminate against anyone. Heck, if a girl chased after him with a knife or threatened his family members' lives, he would be a firm believer in gender equality. It was just . . . every time he looked at this girl in particular, his heart would beat rapidly . . . which in his case might lead to more severe consequences than him pitching a tent.

"There's no way he can fight!" Tom announced. Everyone looked at him, wondering why he had gotten involved. "Xin, he can't fight you because . . . be-because . . . he likes you!"

Tom practically yelled out the last part. The whole hall was dead silent, including Xin herself.

Tom, what the hell are you doing? Why are you confessing to her on my behalf? Gary was screaming in his head at this absurdity while simultaneously wishing the ground would open up and swallow him whole. Just like everyone else, he was speechless, and all he could see was the system displaying his heartbeat, which was rising dangerously close to the 150 BPM mark.

At this rate, I won't even need to use Charging Heart.

"Oh . . . so it's like that?" Xin eventually broke the silence as she placed her hand on her chin. "Well, I'm flattered . . . I guess. I'm not quite sure how to feel right now. I've just transferred here, so all I know about you is your performance during rugby practice and when you were fighting Steven. Oh, and that little red sea of sick you made."

Gary clenched his fists, wanting to run away from this entire situation. If he had known that it would turn into such a giant mess, he would have never challenged this stupid club. At least he was slightly happy that she hadn't outright rejected him . . . although he hadn't missed the fact that she hadn't exactly accepted his feelings for her either.

"I'm sorry, I just can't . . ." Gary mumbled as he began to take off his protective headgear, keeping eye contact with the floor, too embarrassed to look up.

Seeing this, Xin felt a little annoyed, but not as much as Mr. Haruki. Gary had been the one who had started this little fighting session, yet now he was going to give up? While the teacher was still looking for a reason to make him stay, Xin came up with a plan.

"Hey, wait!" Xin called out. "Is it true what your friend said? About you liking me?"

Gary wasn't quite sure how to answer this. Just as Xin had pointed out, they hadn't known each other for long . . . or at all, actually.

"Yeah . . . Sorry that someone like me likes you," Gary answered, mustering the courage to look up.

"How about we go on a date?" Xin suggested. "I can't promise to be your girlfriend, but if you can beat me in a match, then we can at least go out once. What do you say?"

"Huh?" Everyone inside the hall was baffled. Xin was a beautiful girl, and some of the karate club members had tried to ask her out when she joined. She had instantly refused all but one of them. When Steven had tried his luck, Xin had told him that she would consider it before requesting a match against him. Unsurprisingly, that event had cemented his position as second strongest.

"I'll only go out with someone stronger than me," Xin proclaimed with a big smile.

> New Quest received
> Win the date!
> The girl of your dreams has challenged you to a fight.
> Sweep her off her feet and into your arms, lover boy!
> Quest reward: Instant level up (+ a date!)

What the hell is wrong with this system? Gary thought.

CHAPTER 33

XIN'S SKILLS

Gary had been sure that his mind was made up to get out of the hall as fast as his legs would carry him. Heck, he had even seriously considered using Charging Heart to get out faster, and he had been convinced that nothing would be able to change that, yet two things had just made a match against Xin extremely tempting.

For one, there was the quest that he had just received. As silly as the quest description was, the reward was clear enough. If he could beat her, he would benefit from an instant level up.

This system is full of surprises. The fight against that Steven guy had already granted me far more Exp than any other, but it was still a flat amount, so why is it different now? The system seems to function similar to a game, and they usually reward you based on the difficulty of a task, so is it saying that fighting Xin would really be that much harder? But what about Steven? He was weaker than those other guys!

In all honesty, Gary didn't know if the system really worked like a game, so he could only look at the facts that he had in front of him. Beating Xin would result in him instantly reaching Level 4, meaning he would get yet another free stat point to use as he wished.

However, the second reason, which if he was being honest was far more enticing, was that beating her meant she would go out with him. That possibility alone resulted in his mind going haywire once more.

A date . . . shit, I've never been on an actual date before! Where would we go? To the movies? Mini golf? A restaurant? . . . But all those things cost money . . . Maybe I can just take her for a walk in the park. Yeah, that sounds good. There's a river there as well! If someone attacks us, like when I was with Blake, and she gets pushed into the river . . . and maybe she can't swim . . . then maybe I could jump in and . . . and . . .

"So are we doing this or not?" Xin asked after Gary had stopped walking. He remained standing there, which she took as a good sign. She was sure he just needed another little push.

Just then the hall echoed with a chuckle, and it was coming from none other than Gary.

"I say, I'm gonna save your life." Gary turned around, madness in his eyes as he pointed toward her. "Let's fight."

With so many strange things happening one after the other, the students didn't even question Gary's weird response. They were just pleased that they were about to witness another spectacle instead of doing their boring, repetitive drills.

Once again, the only one who couldn't share their enthusiasm was Tom, who was on the sidelines biting his fingernails.

Calm down and check where the exits are. You'll need to grab Gary in case he shows any signs of turning. Now that he thought about it, he had never seen Gary do anything werewolflike, apart from his wild anger, allowing Tom's heart to calm down a little.

He might be just an angry wolf on the inside?

Mr. Haruki was ready, Steven was back to his usual self, and both fighters were in their positions.

"Ready, go!"

The fight had started, and Gary's heart hadn't settled yet. His Charging Heart had worn off, but he was wondering about his heart the way it was now. Maybe he wouldn't need to activate the skill.

It was then that he strangely saw that Xin had charged first. She ran in and suddenly jumped into the air, spinning her body. He saw her back and then her whole leg. At the last second, Gary tilted his head back. His movements were twice as slow without Charging Heart, allowing him to miss her foot narrowly, and he repositioned himself by moving to one of the corners of the mat.

How fast was that kick, and a spinning kick besides? If she had hit me with that, my head would have gone flying off. Is she trying to kill me? Gary wondered as he felt something trickling from his nose.

He tried to sniff it up, but it didn't work, and he looked down and saw blood on the floor. The back of her heel had lightly grazed the tip of his nose.

"Looks like you're a little slower, and I guess if you don't get the first hit, you're useless." Xin shrugged. "I expected more from you for some reason."

The students laughed and mocked him, wanting one of their own to win. "Ha-ha, did you see him running away?"

"Don't go in the corner. Come on, why don't you just use your brute strength like before?"

"Because he knows he's going to get knocked out."

Shit! Was I going easy on her because I didn't want to hurt her? But it looks like I can't hold back.

Skill activated: Charging Heart
All stats have temporarily been doubled
−10 Energy

Placing his hand on his chest, Gary could once again feel his heart thumping so loud it felt like it was going to jump out of his throat. Although nothing seemed to change from the outside, Xin quickly got into a fighting stance again.

"This is what I wanted," Xin mumbled.

Now it was Gary's turn, and he decided to charge in just as he had against Steven.

I'll just take the hit. I took a hit from that large blob guy and I was still standing, so taking a hit from someone like this is no problem at all! Gary gritted his teeth, expecting what was to come.

Xin stayed firm, her leg ready, judging the distance. Then when Gary was within her zone, she spun her body once again and let out a kick, aiming her heel toward his head.

Gary knew that even with Charging Heart, he was still too slow to react to the kick, but he was confident in his recovery skills. He tried to lift his hands, but even they were too slow, and Xin's heel hit him right in the head, under his ear.

He felt an immense pain, and his head was flung to the side. The students even looked away. The kick had landed solid, but Gary gritted his teeth, pushing through, and moved forward again.

I just have to grab her! . . . Huh? Why is she moving away? The image of Xin started to spin, as if he were dizzy. The next thing Gary knew, he was falling to his side and crashing into the seated crowd.

Tom was shocked. *It was a perfect strike behind the ear. His whole head must be spinning. That's why he fell over.*

As for Xin, the one who had delivered the blow, she was shocked herself. *I didn't think he would take the kick head-on like that. I thought he had a better plan. I didn't hold back either. How did he do it? Why is he still standing?*

She was amazed that Gary was even able to stand. He got up but fell back over. Eventually, after getting up the third time, Gary was back on his feet.

It was the quickest she had seen someone recover.

"Reset!" Mr. Haruki said, with a big grin. He knew as a teacher he shouldn't be smiling at something like this, but he just couldn't help himself.

Gary was ready for round two to reset the match and fight again. However, he had received a message from the system at that point.

Quest failed

You are no longer able to complete this quest

Since becoming a werewolf and obtaining the system, Gary had experienced his first loss and first quest failure.

CHAPTER 34

ALTERED HUNTER

Club activities had ended for the day, and for the first time in a while, Tom and Gary had a chance to leave together. The last couple of days, Gary had just rushed home, claiming he had something important to do. Tom had known that he had to be hiding something, but only recently did he find out that it was because of his part-time job as a delivery person.

Then yesterday, Blake had gone home with him for some reason. Now it was just the two of them, and since they didn't live in the same area, the time they would walk together would be short.

Tom had been hoping to crack a few jokes about what just happened, how his best friend had seemingly lost to the girl he had fallen for, but in the whole time since they left the club, Gary hadn't said a word.

The silence was killing Tom, and he just couldn't leave his best friend like this. Since they were about to enter the rougher area where Gary lived, they would part ways soon. If he wanted to say something, he would have to do it now.

"Hey, man, don't let it get to you. Apparently, she's the strongest person in the whole club. I don't think losing against her is anything to be ashamed of. Who knows, if you get better and stronger and learn to control your werewolf powers, maybe you can even beat her next time and get that date!" Tom said enthusiastically, but in his mind, all he could see were images of his friend transforming in the middle of the fight, and he shook his head to get rid of that thought.

"It's not just that I lost . . ." Gary mumbled, but then he went quiet because he knew it was impossible to explain to Tom. Losing to Xin, who weighed far less than him and was the same age, meant that if the Underdogs or anyone else ever found out where he lived, they could easily beat him.

Not just the Underdogs but other gangs had members who were extremely good at fighting in various martial arts. And the Underdogs also had Kirk, an Altered who had won the Altered Rookie Championship. If he was ever sent to deal with Gary's family, could Gary last even a few seconds, the way he was at the moment?

Normally Tom would have left a while ago to head in the other direction, but he couldn't leave Gary like this. He looked down the street and saw some members of the red color gang.

The second they met eyes, Tom looked away.

"The red color gang is in this area now?" Tom whispered to Gary. "I guess the Underdogs aren't in complete control of this area, then? This should be a good thing for you."

"You really think I'm happy that more gangs are roaming around where I live?" Gary scoffed. "It's good because it means the Underdogs have their own problems to deal with, and they won't ruin this place further, but the black color gang and the red color gang have been fighting in this area more frequently. Thankfully, the main gangs haven't gotten involved yet, but . . . let's just say even walking to school is getting tough."

Gary remembered the girl he had seen. He still wondered why the black color gang had attempted to abduct her so openly. Even stranger was that she seemed to be somehow related to Kai, yet he had never mentioned her.

"Oh, that's right, I almost forgot to tell you." Tom facepalmed as he suddenly remembered something. "The other day I decided to go out to the shop, it was pretty late, and these guys followed me."

Suddenly Gary was deeply concerned about his friend. The story wasn't starting well, but Tom had no injuries, and he was relieved. This didn't go unnoticed, and Tom was happy to see that Gary still cared for him.

"I'm all right. What I was going to say was this guy came out of nowhere, all dressed in black, and beat them all up. Honestly, it was pretty badass. Hey, maybe if you had a teacher like that guy, something like what happened earlier wouldn't have happened." Tom wanted to tease his friend, but he quickly covered his mouth, realizing that he had just poked a hornet's nest.

"Huh, not a bad idea . . ." Gary said. "So who do you think he was, a gangster boss out for a walk or something?"

"No, he didn't really look like one." Tom looked at the gang members nearby. The man he'd met didn't seem to fit in with the others. "Come to think of it, he might have been an Altered. That might explain his large frame, and usually they have superhuman bodies even without transforming. Alternatively . . . he could have been an Altered Hunter."

"Altered Hunter, huh? I guess even the Altered have things they need to worry about," Gary said.

Tom couldn't venture too far into the other side of town; he needed to go home. Realizing how far Tom had accompanied him, Gary decided to walk him back until he was in a safer area, since he might not be as lucky to meet such a mysterious stranger a second time.

It was getting pretty late, around six p.m.; the sun was starting to set, and more troubling, people would be roaming the streets. Tom was concerned, but Gary reminded him that he wasn't a regular person anymore and reassured him by saying he would be going straight home.

However, after pulling up his hood, Gary got his phone out and sent a text to his mother and sister.

I'm at Tom's and will be coming home late tonight.

Gary had no intention of going home yet, and he was ready to cause a bit of chaos.

CHAPTER 35

THE NEW WORLD

When Xin left the karate club, she was showered with praise from the other members for doing a good job of humiliating Gary. However, she felt like the fight wasn't over yet. Her opponent hadn't been knocked out and was still well enough to fight again, yet for some reason he had left after the first blow.

Before she left to make her way home, Mr. Haruki had stopped to have a word with her.

"Xin, I'll ask you again, are you sure you don't want to join the winter tournament? If you do well, it's a good chance for you to get noticed, with your talent and in the world we live in . . ."

"Please, Mr. Haruki. I know you mean well, but I really can't," Xin replied. "Besides, I'm not the one with talent in my family." And with the conversation over, she left.

Mr. Haruki was left thinking that an opportunity was slipping away right in front of him. He could tell that something was up. He had never seen any student with such a pained look before, turning such an offer down.

After leaving the club, Xin saw a group of girls watching her. They quickly looked away and started whispering to each other, sneaking glances at her once in a while.

Damn it, did I mess with the wrong girl, like Dad was worried about? But it was an accident! It might be good if I apologize to her tomorrow. Crap, I'm not really good at these things.

As she exited the school gates, a black car with tinted windows was waiting for her. Before Xin could even open the door, the driver had gotten out and opened it for her.

"Good afternoon, miss," the driver said.

Xin got into the car for the ride home, a privilege of being the mayor's daughter.

Usually, an important figure such as the mayor of a Tier 3 city would send their children to school in a higher-tier city. This was because attaining such a position most likely meant that the mayor had a connection to one of the big gangs in the area, making his family an easy target.

At the same time, this also meant that Xin was protected in more ways than one. However, she was sick and tired of her old life: not being able to go anywhere freely, having to be careful whom she talked to, and being guarded at all times. It was hard for her to make friends because of the way she lived.

However, this year she had managed to get her father to relax a little by making a deal with him.

I just have to get through this year and prove to him that everything will be okay. I'll say I'm sorry to Tiffany tomorrow, and I'll make sure everything is all right. But what about that Gary guy? Will I have to worry about him?

She found it strange that someone who was inexperienced in fighting would suddenly challenge a martial arts club. She honestly didn't like people like Gary who had been blessed with a good body and natural strength, easily beating those who had trained for years.

Well, his friend did say he liked me, so I don't think he will be causing any problems.

Eventually, the car arrived in a more private area of the town. It had traveled through what looked like woodlands and had reached a large black gate. Standing outside were men who looked like guards wearing suits; however, if one were to look closer, one could see that they weren't just any guards. They had tattoos running up their necks, and some had piercings.

These were gangsters who had been lent to the mayor for protection. In a way, they were a bigger deterrent against other gangs than bodyguards would be.

Xin's family lived in a large house with six bedrooms, each with its own bathroom. This would be a luxury for anyone living in a Tier 3 city. Not even the mayor of a small town like this one would be able to live in a place like this, not without accepting a few bribes here and there, but she knew her dad wasn't a bad person.

It's just how the world works, Xin repeated in her mind.

Unfortunately, that was the only way to move up in the current world. Still, because she hadn't been here long, it was hard to call this foreign place home. She entered the house and heard a familiar voice from the kitchen.

"Hey, sounds like the little troublemaker is back!"

Xin went in to see her mother and the person whose voice she had heard coming through the doors. Her brother.

"Jayden, you're here! Didn't you say you would be busy shooting now?" Xin asked.

Like Xin, her brother was quite attractive; he had clear skin and a quite chiseled look, yet appeared feminine as well. His eyelashes were so naturally dark that it looked like he wore mascara. Most bodybuilders would strive for a body like his, but that was mostly because of his job.

"Well, one of my appointments got canceled, so I decided to head home early," Jayden answered. He saw a glow in Xin's eyes and let out a big sigh. "Sometimes I don't think you're happy to see me because of me. Fine, let me finish here, and we can go for a round," Jayden said, getting up from his seat.

The two of them headed outside. On the large piece of land where their house stood was an annex set up with gym equipment, punching bags and dummies, and martial arts gear.

"Wow, this place looks nearly as nice as the gym I train at," Jayden said. He waited for Xin to say something, but she was already putting on protective gear. Shaking his head, he knew he had already lost to the fighting-obsessed maniac.

They got into position, and it was time. Xin charged forward, leaping up in the air, and spun, delivering a kick to the head. Jayden leaned back and narrowly avoided it.

It missed, just like against Gary, but this is different, Xin thought.

She was right; the difference was that Jayden had narrowly avoided the kick on purpose so as not to use too much energy and to give him time to return the attack.

Xin continued kicking, with a few punches here and there, but Jayden avoided all of them; once in a while he threw a kick back, but it was just a light tap, showing his sister that he could hurt her at any time.

Eventually, getting frustrated, Xin tried her strongest attack. She was ready; she waited for the perfect time and spun once again, hoping to hit her brother with the back of her heel, right behind the ear.

She could feel it connect, but her brother was still standing with his arm covering the area; he took a step forward, throwing her off balance and causing her to fall to the ground. Throwing out a punch to her face, he stopped an inch from her nose.

"And that is definitely a defeat," Jayden said with a smile. "You really have improved a lot, and those kicks of yours are hard to deal with, trust me," he said, massaging his arm.

Helping her up off the ground, he could tell Xin wasn't pleased. Usually, his compliments made her feel better, but it didn't look like it this time.

"What's wrong?" Jayden asked.

"Are my kicks really that strong? You're not just saying that to make me feel better, right?"

"That's what you're upset about? That kick I blocked at the end. First of all, I'm twenty-five, and your body still has room to grow,"

Jayden said. "Second of all, your brother is one of the top fifty fighters in the country, and to top that off, I am an Altered, so I have an unfair advantage. If you kicked anyone your age, they wouldn't be able to stand up again."

Xin found this hard to believe, because one person *had* stood again after that very kick.

"Maybe that boy is someone to look out for after all," Xin mumbled.

Suddenly, she felt a heat coming from the corner of the room, and as she looked at Jayden, she could see the fire in his eyes.

"What's this about a boy? Did he try touching you? You can tell me, right? You know the rule Dad and I set for you. If anyone wants to go out with you, they need to at least be strong enough to beat me!"

She knew about this rule, but she knew that was also impossible. There were only a few people in the country strong enough to beat her brother. That was why she had changed that rule slightly to herself that they had to at least be stronger than her; hopefully then it would be someone her brother would accept, but whether she would ever find such a person was a different story altogether.

CHAPTER 36

A LEADER

Will there be one today?

Oh, he seems to be getting more impatient; I wonder if something happened to him? Kai mused as he read the message on his phone. At the very top, the name Green Fang was displayed.

There is no need for you to ask me. I will notify you when I need you.

Kai texted Gary back and placed the phone back into his pocket as he continued on his way to a particular parking garage. The structure itself was quite large, six stories, yet it was empty. Although the sky had darkened to night, it wasn't too late, yet there no cars were present.

The structure was empty was because it was another fight night, and the gangs in the area had made sure that those who didn't need to know about it wouldn't stumble upon this place.

"So tell me again, why didn't you invite that Green Fang guy? Are you worried he might go crazy again?" Innu asked, having caught a glimpse of Gary's message on Kai's phone.

The newest member of their yet-to-be-named gang was wearing the new uniform he had been given. The black overcoat with golden trim and matching trousers suited him surprisingly well.

"Because it would be a bit much to invite our leader to such a small occasion," Kai answered with a smirk, not turning around.

"Our leader? That green-haired guy who could barely fight is supposed to be our leader? Didn't know you had a sense of humor, but seriously tell me the real reason," Innu insisted.

However, Kai didn't say another word and just continued to move toward the parking garage. There were two guards up ahead who didn't quite look like they belonged there. Still, it was a perfect way to stop anyone nosy from snooping around.

Innu, for a moment entertaining the possibility that Kai wasn't just pulling his leg, stopped in his tracks, making Marie nearly walk into him. At the last moment, she gracefully sidestepped him.

"He's really not joking? I need to know what the hell I signed myself up for!" Innu asked the girl, who just shook her head before following behind Kai.

The two guards appeared to be in their late twenties or early thirties. They checked over Kai and his entourage briefly yet didn't say anything else as the trio walked past them. Inside, the three could hear people cheering.

Innu knew that once they went farther in, he wouldn't be able to ask Kai as many questions, so he had to ask now.

"Fine, fine, let's say that kid is our leader, then isn't that all the more reason to bring him along? Not to belittle him or anything, but he clearly isn't really used to these kinds of things, and some more fighting practice couldn't hurt either. The way he currently is . . ."

The leader of a gang could be said to be their most important person. In a way, they alone symbolized the prestige of the gang; hence in most cases, the leader was the gang member with the most strength.

Because of the No Lethal Weapons Pact, individual strength was important these days. In cases of disagreement when one side needed to convince another, the most direct method was to do it the good old-fashioned way.

However, this wasn't always the case, especially for established gangs; it was common to have a wise leader at the top, one who wasn't just a musclehead. In those cases, either the leader's right-hand man or those under them with frightening strength would ensure that others followed their command.

Usually, those leaders had something special about them, a unique charisma that allowed them to get trustworthy people to work under them in the first place.

Innu had joined in the belief that Kai would be the latter type, which was why he was shocked to learn that Gary was supposed to be their leader. He didn't even fit the former type, so having him as their gang's representative was practically asking for trouble. Innu could already foresee them getting picked on by other gangs.

"All right, seeing that you're asking out of concern for the new gang you've joined, I suppose I shouldn't keep you out of the loop. You see, in my opinion, there are certain qualities that distinguish a great leader from a good one," Kai replied, not slowing his steps.

"A great leader needs to have a reason to keep growing their territory. Putting it simply, they need ambition and hunger. At the moment, I'm testing Gary's hunger since I want to see just how far he will go. If I'm right, then it's just a matter of time before he starts acting on his own. Once he does, it will be a perfect opportunity to find out just how ambitious he is."

By now the three could see several cars that had been parked in a way to make an arena. Crowds were cheering from behind them, as a fight was already taking place. The first thing Innu noticed was certain students from Eton High. His fists tensed up as images of what happened before flashed through his head.

He said that they will be our next opponent; I guess we are here to scout them today then, Innu thought.

"Don't worry," Marie said. "With the number of different prospect gangs, subdivisions, and color gangs here, no one will be stupid enough to start a fight, so you can stop shaking."

"I'm not scared, I'm angry!" Innu replied with gritted teeth. "I can take on any one of those backstabbing bastards on their own. They only beat me because they ganged up on me!"

The girl just smiled and lightly patted him on the back, then looked for a good spot to watch the ongoing fight. Meanwhile, Kai had been paying attention to something else. On top of one of the cars, a little behind the arena, was a large digital board displaying today's fighting roster and the betting odds.

Strange, I was sure Billy Buster was supposed to be fighting today, Kai thought. *Given his fighting record, the gangs must have already tried to scout him. If he hadn't lost that day, I'm sure he would have gotten a serious offer. Was his pride hurt so badly that he wants to wait for people to forget . . . or did Gary actually manage to hurt him more than I thought?*

At that moment, Billy opened the fridge in his apartment.

I'm so hungry, Billy thought as his eyes latched onto some raw lamb at the bottom of the fridge. Without even a moment's hesitation, he grabbed it, and before he knew what he was doing, he had started ripping it apart with his teeth.

Eventually, when he was done with his meal, he let out a satisfied burp and scratched the mark on his neck where he had been bitten.

CHAPTER 37

TURF WAR

In the town of Slough, there was an unwritten rule concerning the area where Gary lived. When the sun went down, the underworld came out to play. The color gangs and more would roam the streets.

If Gary hadn't told his mother he would be staying with Tom, who lived in a more affluent area, then she would be worried out of her mind. He had also often lied about Tom's parents dropping him off at their apartment.

As a former transporter for the Underdogs, Gary had needed to learn not only where their own territories were but also what territories belonged to which color gang as well as which areas were the most common fight spots. The knowledge that the entire town, except for a few key areas, had been divided into so many areas that the gangs claimed for their own had left quite a bitter taste in his mouth.

It had been vitally important to memorize the safest route, as it was rarely the most direct one. Gary often had to go through several different territories to reach his destination. He had been quite good at his job, which was why he had never failed a delivery until that day.

At least I got this strange system out of it, Gary thought as he quickened his pace. He had his hood up, covering his green hair, not that it stood out among all the other punks who were currently out on the streets. After all, he had chosen that hair color for that reason specifically.

Still, for what he was about to do, he needed to make sure that he wouldn't be recognizable.

Using what money he had left, he bought a few cheap black rags from the convenience store. Then he found an unoccupied alley and ripped them up, then tied them around his arms and legs, covering them fully. Once he was done, Gary headed toward a certain area of town.

It didn't take him long to find what he was looking for. The graffiti on the wall that had marked this area as belonging to the black color gang appeared to have just recently been tagged over with red paint, claiming ownership over this area.

Gary closed his eyes and concentrated on his ears. All his senses had been sharpened ever since he woke up with the Werewolf System. Listening carefully, he could hear some people talking among themselves. Although he was unable to hear exactly what they were saying, he did make out the sound of a spray can. Opening his eyes, he walked in the direction the sounds came from.

It seems like luck is on my side tonight. But for the red color gang to have spread this far out into the black color gang's territory and to do it so brazenly . . . Surely they should know that the black color gang works for the Underdogs . . . are they just brave, or stupid . . . or do they actually have the backing of someone who is willing to go against Damion and his goons? Gary thought as he stepped out.

"Hey, this ain't your territory! Do you really think you should be doing that?" Gary asked, his heart beating louder with every word he spoke. There were three of them, all wearing red. One of them was clearly holding a spray can, in the midst of tagging yet another wall, but as for the others, Gary had no clue what type of weapons they might have on them.

The three young adults looked at each other for a second and started to laugh. The one closest to Gary, who also happened to be the largest, and therefore most likely designated as the lookout, came at him.

"Let's get him!" The man swung at Gary, sure that the height difference would play out in his favor, but Gary was able to duck the first punch.

Good thing I used Charging Heart as soon as I entered the alleyway. Are these gang members always so aggressive? Here I thought I would need to taunt them a bit more. Gary saw an opening, a chance to attack, and quickly kicked the first person right in the stomach, putting his full weight into it.

The man curled over, and Gary mused that if he had gone in again, he could have finished him off, but instead he decided to turn around and run.

I can't underestimate them, and I can't let them see my face clearly! There's three of them and only one of me, he reminded himself as he widened the distance but at the same time allowed the gang members to follow him.

As the red color gang members chased Gary, three soon became six, then nine. The first three hadn't exactly kept quiet, making others notice them and join in the chase.

The sheer number of them, which continued to grow, reassured Gary that he had made the right decision in choosing not to fight. If he had gotten caught up with the first three, then there was a good chance the others would have joined and eventually outnumbered him.

This morning, with Gary's brimming overconfidence after becoming a type of Altered who had even won a fight in the arena, he would have decided to fight the three of them. After all, he had managed to defeat five members of a color gang, but after losing to Xin, he felt humbled. His crush had reminded him that one shouldn't judge someone by their appearance.

"That guy, he's not fast, but he isn't slowing down!" one of the red gang members huffed as they continued to chase him.

Gary couldn't deny it, not when his system had assigned him a mere 3 Dexterity points, which he figured was linked to his speed. Even after he used Charging Heart, his running wasn't much faster than the average person's. Fortunately, he more than made up for it in the stamina department, which he had already confirmed was linked to his Energy level.

Eventually, Gary arrived at his destination, a park with an open platform. Using his sensitive ears, he heard what he had been hoping for.

"I need help! The red color gang has come to fight us!" Gary shouted out loud.

It was only then that the dozen or so red color gang members noticed that they had been following Gary all the way into an entirely different area, one that was under stricter control of the black color gang. A group of black color gang members who regularly used the park as their hangout spot were already present and quickly surrounded the trespassers.

New Quest received
My enemy's enemy . . .
Using your knowledge you have caused quite the stir.
You have instigated a turf war!
Choose a side and make sure they win!
Quest reward: 50 Exp per defeated person

There were around ten of them in total, making the fight more or less even. The red color gang members, seeing no way out of this mess, decided to fight. The two sides clashed, bringing out their weapons in the form of iron chains, pocketknives, and baseball bats. Some just used their fists, and those were the ones who knew how to fight a little better than others.

As for Gary, he didn't just stay a bystander in all of this; he was also joining in, mostly because he needed to. For one, he needed not to blow his cover, and then there was also his quest reward.

Nevertheless, Gary was sneaky enough to wait for the right chance before delivering the knockout blow to the weakened enemy. If all of this had been a game, the gang members might complain about him essentially kill-stealing, but the other black color gang members just regarded him as another member. In this intense moment, they didn't care who got the last punch in, yet for Gary, it was vitally important because the counter that had appeared would only go up when he knocked someone out.

The fight didn't last more than a few minutes, and in the end, the black color gang won. Huffing and panting, three of them were still standing—well, four, including Gary—while the rest had lost consciousness. Surprisingly, although some of them had pocket-knives, nobody was bleeding badly apart from a few scratches.

Quest reward: 450 Exp
Congratulations, you have now reached: Level 4
A stat point has been granted
50/460 Exp

Seeing this, Gary was pleased that he now had two stat points to allocate since he had not yet allocated the previous one. It wasn't that he hadn't been able to decide what to use it for, but he had realized that it was wiser to allow his body to naturally improve until it hit some sort of limit before he started using them.

"Hey, you were quite skilled there, man; what group are you from?" One of the black color gang members approached Gary from behind; he still had his face turned away.

Unfortunately, as a transporter, Gary had only needed to know about the color gang's territories, so he didn't know the ins and outs of the gangs. While he was racking his brain over how to get out of the situation, he heard another sound from the system.

Optional Quest received
. . . is also my enemy?
The truth is you belong to neither of these gangs, and now you can come out on top.
Defeat the remaining gang members!
Quest reward: 50 Exp per defeated person

This system . . .

CHAPTER 38

THE POWER
OF THE MOON

Although this new quest offered him the same rewards for the same type of work, Gary actually felt a bit conflicted. As the description had pointed out, he wasn't really a member of the black color gang, yet these people had helped him out, and he had literally fought side by side with them just moments ago. Gary might be unable to lie his way out of the situation, but he could always just flee.

I . . . I can't backstab them, Gary thought, but just as he was ready to get out of the park, someone let out a scream. Turning around, he could see that it had originated not too far from where he was.

"You should have stayed on your side, bastard!" one of the black color gang members gleefully exclaimed as he whacked his baseball bat down on the back of one of the red color gang members, who were unable to do anything about this sort of bullying.

If that guy keeps hitting him like that, he . . . might even kill him, Gary realized, clenching his fists.

But then he recalled how five members of the very same color gang had tried to abduct that girl not too far away from his home. During his time working for the Underdogs, Gary had seen that not every member was a scumbag. Some still had some humanity left inside them, like Kirk, but this group of ruffians clearly didn't belong in that category.

They robbed people, made the streets unsafe, and didn't even think twice about hurting others. In a way, the big gangs above them were far more respectable, as they at least tried not to get regular civilians involved, yet it was different with the color gangs.

"Hey, didn't you hear me, I asked what group you're from," the black color gang member repeated, but Gary just kept looking at the guy with the baseball bat having fun against his helpless victims. What was more, the third member of their group picked up one of the dropped pocketknives and brought it really close to the red color gang member's face.

"Let me give you a little reminder of what happens if you barge into the wrong territory."

Gary couldn't take it anymore.

"Screw this; the system's right," Gary mumbled. "I don't belong to any of these gangs!"

The black color gang member needed a moment to glean the meaning behind what Gary had said, but by that time, a fist was about to connect with him. Gary had activated his Charging Heart skill, making his fist speed up midswing as he aimed it right at his opponent's chin, sending him flying to the ground.

Gary didn't hesitate as he moved on to the next one. Having watched Gary just knock out his buddy with a single hit, the gang member dropped the pocketknife in a panic, then quickly tried to pick it back up. However, that proved to be a big mistake. The moment he looked down, Gary kicked him square in his face, making him join his buddy in dreamland.

Unfortunately for Gary, the last member of the black color gang who was still up was faster on the uptake. Before he could turn around to deal with him, it was Gary's turn to take a beating. Moments after his kick to the gang member's face, he felt a hit to his back from a baseball bat.

Damn it! Why do all these goons have to aim at my ribs?

–10 HP

Congratulations! After repeatedly taking a beating, your body has grown stronger.

Don't get used to this, though; otherwise people might think you're an M.

Endurance +1

Is this really the time to congratulate me? And what the heck is an M? Gary thought, as the baseball bat continued to pound him. He had curled up into a ball, placing his hands above his head to protect it. The only silver lining was that the subsequent hits only took 5 points off his HP, though he was unsure whether this was because the gang member was exhausted or because of his boosted Endurance.

Gritting his teeth, Gary let the adrenaline take care of the pain. He decided to go for his opponent's legs, charging in and tackling him, a move he had practiced in rugby many times before. Using his strength, Gary lifted him up and then slammed him down on the concrete, knocking him out and causing him to drop the bat.

Quest reward: 150 Exp
200/460 Exp
You are a lone wolf who is growing.
Would you like to activate a Forced Bond on any of those that you have defeated?
During the hunt, you will gain additional Exp for each successful mark you have successfully taken down.

Gary declined the offer to mark more people. He still didn't understand what a hunt was; he had an idea, but he wasn't prepared to kill people, not if it could be avoided.

I still need to figure out how to get rid of Barry's mark. Should I try to talk to him after rugby practice?

It was getting late, and it was time for Gary to head home; otherwise, his mother would start to get suspicious. Thanks to his little bit of fun with the color gangs, he hadn't had time to go to the gym. It looked like he had to give it a miss for today and fail his Daily Quest.

Still, he had gained way more Exp than he would have in the gym. Nevertheless, he imagined that after what he had just done, tensions between the two color gangs were guaranteed to rise, and they would most likely act more cautiously by traveling in bigger groups for the foreseeable future. It was unlikely that he would get another chance to farm so much Exp, but just doing it once had already been worth it.

Gary might be unable to complete the gym part of his Daily Quests, but he could still stop by the shop as he had done before to purchase some more protein. After he finished the raw steak away from the eyes of others, his Energy was restored, which helped him heal his injuries, yet there was still one problem.

My money is going down a lot faster than I thought it would. I still don't have a consistent supply. What should I do? I thought Kai would be calling me more often; how long can this last? Gary had about two hundred dollars left out of his original five hundred, the money from the Underdogs that he didn't want to touch, that he'd planned to give to his mother somehow . . .

On his way home, Gary was surprised by the scent of raw meat. He rubbed his eyes because he could see the scent in the air. It looked like a red mist that led up to a certain apartment.

This . . . looks like the same thing I saw at school. It's the trail that allows me to follow people who are marked, so does that mean Barry lives in this area?

The apartment was only a few streets away from where he lived, and he didn't like this thought at all. Sure, Barry often used his status to get what he wanted at school, but that still wasn't enough of a reason to kill him. He might not have been the nicest person, but there were far worse people than him.

I can't just turn up at his door, especially not this late in the day. I'll have to try to think of something tomorrow instead. I still have some time before the full moon anyway, and who knows, maybe Tom was just making a big deal out of nothing.

When he got home, Gary greeted his mother and sister and ate the dinner that she had left for him quite easily, despite already having eaten two kilograms of meat. His appetite seemed endless ever since he had turned.

But Gary had trouble trying to go to sleep that night. He couldn't stop thinking about what would happen at the full moon. It didn't help that he could see his sister Amy sleeping on the bed next to him.

Then, when the clock ticked past midnight to the next day, the system delivered a new message.

The power of the moon is starting to run through your body.
The fuller it gets, the more powerful you'll become.
Current bonus: All Stats +1

As he read the message, Gary could feel that his body was slightly different. He checked his stats and saw that each of his three base stats now displayed (+1) next to it. This was similar to when he used Charging Heart, which told him that it was a temporary boost.

Wow, I feel so alive right now. Will this seriously continue to happen as we get closer and closer to the full moon?

However, his happiness went away as the next set of messages appeared.

Your bloodlust grows
10 days until the next full moon

CHAPTER 39

BREAKING NEWS

After receiving that message in the middle of the night, Gary didn't get much sleep. Every time he closed his eyes, his brain would play out images of himself turning into a werewolf who would start clawing up his sister, since she was in the bed right next to his.

It wasn't that his body felt like doing it; in fact, although the system claimed that his bloodlust had increased, Gary didn't feel any difference, least of all a sudden desire to harm anyone. He still felt like his usual self, apart from all the super strength and speed he felt from the powerful moon, but that was becoming more ordinary by the second.

You are exhausted from a lack of sleep
Until you get some proper rest, your Energy has been decreased to 75%

Well, whose fault is it that I couldn't sleep, you stupid system? Gary thought irritatedly as he made his way to school. Still, even with 82.5 Energy points he could still use Charging Heart and do plenty of other things. It was also a pleasant surprise that aside from Energy, none of his other stats were negatively affected.

As Gary entered his classroom, he and Xin briefly locked eyes with each other. She had actually been ready to approach Gary, as she had developed a slight interest in him. Alas, unlike yesterday, he didn't pay her any special attention, completely ignoring her greeting and leaving her to just give an awkward wave.

Gary headed straight to his desk, set his bag down next to him, and then immediately put his head down. Now that he was in school, a wave of drowsiness had come over him, so he planned to use the time before the teacher arrived to get a quick nap in.

Did something happen to him yesterday? Could he not sleep because he lost that fight to me? Xin wondered. Having failed to make up with one person who was supposed to like her, Xin was now very worried about how her conversation would go with the girl who was holding a grudge against her . . .

By the time Tom finally arrived, he found his deskmate lightly snoring. Since this wasn't Gary's usual behavior, he decided against waking him up. Be it sheer dumb luck or his teachers not caring or perhaps having some sympathy for Gary, none of them found fault with him sleeping through their class. Eventually, it was break time, giving Tom a chance to talk to his friend.

"Good morning, sleepyhead. Well, technically, it's noon now, so how're you feeling? Was your impromptu nap some sort of statement about how useless all this stuff is we're forced to learn, or was it because it's getting closer to a . . ." Tom looked left and right to see if anyone else was listening. "Full moon."

Hearing those words just reminded Gary of what the system had told him.

"I just couldn't get any sleep yesterday. It's nothing to do with that crap," Gary replied groggily. "Come on, why don't we just talk about something else?"

"Sure, but it's kinda important, seeing as we only have ten more days," Tom said. "We have to figure this stuff out, check if there are any changes . . . Say, are you going to quit the rugby club? If you don't, someone could seriously get—"

"Enough!" Gary was so annoyed that he almost shouted. "You're nagging me worse than my mom. Look, I know you mean well, and I swear I was thinking about that stuff and also worrying about it.

However, I can solve things my own way, and it's hard to explain this stuff, what's happening to me."

It was hard on Tom as well. Honestly, he couldn't remember the last time he and Gary had had an argument, but lately, it seemed like he was stepping on his nerves a little too much. Then again, Tom had to admit he probably was being a little bit too overbearing. Gary was right; he couldn't imagine what it was like to be in his shoes right now.

"Right now, rugby is actually the only thing going well for me, so I don't want to give up on something that can keep my mind off everything else that's happening," Gary said.

When classes had come to an end, instead of heading to the next fighting club like Tom thought Gary would do, they found themselves on the rugby field once again. With the match coming up next week, the team had asked the nonregulars to stay on the bench and observe; this included Tom.

The regulars were split into two groups to have a practice match against one another. Blake and Gary were on one team; on the opposing team were Gil and Barry, who didn't exactly have good feelings toward the newest member of their club.

This is a good chance for me to test a few things out, Gary thought as he looked at his stats.

Strength 5 (+1)
Dexterity 3 (+1)
Endurance 9 (+1)

The boost from the moon was still present, but what Gary wanted to test was how much these small increments of numbers affected him. As soon as the whistle blew, he activated Charging Heart.

His base stats did not change, but he could see that he was also still receiving the one extra point of boost from the power of the moon. The ball was in an opposing player's hands, but Gary ran past the others on the line, seeming to come out of nowhere as he tackled the player with the ball, going straight for his legs.

The large player went down almost instantly but recovered straightaway, yet Gary was able to pick up the loose ball. Two others tried to stop him, but he was able to dodge them with his increased reflexes and their predictable tackle patterns, until he was eventually hit from the side and the rest of the team piled on.

Has he gotten faster? Heck, even his tackling has gotten better, Blake thought.

"What are you doing, broccoli head?" Mr. Root shouted. "I got you so you could mainly play defense. Did you think your slow self could go for a point all on your own? If you manage to get possession of the ball, I want you to lure them and then pass it!"

Gary admitted that he got a bit carried away, but his body felt great. He felt so light when using Charging Heart; it was almost addictive. It was a strange feeling, suddenly becoming twice the person you once were.

As the game went on, Gary showed off his skills, and the other players noticed. Gary was becoming a prime tackler and a reliable player. He had also tackled Barry thinking that he might be able to get rid of the marking with a touch, but it wasn't that easy.

"This is a bunch of crap!" Gil said. "Look how much they're praising that guy just because he's having a good day today! If this keeps happening, Harvey will never be allowed back on the team. We have to do something."

Barry looked at Gary, but for some reason, ever since Gary had stood up to him, a chill ran down his spine whenever he saw him. Either he wanted to avoid him completely, or his instincts were telling him that he needed to do whatever he could to get rid of him before he disappeared.

"Yeah, but there's nothing we can do! Blake made it abundantly clear that we're not to touch Gary. If we do something stupid, we might be the ones who get kicked off the team," Barry replied.

As Gil looked over at the benches, his eyes set on someone else.

"Fine, we might be unable to touch Gary, but there is someone else we can go for instead."

With rugby not really being interesting to Tom, especially knowing that given his physique he would never amount to anything in that sport, he had decided to play on his phone. That was when he received a notification from the local news channel.

Breaking news: Murderer on the loose!

In the small town of Slough in the Montay area, a husband and wife were found dead in their apartment this morning. Police have yet to reveal any information on what exactly occurred, but at the moment they are looking for any tips on the couple's missing son, Billy Bruntin.

Whoa, I know the police haven't said it outright, but if they are looking for the son and he's missing, doesn't that just make him the prime suspect? What would make someone go so bad that he would kill his parents, though? Tom wondered.

Not long after that, Gary received a disturbing message from his system, one that he didn't quite understand.

CHAPTER 40

OMEGA WOLF

After club activities had ended, the members of the rugby team were praising Gary for his skills on the field. Most of them had been worried about Mr. Root choosing him. After all, Gary had been a member of the club since last year, but he had never shown any real talent.

A player getting better overnight might be possible in mangas or novels or on TV, but in reality, it would take a lot of effort . . . and yet somehow Gary seemed to have gone through some sort of growth spurt since the start of the week. He hadn't grown in height, yet he had still vastly improved in terms of speed and strength.

Receiving so much praise was a new experience for Gary. He hadn't really been unpopular in class. In fact, nobody in his class really hated him. If one were to ask his classmates to describe him, most would have probably said "class clown" or "a bit of a weirdo" ever since he came back with his new hair color. However, his relationship with anyone but Tom had never really progressed past the level of an acquaintance.

This feels amazing, Gary thought, with a slightly smug smile. Before the system, he had never been particularly good at anything except perhaps for Altered trivia, so he quite enjoyed getting some recognition from his fellow students.

Walking away from his teammates who had patted him on the back, some playfully, others more seriously, Gary checked over his stats, hoping that one of them might have improved. As expected, he had no such luck. The only change was his Energy, which was now at 58 points, since he had used Charging Heart a couple of times during practice. Fortunately, his earlier sleep session had provided enough rest for the system to revert his Energy back to 100 percent

Huh, what's this? Gary had a new notification that hadn't popped up on its own. *When did I get it? Was it last night when I finally fell asleep, or during my nap?*

The message had appeared at four a.m., which was around the time his desire for sleep had overwhelmed him. Unfortunately, even after opening and reading the message, Gary didn't understand exactly what it was trying to tell him.

An omega has been created

"What the hell is an omega?" Gary mumbled, hoping that the system would shed some light on the topic. Alas, it wasn't that type of system. So far, it had only provided him with insight whenever it chose to. Realizing that he had slept through something important, he quickly checked the Quests tab, and indeed a red dot showed that something had been added to it.

Optional Quest received
Start your own family
You were young and stupid and didn't use protection, so now you gotta deal with the aftermath!
Accept the omega into your pack and turn it into a beta!
Quest reward: Unlocking of the Pack tab

I'm only sixteen! What kind of pervert designed this system to ask someone to start a family at my age? I'm not even able to support my own family, so how could I even afford to start another? No wonder this quest is optional! Gary felt a strong urge to punch the creator.

Nevertheless, since those strange messages had appeared through the Werewolf System, he was sure that they were important. Gary was sincerely hoping that his best friend might be more familiar with those terms and would be able to make some more sense out of them.

"I believe I did stumble upon those terms when looking into your . . . special condition," Tom said as he checked their surroundings, making sure nobody was paying close attention to them. However, that wasn't too much of a problem. The players who had actually been practicing were now in the showers, while those like Tom who had done nothing but warm the bench had quickly changed into their normal clothes and left.

"However, I don't know if they really apply to you. Like I said, there is a bunch of different lore for everything, and who knows what's true. In case you've forgotten, the silver pendant that most sources agree should be toxic to you did nothing at all, whereas chocolate nearly killed you.

"Look, get some good rest today; you still look dead tired. To-morrow's Saturday, so if you want, we can both head to the library and do some research to figure out what these things mean. Well, knowing you, I'll probably end up doing it all, most likely. Say, where did you even hear those terms, anyway?"

Gary was trying to figure out how to answer Tom. After all, he hadn't informed him about the system's part in his transformation into a werewolf.

"Well, given my 'special condition,' I looked some things up by myself. It's a bit of the reason why I'm so tired, actually," Gary answered, touching the back of his head. "But like you said, everything is so confusing, so I didn't really get most of it."

Tom looked at his friend for a few seconds; he still remembered how Gary had told him off just this morning for talking about were-wolves too much, and now he was asking him for help. Were it not for his earlier outburst, he might have yanked his best friend's chain by playfully demanding a date with Amy in return, but in the end, Tom just nodded.

"All right, then, it's a deal. We'll meet at the public library at noon. While we're at it, we could also look up other things about . . . the moon and stars and such." Although Tom didn't say it, he was thinking of ways of learning what exactly happened on a full moon.

Instead of instigating another fight, Gary stopped by the supermarket before heading to the gym. Following the instructions the system provided, he worked out until the system rewarded him with 5 Exp. It was a welcome surprise since he had been half expecting the reward to be cut down to 1 Exp or less, seeing that it had been cut in half once he had hit Level 2.

Still, he was a bit down that he had not experienced any other physical improvements. He understood that it would take him far less time than normal people, but he still couldn't help but be a bit impatient, not knowing when he might need to be more powerful.

For once, Gary was able to head home like a normal high schooler. The phone Kai had given him was still dead silent, so he decided to spend his evening with his family, something he didn't get to do often. As it turned out, just because he had time didn't mean the rest of the world would accede to his desires.

Shortly after he got home, his mother rushed out because her employer had called, asking her to fill in for one of her co-workers, leaving him and his sister on their own. In turn, Amy seemed more interested in spending time with her cell phone than spending precious time with her brother.

If only we had more money, Mom wouldn't have to work so hard, Gary thought.

While enjoying his dinner, Gary watched the news on TV. He was very interested in the local news, since it allowed him to keep up to date with what was going on in Slough.

Especially interesting were updates to the gang situation, and Gary was even more interested in any new discoveries in the case of the recent killings that Gary himself might have been involved in.

Today the station was reporting on a different story, though. The breaking news that had been playing all day was about a couple who had been killed in their own home. Gary had been in the middle of cutting up a piece of steak and eating it like a normal human would when he saw the image of the deceased couple's missing son appear on the screen.

"What the hell? That's Billy Buster!" Gary blurted out.

"Huh, how do you know that guy? According to the news, he doesn't go to your school," Amy said. Although she had been looking at her phone, she had actually also been paying attention to the news, but Gary ignored her.

I knew he was a scumbag for using those brass knuckles on me, but I never figured him for a murderer. What's more, to kill his parents . . . Gary thought, the steak in front of him losing some of its taste.

With Gary having his own plans for the evening, he and Tom had parted ways. Unbeknownst to the both of them, this turned out to be a mistake. Tom had been lost in his own thoughts, walking pretty much on autopilot, when he hit a meaty wall. Looking up, he saw a familiar face, and when he took a few steps back, he bumped into someone else.

"Gil . . . Barry . . . err, how nice to see you. If you don't mind, I kinda need to get home," Tom said nervously, already aware that that wasn't happening. Neither one of them lived in this direction, and judging by the sneaky way that they had appeared, they weren't just there to have a friendly chat with him.

CHAPTER 41

OMEGA, BETA, ALPHA

Perhaps it was because Gary had been so tired on Friday, or it might have had something to do with him having gone to sleep before midnight when he would get a new notification, but on Saturday morning he woke up well-rested.

The absence of the annoying alarm that usually woke him up long before his sister certainly also had a part to play in that. Stretching, Gary checked his status, already expecting to see some changes. Unsurprisingly, his Daily Quests had once again refreshed, but there was also a new notification waiting for him.

Your bloodlust grows
9 days until the next full moon

Unlike yesterday, there were no mentions of any additional stats due to it being closer to the full moon, though. After looking at his phone, he realized that it was already eleven a.m., meaning that he only had one hour before meeting up with Tom.

Holy crap, I slept in too late! Gary cursed internally, getting dressed as quickly as possible before leaving the apartment. Thirty seconds later, he returned, making sure to bring along Kai's phone as well this time.

Gary decided to run to the town center where the library was located. It didn't cost any money, and it would be a good way to check whether he could increase his Energy this way.

Energy and Health were both stats under the Werewolf System, so if he could naturally improve Strength and Endurance, why not those two? It was at least worth a shot . . . although it was mostly about saving money.

The library was a three-story building that had been built on the main shopping street, at the end of all the shops. It was primarily used by college students who had a hopeful future ahead of them. It was one of the few safe areas of town where the police regularly patrolled, which was why gangs left it untouched.

Gary's powerful eyesight allowed him to see Tom already waiting for him, but he could also see that something was wrong with his friend. As he slowed down his stride, his happy face quickly turned sour.

"What happened to you?" Gary asked.

Tom put on a smile and touched his swollen and cut eye.

"This . . . ah, man. I was watching one of Kirk's Altered fights, and then as I went out of my room, I wanted to try out his tornado kick. Stupid me, I fell down the stairs and banged up my eye on the banister pretty badly."

Although a fall down the stairs might explain some of it, Tom also had other markings on his body. Ignoring Tom's dislike for most physical activities, "falling down the stairs" was pretty much the textbook answer someone gave when trying to hide something.

Could it be trouble at home? No, his parents aren't like that. They treasure their golden boy too much to hurt him, Gary thought. He knew that something was up, but Tom's behavior made it clear that he didn't want to talk about it. Given how many secrets of his own Gary was keeping from his best friend, he didn't feel it was right to push him on the matter.

"So what move was it again?" Gary asked, pretending to accept Tom's explanation as they entered the library.

Like any library, it was very quiet, so they kept their mouths shut until they reached the third floor, where they could access the public computers. Tom searched up all the relevant books in the library that they might need. Whenever he found a book he thought could be of use, he asked Gary to go get it, then read through them all and wrote down notes that Gary didn't quite understand, so for now he was just the delivery boy.

Finally, snapping his fingers and rubbing his good eye, Tom was satisfied with the research he had done. "All right, I believe I have learned everything there is to know about alpha, beta, and omega wolves," he said, folding his arms proudly. "Let's start with what applies to actual wolves. According to the lore I found, it should more or less coincide. Still, take all of this information with a pinch of salt." Tom flipped his notepad to a blank page, then wrote the word *Alpha*. As he explained, he wrote out the points and explained everything to Gary.

"Wolves often hunt in packs, so every pack has a leader. These are the so-called alphas. A wolf pack usually has an alpha male and his alpha partner. These two can be seen as the family leaders.

"Beta wolves are pretty much wolves that are under the alpha. They could be their siblings, their children, or even outsiders. However, they all belong to a pack, following the alpha. Do you understand so far?" Tom asked, and Gary nodded.

"Okay, I get those two, but if an alpha is like the leader of a gang, and the betas are like his henchmen and subordinates, then what exactly is an omega?" Gary asked.

His Optional Quest was to turn an omega wolf into a beta, but this was where his confusion was setting in. Assuming he himself was the alpha wolf, was it referring to a sibling, like Amy, or maybe was his mother the alpha wolf and he and his sister were considered betas?

"This is where things get a little interesting," Tom answered, flipping his notebook to a blank page once again. "An omega wolf is usually an outsider to a family or one that has no family. Either way, they're usually at the bottom of the hierarchy. Essentially, after everyone else has gotten their food, the omega has to eat whatever is left."

So far, if Gary was being classified as a werewolf in these terms, he wasn't sure what he was.

"I know you were talking about wolves, but werewolves are part human, right? So how does this work?"

"There are quite a few rules here, and it gets a bit complicated, but essentially a werewolf can turn another with a bite. Alpha wolves bite and turn those they wish to work under them, thereby creating beta wolves. Once turned, the beta wolves can also turn others, making them into other beta wolves that will have to listen to the alpha . . . to an extent, I should add, but let's keep it simple for now."

Hearing this, Gary came to a shaking realization.

A bite can turn someone . . . no . . . no, when the system message came up saying I made an omega wolf . . .

Images flashed in Gary's head to the time he had lost it slightly. At one point during his fight against Billy Buster, his sanity had left him, and he had only wanted to win by all means. As he recalled, he had ended up biting the guy.

Yesterday, the news reported that Billy was on the run and his parents were dead . . . Don't tell me . . . was I responsible for this by fighting him? Is he . . . really a werewolf now?

"Wait, you said that if an alpha bites someone, they would turn them into a beta who would have to follow them, so what about an omega?" Gary asked, realizing that there was something strange about the wording of the quest.

"In most cases, omegas seem to be wolves who have been kicked out of a pack. However, that doesn't always have to be the case. For instance, they could also be the only surviving wolf of a group. In a way, you could say that alpha and beta wolves are just omega wolves who belong to a pack and have a hierarchy among themselves.

"If we take you, for example, right now, you would technically be a lone wolf at the moment, which would make you an omega wolf. I assume if you were to bite someone, it would make another omega wolf. If there are multiple omega wolves, I suppose that they would eventually try to form a pack. However, most likely they would battle it out to decide who among them would be the alpha, forcing the others to submit."

Gary was sure that Tom's guess was spot on because, judging by the quest, he was right. The system clearly stated that there was an omega wolf out there, and to start his family, he would have to make it accept being the beta wolf to his alpha.

Until then, this also meant that at the moment, there was another werewolf in town, and in nine days' time, there was practically guaranteed to be a bloodbath.

CHAPTER 42

AN UNUSUAL GIFT

After Tom was done with his explanation about alpha, beta, and omega wolves, he went into detail about some other possibilities for what these words could mean. Unfortunately, Gary didn't really register anything past that point. After he'd learned what his future could possibly entail, things were going in one ear and out the other as he was too busy to think about what he should do about it.

I was just starting to appreciate this system for letting me shine during rugby practice and allowing me to make money with Kai, but now it seems that this really is more of a curse rather than a blessing.

Suddenly the nine days until the next full moon seemed to be a lot shorter than it had appeared this morning. In the first place, Gary wasn't really sure what would happen; maybe he would just get the biggest stat boost of his life on that day, but that was un-likely.

He had already entertained the thought of either getting Tom to tie him up on that day so he couldn't harm anyone or perhaps hiding someplace where there wouldn't be any other people. However, knowing that there was another werewolf out there, he had to do something about it, especially since he was the one at fault.

So assuming that Billy really is an omega wolf, that should mean that just like me, he hasn't turned yet, right? Gary thought. *But then why did he end up killing his parents? I haven't hurt anyone . . . at*

least, I don't think I did . . . apart from those three guys, perhaps . . .
Shit, do all werewolves have to hurt people?

If Billy really was an omega wolf, Gary had a different problem altogether. Billy was on the run, the prime suspect for killing his own parents. If the police had no clue where he was, how was a six-teen-year-old supposed to find him?

He looked through the system, hoping there might be some way to track the guy down, but so far, other than the red mist he could use to follow Barry because of their Forced Bond, if there actually was a way, the system had yet to grant it to him.

At that moment, Tom had finished explaining everything he needed to, unaware that his friend hadn't been listening, just nod-ding along. He stood up, intending to put some of the books away, when he felt a sharp pain in his side, causing him to almost drop the books.

"The stairs?" Gary asked, taking the books from him as he went to put them back.

"Yeah . . . sorry, I'm not in the best shape," Tom said.

Gary was so concerned about his own problem that he had al-most forgotten that Tom was in some kind of tricky situation of his own. Since Tom had come to help him, despite his own problem, Gary wanted to return the favor. Unfortunately, this was harder than it sounded since Tom refused to tell him exactly what his prob-lem was.

Well, those bruises definitely aren't self-inflicted. Did he run into another gang, only this time there was no mysterious stranger to help him? Gary thought, putting the books back and returning to his friend.

"Tom, I'll be honest, I'm getting worried about this werewolf stuff. I have no idea what will happen to me when the full moon comes up, but I'm going to need someone to help me, and you're the only person who is really helping me. So I want you to promise me that the two of us will be friends no matter what happens. I also promise you that I won't eat you," Gary said, not realizing how hard it actually was to say those words out loud since the possibility actually existed.

He held out his hand, ready for a handshake, and although his words were quite cheesy for someone who was in high school, there was a reason for them.

"Gary, are you on drugs or something?" Tom asked, nevertheless shaking his hand. "We'll always be friends. Besides, I don't think we have to worry about it. Even if you do turn, my scrawny ass won't even be enough for an appetizer."

A spoken deal has been made; would you like to mark Tom Green?

Once they shook hands, the system gave Gary exactly the notification he had been hoping for. His Bond Mark skill was triggered when he made a sincere promise to another party. It would allow him to track Tom at any point in time, which might tell him more about what exactly had happened to his friend.

However, his skill had a very bad side effect. If Tom ended up breaking that promise, he would be assigned a Broken Mark, which would automatically turn him into a hunting target, so Gary had to make sure that the promise was something that neither one of them would ever break. He was also secretly hoping that it might have the additional effect of making Tom immune from becoming a hunting target for as long as he kept his promise.

Yes.

2/5 Marks have been assigned

After mentally agreeing to activate the skill, Gary saw a mark that looked similar to an *M* appear over Tom's head. His friend started giving off a new type of scent, which was similar to yet at the same time different from the one Barry had.

Another thing that was different was the color of the mist that followed with the scent. Rather than red, this one was green, so unless one of the side effects of becoming a werewolf included belated red-green colorblindness, it should be impossible for Gary to get the two of them mixed up.

After leaving the library, they parted ways once again. Tom asked if he wanted to meet up tomorrow to do anything, but Gary claimed that he already had other plans. The truth was, he didn't really want to leave the house more than necessary, in case any members of the Underdogs or people who worked for them were looking for him.

Were it not mandatory, he might have even ditched school altogether until he figured out how to deal with Damion and his thugs. Still, Gary did go to the gym and the convenience store on his way home to continue doing his Daily Quests, as these were vital to improving his body and his strength.

Name: Gary Dem
Level 4
Exp 225/460
Health: 100/100
Energy: 110/110
Heart rate: 62 BPM
State: Normal

Without underground fights, challenging school clubs, or color gangs hunting him, his leveling up had naturally stagnated. School was closed today, and going after the gangs again would be suicidal until they became less wary, meaning he would just have to wait until Kai called him for his next fight.

The rest of his Saturday proceeded as normal, to the point that Gary even went to bed at a reasonable time, simply because there was nothing else to do. Nevertheless, it took him a couple of hours to fall asleep, because of everything on his mind and the decreasing number of days that were left.

In the middle of the night, Gary woke up covered in sweat once again, pulling his bedsheets off. He immediately looked to see if his sister was okay. Apparently, her sleep was so deep that she hadn't even noticed her older brother screaming right next to her . . .

Your bloodlust grows
8 days until the next full moon

Because of the messages, he knew it was past midnight at least.

Damn, I can't keep having these dreams. All this werewolf stuff is causing me to have the strangest nightmares, Gary thought as he went to answer the call of nature. Before he made it to the toilet, however, he was distracted by a scent in the air.

It was something he had never smelled before, and naturally, he followed where his nose led him.

Who could be cooking this late at night? he wondered.

Strangely, the scent was close by, yet it wasn't coming from inside their apartment but from the front door. Gary opened it and right there, on the Dems' doorstep, was what looked like a fresh piece of meat.

The only thing was it still had blood around it, and it was lying there on the floor. Gary had seen quite a lot of raw meat recently, but never had he seen something like this before. His natural human brain was making him feel a little sick, but for some reason, the smell it gave off made him hungry.

The question was, why?

Soon the system had answered that question for him.

Human flesh discovered
For a growing young werewolf such as you, consuming human flesh is the best way to recover your Energy, and who knows, it could make you stronger!

CHAPTER 43

CROSSED THE LINE!

If Gary hadn't felt sick before, he certainly did now, having gotten confirmation of what exactly that was in front of his door. He quickly turned away, fighting off his body's reaction to throw up, but he soon realized that it wasn't exactly going to get rid of the problem.

It was getting hard to think, as the smell was so tantalizing he could feel the saliva dripping down his chin. He pinched his nose, which actually helped him more than he had anticipated.

Why the hell is there human flesh in front of my home? I can't even tell what part of the body that is, Gary thought. *No, it might be for the best if I don't know.*

Gary had developed a knack for keeping secrets from his family, so he quickly closed the door, which further helped him regain his sanity. Although it was not confirmed, all signs suggested that the piece of flesh had something to do with him.

The good news was it was pitch black outside, and after midnight, so it was unlikely that anyone would suddenly come out of their apartment door and see the piece of human flesh on his doorstep, which meant Gary had a little time to think about what to do with it.

He was wondering just who could have done such a thing, and after racking his brain, he came up with three theories.

There's a chance that it might have been me . . . maybe all those nightmares have made me go crazy, and just like Billy, I ended up killing someone? It would certainly explain those weird dreams . . .

Thinking about it more thoroughly, he concluded that it didn't make sense. For one, his clothes had no blood on them, and if he was turning into a werewolf or doing this subconsciously, he would have eaten the flesh by now, not left it outside the door as if to remind himself.

The next suspect was the Underdogs gang. Perhaps they had found his address, and this was their warning that if he didn't return the item, they would do this to him.

He had seen the Underdogs treat humans like dirt before, so he wouldn't put it past them, but that didn't really make sense either. If they had already found out where he lived, why not just abduct and interrogate him? If not him, at least his mother or sister? No, that seemed to be too roundabout for them.

That only leaves Billy . . . but why would he leave this here? I thought he was supposed to become a werewolf, not a housecat. Besides, if we're both omega wolves, why would he leave me a present? Then . . . could this be some sort of declaration of war? Oh shit, what if this is from one of his parents?

Now that he had a prime suspect, Gary still had to decide what to do with the flesh.

Of course, there was the method his system had indirectly suggested, but knowing that it was human flesh, he just couldn't bring himself to do it. Even if the system did say there was a chance it would make him stronger, this was just inhumane. There were always other ways of improving his strength. On top of that, he was also afraid that it would leave behind blood as evidence. If this really was a piece of one of Billy's parents and the police came over . . . Gary didn't want to continue that thought.

He couldn't just throw it into the garbage, either. If one of the neighbors found it, they might call the police. The last thing he wanted was to bring attention to himself. Not only because the evidence was all over their doorstep, but also because it might tip off the Underdogs.

In the end, only one person came to mind who might know how to handle such a delicate situation. Although he still didn't completely trust him, for some reason, Gary had a feeling that he wouldn't disappoint.

Heading back inside quickly, Gary grabbed what he needed and then went outside once again. He had already written a message and hit send on the small phone.

Ding!

Does that guy never sleep? No, I should thank God or whoever is responsible that he's still up.

Jesus, what type of mess have you gotten yourself into? I leave you on your own for a couple of days, and you come back with this? All right, we'll talk more about this on Monday, so here's what you do. First off, with the Underdogs chasing you, reporting it to the police or trying to get rid of the evidence yourself will only make it worse, so DON'T EVEN THINK ABOUT IT!

For the time being, you might want to cover it up with something. I will make some calls, and in about fifteen minutes, some people should come over and make sure that this thing disappears. They're professionals, so let them do what they need to do. Also, consider this a warning: FOR YOUR OWN SAKE, DON'T LET THEM SEE WHO YOU ARE! STAY INSIDE AND IGNORE THEM!

Can't wait to hear your explanation for this one.

As Gary held the phone and read the messages, a wave of emotions overcame him. He couldn't believe that his problem would actually be solved with one simple text.

It can't be that easy, can it? He pinched himself to make sure he wasn't still sleeping.

Although he had been instructed to stay inside, Gary couldn't help but be curious as to how this problem would be solved and just what the big deal was. Eventually, though, about ten minutes later, Gary heard a car pull up outside, and the doors slammed shut.

As soon as they started running up the stairs, he lost his nerve and shut the door, waiting behind it and listening to see if he could hear anything.

Man, what I wouldn't give if we had a peephole right now. From the sound of their footsteps, there should be three of them.

"All right, let's get this cleaned up as soon as possible," one of the men whispered in a deep voice that sounded like it belonged to an adult. Gary heard the men putting on scrubs, and then he noticed the scent of chemicals.

He breathed as quietly as possible while the men worked. It didn't take them long to finish, and Gary heard them starting to head down again.

I might be able to see what they look like from my window. If I climb to the roof, I should be able to still spot them. He ran to his room, but his plans were foiled.

"Gary, what the hell are you doing at this hour? Get back to bed, you idiot!" his sister angrily snarled at him, as his running had actually managed to wake her.

"Sorry, Amy." He couldn't climb out the window now, and by the time his sister fell asleep, the men would be long gone. Still, it made him wonder . . . just who the hell was Kai?

How was a kid his age able to solve a problem this easily? Gary knew that Kai knew people in the Underdogs, and that he was probably still a member of the Underdogs, but what position did he have that he could call on such professionals in the middle of the night?

Perhaps more importantly, how could he not have panicked when Gary admitted that there was what he assumed to be a piece of human flesh in front of his doorstep?

Well, I doubt he'll tell me anything, even if I do ask him. If only he could solve my werewolf problems just as easily. Gary sighed, tensing his fist as he looked over to his little sister, who had started to doze off.

You damn omega wolf, you came right to my family's doorstep! I don't know how you did it, but that crosses the line! It looks like I'm going to have to deal with you before the full moon!

CHAPTER 44

A.I.F.

After the kinds of days Gary was having, one would think that he would be having trouble sleeping, yet for some reason, the closer it got to the full moon, the more his body craved sleep. No matter how much he worried, at some point, he would basically just pass out.

Still, when he woke up Sunday at noon, he hadn't forgotten about what had occurred in the middle of the night. Although Gary didn't exactly know what that piece of flesh in front of his door was supposed to mean to him, it was tantamount to a war declaration.

The omega wolf knew where he and his family lived. This time he might have brought him a "present," but who was to say that next time he wouldn't turn Gary's family members into pieces of meat. He had to find Billy and deal with him.

Luckily it was Sunday, giving Gary the whole day to at least find some clues to Billy's whereabouts. During the week, it would be far more difficult.

First things first. Gary checked every tab in the Werewolf System in case he might have missed anything.

I can't find anything in this system that would help me. Maybe he unlocked another skill, or he managed to track my scent somehow? Gary thought in frustration after going through everything twice. However, the omega wolf had somehow been able to track where he was, so in theory, Gary should be able to do the same.

"I'm going over to meet Stacy; I'll be back by dinner!" Amy shouted, and the door quickly closed behind her.

When Gary heard this, his heart started to beat faster.

Shit, Billy was here at night, so could he have picked up Amy's scent? What if the human flesh was his message that he intended to go after my family? She said she would be back by dinner, and it's not too far to Stacy's; she's also traveling during the day. Billy hasn't been caught yet, according to the news, so she should be okay. Should I just put a Bond Mark on her like I did Tom? But what the hell do I get her to promise me?

With the system not helping him, Gary decided to text Kai, hoping that he might have some useful information.

STOP LOOKING FOR TROUBLE!

Kai replied almost immediately.

You might feel responsible for him since he was Green Fang's debut opponent, but to Billy Buster, it was just another day. Heck, he lost against three other schnooks before you; one of them even beat him three times.

If you go searching after the same guy the police are after, there's a good chance the Underdogs will find you. Remember, they have eyes everywhere, and that includes in the police force as well!

Alas, Kai proved to be far less helpful than he had been before.

Now that Gary took a moment to think about it, he realized that if Kai, or the Underdogs for that matter, knew where he was, Billy would have most likely already been apprehended. For the moment, he was the only one who actually knew that Billy was an omega wolf.

With no better solution, Gary decided to turn on the TV in hopes there might be an update on the situation. It didn't take long for his wish to be granted.

"This just in, this morning yet another murder victim, this time a high school student, has been found in an apartment in the area of Montay. Chief of Police Anton Millstun confirmed that the modus operandi coincides with the murder of the Bruntins. Following the wishes of the victim's family, his name will not be shared.

"So far, police have found no connection between the Bruntins and the latest victim. There has also been no news in regards to Billy Bruntin's whereabouts, and according to Chief Millstun they have to determine whether Billy is the prime suspect or just another victim."

The news didn't look hopeful, and worst of all Gary was wondering if Billy had killed again.

The flesh from yesterday, was that . . . this new person? That would explain why it looked so . . . fresh. Why would he even kill a high schooler? Were they just an easy target . . . or was there more to it?

Thinking about the flesh, Gary remembered the system message that had appeared when he found it. It had told him that there was the possibility he might grow stronger through consuming human flesh.

Since Billy was the first person he had turned, Gary had no idea what the rules were. Was he the only one who could grow stronger by eating others, or was that something shared by all werewolves that he created? Another reasonable question was whether it was a onetime thing or if one grew stronger the more one ate human flesh.

The latter possibility was far scarier. For all he knew, Billy might have eaten nearly three entire human bodies. Billy was already unnaturally strong for his age. The only reason Gary had been able to match up to him was the Werewolf System.

Even if he hadn't gained a system of his own, it was at least safe to assume that he could transform. With that ability, as well as additional stats, would it even be possible for Gary to beat a supernatural omega wolf?

It's my fault that Billy keeps killing people. What's worse, he might just get stronger as the days go by. My best chance of stopping him is stopping him now!

Wearing his usual hoodie to cover himself, he headed out to find Billy's home. It was a little far from Gary's, as it was in a different neighborhood, and it also looked like the next victim was in the same area.

If only I could get into his room and find something that belonged to him. Given my keen nose, maybe I could just find him like a search dog.

Eventually Gary found the apartment building where the Bruntins used to live. The neighborhood was similar to Gary's; the streets were also filled with litter and graffiti. If Gary had to take a guess, Billy must not have exactly lived the best life either. Then again, if he had, he would have had no reason to fight underground.

It was easy enough to spot where Billy lived, even without using his nose, because heaps of reporters were interviewing the people who lived in the building.

From a distance, he peeked around the corner.

Damn, so much for my plan. If I so much as try to go up to the apartment, those reporters will definitely try to question me. I can't afford to show myself on TV! Sniffing the air, Gary tried to pick up any strange scents, but with all the people present, not to mention the sweat and the food that was being sold by some entrepreneurs, it was impossible.

Gary deemed it too risky to go to Billy's apartment, so he would just have to find him another way.

"Hey there, little buddy, where are you in a rush to?" A male voice addressed him from behind.

Gary looked up to see a man and a woman blocking his way. He hadn't noticed them, yet now they stood directly in front of him in their white-and-gold clothing.

"It looks to me like someone doesn't want to be seen. What's that famous saying? 'The criminal always returns to the scene of the crime'?" the woman commented.

"I'm no criminal; I was merely curious," Gary answered in a panic, wondering just who these people were. He was getting ready to use Charging Heart and run away, even if it would make him look more suspicious to these strangers.

"Now, hold on." The woman grabbed Gary as if she had anticipated his next move. "If you've got nothing to hide, then you should have no problem having a little chat with us. You might not be the murderer, but it looks like you might know a few things."

Both of them pulled out their wallets at the same time, displaying a golden badge with the symbol of a white rose with the acronym *A.I.F.* on the top.

Gary gulped. *Oh brother, these guys are even worse than the police. Why didn't I listen to Kai's advice? How the hell did I manage to stumble into the Altered Investigation Force?*

CHAPTER 45

BOILING POINT

The Altered Investigation Force, more commonly referred to as White Rose, was one of the most well-known police forces. Gary had seen them mentioned multiple times on the news for more reasons than one, but mainly they stood out because the force was made up entirely of Altereds.

I might outrun a normal human, but I doubt it will work on an Altered. If I try anything that might seem beyond what a human could do, they'll think I'm an Altered and will investigate how I became one.

Sadie Nimper and Frank Hue had been watching the apartment building for a while. They were supposed to be working on a different case. Earlier that week, in what they assumed to be a gang trade gone wrong, three bodies had been uncovered that appeared to have been killed by an Altered.

The reason they were staking out Billy's apartment was the condition of the corpses. They seemed to have been killed in a similar way, making Sadie and Frank believe that this killer might also be an Altered. They had yet to determine whether it was the same killer or another unreported Altered who had gone rogue.

"I'm just curious. It's not every day that Slough is on the news. I sorta came here to see what all the fuss was about. It just seemed like a cool idea to be where all the action was. Now that I say it out loud, I don't actually know what I was expecting." Gary tried to explain, praying that they would take him for just a dumb teenager.

"So what? You're a teenager, so the suspect isn't much older than you. Come on, now that you know who we are, just spill the beans and tell us what you know!" Sandie demanded.

"Hey, hey, you're strongly implying something there. Just because both of them are teenagers doesn't mean they know each other, right?" Frank tried to calm his partner down. It was obvious to Gary that the two of them were playing a little game of good cop/ bad cop, not that he would dare to call them out on it.

"However, if you don't mind us asking, what's with the hood? If you really wanted to check things out, why would you try to sneak away after seeing the reporters?" Frank asked with a friendly smile, as if to hide the fact that he was calling Gary out on his contradiction.

Since Frank was the good cop, Gary quickly grasped that he would be the way out of his mess. His "just a dumb teenager" act seemed to have failed, but he was sure there was one way to convince them. He looked around left and right, then slowly pulled down his hood, revealing his bright green hair.

"I . . . I had my hair done recently, but it turned out far brighter than I wanted. Once I saw the reporters, I got scared that I might get interviewed. It's already bad enough that my friends are teasing me in school about it, but if my current appearance gets shown on TV . . . yeah, I would never live it down.

"I swear, I was only here because I was curious. Me and that Billy guy, we don't even go to the same school. First time I ever heard about him was on TV," Gary insisted, making a "scout's honor" sign, even though he had never been a scout.

Frank was trying to hold in his laughter after seeing Gary's hair; his explanation certainly sounded like a tragic tale.

"Oh, really? What school do you go to and what's your name?" Sadie asked, seemingly not fully convinced yet.

"Westbridge, Gary Dem, ma'am," Gary answered immediately. "You can check at the school."

Sadie gave him an odd stare that just wouldn't go away, and she was still holding on to his hand. A few seconds passed before she finally let go.

"Get out of here! A stupid kid like you shouldn't hang around crime scenes. I swear if we ever catch you near another one again, I'll personally bring you in for questioning!" Sadie threatened, and Gary quickly ran off, thanking his lucky stars that he had just escaped a close call.

"Why did you let him go?" Frank asked.

"Well, you heard him, he and Billy don't go to the same school, but for someone who's not involved in the case, he sure did know enough about it. Do kids really pay attention to what's on the news these days?"

"Perhaps I'm just being too cautious, but it was a death that happened in the neighborhood, so maybe he did know about it, but just in case, take a note of the kid's name and school. If we find something linking Billy to him, we should pay him another visit at some point."

Damn it, what do I do now? That woman made it abundantly clear that if they ever see me anywhere near the spots where Billy might have been, it will just make matters worse.

In the end, since Gary was unable to locate Billy anyway, he decided to head home after doing his regular Daily Quests. Before he knew it, the next day had arrived.

Your bloodlust grows
7 days until the next full moon

For the love of God! You stupid system, don't you have an option to turn this off? I don't need a freaking reminder every day. I do have my own calendar, you know!

With the next full moon approaching, Gary's temper was rising. He understood that getting frustrated at the situation didn't help, but cursing did help him calm down.

The only good news was that at least today there was nothing in front of his door.

As always, the weekend was over far too soon. Tom was looking at himself in the mirror. His eye had healed up, but the bottom of his eyelid was still a little swollen, causing him to squint a little. His parents had been very concerned about his wounds, so he had made up a lie that he had helped Gary, who had been accepted on the rugby team, with some training.

If those two bastards had only listened . . . There was no goddamn need to beat me into submission when I was already doing my best to make Gary quit the rugby team on my own! What should I do? Once they see him play again, will they come after me again? Tom wondered, still feeling the pain from last time. *Maybe I can ask Gary to accompany me home. Or perhaps I could hide at his place for a bit.*

There was a specific reason why Tom hadn't told Gary about the incident. He was worried that his best friend might snap and do something stupid to them if he found out. Now that he knew that Gary was a werewolf who could transform, getting him angry wasn't exactly the best idea, especially so close to the full moon.

After arriving at school, Tom eventually saw Gary in the hallway. Coincidentally, he came at the perfect time to see that someone else had blocked Gary's path. Surprisingly, it was neither Gil nor Barry.

"Hey, Gary, I don't know what was up with you coming to the karate club the other day. That was really not cool what you did back there," Steven said. "You only won because I was off guard! If it had been a real fight, don't think it would go the same way!"

Gary didn't even look at Steven as he was talking down at him. He had too much other stuff to worry about, and his mind was fully occupied with trying to figure out how to get rid of his problems, which already stressed him to the max.

Steven, noticing that Gary was bluntly ignoring him, naturally took this the wrong way.

"Hey, man! Do you really think you're some hot shit? I know you, man, you did all of that to hit on Xin, but if she isn't going out with *me*, then there's no way in hell she'll be going out with *you*!"

"Can you please just let me through?" Gary almost shouted, and barged past him, pushing him off to the side. He was so loud that the other students who were conversing in the halls went silent and turned around to look at the commotion. Hearing what was going on, they started whispering, and Steven heard them.

They're talking about me! They must have heard about how I lost to him in a fight! Now he's even pushing me in the hallway! Believing that the other students were talking about him, Steven felt like he had to set the record straight to prove himself and make up for his loss.

However, as a karateka, he couldn't just start swinging his fists. He needed Gary to start the fight so he could claim it was self-defense, but not even mentioning Xin had annoyed him.

"You have a sister, right?" Steven asked, and at that moment, Gary stopped inches before entering his classroom. It was obvious that this had gotten his attention. "I heard that she is quite the looker. Tell you what, you can have Xin, and in turn, I'll have your sister."

Gary turned around and started to walk up to Steven, stopping just in front of him.

"Hey, Steven."

"Wha—" Before Steven could finish his sentence, Gary grabbed the side of his head, then slammed it with great force into the side of the wall. He let go and Steven's body slid down onto the floor.

"Shut the fuck up," Gary said.

CHAPTER 46

ANGER

The corridor was silent until one of the girls started screaming as Steven lay on the floor unconscious.

"He killed him! Gary just killed somebody!" Tiffany screamed.

Although it was unheard of that a scrawny high schooler would have the strength to kill someone with one hit, Gary was far from being an ordinary high schooler. In his rage, he had struck Steven without holding back. Tom ran past the gathering crowd and checked out the situation.

Gary was still in disbelief about what he had just done. He just stood there, looking from the hand that had slammed Steven into the wall to the body to his feet. Meanwhile, Tom had noticed the specks of red that had started to run down the karateka's head. Examining Steven's carotid artery, he let out a sigh of relief when he felt a pulse.

"Gary, snap out of it! He's okay, but we need to get him to the nurse ASAP! I mean, he's not okay, but at least he's alive; now help me carry him," Tom called out to his friend. Gary quickly went to the other side and lifted him off the ground, and they carried Steven to the nurse's office.

The crowd just watched them with their mouths wide open. None of them knew what they were supposed to do. Should they help? Should they call a teacher? Perhaps an ambulance? In the end, what they chose to do . . . was to spread the news about this event to those who had missed it!

Tom and Gary were lucky that no teacher was in the hallways, but they encountered someone else. Xin had just come from the bathroom and was surprised to see them.

"What happened?" Xin asked.

Gary would have loved to explain himself to her, but he honestly didn't know how. The truth was, he had just bashed in his schoolmate's skull. Sure, Steven had provoked him, but even Gary saw that he had vastly overreacted. So he and Tom just walked past, leaving Xin to listen to the rumors that had already begun to spread.

"He slammed him into the wall with just *one* hand!"

"Caspar told me that Josh even heard the poor guy's skull crack. Steven might never be the same again!"

"Does anyone know what he told broccoli head to piss him off that much?"

"I don't know; I heard the name Xin."

Hearing this, Xin felt a bit guilty. Was she somehow the cause of this mess?

Were those stupid boys seriously fighting over me?

Eventually, Tom and Gary reached the nurse's office. After briefly checking his vitals, the nurse decided that this was above her pay grade, so she called an ambulance. Steven was breathing, and she did what she could to keep him stable, but he wasn't responding, nor did he show any signs of regaining consciousness.

When asked what had happened, Gary mumbled that Steven had been hit in the head but gave no other details. The nurse agreed to let them stay and miss their morning classes, believing that the three of them were friends.

It didn't take too long for the ambulance to arrive at school. After getting a brief account of what had happened, the paramedics took Steven away, leaving Tom and Gary behind. Once her patient was gone, the nurse left to make a report.

"What . . . what happened there, bro?" Tom asked after making sure the nurse wouldn't come back because she forgot something.

"I-I don't know. Suddenly all this anger, this rage just came over me. The moment he mentioned Amy, images of him hurting my family came flooding into my head. All my senses were telling me that I needed to do everything I could to stop him. Before I even realized what I had done, he was on the floor."

Nevertheless, Gary didn't tell Tom everything. If he was honest, he had actually wanted to hurt Steven more. The only reason he had stopped was he had begun to panic at the sight of Steven's motionless body. His rational side returned, stopping him from worsening the situation.

Tom didn't ask him any more questions after that. However, he was very glad that he had decided to keep the truth about what had really happened to him on Friday hidden from his best friend. If Gary could get this crazy at the mere thought of someone hurting those close to him, Tom's attackers would have most likely ended up in a morgue rather than the hospital.

Eventually, the two of them headed to class. All eyes quickly turned to Tom and Gary when they entered the room.

"Gary, you're finally here. There's no need for you to sit down. Principal Young wants to see you in her office. I'm sure you know why," Mrs. Bedford said, after briefly looking at who had disturbed her class.

It didn't go unnoticed, and for some reason, Gary felt pissed off at being ignored like that. Fortunately, his rational side was still in charge, so he just started walking to the principal's office, leaving Tom to sit down in class.

What is wrong with me? How come everything is getting on my nerves today? Are people just assholes today, or am I being super sensitive? Gary was worried that this might be the effect of the blood-lust his system kept mentioning.

Above the double doors, a plaque read *Principal Young*. He knocked at the door, and someone said "Come in" from the other side. This was the first time he had been called here. Cautiously, Gary opened the door and entered the large office, which was big enough to fit a sofa and coffee machine inside.

"I would love to say that it's good to see you, Mr. Dem, but you should already be aware why you're here." Ironically, Mrs. Young's family name didn't match her outer appearance. She was an older woman with mostly gray hair. The light in her eyes showed that she was actually younger than she looked and that the graying of her hair was mostly due to the stress that came with her position.

"We have already gathered the testimony of the students who saw this morning's event unfold, and a few minutes ago, the hospital sent me a report about Mr. Richardson's condition. You might be elated to know that your schoolmate is awake and is doing relatively fine. There are no injuries other than some bruising on the outside of his head and a bump. Luckily after some rest, he should be good as new.

"Unfortunately, this doesn't change the fact that his mother is out for blood. She wants something done, and I'm in no position to deny her request. We can't exactly allow you to get away scot-free after doing what you did.

"Fortunately, you have never really been a troublesome student. While I personally don't understand why a young man like you would choose to dye his hair that horrible color, it doesn't violate school regulations. It's also your first offense, so I would have usually just let you off with a warning, but because of the severity of this case, I'm afraid I can't do that."

Honestly, Gary had expected to be shouted at the moment he came in. He had been prepared to get a lecture about how dangerous and wrong his actions had been and how easily he could have ruined Steven's and his own future.

The way Mrs. Young had chosen to talk to him was less harsh than he had expected, yet the tone in her voice made him fear the worst about what was going to happen next.

"I expect you to write an apology letter to the Richardson family about how deeply you regret your actions. Now I don't care if you really do or not, but for your own sake, you should make sure that it at least sounds sincere enough so that Mrs. Richardson won't pursue any legal action against you."

"Apart from that, effective immediately, you're suspended from school for the rest of the week."

"Suspended?" Gary repeated, standing up from his seat. "You mean I won't be allowed to come to school for an entire week?"

CHAPTER 47

FOLLOW THE MIST

Most teenagers disliked going to school and only did so because they had to. Every holiday was a joy since it meant a day of not having to go to that dreaded place, so the concept of "punishing" someone by making them not go to school had always seemed rather bizarre.

For a troublemaker, being suspended essentially meant they got a free week to do whatever they wished. However, now that Gary was suddenly faced with that situation, he began to realize the horror of it.

What the hell do I tell Mom?

Their high school had a relatively good reputation in Slough. Getting suspended for a week was unheard of. In fact, the only harsher punishment would be expulsion.

Was this Mrs. Young's way of telling him how close he had come to being . . . expelled?

Suddenly Gary started to consider the consequences if that were to happen. He would have to change schools, probably forcing his family to move to another neighborhood. It might mean his mother would have to find new jobs.

Essentially, it would ruin the lives of the entire Dem family.

On top of that, with nothing to do but to stay at home on his own, he was worried that he might go mad . . . or, worse, do something extremely stupid like go out and look for Billy.

"Since you are suspended, you won't participate in any more classes today. For the time being, you're to stay here. Feel free to start on that apology letter, and I will have my secretary bring you your schoolwork later," Mrs. Young explained. "Honestly, I would have just sent you home immediately, but there is a reason why I'm keeping you here.

"By now, the whole school is aware of what has occurred, including the teachers. One teacher in particular has strongly insisted that you be let off."

Gary was baffled to hear this. He wasn't particularly friendly with any of his teachers, nor did he excel at any subjects. His relationship with his homeroom teacher wasn't out of the ordinary either, so it was hard to pinpoint who exactly it could be.

"I never would have thought there would come a day I would see Mr. Root begging me to not expel a student like you. Unlike what your stature suggests, he claims that you're a very gifted rugby player, one he simply can't do without."

Mr. Root would have been the last person Gary would have suspected, even if he had been doing better in their training matches. Was it really to the point where they needed him this much?

"I have therefore agreed to make a special exception for you. Despite being suspended, you're allowed to attend your club lesson after school for the whole week, and that will include today. I will look forward to your performance on the weekend."

For some reason, Gary felt quite happy with the news. At the moment, playing rugby really was the only distraction he had left. Given his performance, he was very excited to test himself in their first official game.

After giving him paper and a pen to write his apology letter, Mrs. Young stayed in the room doing her own work.

Mom should be at her first job, so I doubt she already knows. Mrs. Young's secretary will probably send Mom a letter, so all I gotta do is

MY WEREWOLF SYSTEM

get to it before she does. I sorta got a week off . . . maybe I can use this to my advantage. It gives me more time to figure things out.

Class had continued without Gary, yet Tom was constantly looking over at his friend's empty seat. He was worried for him in more ways than one. When Mrs. Bedford's class was over, Gary still hadn't returned, which told Tom that his best friend must be in some serious trouble. Tom had tried texting Gary during the breaks and at lunch, but he hadn't answered yet.

Eventually, it was time for rugby practice. During his walk to the changing room, he encountered two large figures. Immediately, Tom put his head down, hoping to avoid eye contact, yet it did nothing. A few moments later, two heavy arms were over his shoulders.

"Hey, Tom, old buddy. Why don't we have a talk before heading to practice today?" Gil suggested with a smile as he started to push Tom in the other direction.

Tom wanted to walk forward, but both of them had gripped him tightly. They were practically forcing him to come with them as they dragged him, lifting him slightly off the ground all the way to the closest bathroom.

As soon as they entered, they shouted to see if anyone else was inside. Once it was clear that it was just the three of them, they locked the door behind them.

"Sooo, me and Barry went to check out the roster this afternoon, and for some reason, Gary's name was still there. Why is that?" Gil asked, shoving Tom's small body to the floor.

"I didn't get a chance to talk to him yet! You must have heard what happened this morning!" Tom tried to explain, quickly checking the room for any way to escape his captors.

"Grab him!" Gil ordered, and Barry picked him up off the ground, holding his hands up so he couldn't use them to defend himself. The next second Gil landed a hard slap right across Tom's

231

face. His cheek turned bright red, and he could taste blood as the inside of his mouth smashed against his teeth.

"You could have texted him or talked to him over the weekend. Aren't you guys close? No, it looks to me like you didn't take what we told you seriously." Gil grabbed Tom by the back of his head, shoving him into one of the toilet stalls.

School toilets, although they were cleaned regularly and this one hadn't been used today, weren't exactly the most clean places.

"Hey, Gil, don't you think this is taking things a bit too far?" Barry asked, but Gil didn't seem to be listening.

The next moment, he shoved Tom's head into the toilet for a few seconds, pushing him down and watching him wiggle and struggle, and smiled. The feeling of having total control of another human life was exhilarating.

Why? Why are they doing this to me? What did I ever do to you? Tom thought as he cursed his life. *I didn't even tell him what you guys did to me because I'm trying to protect your sorry, miserable lives!*

Lifting his head out of the water, Tom gasped for air. He couldn't even say anything because all he was doing was trying to breathe.

"This isn't enough," Gil declared after dunking him a couple of times.

Barry realized that his friend had lost it, yet it seemed too late to stop him, and worst of all, now he himself was a part of whatever was about to happen.

Out on the field, Gary had joined rugby practice. He noticed that Tom wasn't out yet, but judging by the green mist he could see that he was still somewhere in school. Tom didn't enjoy rugby in the first place, so he didn't care if he was on time, and it didn't seem like the teacher did either. Which was why Gary thought it wasn't so strange.

Before the lesson started, Mr. Root pulled Gary to the side.

"Listen here, broccoli head, I don't know what exactly made you do what you did this morning, but let me tell you this. I'm used to dealing with kids who have anger problems and who have an aggressive nature. You don't really seem the type, but you have proven me wrong more than once already. The good thing is, there is an easy fix.

"Use that pent-up anger, frustration, whatever is inside you, out on the field. Use it to run faster from the others, use it to snatch the ball out of their hands, and use it to tackle them to the ground, because on the field, all of that is allowed."

The practice started, and Mr. Root's words spurred Gary on. Today he was playing even better than before. He was sharper, as if his eyes were glued to the ball. It was strange because his technique and playing tactics weren't as sharp as those of someone like Blake, but he made up for it with his talent.

Eventually, Gil and Barry also arrived on the field. Naturally, they got a scolding from Mr. Root, and after running a few laps, they were allowed to join in the practice game.

Both of them tried to tackle Gary when he was in possession of the ball, but they were too slow. Instead, a couple of the faster, lighter students managed to get hold of him. Still, Gary was able to move forward until he passed the ball to Blake, allowing him to score the try that won them the practice game.

Both Blake and Gary were praised as if they had won the World Cup; the two of them had proven to be an unexpectedly good match as a team.

"You two!" Mr. Root said. "If you can repeat what you did today on the weekend, we are going to destroy Eton High!"

Gary was enjoying the praise just as he had on Friday, and his mood was better than before, but he noticed something. Although rugby practice was nearly over, Tom wasn't on the bench; his mist was still in the school. He never appeared, not even by the time practice ended. Instead of heading to the locker room, Gary decided to go into the school and follow the mist to his location.

I know I'm not supposed to be in school, but classes are over anyway, so it won't matter, right? Gary was too concerned about his friend to care.

He was surprised to find the mist leading him to the bathroom, especially since it wasn't far from the changing rooms. Just standing outside, though, Gary was now even more concerned because his nose picked up a scent he had recently become overly familiar with.

Blood!

He quickly pushed the door open and followed the mist to one of the stalls. Opening it, he found Tom lying on the floor, his front teeth broken and blood spilling out onto the tiles.

CHAPTER 48

DON'T FIGHT!

When Gary saw Tom lying on the floor in the bathroom stall, a mix of emotions came over him: most prominently worry about his best friend's condition, followed by anger at whoever had done this to him. Yet there was one feeling he hadn't expected.

Hunger.

The smell of blood coming from Tom's mouth was strong. While he was out on the field, Gary hadn't been hungry at all, but suddenly, confronted with this tantalizing scent, he felt as if he hadn't really eaten in days, only to stumble upon a freshly grilled steak. Saliva started to escape his mouth.

Fortunately, Gary's other feelings quickly snapped him out of his daze. He shook his head to regain his clarity and wiped off the drool. He carefully grabbed Tom by his shoulders and put him into an upright position.

With Tom's face no longer on the floor, Gary started to inspect his condition. From what he could see, one of Tom's front teeth had been knocked out, while the one next to it was slightly chipped. There was also the wound on his head, but Gary had no idea whether he had any internal injuries.

The water in the toilet bowl had turned red. Although his best friend's wounds didn't seem fatal, he could tell that Tom had been put through a lot of pain. He didn't even want to imagine how long he had been tortured like this, since he had missed the entire rugby practice.

"Tom, are you okay? Talk to me, please. What should I do?" Gary asked, despite realizing how dumb the first question was, given the situation.

Having been lifted from the floor and hearing his name being called out, Tom slowly came to. He hadn't been knocked out, yet the pain had been too much for him. The experience of getting tortured had been so tiring that by the time Barry and Gil had left, his body had practically shut down to concentrate on healing.

"G-Gary . . ." Tom whispered weakly. The pain was still overwhelming. After seeing who it was, he closed his eyes again, wanting nothing more than to return to sleep.

Seeing his best friend still alive, Gary let out a sigh of relief. He knew that he couldn't just leave him there; Tom needed medical help. He carefully lifted Tom off the ground, placed him on his shoulders, and started running straight to the nurse's office.

She was naturally surprised to see him for the second time today. She wanted to say something to him about this morning's situation, especially since she had learned the truth.

However, Gary didn't stop. He went right past her and gently placed Tom on one of the cots.

"Help him!" Gary pleaded with tear-filled eyes.

Seeing the amount of blood, the nurse rushed to Tom's side. Once again, there was only so much she could do. She gave Tom some painkillers, since his teeth were the area that had suffered the most damage. This wasn't an urgent case, so there was no need to call an ambulance, but she did have to make a report, and she strongly suggested that Tom go to the hospital as soon as possible to get his mouth looked at.

"Are you sure that is how you found him, and it wasn't . . ."

"It wasn't me," Gary replied aggressively, realizing what she was implying. "I admit that I injured Steven, but this time I'm innocent.

Mr. Root and the other students can testify that I was at rugby practice the whole time! After that, I went to the bathroom because I had to go, and that's where I found him!"

The nurse still gave him a questioning look, but she had to leave. Not only was school over, but now she had to inform someone of what had happened, leaving Gary and Tom alone once again. Nevertheless, she was inclined to believe that Gary was telling the truth this time. Not only because he claimed to have witnesses who could prove his innocence, but more so because he had genuinely been concerned for Tom and had even been tearing up when they came through the door.

Gary stayed by Tom's side until he eventually woke up again. This time, because of the painkillers, he wasn't in as much pain as he was before, allowing him to stay awake for longer.

However, before Tom could even say anything, Gary asked his own question.

"Who did this to you?" Gary asked. "Why did they do this?"

Tom saw that look in his best friend's eyes again.

"Gary, please . . . just . . . just forget about it."

"Forget about it? Forget about it? After they did all of this to you? Do you realize how lucky you are that I even found you? If you let people like that get away without any consequences, what will happen next?

"Next time, you might not get so lucky. What if they do worse things to you? Whatever they did to you, I'll make sure they experience the same pain as you did!" Gary said, holding the side of the metal bed frame and squeezing it tightly.

When Tom didn't answer, Gary got up and began pacing up and down, trying to calm himself. Tom looked down at the metal bed frame and saw that it had bent slightly.

I can't; I can't tell Gary who did this. Otherwise, those guys . . .

"Gary, I'm not denying that you have a point, but think about your circumstances. The whole school knows what happened with

Steven. You've been suspended. If you do anything like that again, no matter how minor, you'll be expelled right away.

"I know your family situation. Have you thought about what would happen with Amy and your mother? I appreciate the gesture, but do you really want to do this to them?"

Listening to what Tom was saying lessened Gary's anger slightly, as images of his family appeared in his head. In the first place, everything he was doing was for them. He wanted to get revenge for Tom, and he wanted to help him out, but he did realize that his best friend was protecting him in his own way by not telling him who these people were . . . even though he already had a slight suspicion. Aside from Tom, there had only been two other students who hadn't been there the whole time.

Gary was about to leave it there, but then he remembered that Tom had arrived at the library with a black eye. Putting these two incidents together, he realized this wasn't the first time Tom had been hurt.

"Do you think they won't attack you again?" Gary asked.

Tom gulped because he wasn't sure of the answer himself. He had expected to be bullied a bit because of Gary, but something was clearly wrong with Gil. He seemed to have really enjoyed the power he had had over Tom, rather than doing it for his teammate's sake.

Suddenly Gary got up and strode out of the nurse's office. However, he wasn't empty-handed. When the nurse examined Tom, she had taken his bloody shirt off and changed it for a clean robe.

Right now, Gary had Tom's shirt in his hand.

Tom was bleeding a lot, so whoever hurt him, their scent should also be here.

CHAPTER 49

GRAY ELEPHANTS

Gary had been a normal teenager up until last week, so becoming a werewolf and acting this way didn't come naturally to him. Unfortunately, his system wasn't helping him find the culprits in any meaningful way.

While it was easy enough to follow the mist of those he had marked, it was a different story when he had to try to pick up a scent from the bloody mess that was Tom's shirt. He would take a few steps, and every so often, he would take another sniff of the shirt. Being in a school that had a few hundred students didn't make his task any easier either.

It's somehow easier to focus when I close my eyes . . . there, I think it should be in that direction! Gary opened his eyes and found himself outside on the field. It hadn't been too long since rugby practice had finished, so the scents of his teammates were still fresh. Surprisingly, he noticed that the scent that he had picked up had split in different directions.

I'm sure of it; there really was more than one person behind it. So much for giving them the benefit of the doubt. Here I even had some sympathy for that stupid bastard Gil!

Two team members had arrived late for rugby practice. Everything was starting to fall into place. Gary took a big sniff, and now he was sure of it. One of the scents was in the same direction as the strange red mist that led him to Barry.

Why the hell did they attack Tom? Gary tensed his fists so hard that it felt like his veins were going to pop from his hands. *Is it really just because they don't want me to be on the team? They couldn't go after me, so they went for Tom? What bullcrap is that?* Gary swung out his hand, hitting the school wall.

Usually, a swing so fast and so hard would have shattered his wrist. But he didn't feel any pain. Fortunately, he hadn't directly aimed for the wall; otherwise, he might have left his fist print.

The mist told him that Barry was still in school for some reason. Since he had been marked, Gary didn't worry about losing him. No, he was far more interested in Gil. His scent had left the school grounds.

Tom's words still rang through his head: that if he did anything, he would be expelled, especially after the incident this morning.

Whatever I do outside of school shouldn't be a problem as long as nobody recognizes me!

Lifting his hood, Gary left the school.

He'd put Tom's shirt in his bag, and whenever he lost Gil's scent among the myriad of others, he took another sniff to catch it. Once he entered more dangerous areas, the number of scents decreased sharply.

On his way, he also made his routine stop at the convenience store for fresh meat, restoring his Energy after the rugby match just in case he needed it.

Exp 230/460
Skill activated: Charging Heart
All stats have temporarily been doubled
–10 Energy

He started running through the streets, tracking down the scent, afraid that Gil might reach home soon.

Eventually, he noticed that he had entered a certain area in Slough.

Doesn't this area belong to the Gray Elephant Gang? The Gray Elephants were the second biggest gang after the Underdogs; they also controlled the gray color gang. It still wasn't completely dark out; the sun was just starting to set. The gangs usually didn't bother others at this time of day anyway, not that Gary was particularly worried if they chose to attack him.

Following Gil's scent, Gary left the residential neighborhood and followed it to an industrial area, arriving in front of some abandoned warehouses. He had never been here, but he recognized that such a location practically screamed "gang hangout."

He had to be extra cautious; fighting off a small group and an entire gang were two completely different things. Having tracked the scent to one warehouse in particular, he saw gang members wearing gray clothing outside. He could hear them cheering all the way from his location.

He sneaked around the outside until he found a pipe that led to the roof. Gary wasn't the best climber, but he had been practicing and with Charging Heart still active, jumping up and grabbing onto the pipe was easy. He soon found himself on the metal roof.

Gary was careful with his footsteps since they would make quite a bit of noise, but luckily there were also plenty of seagulls on the roof. Whenever they moved, they made the roof clang regardless of how quiet he was, and it seemed like whatever was happening inside, the gang members were far too preoccupied with that to care was happening outside.

He found a hole in the roof and was happy to see that it allowed him to watch what was happening underneath. His enhanced hearing also allowed him to hear what they were saying.

"Not bad, kid." A male voice was praising someone. "Your skill, your strength, and most of all your ruthlessness are the real deal. You're perfect. There's just one last thing for you to do before we let you in our gang."

One person stood there, bloody and battered, yet he was in far better condition than the other guy at his feet. Gary had only heard about the gray color gang's "auditions," but he assumed he had just walked in on one.

There were a couple of ways to join a color gang, but the most direct one was the scene Gary had just stumbled upon. Those willing to join could challenge active members, and if they proved themselves, the color gang would usually offer to recruit them.

That's him . . . he's the one who hurt Tom! Gary could still smell Tom's blood on his clothes, even though it was now mixed with the blood of the person on the floor.

"You will join us on our rounds today. After that, we'll discuss your payment and more. I have hope for you. If you do well and rise up, then you might even be accepted into the Gray Elephants."

Gary would love nothing more than to jump down and pay Gil back, but his rational side was still present. His first instinct was nothing but suicidal. There were around thirty gang members inside, and the person Gil was speaking to seemed to be their leader.

No leader of any gang would be an easy person to deal with, especially belonging to the color gang under the Gray Elephants. He could continue to follow Gil and his scent, but from the sounds of it, the leader himself might be the one to show Gil the ropes.

There was no guarantee that Gary would get a chance to get his revenge today, and there was also another problem. He still needed to hurry home to intercept the letter about his suspension from school. His mother was working late tonight, so he should still have some time.

It was then that the system answered his prayers, solving his issue once again.

You have successfully tracked down a target using your keen nose!
You are acting more like a werewolf and less than a human by the day!

Bloodlust has been detected

Last time he had marked Barry by accident, though he had been holding him by the wrist. Now it appeared that physical touch wasn't a requirement. Now that he thought about it, Gary realized that back when he had defeated the color gang members, the system had also offered him an opportunity to activate a Forced Bond, even though he hadn't touched them.

At the time, he had declined, but now that Gary saw the message with his emotions running high, he didn't hesitate.

Yes!

Forced Bond has been activated
3/5 Marks have been assigned

CHAPTER 50

THE LETTER

Gary hadn't considered the consequences of marking Gil. He wasn't sure what would happen when the full moon came out, and quite frankly, he didn't care. Now that he had made sure that he would always be able to find Gil, it was time for him to head home.

As he left the area, he could see that the marking worked as intended. A visible red mist trail drifted in the air leading to him. Now he had two red markings, one for Barry and one for Gil, but he could tell the difference by the different scent each mist gave off.

Using Charging Heart for the second time, Gary rushed home, skipping his daily gym workout. As he did so, images of Tom appeared in his head.

Those guys, why . . . why . . . why would they hurt him that badly? Gary ran faster and faster, leaping over trash cans in the middle of the street without slowing down.

Tom, why didn't you say anything? With how late they were, they must have been torturing you all that while. How could you protect those scum? The smile on Gil's face . . . that was not the face of a human. He's a monster worse than me! He will just come back to hurt you again and again, so I need to make sure he doesn't get the chance!

The good news was that the running had quenched Gary's anger a little, and he made it back to his apartment far quicker than he had anticipated, even with his newfound powers. Opening the door, he quickly looked down to search for the letter that his school surely must have already sent out.

However, it wasn't there. More accurately speaking, there was nothing there. Usually, there would at least be junk mail, if not overdue bills. Unfortunately, someone appeared to have already collected it.

"Are you looking for this?" Amy asked, holding up a letter in her hand while standing in the kitchen. The rest of the missing mail was also on the countertop.

"Amy!" Gary rushed over and snatched the letter from her hand before she had any chance to hide it behind her back. Just as he had expected, the letter was to inform his mother that Gary had been suspended for a week for getting into a fight to the point of sending a schoolmate into the hospital.

"Hey, you know I'm still going to tell Mom!" Amy said, pouting. "Ever since you came back with your green hair, I was worried that one day you would do something stupid, but this? Seriously, I know that you like watching those Altered fights, but you've never gotten in a fight before! What was it even about, that you sent the other guy into the hospital? A girl, or a boy, or maybe just some stupid boy stuff?" Amy couldn't stop asking him questions, driven by a mix of worry and curiosity.

There's no way I can tell Amy that I got into a fight because he threatened to date her! That would just be too . . . too embarrassing. Gary's face was going red just at the thought of it.

Still, he needed to figure out a way to stop Amy from telling their mother; not only would he get an earful and worry her to death, she probably wouldn't let him leave the house either. He would be grounded, and he just couldn't afford that in his current situation.

"Why did you even open the letter in the first place? It's not even addressed to you!" Gary tried to change the subject, clearly annoyed that his sister wouldn't back down.

"Because I saw your school logo on it. Schools only send letters home if it's good news or bad news, and come on. With your hair, what the hell kind of good news would there be? If it was something I wasn't supposed to see, I planned just to reseal the envelope and put it back as if I never opened it," Amy smugly replied, aware that she had the moral high ground on this one.

With no way out of the situation, there was really only one thing Gary could do.

"Please, I beg you, just don't tell Mom. You know how much she would worry. It's just a week; I'll manage to keep it hidden from her somehow," Gary pleaded. "I promise to make it worth your while!"

Unexpectedly, his little sister held out her hand, turning her head away.

"Fine, but you owe me! If you want me to keep it a secret, then it's going to cost you."

A few seconds later, she felt something in her hand. Opening her eyes, she saw a fifty-dollar bill in her hand. For a moment, Gary could swear that he saw Amy's eyes turn into gold bars.

When his little sister had asked for payment, she hadn't literally meant money. She had intended to blackmail Gary into taking over her chores for the week. Either that, or perhaps make him act like her servant or bodyguard next time she visited Stacy, but this was much better than all of those options.

"Where . . . how do you even have this much money?" Amy asked. "Don't tell me you robbed the guy on top of sending him to the hospital?"

The truth was, other than the five hundred he had stashed away in their room, Gary had been down to the last hundred from the first paycheck he had earned that day fighting against Billy Buster . . . and now he had given Amy half of that, just so she would keep quiet.

"Nothing like that! What do you take your brother for?" Gary protested, but Amy pointed to the letter he still held in his hand.

"You know how I've been claiming to visit Tom a lot lately? Well, the truth is I've been helping out another friend of mine with their family business. They give me money for helping out. At the end of each day, I get paid in cash. I haven't told Mom because you know what she's like. She would just feel bad and tell me to stop, that it's an adult's job to take care of their family, but . . . you know, I'm also part of this family."

Hearing this, Amy felt a little bad for taking the money. Gary had worked hard for it, and he had done so for all of them.

"Arghh, here, take it back," Amy said, shoving it back into Gary's hand. "After you tell me all that, what kind of person would I be to take it? You think about others too much." She sighed, making her way back to their room.

"Wait, are you going to tell Mom?" Gary called out after her.

"No, just do what you want." Amy turned around and smiled. Although her brother wasn't the brightest, he really was the best brother she could have. "I'll try to think of a way for Mom to accept the money if you have more of it."

Now, knowing that his sister wouldn't reveal the situation, Gary headed toward the front door with the letter; he would destroy it later.

"Wait, it's already late. Are you going to work again?" Amy asked worriedly.

"Nope, I need to return something to someone," Gary replied, and shut the door.

It was time for him to hunt.

CHAPTER 51

PERFECT TIME

Once outside, Gary found it easier to distinguish between the two Forced Bond markings. In addition to their different scents, the closer he got to one of those who were marked, the darker the color of the mist would get. It made Gary wonder if there was a limit to his marking. Perhaps once he was far enough away, the red mist would completely disappear, but even in his own home, he could still see all three marks.

His dark hood was covering his head, but he had no time to replenish the Energy he had lost so far from using Charging Heart twice and the general Energy he had used up rushing home and trying to catch up to Gil in the first place.

88/110 Energy

The gray color gang shouldn't stray too far from their territory, but they'll probably want to head into a more residential area.

Thinking about this, Gary realized that the gray color gang area also happened to cover where he had been on Sunday, the residential area where Billy's apartment building was located.

One problem at a time, Gary thought. *Besides, given how many reporters there were just yesterday, they would be stupid to go anywhere near it.*

While the Underdogs covered most of the town's nightclubs and profited from selling drugs, among other things, the Gray Elephants specialized in protecting the factories and warehouses in Slough.

The organizations needed protection from other gangs that might look to profit by stealing their equipment or products or might come around to harass their employees. It wasn't uncommon for a business to hire some gangs to use those means to make life more difficult for their competitors.

So the Gray Elephants would send out their members as body-guards, and they spread the word about who was under their protection. They usually got a percentage of profits, but for the business it was far better than the alternative, making it an arrangement that ultimately profited both sides.

As for companies that wanted to rent or set up a factory without relying on a gang . . . well, the gangs naturally had their ways of convincing companies how much their "service" was needed.

The air was filled with a gray smoke that hovered over every-thing, including the lampposts, and it was messing with Gary's nose a little. If it weren't for the red mist he had followed on his way here, he would have struggled a lot more to find them.

From what I've heard, the Grey Elephants and their color gang have quite the fighting strength given their job scope. If I see one of them, I'm going to have to get out of there. News about my little trick must have already spread in their circles, so I doubt they will follow me, not that there are any nearby areas that I could lead them to.

As Gary continued to stalk them, the color gang eventually stopped in front of a small workshop that looked to be a shoe repair and key-making service. Gil was there with four other gang members, but there was no sign of any other members nearby.

The problem was they were on a pretty open street; there was a chance that other gang members could come along quite easily, so Gary needed to wait for the perfect opportunity.

"Break it, new boy!" a member with a gray bandana tied around the top of his head yelled out. Gil picked up a large brick on the side of the road and hurled it at the window, but it immediately bounced off, nearly hitting him in the head.

The other gang members laughed.

"Ha ha, that's reinforced glass, you idiot. All the shops in this area have it; otherwise, they'd have to buy replacements every day." The gray color gang member who had ordered Gil around seemed to be the leader of the small group.

Gil did not look pleased with this little joke they had set up. A few seconds later, a frail old man came running out. He held a broomstick in his hand and pointed it toward the gang.

"What are you hooligans doing? This is my shop! How many times do I have to tell you that I have no money? My shop has been here for over thirty years! I won't give it to you; you'll have to take it off my dead body!" the old man shouted as he swung the broomstick widely, but all of the gang members, including Gil, were easily able to evade it. He never managed to hit any of them, making them laugh at his antics until he was tired out, huffing and panting loudly.

"Okay, new boy, here's your first task of the day. We need new business in this town, and this geezer hasn't been willing to play ball, so it's time we let someone else in who will be more willing to cooperate. You've heard the old coot; apparently, we'll have to get it over his dead body, so let's put his conviction to the test!"

Gil understood what the leader was implying. He went up to the old man and smiled. The other gang members stopped laughing, interested in whether Gil could actually follow through.

There were many reasons why people chose to join a gang. Some, like Innu, did it because they were unable to find a place for themselves in the world, their only talent being that they were decent with their fists. Others, like Gary, did it because, in the current times, gangs were one of the easiest ways to earn money.

However, those like Gil did it for a completely different reason. His type was the most dangerous. The sadistic smile on his face said it all. He enjoyed the feeling of dominance, making others submit to him by using violence.

The old man tried to muster all his strength, grabbing the broom and swinging it toward Gil, but the large high schooler managed to grab it quite easily.

"Old man, your strength is nothing against a member of the rugby club," Gil said, pulling on the broomstick and yanking it away as the old man tumbled to the ground.

"You know, although these things are made from wood, they're pretty strong. You just tried hitting me with it, so now this is just self-defense. Let's see how much it hurts!" Gil shouted as he raised the broomstick and slammed it against the old man's side.

The others watching could see that Gil showed no hesitation. It was one thing for someone to fight their way into a gang by beating up another gang member, but new members usually hesitated to fight civilians.

"Ahh!" the old man screamed, rolling on the ground. "It hurts! How could you do this? Imagine if I was your gran—"

"Shut up!" Gil shouted, whacking the broomstick on the old man's legs again. "Shut up! Shut up!" Each time he used his full strength, and the old man's moans only got stronger.

"Hey, shouldn't we stop him? We were only supposed to scare him, but if he kills the old man, the Gray Elephants might tell us off," one of the gang members asked the leader.

"Humans aren't as weak as you think. He hasn't even really started to beg us to stop. The old coot still has some fight left in him. Is that all you got, new boy?" the leader shouted, trying to spur on Gil even more. "How long does it take you to convince one frail old man to do the right thing?"

Up until this point, Gil had been holding the broomstick with one hand, worried that if he used both hands he would break it. Getting the okay from the leader, he lifted it above his head and used his full strength and weight to swing it down on the old man.

Suddenly, a hooded person appeared almost out of nowhere and grabbed the stick before it could reach its intended victim.

"Screw waiting for the perfect time! I can't just watch you torment an innocent old man!" Gary yelled out.

"System, put both points into Strength!"

2 Points have been allocated into Strength
Your base Strength is now at 7
Current Strength: 14 (+1)

With Charging Heart and the power of the moon, Gary pulled the broomstick out of Gil's hands. While the bully was still confused about the situation, Gary used both hands to swing the stick from the side like a baseball bat, hitting Gil across the face, flinging his head back, and causing him to fly through the air for a few meters until he hit the ground . . .

A single tooth had fallen out of his mouth.

"That's a start!" Gary thought about Tom's missing tooth, but it still wasn't enough.

CHAPTER 52

ILLEGAL WEAPONS

Although Gary was already at Level 4, he had assigned only one of the three stat points he had received from leveling up. He'd considered what stat he might use them for but decided it might make more sense to increase them at the gym, until he hit some kind of wall.

However, when Gary saw Gil attacking an old man who could hardly defend himself, something snapped. It was similar to what happened when Steven had "threatened" him by telling him he would go out with Amy. He imagined Tom lying on the ground, getting bullied by Gil.

Unable to wait for a perfect opportunity, he dived right in, running past the gang members while placing his stat points into Strength. The broomstick snapped after connecting with Gil's face, and Gary still held half of it in his hand, his head hanging downward slightly so the others wouldn't be able to see his face.

"What the hell? I thought the new guy had some strength, but it turns out his muscles are all hot air. Hey, aren't you embarrassed getting taken out by such a scrawny kid?" One of the gray color gang members turned around to make fun of Gil, not having grasped the seriousness of the situation.

However, the same could not be said about their leader. Unlike the other three, he had watched Gil fight, so he had seen his strength. His body didn't just look strong, and not many people could make someone so big fall so easily. What was more, the "scrawny kid" had managed to snap the broomstick with one blow.

"What are you guys doing? He might just be the new kid, but since when do we allow anyone just to hurt one of our members? Stop gawking and bring him in!" the leader shouted.

Seeing the other three charge in, Gary was thankful for one thing. None of them seemed to be using weapons. One of the traits of the gray color gang was that they relied on brute strength.

Still, Gary went to the injured Gil and lifted him by the scruff of his uniform.

"Don't think this is over; I'm not done with you yet."

Blood was dripping from the rugby player's mouth, and he was possibly in a worse state than Steven, but Gary had no sympathy for him, not after what he had seen him do. Making use of Charging Heart's duration, he lifted Gil above his head with both hands.

Even with an effective total of 15 points of Strength, the weight seemed to be a bit much for Gary, but his frustration allowed him to power through. He managed to throw his schoolmate toward the gray color gang members, crashing him into two of them.

The third one turned around to check on his friends, disbelieving what he had seen. This turned out to be a big mistake, as by the time he turned back, Gary was already in the midst of a punch, aimed straight at the gang member's face.

"You guys are just as bad!" Gary shouted.

He could only imagine what the gray color gang members must have been doing in this area for so long. All the chaos and trouble they had caused. The truth was, Gary wasn't the only one who wanted them gone, yet nobody ever did anything because they were afraid.

In the past, if Gary had come upon such a scene, would he have been brave enough to help out? The truth was, the answer was no.

New Quest received
An eye for an eye, a tooth for a tooth

Your anger has finally led you to this.
Deal with the one you're after, as well as everyone protecting him!
Quest reward: 50 Exp per defeated person
Your opponent has been knocked out
50 Exp received
Exp 280/460

Receiving this message made Gary realize something: that Gil still had some room for a beating. As he walked over, the two who were trapped under Gil's heavy body pushed him off and got up from the ground.

"Don't just stand there, Bowden; give us a hand!" one of the members shouted. Since they still had the advantage of numbers, he was confident they could win.

"No real names, you idiot!" the leader shouted, slapping him from behind, while he waited and watched Gary.

The three of them stayed back, and when the leader took a step back, so did the other two. That was when the leader noticed that their attacker wasn't looking at them. Instead, he only seemed to have eyes for Gil, who was on the floor.

After being hit by the broom, Gil's head was spinning slightly. He wasn't knocked out yet, and he could hear the chaos around him, though he was unable to react to it. He tried to stand back up, but his legs felt like jelly.

Recovering a little, he felt someone above him, and the next second that someone slapped his face.

"Oh no, you don't just get out of the situation by losing consciousness. You still have plenty of teeth left in your mouth," Gary said.

Gil was still struggling to open his eyes, yet before he could, his head was slammed into the concrete and lifted again. His forehead had been cut and blood was dripping down, obscuring his vision even more.

It was then that the gray leader was sure that his hunch was right.

"Let's just get out of here, boys; that person isn't here for us."

The three ran off, leaving Gil behind as well as the other gang member. The leader thought it was safe to abandon him; he would wake up soon, and the leader was more concerned about what would happen if they tried approaching the attacker again.

That person . . . is just another beast. Let the two of them deal with each other, the leader thought as he left.

Holding Gil's head up, Gary could tell he was still conscious. It seemed to have been the right call to cancel Charging Heart instead of using his full strength.

"Tell me, how does it feel? Not so great when you're on the receiving end, now is it? You still like to hurt people? I don't get how you can enjoy this so much!" Gary shouted before getting ready to whack his head against the concrete once more.

Gil, in his desperate situation, used his hands to cover his head as it hit the ground, but the impact was still strong.

"Who . . . are you?" Gil blurted out, his mouth filled with blood while his entire body still hurt from being used as a projectile. He hadn't even realized yet that the side of his face had swollen up from getting hit with the broomstick.

Gary still wasn't done yet, and he wouldn't be until the system gave him the Exp for knocking Gil out. Grabbing Gil's head once more, he was ready to slam it onto the ground again, but then he felt someone grab his wrist.

"Stop! If you keep doing that, you'll end up killing him," a male voice cautioned him.

Gary looked up, trying to see who could possibly have the strength to hold him. It was a man in a large black trench coat and a scruffy beard who was also wearing a large hat that covered most of his head.

"I've been watching you. You managed to knock out a gang member all by yourself, and you even managed to lift this kid over your head despite the size difference. Are you sure you're human?"

the man asked as he reached into his pocket to grab what looked like a baton.

"You know, there have already been a couple of killings in this area, and it seems their wounds were not inflicted by normal humans." The man pressed a button, and the baton lit up. Blue sparks started to buzz around it.

Once upon a time, these batons were used for self-defense, yet under the No Lethal Weapons Pact, they were still considered taboo. Only one group still used them: the Altered Hunters.

CHAPTER 53

SURVIVE!

New Quest received

There's always a bigger fish

As a werewolf who hasn't even experienced his first turning, you're still too weak.

Survive!

Quest reward: ???

Gary was quite surprised that for the first time, the Werewolf System didn't even hint at the type of reward he would receive if he fulfilled the quest. Did this mean that it hadn't decided what he would get, or did it doubt his ability to survive the fight?

At the same time, the conditions for completing the quest weren't really clear. What would happen if he ran away? If he was knocked out, that would count as surviving, right? Or did it mean that the person in front of him wanted to kill him?

It's impossible for the system to know all of that! It's just a system!

Whatever the case, now wasn't the time to worry about that. Seeing the baton light up, Gary was in no way inclined to allow his opponent to hit him with the weapon. He had experienced being electrocuted when he was younger, when he accidentally touched a bare wire, and this looked far worse.

As he had discovered during his rugby training, one of the benefits of canceling the Charging Heart skill early was that the cooldown between each use would also be shortened. The downside to this was that no matter how long the skill lasted, he wouldn't get back any of his spent Energy points.

Gary tried to pull away, only to find himself unable to do anything. He could barely tug his arm away from the strange adult who was gripping it tightly with his giant hands.

This is insane! Just how strong is this guy's grip? Gary thought. With the baton coming closer, he had no other choice but to use Charging Heart again.

61/110 Energy

The last time Gary had been forced to use up so much Energy was in his fight against Billy. As he yanked his hand once more, the sudden spike in strength surprised the Altered Hunter, and his grip weakened for a moment.

Unfortunately, Gary failed to pull away completely. His captor managed to grab his other hand, this time even firmer than before, completely ignoring the teenager's boost in strength.

Even with Charging Heart, he is still just as strong! No, this guy might even be stronger.

These guys hunted Altereds for a living, and they had to have some way to combat them. At this rate, Gary was suspecting that the Altered Hunters were Altereds themselves, but what kind of hypocrisy would that be?

Using Gary's struggle against him, the man threw him off balance and followed up with the electrified baton. The second it touched Gary's stomach, his body tingled all over, his green hair stood up, and all of his body hair stood on end. No matter how hard he tried to move while the baton touched his body, none of his muscles were responding.

It was strange that the pain was minimal, but he was unable to do anything. Although he saw the large fist coming toward his face, Gary was unable to block it. The blow hurled him into the air; he landed hard and skidded across the ground, and for what felt like the second time, his nose was broken.

You have incurred a grave injury
–27 HP
68/100 HP
Would you like to activate emergency healing?
If you wish, you can set a limit to when emergency healing will be activated.

The only time he had experienced emergency healing was after Billy had broken his ribs by using the metal plate in his glove. It had used Energy, allowing him to heal his wounds and continue fighting. However, in this situation, Gary didn't have a lot of Energy points to use. At the same time, he didn't really need his nose to help him fight.

"You clearly have abnormal strength for your size, so what are you waiting for? Why don't you transform?" the Altered Hunter asked.

Wiping away the blood trickling down his nose, Gary got up again. He wasn't sure if he could win this fight, but he was pissed. Beyond pissed that this person had interrupted him in the middle of what he had been doing.

After all, there was still another quest active that had to do with Gil.

Trust me, if I knew how to transform, I would have done it by now and ripped your freaking head off! Gary kept his eye on the baton. The man pressed the button and it electrified up again.

It looks like his weapon can only stay on for so long, otherwise he would have just kept the stupid thing electrified.

Realizing this, Gary charged at full speed, using Charging Heart to power his attack. The man confidently swung the baton toward

Gary's head with perfect timing, but Gary ducked, and the baton went over his head. He then threw an overhead punch as hard as he could toward the man's face.

Impressive, you fooled me into thinking that you were using your full speed the whole time. It's just too bad that you weren't the only one who held back, the man mused as he blocked the incoming punch.

As it hit, Gary felt something hard, far harder than bone, and his knuckles ached. In return, the man seemed surprised at how much force the punch had behind it.

Is he wearing armor under his clothes? Goddammit, of course he is! How could an Altered Hunter work without that type of stuff?

Gary jumped back and considered the situation. He was getting low on Energy, yet his opponent still seemed fine, not even hurt. Gil appeared to be barely conscious, rolling about on the ground, while the abandoned gray color gang member had regained consciousness and was getting up on his feet.

Right now, Gary was sure that there was nothing he could do against the Altered Hunter. He didn't like it, but he had to run. Turning away, Gary started to sprint as fast as he could. Slightly regretting not having put any points into Dexterity, he prayed that the Energy he still had would allow him to escape.

However, the Altered Hunter didn't bother to chase after him. Nevertheless, Gary didn't stop running, not even after he received a notification that the quest for catching Gil had failed for getting out of range.

Quest failed

On his way home, Gary stopped by the convenience store. Although he had already completed his Daily Quest, he was in dire need of replenishing his Energy. He was already feeling hunger pangs the closer he came to reaching 0 Energy.

After spending the last of his money, Gary practically gobbled up the meat in an alley. He used some of that Energy to restore his broken nose before continuing on his way. Gary made sure to go through some alleys and returned home only when he was absolutely sure that he hadn't been followed.

His mother had already arrived, but Gary played it cool. Judging by the fact that his mother didn't immediately give him a lecture, Amy had kept her word. After spending some time with the two of them, Gary headed back to his room; his head and body were shaking as he sat down on the bed.

That . . . that was so freaking dangerous! If that Altered Hunter had caught me . . . or if he had come in a bit later when I was weaker from fighting the others . . . Damn it! Gary wanted to punch something in his frustration, but before he did, he recalled what had happened to the wall at school.

Above all, he was most upset that he had been unable to teach Gil more of a lesson. Sure, the 50 Exp he had failed to earn had left a bitter taste in his mouth, but now he was worried about what the bully would do. Not knowing why he had been punished, he might try to do something to Tom again.

Gary swore that he wouldn't let that happen.

Still, there was at least one piece of good news that came from the unfortunate encounter.

Congratulations, you have managed to avoid getting captured by the suspected Altered Hunter!

You've learned the importance of a strategic retreat in the face of an opponent who vastly outclasses you! Fortunately, as an apex predator, you'll be able to grow in due time. Here's something to pay him back, if you ever see him again!

Quest reward: Skill selection

CHAPTER 54

TARGETED

Tuesday morning was far quieter for Xin than Monday. A big reason for this was the absence of Gary and Tom. She didn't know why, but ever since the two friends had shown up at the karate club, Xin had started to pay more attention to them.

She turned and stared at their empty seats.

I heard that the green-haired boy got suspended for fighting with Steven, but what about his friend? Is it just a coincidence that he's also missing, or has he decided to skip classes so the two of them can hang out?

As she wondered about the reason, she heard a group of girls whispering things about her, no doubt spreading nasty rumors, as they were staring daggers at her.

Right, I should probably worry about my own problems first. Why is it so hard to find an opportunity to apologize and clear things up between us? Just when did Tiffany convince the entire class to avoid talking to me as if I have the plague?

Ever since Xin had accidentally thrown Tiffany into Gary's puke, she had tried to apologize. Last week, she had failed to make any progress. Xin had sincerely hoped that after the weekend, the queen bee might have forgiven her or at least shown herself more willing to listen to reason, but she had no such luck.

Yesterday, Tiffany's two goons had gotten in the way each and every time, not even letting her speak with their ringleader. It had gotten to the point that Xin just wanted to beat them up to get past them. The only reason she hadn't done so was that she feared it would only escalate her situation.

When the bell signaled their lunch break, Xin planned to catch Tiffany on the way to the canteen to finally settle things between them. Following her down the hallway, though, she eventually encountered a boy walking through the halls with a bandage on his head.

"Steven? Is that you?" Xin called out to her clubmate. The karateka seemed pretty zoned out, so she wanted to make sure he was okay. "Is your head all right? I heard what happened. What made that guy attack you like that?"

Based on the few interactions she had with Gary, he hadn't seemed like the type of person to just attack someone for no reason. Then again, she hadn't exactly expected to find him challenging their karate club either. Still, unlike Gary, Xin felt like she knew more about Steven and his character.

It wouldn't surprise her to learn that he had felt embarrassed about the loss and had decided to fight him again, only this time without any gear on. Of course, the amount of force Gary had used was undoubtedly excessive.

Steven looked at Xin for a few seconds and just brushed her off, walking past her. Although part of him knew that it wasn't her fault, another part blamed her for what he had gone through yesterday.

"He can have you," Steven mumbled as he walked away.

His words were cryptic, and she was about to push Steven for more answers, yet just then she saw Tiffany enter the bathroom . . . alone!

Wait, are those other two not with her? Xin rushed over, finally getting the chance she had been waiting for!

When she opened the door . . . a trash can landed on her head.

Xin didn't understand what had happened. One moment, she had followed her classmate into the bathroom; the next, she was covered from head to toe in banana peels, food scraps, and other garbage. Xin immediately threw the trash can to the side, only to see Tiffany pointing at her, laughing with her two friends who had already been inside.

"Ha ha, well, I can safely say this is far worse than you throwing me in that puke, but it's not enough. This is just the start. You humiliated me in front of everyone, so you have to pay for this!"

Xin picked up the trash can. Walking over to one of the two goons, she swung it over her head, causing the girl to fall to the floor and accidentally bite her lip.

Seeing this, the other goon stepped back and fell down on her butt. Before Tiffany could react, Xin headed straight for her. With her forearm, Xin pushed her back until the queen bee was against the wall, with Xin's forearm pressed against her neck.

"*Enough!* I have had it with you. I've been here barely a week, and you've done nothing but torture me for something I did to you by accident!" Xin shouted. "Ever since, I've been trying to apologize to you, but you've made it abundantly clear that you don't want me to. What's wrong with you? Are you on some sort of power trip or something?"

It was then that Xin saw a smile on Tiffany's face, a reaction she hadn't expected.

"You screwed up," Tiffany declared. "As the mayor's daughter, I bet you thought you were pretty safe. Truth be told, I actually planned to keep this between the two of us. Pay you back for another week or so before I would eventually leave you alone, but now you laid your hands on me . . ."

With this threat, Xin wanted to finish her off. She was ready to use one of her powerful kicks, but the words of her father rang through her head, and she decided to let go and left the bathroom.

She slammed the door behind her, catching the attention of a few students, as did the smell of the food and other garbage that was still stuck to her clothing.

Things never seem to change around here, Kai mused as he walked down the hallway, staring at his phone. Frankly, he enjoyed observing his fellow students and their problems, but he had just received a text from an important person.

Thank you for helping me out the other day! I seriously don't know who would do something like this, but I'm just glad you knew the right people who could get rid of the problem. Anyway, I owe you a big favor.

Innu had called him in the middle of the night to inform Kai that a human arm had been left outside his apartment. Panicked and not knowing what to do, he had called Kai to see if he could do anything. To his surprise, his fellow gang member had fixed his problem with a simple phone call. The fighter hadn't asked any questions and had simply done as instructed.

Just what is going on for both Gary and Innu to find human flesh in front of their doors? This isn't something the Underdogs would do. Could it be a rival gang trying to scare them? . . . No, that doesn't make any sense. We're barely a gang, and even if those guys from Eton High found out that we'll be fighting them in the tournament, they would simply beat them up. Whoever did that must have wanted to leave a message. In that case, what exactly do they have in common to receive such a thing?

CHAPTER 55

NEW SKILL

Waking up that Tuesday morning, Gary had expected his body to be sore from yesterday's fight against the Altered Hunter, but thanks to his new supernatural body, he felt good as new. However, he noticed something strange. For some reason, he seemed overly hungry, and this didn't seem to be his normal type of hunger that a simple breakfast would solve.

What was more, he should be overly full from yesterday. Before heading back home, he had stopped by the convenience store to replenish all the Energy he had used up in his fight. After that, he also had a nice dinner with his mother and sister. If anything, he should still be full, not hungry.

Wondering what was wrong with him, he decided to check his system, and the first thing he noticed was a few notifications he had missed, since he had gone to bed before midnight.

Your bloodlust grows
6 days until the next full moon
As the date of the full moon approaches, the power of the moon strengthens you further.
Current bonus: All Stats +2

Whoa, another boost! How many more will I get? Since it's a bonus, my guess would be that after the full moon passes, the bonus stats will go away. However, what happens after that? After each full moon, there will be a new moon. If the moon is what grants a werewolf its powers, doesn't that mean I'll have to worry about getting weaker and suffer penalties?

Gary chose to ignore the countdown notification, as it seemed impossible to turn it off. Instead, he looked over his base stats, all three of which displayed (+2) next to them.

Strength 7 (+2)
Dexterity 3 (+2)
Endurance 9 (+2)

It was scary to think how strong he might possibly be in a week and when he actually transformed. Looking over his Energy and Health, he saw that they still didn't benefit from any bonuses, but then he noticed something strange.

81/110 Energy

What the hell? Why is it lower than before I went to bed? Was I sleepwalking and using Charging Heart or something?

Thankfully, the Werewolf System decided to enlighten him this time and offered the following explanation.

The more your bloodlust grows in tandem with the state of the moon, the more Energy is required to empower you. It would be advisable to increase your Energy.

Goddammit, why do you tell me this now, when I no longer have any stat points? Shit, I still haven't found a way to increase that stat naturally! Why doesn't this stupid thing have a tutorial or a help function? Who the hell designed this junk system?

Gary's cursing, unfortunately, didn't result in anything. He didn't know whether the system felt insulted and had decided against cooperating or if it was just the way it worked; however, he had no way of finding that out. Instead, he chose to do something about the problems he could fix, albeit temporarily.

I should have known that the system doesn't give me anything for free. All right, I should be able to fix this by purchasing more food to replenish my Energy that way. I'll also have to avoid getting into any fights and probably refrain from using Charging Heart during practice.

After quickly getting dressed to keep up the ruse of going to school, Gary headed to the fridge. It seemed like he had only recently filled it, but as he thought about it, he realized that was a week ago. He wasn't the only one who had access to it, so right now, it was rather empty. It contained an opened milk carton, some juice, eggs, butter, and jam, but he craved something else right now.

Damn, I already used up the rest of my money yesterday to buy meat, so what the hell am I supposed to do now? Gary wondered. He knew that he still had his emergency fund of five hundred dollars, but he was adamant in wanting to use it to help pay off some of his family's bills. Alas, if he didn't come up with a solution soon, he might have no other choice but to use it.

It was already time for him to leave for school. He was thankful that his sister hadn't told his mother, and because of this, he was free to do what he wished, which happened to be finding solutions to his ever-increasing problems.

After walking around downtown for a couple of hours, Gary noticed that his Energy had gone down by a bit.

78/110 Energy

I still have a week to go; just how bad will it get ? If I get into more fights or get called by Kai to fight, this could end very badly. I don't want to create any more Billys. Gary kicked a pebble out of frustration.

Following its flight path, he noticed a poster in one of the shop windows. He had actually been hoping to see if there might be any odd jobs he could do, but this one caught his eye because it had certain words that stuck out to Gary.

AFC Academy. Train to become the next big fighter!

An Altered Academy that trains Altered? How great would it be if I could attend something like that? It's not like I can fake it; Altered are able to transform at will. Too bad, with how much money Kirk makes, I bet I could get rid of nearly all of my problems at once. Gary began to daydream.

Trying to think of something positive was a nice little escape from reality, but eventually he left downtown and headed toward the park, where there was a nice woodland area nearby. He had chosen this area for a specific reason.

After entering the woods, he looked around to see if he could spot anyone, but it didn't look like anyone was nearby. Despite all his setbacks yesterday, his system had surprised him with one good reward at the end of the day.

Showing skills that are available to be unlocked at current level
1. Claw Drain
2. Hardened Will

Don't you usually get a choice of three? Whatever, I can't really complain about getting a free skill. However, this system could have at least given me a slight description. I have only the name to go off of to guess what they do.

From the notification, he inferred that his skill choice was limited by his current level, so there was a chance that whatever he didn't choose might become available later. Claw Drain sounded like an offensive skill, whereas Hardened Will sounded like a defensive one.

Seeing as Endurance was still his highest base stat, even without having put any stat points into it, he wasn't very keen on the latter. Besides, what would be the point of him being able to take a beating for a longer time? It wouldn't have changed anything in his fight yesterday. No, what he needed was some firepower.

Are you sure you would like to select the skill Claw Drain?
Yes / No

After he selected *Yes*, a set of information entered his head. He knew he would just need to think of the skill name in order to use it, but he needed to know how it worked first.

Claw Drain (Level 1)
Once activated, half of the damage inflicted by the user will be used to recover Health.
The skill will use 15 Energy points.
The skill will last 2 seconds.

This is awesome! Up until now, I could only heal passively by converting Energy into Health. It would be even greater if it had some function to boost my strength like Charging Heart, but that might be a bit much to ask. Still, now I can actually trade blows with my opponents without having to fear hitting 0 Health.

The only downside seems to be the short duration . . . and the Energy cost. If I use Charging Heart and Claw Drain together, that's 25 Energy points, which is nearly a quarter of my overall. Looks like skills, although helpful, really have quite the burden.

Gary wanted to test out his new skill, which was why he had come to the woods in the first place. The only problem was that he was now worried about his Energy. He was already losing it passively, so was it really wise to experiment with it? On the other hand, not experiencing the skill seemed dumb as well.

As he debated whether to test it out, his phone vibrated. Grabbing it from his pocket, he saw a notification about breaking news.

Shit, so this time a college student has been killed, and it says their body was mauled.

Gary had a bad premonition that it was Billy. He put his phone away to try to solve his Energy problem, but at that moment, his secret phone vibrated. He didn't want to make Kai wait, especially after he had helped him recently.

Gary, we need to meet up ASAP and discuss something. It's about Billy!

CHAPTER 56

BILLY'S TARGETS

After reading the message, Gary had worrying thoughts going through his head. Why would Kai bring up Billy now of all times? Had he somehow discovered that all of those recent murders might have been his doing? Or could he have encountered a hairy creature at night and linked the whole mess back to him?

Hang on, if Kai has actually found a lead on Billy, then that would be a great thing! I might finally be able to track him down and stop him before he can do any more harm! Gary thought, pacing up and down in the woods.

He looked at the clock on the phone. It was nearly lunchtime, and although he was only allowed in school for club practice, which would be around three p.m., he just couldn't wait that long. Kai's message sounded pretty urgent, and if he had reached out to him about Billy, then it was vitally important to hear what he had to share.

Gary decided to rush back to school. Although he was still worrying about his Energy, this clearly took precedence, though he refrained from using Charging Heart, as he should still make it in time.

When he arrived at school, it was quiet; the lunch bell hadn't gone off yet. Given his uniform, it was unlikely that someone would report him if they saw him. Even if someone did recognize him, they would likely just think that he had been called in by Principal Young.

After all, who would use the free holiday that was suspension to get back onto school grounds?

Gary hurried through the hallways, trying to avoid any teachers or students who might be around. Everyone was busy with their own thing, but it couldn't hurt being cautious. Right now, he was following Kai's instructions and heading to a certain storage room.

Gary had expected that Kai would call him up to the school's roof, but the bell would be ringing any moment now, and some students went up there to enjoy their lunch. The fact that Kai seemed to care about secrecy in the matter concerning Billy just added to Gary's worries.

He texted Kai that he had arrived and was now pacing up and down in the small storage room. Unfortunately, he could only take four steps before having to turn around. This "room" was basically an oversized supply closet filled with cleaning supplies and toilet paper. A few paces later, the school bell had rung. Students had begun running through the halls, but Kai had yet to reply.

There was a sudden knock on the door. Gary panicked, looking left and right, searching for a hiding spot, but there was none. For once, it didn't seem like any of his werewolf powers were going to help. As the door slowly opened, Gary turned around, stopping his breathing.

"Yeah, you might wanna try that again when you don't have green hair. It sticks out like a sore thumb, and what was the point of turning around? 'If you can't see me, I can't see you.' What are you, five?" Kai held back his laughter as he closed the door behind him. "I knocked to let you know that it was me. I mean seriously, who else could it have been? The only ones visiting this room would be either the janitor or some horny teens looking for quiet time. Do you think either one would have knocked?"

Realizing how stupid he had been, Gary felt a little embarrassed about what had just happened. He brushed off some dust from his clothes. "So, how come you brought up Billy so suddenly? Have you seen him lately? Did he look any different?" Gary asked, changing the subject.

Kai thought it was a pretty strange question, but he decided to tell Gary why he had called him in.

"No, I haven't; otherwise, I would have already reported him to the police. Anyway, just be quiet for a moment and listen to what I have to tell you. Also, try not to panic since it won't help you, and I would like you to help me figure out what to do next," Kai answered, looking into Gary's eyes.

He didn't miss that Gary was gulping just from his warning, so Kai didn't have high hopes about Gary not panicking. However, he couldn't exactly fault him for that. Gary had already tried to reach out to him about Billy, yet Kai had shot him down at the time, believing that Gary had just been looking for trouble.

"You know about all those murders that have been happening on the news lately? Well, I'm convinced that they are Billy's doing. I mean, 'Son goes missing after his mother and father have been found dead, yet doesn't show up despite news outlets stating that police are looking for him' doesn't really take a genius to figure out that unless he's dead, he's the prime suspect. Heck, I think you figured that out when you sent me that text. And if you've watched the reports, you know that one of the murder victims was a high school student like us, whereas the most recent one was a college student . . . and wouldn't you know it, both had connections to our fugitive friend."

Hearing this, Gary felt relieved. He had strongly suspected that Billy was the murderer, yet learning that his victims were people Billy knew meant that at least Gary's family members were likely safe.

"What are the links, and how did you figure all of this stuff out?" Gary asked.

"To be honest, that was a bit of a coincidence. I was actually looking for a link between you and Innu. You remember the new guy that recently joined our gang?" Kai asked, and Gary just nodded. He had only seen their newest gang member once, though, so he wasn't sure what kind of link they could have had. Most importantly, how did Billy fit into all of this? Or the murders, for that matter?

"See, turns out you weren't the only one who received a nice little gift from a secret admirer in the middle of the night. Fortunately, Innu was just as smart as you and let me take care of that problem. As you can imagine, I have no desire to keep sending over people and taking care of such things. So I did a little digging into who exactly would do such a thing. Unlike you, Innu doesn't really have any connection to the Underdogs, nor does he have a beef with any of the other gangs. The only thing I could find that the two of you shared, apart from both being in the same gang now, was that both of you participated in the fighting club.

"You know who else was participating? That's right, Billy . . . and so were his two latest victims. Now, here's where things get interesting. Not only were the murdered high schooler and college student both fighters, but both of them also fought against Billy Buster!"

Knowing that Billy was out for revenge made Gary wonder a number of things.

"So does that mean he's after everyone he ever fought?" Gary asked. "Say, how do you know their names? I don't recall the news mentioning them. Heck, didn't the family of the high schooler even request that his name not be released?"

"Does that really matter now? Just be glad that I did find out and that I discovered the connection. As for your first question, it's not as simple as Billy going after those he fought," Kai replied. "In fact, he seems to be targeting those who beat him!

"I have a feeling that the body parts that the two of you received might have come from his other two victims. I need both of you to be careful. Heck, it might be for the best if the two of you could start hanging out and look after each other."

Since Kai had figured all of this out, Gary started to wonder. Was there actually a way for Billy to track him down? Gary had never found a way, but Billy had somehow found the houses of all of those who had beaten him.

That information had to come from somewhere!

Maybe Billy hadn't found Gary's home because he was a werewolf but had sought him out for revenge. Otherwise, how would he have found Innu's home?

Now Gary knew that Billy was out for more blood, and it looked as if Innu had made it onto the omega's hit list. And all of this . . . was his fault!

All of the people who had died so far had died because he had bitten Billy. On top of that, if Billy could find out where he lived, it certainly meant that the Underdogs could.

Gary hesitated a little before asking the question that was on his mind: "How many people did Billy lose to?"

"Four, including you. Two of whom are already dead, and you can pretty much guess who he had lost against three times, right?"

"Fuck."

CHAPTER 57

GET HIM BEFORE ME!

Now that Gary had learned a bit more from Kai about the other victims, it seemed like Billy had been going through his revenge list in order of those he had lost to. Which meant that Innu was next.

From what I remember, Innu is a strong fighter. He might be able to handle himself in most situations, but that's with a human as his opponent, not against a werewolf, Gary thought. *It's also possible that Billy has gotten stronger because of the moon, like me, and to top that off, he's apparently killed at least four people if we include his parents. Yeah, there's no way Innu will survive that on his own.*

"You're a more caring person than I thought. While that might not be the best quality for your average gang leader, for our little group, it's not exactly bad," Kai said, making Gary flinch, as he had completely forgotten about his role in their little gang.

"Anyway, I think it's for the best if you two start to hang out together. Although Billy seems to go after his victims in the order he lost against them, we have to account for the fact that you got your 'present' before Innu got his. If that's his calling card, then he might be coming for you first. Either way, there's safety in numbers, and at least you know that he's coming after you.

"After your practice, give Innu a call. Let me add his number to your phone. I was going to get you two to meet up with each other more often anyway. Use that time to learn how to cooperate for the next underground fight."

Gary was in the middle of giving his secret phone to Kai when he realized something.

"Come again? What's that about an underground fight?" Gary asked.

"Oh yeah, I never got a chance to tell you, since someone managed to get himself suspended yesterday. Next week our little gang will have their gang debut, and the two of you will be entering in a tag team match against Eton High. Don't worry; it's not on the same day as that rugby match of yours. Who knows, maybe you'll see your opponents out on the field," Kai said casually as he turned toward the door.

Shit, out of all things. I've barely had a single match, never mind with someone else. Heck, it was because of that stupid match in the first place that I ended up turning Billy!

"Wait," Gary called out, stopping Kai before he left. "I wanted to ask you about something."

Kai sighed, as if he knew what the question would be. "Let me guess; you're worried that since Billy found out where the two of you lived, the Underdogs might as well. You don't have to worry about that. It's in my own interest to prevent them from finding you. I've already begun looking into how he found out about you in the first place, and once I do, I will make it impossible for them to do the same."

Although Gary was worried about this also, he was more worried about something else. At least he knew that Billy was only attacking opponents he had lost to, so maybe his family wasn't in any danger, but there was another problem.

"Thank you very much, but I was actually going to ask . . . if you could spot me some money. I used up everything I've earned to help my family pay off some overdue bills, but we got some new ones coming in, so I kind of need some more. It won't be for long; you can just deduct it from whatever we'll earn in that tag team match!"

Kai's hand left the door handle, and he smirked.

"Borrowing money from a gang, now that would be quite troublesome, wouldn't it? Although I would like to say yes, you're not the only one who's a bit short on cash. You see, I never really accounted for having to call for the cleaners, much less having to do it twice in a row. As you can imagine, it's not exactly cheap to get them to work without asking questions, much less to keep it off the record.

"I'm down to what I've earned by betting on you, but those are gang funds. The rest of my cash is tied up with the Underdogs, so there's no way I can access it without someone getting suspicious. You wouldn't want to be borrowing money from an Underdog member, now would you? That could end up being very dangerous.

"If you need cash that badly, try Innu. Otherwise, you'll just have to make do until the tag team match. I promise you'll get a big payday then, as long as you win, of course," Kai said, leaving the room before Gary could say anything else.

Gary didn't have high hopes for Innu. They didn't really know each other, so why should he give him any money? Gary was the gang leader in name only, and they both knew that. Since there wasn't much for him to do, Gary simply decided to stay in the storage room with his thoughts until lunch was over so no one could see him.

In the end, he hadn't figured out anything at all. He had pondered going back to the woods, but then he would just have to get back to school, which seemed like a waste of time and probably Energy. So he decided to just wait out the last two hours before club practice started.

The Bond Mark on Tom was barely visible today, indicating that his best friend was far away, most likely still in the hospital. Gary couldn't imagine how worried his parents must have been after being notified that their boy had been assaulted to that degree.

Then there was Gil. The mark from their Forced Bond was also very weak, so apparently he hadn't come to school either. If Gary were to wager a guess, the bully was also in the hospital, though Gary hoped it wasn't the same one as Tom.

Gary didn't want to see Gil's face very soon again anyway. The only one whose mist had been very noticeable ever since he entered the school grounds was Barry. Gary knew that he had been there when Tom was bullied, so he intended to pay him back.

Eventually, it was time for rugby practice. When Gary arrived, people were actually pleased to see him, most noticeably Mr. Root and Blake. The latter came up to Gary and gave him a friendly handshake and pulled him close. It was something that Gary had only seen very good friends do. It wasn't quite a handshake, nor was it a hug at the same time. To say the least, Gary found it a little awkward.

"What was that?" Gary asked.

"The two of us went through that crap with Eton High together, and honestly, I've been thinking about that day for a while now. Without you, I could have seriously gotten hurt; it might have even ruined my entire rugby career. And I see you're getting better at rugby by the day. I think it will be good if the two of us stay close together."

Before, when interacting with Blake, Gary had shrugged him off, and he was only starting to realize that it was because he had been . . . jealous. The fact that Blake was so perfect had only highlighted how imperfect Gary was. However, now that those on the rugby team had started to accept him, he was realizing that Blake was just a nice guy.

Not everyone was happy to see Gary, though. When Barry saw him and Blake exchange their greeting, his eyebrows furrowed. The strange thing was that Gary seemed to notice and turned around, though Barry also looked away as if avoiding a death stare.

"Are any of the team members still causing you problems?" Blake asked, noting the change in Gary's mood. For a second, Gary considered confiding in him but ultimately decided against it. Even if Blake had the power to punish the two goons who had done that to

Tom, most likely by getting them kicked off the team, that wouldn't satisfy Gary's anger.

"Thanks for the offer, but it's okay; it's nothing that I can't deal with." Gary shook his head, walking past Blake, not even looking at him again but just staring at Barry.

Rugby practice that day was probably the worst performance Gary had ever put on since he had become a werewolf. The main reason was his Energy problem. With no reliable way to replenish it, he hadn't used Charging Heart even once, and he was trying to conserve his Energy as best as he could, which translated poorly for his team.

He might have gotten into trouble, but as it turned out, he wasn't the only one whose performance was subpar. Barry had missed catching the ball a couple of times, fumbling and allowing it to fall to the ground.

After yelling at them all a couple of times, Mr. Root decided to end practice early in hopes that maybe some rest would do them some good. He hoped that by tomorrow, Gil might be back as well. As the others left the field, Gary turned around to stare at Barry again, causing him to flinch.

Barry thought, *Damn it, I couldn't concentrate at all today, and it's all because of him! Gil . . . he's in the hospital, and he was badly beaten. I can't prove it, but it just has to have been that green-haired kid! He may not look the part, but after what he did to Steven, it's clear that he's hiding a few things. I knew we shouldn't have messed with his friend, and look what's happened now. The way he's looking at me, I just know he's going to come after me next.*

In the locker room, everyone was happily getting changed, but Barry had yet to open his locker to change out of his rugby uniform. His hand was visibly shaking as he reached to open it.

That stare . . . I can tell, he's . . . he's going to kill me! If it weren't for the guy saving Gil from his assailant, Gary would have surely killed him! I can't let it end like that! Barry thought as he opened his locker, and inside was a four-inch kitchen knife he had brought from home.

He can't kill me if he's dead!

CHAPTER 58

LOW ON ENERGY

Gary had left as soon as rugby practice was over, following an unexpected message on his secret phone from an unknown number. Given the content of the message, it wasn't hard to figure out who it was, though.

Kai gave me this number and told me to text you. He told me that the two of you have already talked about our little Billy situation and our upcoming tag team match. I'll be waiting here. Innu had attached his location on the map, marking his position.

Honestly, Gary wasn't looking forward to meeting Innu so soon, mainly because he figured that Innu would want to either have a sparring match or just train together. Until he had a way to solve his Energy problem, neither option seemed like a good idea.

52/110 Energy

His Energy points were going down far faster than he had expected, even though he didn't feel like he had actually done much during rugby practice. It seemed as if just staying awake was taking up Energy today.

The primary reason why Gary had decided to meet up with Innu was in hopes of solving this very problem. He intended to follow Kai's suggestion and ask his fellow gang member if he could borrow some money.

Arriving at the location, Gary was surprised to see that it was quite a nice-looking park. There was a large open green field where people were playing football, a set of swings, and some families. It was halfway between Gary's school and Innu's school.

I don't even know what gang runs this part of Slough. Although the Underdogs have most of Slough under their thumb, they don't own all of it; this place is so . . . peaceful, Gary thought, wondering why Innu had asked him to meet up in such a place.

"Over here!" Innu shouted, waving with one hand in his pocket. The first thing Gary noticed was that both of the fighter's hands were still bandaged up. He looked almost exactly the same as when Gary had first seen him in the arena; the only difference was that he was wearing familiar-looking clothes. It took him a moment to recognize them as the gang uniform that Kai had prepared for them.

"What gives? Here I do my best to make myself presentable by wearing our gang outfit, yet our mighty leader isn't wearing the clothes himself?" Gary wasn't sure whether Innu sounded more annoyed or embarrassed about the fact that he was the only one who seemed to have put some thought into this meeting.

"Sorry? I didn't really consider this a gang meeting, and I also just came out of school. Besides, is it really wise to wear our colors so openly? Isn't this like sending a challenge to all the other gangs?" Gary asked.

At this point, Innu couldn't hold it in any longer and let out a big sigh. Someone who was in a gang wasn't supposed to act like that in front of their leader, but the more he interacted with Gary, the more he was convinced that Kai must seriously be pulling his leg about who the actual leader of their gang was.

"As long as the big gangs don't know who we are and who is supporting us, they won't mess with us. They just don't roll that way. Why do you think so many color gangs are able to roam around freely, sporting their colors? Unless it gets pretty serious, those behind them don't usually get involved.

"Second, displaying your colors is the whole point. A gang isn't supposed to show any fear or back down from those around them. If you're serious about starting this gang stuff, then you need to do it right!"

Gary wanted to stop Innu there. This whole creating-a-gang business had never been his idea in the first place. However, explaining to Innu that Kai had practically forced him to act as their leader didn't really seem like it would actually help in this situation.

Innu had already gotten into a fighting stance, pointing for Gary to go opposite him in the large grass field. They weren't even very far away from where the kids were, so the parents could easily see them.

"Really, here?" Gary asked.

"Well, from what I've heard, it's not like we have a hideout yet, so yes, here. Don't tell me you're shy, Green Fang. When I fight, I always intend to win. You're my partner, so I need to see what you've got," Innu explained, and he threw out a kick.

Out of reflex, Gary tried to evade it, but he was too slow and only partially blocked the attack. As soon as it hit, though, he realized how powerful the strike was.

–5 HP

Damn, that hurt, and it didn't feel like he was serious yet. Shit, if I keep losing Health, then my Energy will be used up to heal me once I'm idle, which will just worsen my situation!

Innu didn't give his opponent much time to think and just kept on attacking. Gary couldn't do much but try his best to evade and block, but it was near impossible for him to counter, given his passive fighting style. Thanks to the buffer the moon provided him, Gary's speed was faster than usual, but it was a far cry from using Charging Heart.

After some more of what could only be called one-sided bullying, Innu called off the fight. Gary was very thankful for that, since he was left with merely 31 Energy points, and the pangs in his stomach were getting stronger.

"What's wrong with you? You seem distracted and a little . . . weak?" Innu asked. "Are you that worried about that whole Billy situation?"

Gary shook his head. "No, it's just that I'm exhausted. As I told you, I just came from rugby practice, and these days I can't really afford to eat anything decent. Actually, I was hoping you could—"

"I can't," Innu replied straightaway, not even letting Gary finish his sentence. "Financewise, I'm not exactly in the best situation myself. Otherwise, I would have never ended up joining your gang. If you're really hungry, you'll figure something out; I had to do the same. Whether you need to hunt for food yourself, steal, or whatever, a really hungry person will find a way.

"Being hungry might explain the lack of energy, but not you being distracted. Look, I know Kai said the two of us should look out for each other, but honestly, you just need to look out for yourself. You don't need to worry about me. I don't have time to babysit you. Heck! I beat the guy three times already, and now that I know that he might be after me, I won't mind beating him a fourth time. Maybe I'll even get some sort of reward if I can hand him over to the police."

Gary wanted to say that Billy had changed since then, but there was no way that Innu would believe him if he started talking about werewolves. He would probably consider him crazy on top of being an incompetent leader and fighter.

"Anyway, that was my pep talk. We can meet up and train here before the match. When you have more energy I'll show you a few things you might know about fighting, but you don't know how to fight," Innu said, and he got ready to leave. "Next time, make sure to have more energy! Also, come in uniform, so I won't look like an idiot!"

"Wait!" Gary called out. "If . . . something happens . . . if you happen to see Billy or if you think he's somewhere near you, promise you'll text or call me! I'll be there right away!"

"I already told you, there's no—"

"Please, just tell me!" Gary insisted.

Innu looked into Gary's eyes. He didn't know why it was so important for his leader, but there was more fire in his eyes when he made his request than the whole time the two of them had been fighting.

"Sure, whatever." Innu shrugged and waved goodbye as he walked off.

30/110 Energy
Your Energy is now extremely low
In order to conserve Energy, marks will no longer be visible

Huh? Wait, that was an option? Couldn't you have told me about that earlier? Gary felt a migraine coming up thanks to the system's scheming antics. *Well, it's not as if knowing that would have solved the issue anyway. Looks like I have no choice now. I'm going to have to use the secret stash. I've never felt this pain before.*

The mist from the marks that usually hovered in the air had disappeared. The only good thing was that his Energy was now decreasing at a seemingly lower rate. It seemed like nearly everything the werewolf body did required Energy.

Gary thought about how much meat he had already eaten since he had become a werewolf and, more importantly, how much money it had cost him. He shook his head to think about something else. Gary passed by his school and headed home. The more he thought about food, the hungrier he was getting.

Is . . . is this hunger or is my eyesight worsening as well? . . . No, my sense of smell is also . . . could it be that I'm becoming more normal? Gary checked his menu. Although his Energy points were low, his stats remained unchanged, which was good.

As he walked down the street, Gary pondered whether he should stop by the gym after replenishing his Energy. He had missed yesterday's session, and now that he had increased his base Strength, he was sure he would have to train even more if he wanted to raise it further.

Although his hearing had also suffered, he heard someone coming up from behind. Gary didn't think anything of that. It was still the middle of the day, and he was on a public street. At most, he thought that he might have dallied too long, and someone wanted to pass him. He turned around to let whoever it was pass him, but at that moment, he recognized the guy behind him.

"Barry?" he called out in surprise.

The next second, Barry had closed the distance between the two. Suddenly, Gary felt a familiar pain, a dull ache that continued to worsen, and a warm liquid trickled down his leg.

You have been stabbed!

CHAPTER 59

FIRST KILL

You have been stabbed!

–30 HP

70/100 HP

While your Energy is extremely low, emergency healing function is unavailable!

Replenish your Energy by consuming meat.

You are bleeding!

Your Health will decrease by 4 HP per minute until you're patched up or healed.

Gary didn't need the system to figure out that he had been stabbed; it was a memory that he would probably never be able to forget. The really worrying part was the messages following it. Unless Gary could somehow replenish his Energy to have his system automatically heal the wound, or at least bandage it, he would bleed out and die.

Barry, you damn bastard! Where the hell did you come from, and why did you stab me? First, you hurt Tom, and then you do this? I should just . . . just . . . As he gritted his teeth, his bloodlust was leading him to only one logical conclusion. *I should just kill you!*

Barry looked up, yet instead of looking afraid, Gary was the picture of pure unbridled anger. Barry had expected him to be either screaming, scared, or in shock, but instead, his schoolmate seemed ready to take him along to the next world.

Instinctively, Barry stepped away from him. His hand was still on the knife handle, and he ended up pulling the weapon out. He had never stabbed anyone before, so he himself was still in shock at what he had done.

"I'm sorry, but I don't want to die!" Barry cried out, attempting to stab Gary one more time. However, Gary was already waiting for his attack.

"Screw you!" he thought as he activated Charging Heart.

18/110 Energy

Showing no hesitation, he grabbed the knife before it could stab him again. Gary held it in place with his Strength, even though his hand was now cut.

–5 HP
65/100 HP
A deep cut has appeared on your hand
Your blood loss quickens
–2 HP
63/100 HP

What kind of psycho is he? How can someone just grab onto a knife like that? How isn't he hurt or scared from all that bleeding? "You're a monster!" Barry blurted out.

Not wasting time on talking back to his assailant, Gary swung his fist out. It was too fast for Barry to even see, as Gary hadn't held back. The strike connected with the right side of Barry's head, close to his temple.

His whole body turned, and he nearly fell over. Lacking strength, he let go of the knife in his hand, and Gary kicked it down the alley-way before kicking the bully in the same direction.

"Why . . . did I even try . . . why did I even think about getting that marking off!" Gary muttered, yet it seemed more as if he was speaking to himself than to Barry. He knelt down and punched Barry in the head once more, leaving the larger teenager dazed. Gary's punches were harder than anything he had ever received, even though he had actually seen and had his fair share of fights.

Barry soon found himself being dragged deeper into the alleyway, pulled by the hoodie he had worn not to get recognized immediately by passersby. He didn't know why Gary was doing it, but whatever his reasoning was, it couldn't be good for him. Desperate to get out of this situation, Barry looked for anything that might help. He found a brick on the ground and quickly picked it up.

Gary was still busy dragging Barry along, so he was surprised when he suddenly jumped up and smashed him in the head with a brick.

−10 HP
51/100 HP
Your skull is partially fractured
Congratulations! After repeatedly taking a beating your body has grown stronger.
Don't get used to this, though; you might lose some brain cells.
Endurance +1

Unsurprisingly, Gary let go of Barry. For a moment he saw black, and by the time he recovered, he only saw the back side of Barry running away. Following an instinct, he immediately started to run after his target. After closing the distance, he leapt into the air and landed on Barry's shoulders, causing him to fall and smash his head on the ground. He quickly turned him over; Barry was now pinned by the weight of his knees but was too weak and had no energy to try to lift Gary off him anyway.

"What the fuck is wrong with you? Not only did you torture Tom to the point he had to go to the hospital, you freaking stabbed me in broad daylight and tried to bash my head in! All because your stupid friend might have to sit on the bench!" Gary shouted at Barry as he held him down. He no longer cared about what would happen to him.

He wasn't using fists; instead, he was attacking Barry as if his hands were made from claws. His nails had ripped through Barry's school uniform and were now piercing his chest. His skin was being ripped off as he continued to scream in pain.

"*Stop! Help!* A monster . . . he's a monster!" Barry could only pray that someone would hear his cries for help.

"Did you stop when Tom asked? If it's my life or a scumbag's like yours, I'll easily take yours!" Gary shouted as he lifted his hand once more.

"Police, put your hands up and get off him!" a man shouted.

Gary could tell that the voice was coming from in front of him, but instead of listening to the police officer, he pulled up his hood and ran back into the alleyway.

The middle-aged police officer ran forward; he wanted to chase the culprit, but it was obvious that the person on the ground needed first aid and an ambulance right away, and it might even be too late by the time they arrived.

"This is Chief of Police Anton Millstun, reporting in. We have an assault suspect heading down the 163rd Street alleyway. Need an ambulance sent to my location ASAP."

Anton could see that the kid's chest wounds were deep, and the markings looked as if they were made by claws. It didn't look like something a normal human would be able to accomplish.

That was when he noticed that the boy was mumbling something under his breath.

"It's okay, conserve your energy. The ambulance is on the way," Anton said.

Listening carefully, he could just make out what the boy was saying.

"M-monster . . . monster . . ."

Was it an Altered? Anton wondered.

Running through multiple alleyways as fast as he could, Gary was still bleeding out and, making matters worse, his Energy was still incredibly low. His Charging Heart had also run out, and he thought he at least had made it far enough to get away from the police officer.

Stupid police! Only there when you don't freaking want them to be . . . why don't they go and stop some real criminals for a change! Gary cursed as he leaned against a wall and applied pressure to his wound.

"Crap!" he shouted in pain. *What do I do now? I was going to . . . I was going to . . . What was I going to do?*

Then it hit him.

Was I really just about to eat another person to replenish my Energy? If the cop hadn't stopped me . . .

Gary shuddered at that thought. Not being able to move much, and with his Energy about to hit 0, he didn't have many options left. He was far from home, not even sure where exactly he had run off to.

Suddenly he heard a squeaking sound. Squinting, he made out the shape of several rats that had scurried over to him, curious as to what was in front of them.

"I'm so . . . hungry," Gary mumbled, and when one of the rats got within reach, he immediately grabbed it.

The struggling rat bit down on Gary's finger.

"I . . . deserve that for what I'm about to do . . . I'm sorry, little guy, but I need to live."

+10 Energy

CHAPTER 60

THE HUNTING TARGET

Gary wasn't sure how many times he had to close his eyes and just continue chewing, but eventually, the message that he had been waiting for finally arrived.

Your Energy has been fully restored
110/110 Energy

The alleyway had been filled with rats, and after he consumed the first one, his Energy started to be replenished, allowing him to catch more. Three rats later, his emergency healing finally kicked in, though it meant that he would have to eat even more of the rodents.

On the plus side, his wounds had started to heal as if by magic, but what he had done, what he had eaten to get to this point, felt like a distant memory in his mind.

The taste of the rats themselves had actually been far better than he had anticipated, though he had the feeling that this was thanks to him being part werewolf now. He was sure if he were still a complete human, he would have thought very differently. Nevertheless, they had the same ironlike taste that he had begun to enjoy in the steaks he had been purchasing from the convenience store.

Daily Quest complete
Eat 2 kilograms of meat
285/460 Exp

Walking out of the alleyway, Gary used his enhanced senses to check if anyone was following him, but so far, he seemed safe. However, he had to do something about his clothes. They were a bloody mess, not least of all because of his impromptu snacks.

Blood is so hard to get out of a white shirt . . . yeah, I'll have to dump this one. There's no way in hell I can get the stench of rat entrails out of it. I'm going to have to buy a new one. Here I tried so hard to save that emergency money and yet I'm still going to have to use it, Gary lamented.

For the time being, he kept the uniform with him as he needed to find some way to dispose of it discreetly later, preferably somewhere far, far away from his fight with Barry. He still hadn't figured out what to do with his other clothes that were covered in blood from the construction site, and he had no desire to have a closet full of evidence.

The taste of those rats . . . They weren't that bad, and it's cheaper than buying meat. Still, the thought of what he had just done was making him feel quite sick. It was then that he heard some pigeons flying above.

I suppose it doesn't have to be rats necessarily. It should also work with other things, right? If I can keep up my Energy without having to spend money, and if it stops me from . . . Gary didn't want to finish that thought. He changed into his rugby uniform, placed the bloody clothes in his bag, and headed home. He decided against going to the gym for now, and he wasn't sure he would go there after dropping off his bag at home.

The good news was that Gary not only had replenished his Energy but had also essentially solved his problem of how to get a free food supply. At least for the coming days, he could test out his new skill and more, but there was still the problem with Barry.

Will he say anything to the cops? I mean, he was the one who stabbed me. Everything I did was pretty much just self-defense. If he tells the truth, he'll get in trouble too."

After he got home and spent some time with his mother and sister, this thought made it hard for him to fall asleep. Eventually, he saw a familiar message as the clock hit midnight.

Your bloodlust grows
5 days until the next full moon

Earlier in the day, Anton Millstun had stayed behind to investigate the crime scene. More police had arrived to help him while the ambulance treated the injured high schooler before taking him to the hospital.

After reporting what he had witnessed, the chief of police left his subordinates to gather clues while he went to the hospital, hoping to talk to the victim. Despite the late hour, he waited for the boy to wake up.

In the hallway, a young police officer named Roo Game walked up to Anton with a few files in his hand, but he had a worried look as he approached.

"Just tell me what it is." Anton sighed and waved to Roo to hurry up.

"Yes, sir. Unfortunately, it seems like we will have to hand over the case to White Rose. We tested the weapon that was found at the scene for fingerprints. It appears that the person we apprehended isn't the victim but actually the assailant. However, we have also found the blood of what we can only assume to be the actual victim.

"The blood spatter report states that the injured boy most likely stabbed the suspect you scared away. Now here's where things get interesting. While we don't have the suspect's identity in the database, we do have his blood on record. Remember the gang members we found at the construction site? Well, the blood matches up. Whoever that person is, he was at the construction site on that day."

Anton let out an even bigger sigh because he now understood why White Rose would grab this case. If the blood matched up, it was most likely the same Altered who had killed the gang members that had attacked the high schooler.

"What about Billy Bruntin? He's a high school student, and his last two victims were teenagers. Is there any possible link to him?" Anton asked.

"Not that we are aware of. We have Billy's suspected DNA on file that we recovered from his home. White Rose has made a forensics check, but his DNA wasn't found at the construction site or near the alleyway or the other cases. It seems these are two separate Altered killing cases."

Shaking his head, Anton wondered what the world was coming to.

"Thanks, Roo. Report this to White Rose, and while you're at it, try to look for some links between the two. I know that there hasn't been anything so far, but with the fact that these are both high school students and have had run-ins with suspected Altereds, I have a feeling this whole thing is connected."

Just then they heard sounds of panic not too far away. A nurse came rushing out of the room and quickly brought a doctor back with her.

Even more panic started to ensue, and they wondered just what was going on. Inside the hospital room, Barry was shaking. His whole body seemed to be undergoing some type of fit, and foam was coming out of his mouth.

Not too long after, someone received a notification.

Congratulations, you have successfully hunted your first marked! Quest reward: Additional stat points

"Huh?"

CHAPTER 61

A DEAL

This was the second night that Tom had to stay in the hospital. Following the advice of their school nurse, Tom had gone to the emergency room, and given his situation, he didn't have to wait for long. He had quickly been assigned a private room, though he ended up having to sleep there Monday night since the surgeon didn't have a gap to get to him.

Tom didn't mind that. The hospital staff had given him enough painkillers that he easily slept until Tuesday morning. When he woke up, he saw that he had seventeen missed calls from his mother and nine more from his father. At some point, his father had messaged him that the hospital had already informed them where he was and that they would be with him this evening.

With a few more hours to go until his dental surgery, Tom had browsed the web via his phone. The first thing he searched for was recent news. He half closed his eyes as he read the headlines, expecting to see Gary's name or headlines reading *Werewolf Caught*, but there was none of that, just news about Billy.

His surgery was rather uneventful. From what he had been told, implanting a new tooth was a rather routine procedure, and they had also taken care of the cuts in his mouth.

I wonder how Gary is coping. Where did he run off to after leaving me at the nurse's office? I'm seriously worried. I mean, if he ever found out who did this to me, there's a good chance he could . . . Tom gulped. *Kill them.*

At that moment, his parents burst into the room, looking worried.

"Tom, how are you feeling? Did the surgery go well? Let's see that beautiful smile of yours," his mother called out as she rushed to his bedside. She hugged him to the point that Tom had trouble breathing. He tapped his mother on the shoulder, asking her to release him.

She pulled back and allowed Tom to give her a shy smile. It had been a while since he had seen his parents, so it was a bit saddening that he had to be in the hospital for them to find the time. They were still wearing their white lab coats, indicating that they had rushed over from work to visit.

Holly and James Green were living embodiments of what one pictured when hearing the word *scientist*, including the thick black glasses on their faces. Tom's mother was blond and rather good-looking. Her son sometimes lamented that he apparently got his looks more from his father than his mother, including his brown hair, which was hard to see given his haircut.

James Green wasn't bad looking, but he wouldn't exactly be described as handsome either, which sometimes made Tom wonder how his father had managed to get his mother. His pet theory was that among all the other scientists, he was probably the best-looking one.

They must have even asked for time off to visit me, Tom thought with a guilty conscience. Both of them worked in a Tier 2 city. Because of the long drive, they didn't always come back every day.

"Tom, your father and I have been talking about your situation. We've decided that it would be for the best if we move you from Slough to Brocknell."

It took Tom a second to comprehend what his mother had just said. It was one of the many possibilities he had thought his mother would say when she found out. Although he wouldn't mind seeing his parents more often, it wasn't a given that would actually happen. From what he had heard, their company actually had sleeping rooms for their personnel.

"We can sell the house and all move into a nice apartment in Brocknell. We're not too far off from completing our big project. With the bonus we will receive and our contracts being up for renewal soon, we'll be able to afford a place that is just as nice as this one and move you to a new school. It will be much safer there." Her approach was gentle, but Tom had already prepared what he would say to that.

"You know that's not true, Mom! It's only safer on the surface," Tom replied, looking into her eyes to stress that he wasn't having any of this. He understood that his parents were just trying to look out for him. "There are even bigger gangs in the upper-tier cities; you know that! It's just more behind the scenes. Besides, Westbridge is plenty safe. Something like this has never happened to me before; it was just a onetime incident! I was just at the wrong place at the wrong time!"

Tom tried his best to downplay the situation, since he honestly didn't know what would happen the next time he met the bullying duo. He didn't want to leave his school, and most of all, he didn't want to leave his best friend behind. He had never liked talking to people, but somehow Gary had made it seem less bothersome, making him treasure their friendship all the more.

There was a time in Tom's life when he had needed someone, yet his parents had been too busy with work, and his teachers didn't seem approachable, so the only one he had been able to rely on had been Gary. Now that his best friend was struggling with a supernatural problem, he couldn't leave him to his own devices. He somehow had to convince his parents to let him stay in school.

"Even if it was a onetime thing, the important point is that it *did* happen, which means it could very well happen again. We've already been notified that you have refused to say who exactly did that to you, so how can we believe that this was merely a onetime thing?

"We live in a good part of Slough, so we're lucky to not be affected by what's been going on, but at the same time, we can't bear to be away from you and allow such a thing to repeat. As if that weren't enough, we've heard about the recent high school student killings! That alone would be enough reason for us to pull you out of this place!"

His mother made good points; better than her son did for wanting to stay in this dangerous town. It seemed she had already made up her mind, which meant there was only one person who could help him win over his mother.

Although he lost more times than not, once in a while, his father managed to come through.

"Dad, I get good grades; I have good friends and even my teachers somewhat like me. If I get put into a different environment, it could really affect me, and this year I'll have my SATs. I can't afford to fail! Don't you two always talk about how compromise is often important for your experiments and research? Isn't there a way we can compromise?" Tom pleaded.

His mother was more than a little annoyed that Tom had decided to ask his father for help. Nevertheless, she also knew that her son only did so when he regarded something as very important. His father, who had been quite calm during their visit so far, placed a hand on his wife's shoulder.

"We can compromise and allow you to stay until the end of this school year," his father offered. "By that point, we should have finished with our project, so we will be ready to move you out once you get your test results. You can't say we are affecting your studies then, can you?"

It was clear from his mother's demeanor that she wanted to argue that a school year was too long. Tom knew his parents well enough to recognize that this was the best offer he would get out of them.

"Deal!"

I just hope that time will be enough for us to figure out what to do with Gary's condition. How and when am I supposed to tell him I'm leaving, though?

After this, the Green family ended up talking about a few other things like school, whether Tom had perhaps found a girl he liked, and how things were with Gary. Eventually, his mother left the room to talk to the doctor and sort out a few things, like the cost of the private room.

"Dad, you said your research is about Altered beings, right? You must have seen a lot of them, but have you ever seen an Altered based on a wolf?" Tom asked when it was just him and his father.

His father thought about it for a moment.

"Now that you mention it, I haven't so far. Many of them resemble some type of dog breed but not a wolf per se. Still, with so many types out there, and with new ones getting discovered every so often, I don't doubt that there is one. Maybe not what we think of, since they're based on animals that don't seem to come from our world, but at least something resembling our wolf. Although when I say the words 'wolf' and 'Altered' together, it just makes me think of werewolves." His father started to chuckle softly.

Tom joined him, only his chuckle was more due to nervousness. He wondered how his friend was coping.

Gary had still been unable to get any sleep. Pulling his sheets over his head hadn't really helped. After getting the notification, he had come to a realization. He pulled his sheets down and looked around. He could see the vague outline of a red mist and a green one, but that was it. The other marking was no longer there; he could no longer see it.

I-I . . . I killed him . . .

CHAPTER 62
KILL AGAIN

If I can't find a way to get rid of this marking in six days' time, Gil could be in serious trouble. Whoa, what the hell just happened?

His body suddenly started to feel stronger. His muscles bulged for a few seconds, and his insides started to adjust before relaxing again. It was a similar feeling to when Gary distributed his stat points, so he immediately checked his system screen.

Name: Gary Dem
Level 4
Exp: 385/460
Health: 100/100
Energy: 110/110
Strength 7
Dexterity 4
Endurance 10

The first thing Gary saw was that he had gained 100 Exp points. As for his stats, one thing had improved among them all, and that was his Dexterity.

After successfully hunting a target, a single stat point has randomly been allocated

Reading the notification, Gary understood what had happened. Still, he wondered if the stat could go into Health or Energy. If it couldn't, then it was better to put the stat points he'd earned by leveling up and put them toward Health or Energy.

While he was checking out his system, Gary saw another notification screen.

Marks: 2/5

Although you have successfully hunted your first target, you didn't eat him!

In order to grow stronger, consume your hunting targets for additional stat points!

At first, Gary was just happy about receiving additional strength. His goal was to get stronger so he could help his family, but then he realized what had happened and whose marking had disappeared. Everything was starting to make sense. The system message had explained it to him. It could only be one person.

Gary pulled the sheets back over his head, shaking at the thought.

I ended his life, his life. *He won't live to see tomorrow. He won't ever think or feel again.* Gary tried to reason with himself. *But he tried to kill me! It could have easily been me not seeing the next day. He actually stabbed me, that . . . that bastard stabbed me!* Thinking about this, Gary tensed his fist. The more he repeated the scene in his head, the angrier he got.

Images appeared from when he was in the alleyway, of Gary on top of Barry, having pinned him to the ground, before the police officer had interrupted him. Gary saw himself digging into Barry and eating his flesh.

If you were going to die anyway, you could have at least let me eat your flesh. What a waste of Energy and probably stat points as well.

At this lapse in thought, Gary pulled the bedsheets off his head.

What was that? Why did I just think like that? I . . . I don't feel like myself anymore. It's like another personality is inside me, trying to get out! Gary was sweating.

"Arghh!" he moaned, pulling the sheets toward him and ripping them slightly with his fingernails. He'd killed someone, and he didn't even feel bad about it. He didn't understand what was going on.

"Gary . . . is everything okay?" his sister asked, rubbing her eyes. "You're covered in sweat. Did you have a bad dream or something?"

A bad dream. Gary wished it were all a bad dream, but for some reason, seeing his sister next to him had calmed him down. He chucked the strange thoughts he was having to the back of his mind. He couldn't let his sister see him like that.

Amy got up and started to rummage through the drawer by her side, eventually pulling out what looked like a pendant. She walked over from her bed to Gary's, and he flinched a little. It was a strange reaction, but his sister wasn't scared, and she slowly placed the pendant around his neck.

"I want you to have this. I realized the other day that you have a lot on your mind, and for you to act out like that at school and have trouble sleeping, you must be under a lot of stress.

"When I have exams and stuff, I just hold on to this pendant and start thinking about Dad. It's the only thing I have left from him. I think you need it more than I do right now."

Gary wasn't sure what Amy had done. Placing the strange pendant over him felt like a magic spell. All his worries were disappearing. He wasn't sure if it was a placebo effect or just because it had come from his sister.

"This was from Dad. I can't take this," Gary said, attempting to pull it off, but she pushed his hand away.

"Please, I need some sleep, so wear the damn thing." Amy returned to her bed, pulled her sheets up, and went back to sleep.

This small interaction with his sister had cleared his mind, but it didn't let him escape from the reality of what he had done. As tried to get some shut-eye, his sensitive ears picked up on something else.

It sounded like someone was sobbing. Looking to his left and seeing that his sister was fast asleep, Gary got up and headed toward the noise. His mother was sitting in the kitchen at the dining table with a bunch of bills in front of her. She was rubbing her face as if she was highly stressed out.

Suddenly a shadow fell over the papers, and she looked up and noticed Gary had something in his hand.

"Take it, Mom, it's money. I've been saving up for a long time, doing things here and there, coming up with business ideas with Tom," Gary said. He'd tried to come up with a better lie, but in the end he couldn't.

His mother looked at the money in Gary's hand. There were a lot of bills, no small amount for a high schooler. "Gary, we're okay—"

"We're not," Gary replied. "Amy and I both know we are not okay. We know how hard you work, Mom. I've always wanted to help. Now's not the time to be stubborn. If we can't pay some of these bills, we'll have to move. So just take the money," Gary said, leaving it on the table and walking back to his room.

He had learned something from Amy. If someone refuses to take something, then just give it to them and run away before they can object.

"Gary," his mother called out. "Thank you."

As he got back into bed, Gary realized something. His sister and mother were his motivation for doing everything he had done. He needed to make money to protect his family from the Underdogs.

Damion and the others had killed plenty; of course they had. Gang members in the area killed people every day. They didn't hesitate, and these were the type of people he was up against.

There's a good chance that at some point I may need to kill again, and if it's for the sake of protecting my family, I'll do it in a heartbeat, Gary told himself.

What Gary didn't know was that this scenario would arrive far sooner than he thought. Outside, a figure stood in the smog staring up at Gary's apartment building.

CHAPTER 63

ALTERNATIVE

Gary still had three days of suspension left, which meant that today was another day that he was technically free to do as he wished until rugby practice, while everyone else his age was stuck in school. Most kids would have enjoyed this time off, yet he couldn't.

For one, Gary didn't want to worry his mother, so he had to keep up the ruse that everything was fine by leaving for school. However, even if that hadn't been the case, he had far too much on his agenda to be sitting around watching TV.

There was still so much for him to figure out about the Werewolf System. Barry's mark might be gone, but there was still the one he had placed on Gil just two days ago. Judging by the direction of both remaining marks, it appeared that Gil and Tom had already gone to school today.

Then there was still the omega wolf on the loose, but if the police were still looking for him, Gary would have a hard time finding him too. After yesterday's run-in with the police, going after Billy was even riskier. He had been stabbed by the deceased bully, so his blood had been left all over the scene. If they hadn't been looking for him before, they would surely do so now that Barry had died.

Gary was lucky that he had no criminal record, so they didn't have his DNA on file. However, if he ever did get taken in as a suspect, it would be easy enough to match his DNA with the other two events.

If he became a criminal, he could help no one. The better option was to look out for Innu and just wait for Billy. Not really knowing much about Innu, though, all he could do was hope he texted Gary if he got in trouble.

For the first time this week, Gary was making his way to the gym. The last two days, he had been unable to go there. Monday, he had encountered the Altered Hunter, and yesterday he had been stabbed. He was also eager to test how his extra Strength translated in terms of power.

Gary noticed the questioning looks he received from the other gym goers. They seemed to wonder why a high schooler was there this early in the morning. Some thought he was skipping school, while others gave him the benefit of the doubt and assumed his school started late, yet in the end, nobody bothered him. All of them seemed to agree that it was better for Gary to be here than to roam the streets.

He followed the system's instructions while reminding himself what he had learned today. *I know now that I can gain additional stat points for successfully hunting a mark even when it isn't the full moon. I only got a single point, but I would have gotten more if I had eaten him as well . . .*

I have no idea whether Billy also has a system, but if he gets stronger the same way I do, then he must have gotten a lot stronger after eating his victims. There's a good chance that he'll be as strong as me if not more so using Charging Heart. I have to find a way to close that gap by playing with my system!

Daily Quest complete
5 Exp received
390/460 Exp

Gary received the notification after his last rep. He took a quick shower before heading to a nearby park. It wasn't the same one Innu had called him to, but this one was closer to his apartment, and most importantly, it contained a forest.

Gary was completely broke after giving his mother his emergency fund, though he would do it again in a heartbeat if it meant that they wouldn't have to move away.

I just hope that winning that tag team match will pay as well as the fight against Billy. Until then, I have to make sure I don't go crazy from this continuous loss of Energy. Whether I like it or not, I'll have to go feral on some animals.

His second Daily Quest required him to consume two kilograms of meat a day. Thanks to yesterday's unexpected meal, Gary now knew that the system didn't care where it came from or how processed it was. In fact, he started to suspect that it had been goading him toward going out to hunt all along.

The thought of eating wild animals was still somewhat gross, but it was far better than the alternative. It also had the benefit of keeping down his bloodlust, so he wouldn't try going for something bigger. He was here today because rats weren't exactly on the top of his "to eat" list, even if they hadn't tasted that bad.

It didn't take long for Gary to find a squirrel running through the forest. His first attempt to catch it failed completely. Not used to this sort of thing, he stepped on a branch, alarming the critter. Seeing that his stealth approach had failed, he immediately sprinted toward it, but the small creature was faster and closer to a tree, which it promptly climbed.

Climbing a tree would have probably been impossible for the old Gary, but thanks to his stats, it was easy enough now. Unfortunately, his transformation hadn't made him an expert tree climber overnight. He followed his prey, but by the time he climbed to where the squirrel had been, it had already leapt to a nearby tree.

Gary didn't want to give up yet. He memorized the scent of the squirrel and waited for it to get down again. After widening the distance between them, the squirrel was on the ground, foraging for food. This time, Gary made sure not to alarm it, but alas, when he tried to snatch it at the last second, the squirrel somehow sensed him and hopped onto Gary's arm, then onto his shoulder, and fled to another nearby tree for safety.

That was the second time he failed.

Unsure what he could do better, Gary decided to try his luck with another animal. In the forest, most of the pigeons stayed up in the tree branches, but others remained on the ground. Regardless, the same thing happened. The second Gary got close, his feet would cause the leaves to rustle, scaring them away.

He knew he had to decide on a different approach. This time, Gary decided to climb up high in one of the trees. He looked for a strong branch and waited . . . and waited . . . and waited . . . until the pigeons had gathered on a tree not too far away.

Damn, so I really have to act like one of those animals who are out hunting on those TV shows, huh?

He crept slowly along the tree branch. It started to bend slightly under his weight, which made him worry. Still, he kept his eyes on the one pigeon that looked at him, bobbing its large head backward and forward.

Just stay still, you stupid bird! Gary cursed in his head.

That was when the bird started to move.

No! I waited too long for this to fail!

Skill activated: Charging Heart
All stats have temporarily been doubled
–10 Energy

With all of his stats doubled, he leapt through the air. The birds scattered, flying from the other tree branch. At this moment Gary was fearless, and he just wanted to catch one of these damned flying rats after trying for so long. He reached for the bird, but it was already out of range.

Something inside him was telling him that there was a way. Images he had seen while researching werewolves came to mind: their large clawlike hands.

Skill activated: Claw Drain
–15 Energy

His fingers started to extend slightly, and his nails grew slightly larger and sharpened. Gary managed to cut the pigeon's belly open, his nail slicing through it easily, and it tumbled to the ground.

Oh, that hurt a bit, Gary thought, but at the same time, he had done it.

Was I . . . imagining things? His hand seemed to have gone back to normal, but he was sure it had happened.

Well, I suppose I should have figured that a skill called Claw Drain *would do something like this, but would it have killed you to maybe mention it in the skill description, you stupid system? Thank God I didn't try it out in the middle of a fight. I can't exactly be using this in public like Charging Heart, now can I?*

There was another problem. Although he had finally managed to kill a pigeon, he had been forced to use both of his skills to do it. If even a rat had only been good enough to replenish around 10 Energy points, he doubted the pigeon would be much better.

I guess until I get faster, it's back to the rats for me . . . Will it help if I use some condiments, or will that just make matters worse?

Just then the secret phone in Gary's pocket started to vibrate. To his surprise, the sender wasn't Kai this time, and even more baffling was the content of the message.

I found him.

CHAPTER 64

BRING IT ON!

Gary immediately asked for more information. He needed to know whether Innu had actually run into Billy or simply found him. Unfortunately, he didn't get an answer. His message wasn't even marked read, which worried him.

Not knowing anything about his fellow gang member, Gary texted the only person who could explain: Kai. When he asked where Innu might be, the answer was so obvious that Gary was ready to facepalm. As if anticipating the follow-up question Gary was about to type, Kai sent the location of Innu's school.

Gary munched on the pigeon and was surprised to see a notification that he had regained 10 Energy points. Running through the forest with the help of Charging Heart, he was able to grab an unsuspecting squirrel. Before the critter even had a chance to struggle, Gary squeezed tightly. A few moments later, Gary had learned that a squirrel helped him regain 6 Energy points.

83/110 Energy

Gary would have loved to regain even more Energy, but he couldn't waste any more time. He knew that this one squirrel was just a fluke and that he couldn't gamble on being so lucky again. So he used Charging Heart to get to Innu's school faster.

He wasn't sure if he could afford to use the skill again since he would need as much Energy as possible to fight Billy, yet at the same time, if he was late, the omega wolf might escape . . .

This is it . . . I'm really going to face Billy . . . I thought I would be more scared meeting him, but for some reason, all I feel is . . . excitement? Gary thought just as the Charging Heart skill had run out, and he activated it once more.

73/110 Energy

Meanwhile, the reason for Innu not answering wasn't that Billy had attacked him. He also wasn't ignoring Gary; no, it was something far more mundane. His teacher had caught him using his phone in the middle of class, so he had confiscated it.

The teacher didn't care that Innu, like many other students in his class, wasn't actually paying attention to his math lesson; he had a zero-tolerance policy regarding phones. It was one of the many schools in the area where students who were deemed "a lost hope" were sent.

I did what he asked, I sent him a text so he can't go nagging me, but he's really here, huh? Looks like Kai is right. He's after me, but why did he seem so different? Innu wondered.

This morning, on his way to school, he had noticed a large figure by the gate for a brief second, but by the time he turned around, nobody was there. The students nearby hadn't cared, but Innu had found it strange since the figure hadn't been walking into or out of the school, just standing there on the sidewalk staring straight ahead.

It had been too short a time frame, but Innu could have sworn that underneath the hood had been none other than Billy. What was more, he seemed to have a creepy smile on his face.

What's your game, Billy? After your last stunt, do you want to try to scare me by showing me that you know what school I go to? Or are you going to jump me after? Whatever you bring, I'll take you on.

Gary's white school shirt had gotten bloody yesterday, he wasn't wearing his school uniform. There was, of course, his blazer, but he hardly ever wore that. Going near other schools wearing your own blazer was a sign of trouble.

A lot of the schools were influenced by the gangs in the area, and eventually, the bad kids in school had started to imitate them, believing that belonging to one school was like belonging to a gang.

The good thing was that it had practically become second nature for Gary to travel with his trusted hoodie. This time he had opted for one that was even darker than his usual one, because this time he was planning to go hunting.

It didn't take long for Gary to reach Innu's school, and his immediate opinion was that it looked like more of a dump than his place.

This must be one of the schools Mom kept warning us about, that we would end up in if we didn't study, Gary thought as he walked right in. There wasn't even a teacher there to stop him; the only person out on the field appeared to be a janitor, yet he didn't say anything as Gary walked past him.

Shit, Innu must still be in class. Kai only sent me the school address, but not what class he would be in. Seems like he doesn't know either. Well, I don't hear any noise, so that should at least mean that Billy still hasn't done anything outrageous so far . . .

Gary sniffed the air, hoping to catch some type of foreign scent, but since he was in a school, the area was riddled with unknown scents. It was impossible for him to isolate Billy in particular like that.

If I'd known I would have to hunt him down, I would have tried to memorize his stupid scent. He's a frigging werewolf like me now, so why can't I get some help via the system? Looks like I have no choice but to rely on my eyes instead.

As he walked past the classrooms, he could see just how out of hand the school actually was.

He thought about his mother and how much she had pushed for him and Amy to go to a good school in Slough. Although, more so for Amy's sake, he understood. If Amy went to a school like this, then Gary would probably be getting into fights every day.

Eventually he reached his destination: the school roof. He quickly ran up to the fence on the edge, looking down to try to spot anything that looked out of place.

"Who are you? I haven't seen you before!" a voice said from behind.

Turning around, Gary saw a student smoking a cigarette. He looked to be slightly older than Gary, and for some reason, he was sporting a pompadour, a hairstyle that was clearly out of fashion, yet he was quite well built for his age.

What the hell is it with high schoolers these days? Has someone been handing out steroid-infused candies, and I was just absent that day?

"I'm just trying to find someone. Once I do, I'll be out of your hair," Gary replied.

"Well, it's clear you're not from around here; otherwise, you would have known that this is my spot!" the student shouted, and Gary suddenly felt a strong blow to his side.

–8 HP

Did that guy just hit me? What is wrong with him?

"This is my place, bitch!" he cursed at Gary, yet the werewolf was in no mood for games. This person was not the one he needed to face.

At that moment, something happened that hadn't happened in a long time; Gary's heart rate was rising in anger, so much so that it had crossed the 150 BPM mark without the need for him to use Charging Heart.

Meanwhile, the bell was about to ring for lunch. Lifting his head, yawning and stretching, Innu saw someone in the hallway through the window in the classroom door. It was the same large hooded figure.

What the fuck is he doing in school—

Before Innu could finish his thought, Billy threw his fist right at the glass window. Like in a movie, he smashed through it with a single hit and shards flew everywhere, and the students covered their faces and screamed as Billy charged in.

"Ha ha." Innu smiled, wiping blood off his forehead, as a piece of glass had managed to scratch him. "Bring it on!"

CHAPTER 65

DOUBLE TROUBLE

Perhaps if Gary had been paying more attention, he would have never allowed the other student to get a hit in that easily. The most surprising thing to Gary was how much it hurt.

Endurance had always been his strongest stat, and it had increased twice during his recent fights. On top of that, he had the power of the moon helping him, yet that one strike had taken off nearly as much Health as Barry's brick attack.

"I'm surprised someone like you is still standing after a hit to the side like that," the boy, whose name was Austin, scoffed. "I knew you had to be someone special to just walk into our school like that!"

Gary was ready to show this arrogant kid the real meaning of pain, but just then both of them heard screams coming from inside the school. Concentrating on his hearing, Gary located the source of the sound.

Austin was momentarily distracted by the screams, and when he turned back around, the strange boy was running straight at him.

"Get out of my way!"

Austin was known as the top dog at his school. He had been fearless when he came here, facing every person who was willing to challenge him to a fight, but then there was an incident with a certain transfer student.

Something had told him that fighting that person would be too dangerous, and now for the second time in his life, he had the same feeling about this stranger.

This is impossible! Austin thought as he threw a punch, aiming to hit the strange boy right in the face.

In the classroom, some of the students tried to make a run for it after Billy forced his way in, while others remained but now stood toward the back of the classroom.

Even the damn teacher ran off, not that I can blame him . . . Did this guy have a growth spurt since the last time I saw him? Innu wondered.

Billy certainly had grown in size. He had always been large for his age, but even his 4XL clothes didn't seem to fit him, as his belly was sticking out through his shirt.

"What is this pig doing in our class?" one of the students yelled. He was part of this class's delinquent trio. Ever since he had transferred here from Eton High, he had laid low. There was no reason for him to waste time fighting a bunch of delinquents and wannabe gangsters. They just weren't on his level.

However, they didn't cause Innu any trouble because of one guy: Austin Foster. Austin had claimed reign over the whole school. The two of them had met only once. They had stared at each other, but eventually Innu just shrugged and went past him.

Austin was the only person that Innu suspected had some type of fighting skill, but challenging him and potentially winning against him sounded like too much of a hassle. He had no desire to run this school, not after being betrayed by his "friends" in Eton High.

If only my tag team partner in the match were someone like him, we might actually place highly in the tournament. Someone like him has the aura of a real leader. No idea what Kai sees in that Green Fang guy . . .

While Innu was thinking these things, the trio went in for an attack against Billy. The other students smirked, excited that they were about to witness a good beating, thinking that the pig deserved it after scaring them like this.

However, before the first student could hit him, Billy grabbed the incoming fist. With his free hand, the oversized intruder punched his attacker's forearm, and a devastating crack resounded throughout the classroom, followed by a blood-chilling scream.

It looked so effortless, but it was obvious to everyone that the student's bones were broken. The other two, who were now close to Billy, had successfully landed a punch each, but they were unable to reach his head because Billy was too big.

They had aimed for his stomach instead, expecting to hit rolls of fat. Instead, they hit what felt like a massive rock, their knuckles bleeding while their fingers bent into unnatural positions. Before they could do anything else, Billy grabbed their heads, lifted them off their feet, and threw them on the floor, causing their bodies to bounce like rag dolls.

The students who were watching screamed, fearing for their lives. One of the students headed for the door, trying to make a break for it. He was a shorter boy who had been holding his girlfriend's hand until a second ago, but now he just pushed her to the side.

However, Billy wasn't going to let anyone leave, and he immediately blocked the only door. Standing in front of the student, he kicked him in the stomach, sending him skidding across the floor until he landed in the shards of broken glass.

What the fuck is going on? Since when is that blob of fat this fast? What the hell did he take to not only grow bigger and stronger but also faster? Innu's previous confidence started to dwindle, but he still needed to do something, aware that Billy was after him primarily.

The first thing Innu did was kick at a desk, sending it sliding toward Billy. Its wooden top hit Billy's knees, causing him to flinch slightly. Innu wasted no time. He followed straight behind the desk and jumped on top of it, and then, using his momentum from running in, he followed up with a knee strike.

All the students rubbed their eyes to make sure they weren't dreaming. This kind of performance usually only happened in movies, yet Innu had done it in one smooth motion. Their classmate's knee connected with Billy's face, and the force caused the bully's head to fall back a bit . . . but only a few inches.

Billy smiled and swung his arm out, punching Innu from the side, sending him rolling onto the floor. Innu quickly got up, but his hands immediately went to his ribs.

It feels like they're broken . . . Shit, I should have listened to Kai. Unfortunately, his regrets came far too late. Even if he could call for help, how long would it take to arrive? Then there was also the question of whether his fellow gang members actually *could* do anything to help, or if their presence would just doom them all.

Billy spit out a few teeth and some blood. His nose was also bleeding, yet it didn't look to be broken. As the blood ran down his face, he licked his lips, tasting it. He didn't look to be hurt at all.

He lifted the desk in front of him with both hands, a great big smile on his face. He walked toward Innu, ready to flatten him.

"If he hits him with that, he's going to kill him!" one of the students pointed out, too scared to do anything about it.

"Quick, throw whatever you have!" another suggested.

The students grabbed their chairs and hurled them toward Billy. Then they grabbed their bags, books, whatever they could find in the classroom, but even though he was a hard target to miss, the attack didn't seem to be doing much. His eyes didn't leave Innu for even a second.

Despite their good intentions, nobody seemed to have realized that throwing things actually made it impossible for Innu to flee, because he would risk getting hit by something. Unlike Billy, he didn't feel confident in being able to ignore those makeshift projectiles.

"Guys, stop! You're just making it worse!" Innu shouted, but the students had fallen into a panic, and none of them had registered what he meant. Because it was the only thing they could do, the frightened teenagers continued throwing stuff.

Suddenly someone entered the classroom and ran toward Billy. A chair came flying his way, but he knocked it out of the way, only to be hit by a book, yet he continued to run.

Who is that crazy person? Innu wondered.

Another student entered behind him, but seeing the condition of the room, he stopped.

The desk was in midswing; Innu tried to move, but the pain from his broken ribs was slowing him down. He knew he would be a fraction too late.

That was when he noticed that the student who was running in wasn't going for Billy, but instead ran past him and pushed Innu to the side before rolling across the floor. The desk hit the ground and broke on impact from the powerful blow.

The desk had missed him by only a few inches.

"What are you doing? You could have been hit by that thing and died!" Innu complained to his savior. "That bastard is after me, so stay out of it!"

"Yeah, that won't work. He's after me too," the hooded person replied.

CHAPTER 66

OMEGA VS. OMEGA

It took a second for Innu to see the green hair and realize that the hooded person was Gary. Although he had texted him as requested, he didn't think that his supposed gang leader would be so desperate to find him that he had come all the way to his school. For that matter, he didn't recall telling Gary what school he went to.

Wait, does he think he can take on this guy? He wasn't here when Billy came in and wreaked havoc!

"Don't be an idiot," Innu warned Gary. "I know you might have defeated this guy before, but he's clearly not the same. You can't beat him."

Naturally, Gary could see that Billy had changed. Even a growth spurt wouldn't explain his sudden increase in size over such a short period of time. What was more, he could feel a new type of pressure exuding from the large fellow. His system also finally confirmed something he had been wondering about for the longest time now.

You have finally met the other omega wolf

Well, thank God he isn't actually a werewolf, and he's just like me, Gary thought.

"I want to thank you for what you did to me!" Billy said suddenly. No one really knew whom this was directed at, apart from Gary, of course, but Billy turned around as if he was looking for a way out.

"No, you don't!" a voice announced. "You don't get to just come into my school and mess with everyone this badly!"

The person who was now standing behind him was Austin, who had followed Gary, and he immediately threw an uppercut toward Billy's stomach. It was a powerful blow, but unlike the delinquent trio, Austin's hand wasn't injured.

Austin had a feeling that a guy that big wouldn't go down with just one hit, and he followed up with a punch to the side. Just like the others, he was surprised by Billy's nimbleness as he turned around, grabbing both of Austin's hands.

"You're strong. Stronger than anyone else I fought before, so maybe you deserve this," Billy said as he opened his mouth wide, revealing a set of sharp teeth.

"Vampire!" someone screamed.

Is he going to eat him? Innu wondered. At this point, he felt like nothing would surprise him when it concerned Billy. He had seen people bite others before, but only when they were desperate. Green Fang's debut fight would be an example, though Gary had seemingly done that more because he had lost himself in a battle frenzy.

This was the first time Innu had seen someone open their mouth this widely.

While the spectators were frozen in place, only the hooded figure moved, and to everyone's shock, he dived right into the situation.

Damn it! If only I hadn't been hit so bad! The three of us together might have been able to do something. Innu cursed his injury.

He could only watch and pray that Gary knew what he was doing . . . but then the strangest thing happened. His gang leader didn't go in for a punch; instead, he got right between Austin and Billy and shoved his forearm into Billy's open mouth!

"Oh, no you don't! It's bad enough with just one of you!" Gary shouted as he pushed forward with his forearm. Billy's jaw was strong, and his teeth had already sunk in. Blood was dripping down Gary's arm.

The students couldn't understand why someone would allow himself to get bitten instead of someone else, especially since the hooded person didn't seem to be from their school.

Is this why? Is his reckless will to sacrifice himself the reason Kai wants him as the leader? Innu wondered. He felt horrible; he was using his injured ribs as an excuse not to fight, while this guy who hardly knew anything about fighting had just shoved his arm into Billy's mouth.

It was then that both Austin and Innu each picked up a chair and slammed them down on the intruder's back at the same time. But Billy still didn't let go.

"FUCK!" Gary screamed. He tried to push back, but Billy's jaw strength alone turned out to be far above his own. "You bite me, I'm going to bite down on you!" Gary opened his own mouth, ready to bite back, but just then Billy let go. He turned around and jumped through the broken window.

As Billy ran away, Gary was left there with his arm bleeding.

"Hey, man, you took that bite for me. Are you all right?" Austin asked, checking on him. However, for the second time, Gary ignored him and ran after Billy himself, jumping through the window.

"You're going to chase him in your condition? Just leave it!" Innu shouted, yet Gary was already running down the hall.

I can't leave it . . . Billy tried to bite down on that strange guy I met on the roof. I might be overthinking it, but it didn't seem like he planned to eat him. In that case, he must have wanted to do the same thing that I did to him! He wanted to turn him! I can't allow him to start his own pack!

Gary could see Billy up ahead, but despite his large size, he was fast. Gary had already activated Charging Heart when Billy bit down on him, yet despite his boost, his legs still couldn't keep up.

System, use Forced Bond on him, so I'll be able to track him down!

323

Error: Your marking skill only works on human targets!

What a piece of crap! Gary wanted to yell out, but then he saw Billy not slowing as he crashed through a window. Gary caught up and looked out, only to see that Billy had already left the school grounds. They were on the third floor, and Gary wasn't sure if he could survive such a fall and then catch up with Billy.

Crap, crap, crap! Gary thought. He heard police sirens in the distance. He took that as his cue to get out of the school. It was already bad enough that he'd had to intervene and reveal himself, but he couldn't allow himself to become a witness. Heck, he couldn't even explain any of it anyway.

While running, he texted Innu.

If they ask, you don't know me!

Gary was left undecided over what to do. Just as he had expected, Billy was the other omega wolf. He was faster, stronger, and better at fighting. On top of that, he wasn't worried about hurting or killing people.

So much for the system giving me some sort of edge. How the hell am I supposed to beat him? I need help . . .

CHAPTER 67

WHO IS HE?

The police arrived at the scene and quickly went to work. The teachers provided them with a classroom so that they could start taking the students' testimony about what happened. Although none of them had outright been able to tell that the attacker was Billy Bruntin, the police were confident that it was him based on the few details they received.

The only thing they couldn't really figure out was who this hooded stranger was who had apparently saved both Innu and Austin.

"You should have seen his entrance; it was right out of a movie! He came running in, pushed Innu out of the way, and rolled to safety like a millisecond before that monster slammed the desk down! He was like a hero who came at just the right moment! I swear if he had been a moment later, Innu would have ended up as a pancake!" one of the students reported in excitement.

"That guy's crazy, I tell you! I mean, seriously, who would shove their own hand into the mouth of such a monster? That fat bastard was even worse! It looked like he planned to eat the smaller guy! Blood was spilling everywhere! We tried helping, everyone did, but we didn't want to get close after we saw what he did," another student said as he told his version of what happened.

The two police officers who were talking with the students were none other than Chief of Police Anton Millstun and his younger assistant, Roo Game. As crazy as it sounded, by now both men had accepted that the students weren't pulling their leg. The students had been called in one after the other, and unless they all had collectively decided on a story beforehand, their testimonies matched, though some seemed more exaggerated than others.

Initially, they had been far more skeptical. The first person interviewed was Innu, as he had fought Billy the longest and was also closest to their target. They had hoped that he might be able to tell them why their suspected killer might have so publicly attacked the class in the first place, or at least who the other mysterious person was.

Unfortunately for them, Innu had retrieved his phone from the broken desk, read Gary's message, and, just to be safe, deleted it. So he had pretended not to know either one of them. The two police officers had noticed his slight change in attitude when asked about Gary, but without any further evidence linking the two, they had let him go and continued questioning the rest of the class.

The last person on their list was Austin Foster, since he was a student from a different class, yet he had joined the fight after Gary. He entered the room with his hands in his pockets as calm as ever, and the questioning began. They asked whether he knew Billy or had at least seen him before.

Austin just shrugged, telling them that his face seemed familiar and that he might have seen him in passing somewhere. When they held up Billy's picture, Austin gasped in surprise.

"That's him! Only the dude was like a head bigger. Who is he?" Austin asked genuinely.

By this point, the two officers weren't surprised anymore. Barely any of the students had recognized Billy, but they couldn't fault them just because none of them had bothered to follow the news, making them clueless that they'd had a run-in with a suspected killer. Like the others, Roo just told Austin that he was a suspect in another case without going into further details.

"Your fellow students reported that they saw you come in shortly after the hooded person. Do you know him? If not, could you at least make out what he looked like?" Roo asked.

Austin sat there for a while, making it seem like he was trying to remember something. The truth was he had seen what the boy looked like after punching him, quite clearly at that. If he were to tell them about the boy's hair color, it would most likely help them immensely . . . yet he didn't.

"Nah, I've never seen him before today," he answered truthfully. "He came out of nowhere, so I started chasing him, thinking he was an intruder in our school. He wore a hood, but it was a no-name brand, so all I can say is that it was dark. Then I saw that Billy guy, so my attention was more on that giant pig bastard than the guy who was helping me. He was gone before I could even thank him."

After a few more questions, Austin was free to go, but Anton didn't feel like he had made much progress at all until he received a text from his phone.

"They . . . match," Anton murmured.

"What matches, sir?" Roo asked.

"The blood in that classroom from our mysterious stranger is the same as the blood from the guy who attacked that deceased high schooler and the sample that was found at the construction site. They all match! I don't know how yet, but he seems to be also connected to this Bruntin case!" Anton looked to be over the moon, almost jumping up from his seat as he spoke.

"I knew that these cases had to be linked, but what . . . what is going on? According to the students, he came up, saved some strangers, and then chased after the killer?"

Anton thought back to what he had seen in the alleyway. Could it be that the killer was actually this mysterious person they were chasing, and Billy was just trying to find out the truth? No, that didn't seem right to Anton either, especially given that Billy had undoubtedly been the aggressor.

In all of the cases involving Billy, his blood hadn't been found at the scene. In all the other situations involving this stranger, the circumstances just seemed more life-threatening, as if he was fighting for his life. It was hard to make out the full picture without all the puzzle pieces, but at least there seemed to be a connection. Catching one of them might allow them to catch the other . . .

A little down the hallway, Innu was waiting for Austin to get out.

"Did you say anything?" Innu asked quietly after making sure that nobody was around.

"I'm no snitch. Since he was running away from them, I'm sure he had his reasons." Austin shrugged it off and continued to walk down the hall.

"Thanks," Innu called out.

"I didn't do it for you," Austin replied. "I did it because that guy saved me from getting bitten."

He took a few steps, stopped, and turned around. "Hey, he's your friend, right? Who is he?"

"Why . . . you want to thank him in person?" Innu asked cautiously.

"Nah, he was just . . ."

Austin thought back to the roof. When he threw his punch, the boy suddenly did a strange spin to avoid the hit; it seemed slow, but the timing was perfect. Austin had been ready to try to kick him, but he could see at that moment that the boy wasn't aiming at him; his gaze was focused on something else entirely.

He'd stopped his leg as the green-haired boy punched the metal door behind them. The door hinge snapped right open, and the boy continued running forward, fixing his hood. Austin wasn't sure what to make of it, choosing to believe that the boy was just trying to run away.

But the metal door had been dented slightly. That wasn't the strength of an ordinary person, and he shuddered to think what would have happened if he had fought him seriously.

". . . he was just really strong." Austin said.

This came as a surprise to Innu. Although Gary had undoubt-edly saved both of them, he hadn't exactly fared that much better against Billy. If anything, Innu would have used the word *brave* if he wanted to compliment Gary, though he was bordering on *idiotic* and *suicidal*. Nevertheless, it was obvious that their school's official top dog was interested in him.

Did something happen between those two or something? Innu wondered, especially since they had both entered the classroom around the same time.

"You don't have to tell me, just . . . if he ever needs some backup, let me know," Austin said, continuing his walk back to his class-room.

It was then that Innu realized that he had already accepted Gary for who he was; if he hadn't come today, what would have hap-pened to Innu? So if someone asked him who Gary was to him, he shouldn't shy away, but tell the truth.

"Hey!" Innu called out. "About your question . . . that guy is my leader!"

CHAPTER 68

THE KINGS

The Basement was a popular nightclub in Slough's town center, yet today its front door had a sign that read *Closed*. However, the guards around it were a telltale sign that something was going on inside. Unbeknownst to the normal populace, the club was merely a front for the Underdogs, one of the town's most successful gangs.

What was more, the Basement wasn't the only business that would remain closed today. Damion Hawk had used his influence to make all the shops on the block treat today as a sort of impromptu holiday so that nobody would disturb their special meeting.

Inside one of the VIP rooms, Damion had been sitting calmly, talking to another person on the other end of the table; the conversation was about to come to an end. The other person stood up.

"I thought the Underdogs were supposed to be the best in Slough, which was why I hired you. Believe me when I say that package is important for both of us. Get it back, or it could be both of us on the chopping block," the man said before leaving.

Damion remained seated until the man was escorted out. He picked up the large wine bottle in front of him and threw it against the wall, smashing it to pieces.

"It's been over a week! How is it possible for you to not have so much as a *single clue* about that damn traitor's whereabouts?" he shouted at his subordinate, who was in the unfortunate situation of having only bad news to report. The ringing in his eardrums was the least of his worries as he braced himself for what was coming next.

He had known his boss long enough to anticipate the large fist that hit him across the face, sending him flying down to the dance floor. Damion wiped his hand with a little cloth he had in his suit pocket and walked down the stairs to the injured man.

"Do I need to remind you just how important that package is?" Damion asked.

The man was in pain. Touching his face, he felt an imprint left from one of his boss's rings. His cheek was bleeding, but he knew that unless he replied immediately, the Underdogs leader would just continue beating him up.

"No, sir! I understand it perfectly, sir! The problem is that everything that boy has told us was fake. Right now, the color gangs are causing chaos in our territories, so it's hard for us to gather any reliable information on him, especially since we only have his hair color to go on. There are so many punks that dye their hair green, and he might have even dyed it another color by now. The red color gang, in particular, has been getting more and more brazen, challenging us for multiple areas." The man answered truthfully, yet he was frightened that Damion would hit him again . . . Instead, Damion squatted, grabbed the man by his hair, and pulled him up to his eye level.

"How long have you been in this gang?" Damion asked.

"Around one year, sir! I was recognized for my work and got promoted to the Pitbull Unit!" he replied quickly.

"A hard worker, eh? I can respect that. Fine, I shall let you off with this much. You better show me the results, or I'll make it so that you will fit in that package. We still have to deliver that fucking thing to one of the Kings! You know who they are, right?" Damion asked, not letting go of the poor man.

The gangster nodded instantly, even though nodding caused his hair to hurt even more. *The Kings* was a colloquial term for the top gang leaders of their county, those who controlled the Tier 1 cities, making them the richest and most influential people in the world.

If one of these Kings asked one of the lower cities for a favor, the other party was unable to refuse, no matter how ridiculous that favor might be. Still, it wasn't all bad. The Kings also observed noblesse oblige, making such a thing high-risk, high-reward, and Damion had no desire to take the fall.

"The reason the red color gang is kicking up a fuss is that another King must have ordered them to intercept the package. They don't seem to know that we don't have it anymore, so they're trying to get rid of us!" Damion shouted in anger, and he stood up so quickly that he ripped out some of the gangster's hair before heading back upstairs.

"We're lucky that it's just the red color gang for the time being! If we don't give that King what he wants and earn his protection, the rest of the gangs might attack us to get the package!"

Everyone in the clubroom wanted to take a step back for fear that Damion would take out his anger on them next, but they knew that if they did move, they were more likely to be picked.

"Kirk!" Damion called out. Hearing his name, Kirk stepped up, wearing his usual flashy red suit.

"Your schedule has been cleared for the rest of the month. As you can tell, everyone else is pretty much useless. I want you to do me a little favor. Let's remind Slough why you're my right-hand man and why the Underdogs shouldn't be messed with. Get rid of the red color gang for me, and while you do, find out who was backing them.

"Now that the Cheetah Squad will be dealing with the color gang, I expect *results* and not *excuses* by the end of the week! *Find that damn greeny!*" Damion shouted.

CHAPTER 69

WAITING FOR THE DAY

It had already been an eventful day for Gary, but there were still many things he needed to do even after facing Billy. First things first; it was time to regain some Energy. To do that, he visited his new favorite alleyway. The number of rats didn't seem to have reduced, something he was actually thankful for.

His natural speed was slow, making it hard to catch the critters. Fortunately, Charging Heart allowed him to turn the tables. He could also catch several of them at a time before the effect wore off, making him earn a net plus. Gary continued even after his Energy had completely filled up, only stopping once he got a notification.

Daily Quest complete
5 Exp received
395/460 Exp

I didn't get anything for risking my life fighting Billy . . . I need to figure out how to beat him somehow, Gary thought as he made his way to school to not be late for rugby practice.

On the way, he received a text from Innu informing him that Billy might have broken his ribs, so their training would have to be put on hold for a while. He also said that he would go to Kai to sort something out.

Gary had actually been looking forward to their training, hoping Innu might be able to teach him a few things. The fighter had been his best shot at gaining some sort of edge over the omega wolf. Unfortunately, it seemed as if they would have to wait for Innu to get better first. Gary texted him back.

Another time, then.

The only question was, how much more time did they have if Billy attacked his targets out in the open now?

At the start of rugby practice, Mr. Root had an important announcement.

"I know the school has already had a memorial service, but Barry was an important part of our team and loved rugby. So if there is anything we could do for him, it would be . . . *to win this upcoming game!*"

The students found it a bit awkward that Mr. Root was trying to use Barry's death to encourage them, but they weren't really that affected by it. To them, it just felt like Barry had moved or something; it was hard to process a death like that.

Still, there was one person who was affected and had returned to the field . . . Gil. The only thing was Gil didn't look the same as before. He had dark bags under his eyes.

But there was also good news. Tom was sitting over by the bench watching the game with his typical attitude of not caring in the slightest about it. Seeing this, Gary raised his hand after a good twenty minutes of practice and requested a break.

Mr. Root, seeing that unlike yesterday, Gary was playing well, actually agreed to this. He was far more concerned with Gary getting an injury at this point.

"Hey, so you look a lot better," Gary said, sitting down on the bench next to Tom.

"Yeah, I'm all fine now. I think they might have straightened my teeth even better," Tom said with a smile. "Fortunately, they didn't make me too handsome to hang out with you."

Both Tom and Gary laughed for a few seconds, but then there was an awkward silence. It was like they had forgotten how to interact with each other. The truth was, Tom wanted to ask Gary something but was too afraid of the answer.

He had heard about Barry's death, and there was something telling him that Gary . . . might have had something to do with it. Of course, it wasn't like he could outright ask him. If it wasn't true, then Tom would have just insinuated that his friend had killed someone in cold blood.

And if it was . . . well, then Tom felt like he was also partially responsible. If he had told Gary about the bullying before it got out of hand, things might have ended very differently.

Neither option had a happy ending, so instead, Tom decided to ask something else.

"I can see that there's something on your mind. I just want you to know that you don't have to worry about me anymore. Whatever happened to Barry, it looks like Gil is feeling too down to be targeting me anymore."

Gary would normally have been elated about Gil no longer bothering his best friend, but Tom was right, his mind was elsewhere, and it wasn't focused on Barry or his involvement in the bully's death. He had gotten over that far quicker than he believed normal, suspecting either his system or his new existence to have some role in that, but right now, all he could think about was Billy.

"Tom, I have to tell you something," Gary began. "I thought . . . no, I was pretty sure there was another one like me out there. I mean another . . . you-know-what," Gary finally admitted. This was news to Tom. Out of all the things he had expected Gary to say, this wasn't one of them. He was at a serious loss for words.

"I could kind of feel it. It was like the two of us seemed to be fighting over who should be the leader, the alpha like you said, and today . . . I ran into him."

"You ran into another one of your kind? Was he older than you? Was he always a werewolf like you? What did the two of you talk about?"

Gary just shook his head. Looking into his eyes, Tom could tell he was concerned about this, almost frightened.

"He's not like me. He didn't exactly invite me over for tea and cookies. No, I found him attacking innocent people, hurting others, so I tried to stop him. It was strange. It felt like he was stronger than me, but for some reason, he ran away from me. I've been thinking about it ever since, and I can't wrap my head around it. I was hoping you might have an answer."

Tom thought about it for a while. He had actually done the research in that regard before spoon-feeding it to Gary, who had tuned out at first. In the end, he could think of only one thing.

"I'm not sure. I only know as much about werewolves as what we've learned. Maybe he's waiting for the upcoming full moon? I mean, according to lore, that's when you're both supposed to transform and be at your strongest. If he's an omega like you, maybe he wants to fight you at your strongest, so he can make you submit fully to him," Tom theorized.

For some reason, a part of Gary agreed that this would be the honorable thing to do. Whenever he thought about time, Gary was always thinking about the full moon. It was almost as if that were the date set for when their match would be held. If so, that would mean Gary had until the full moon to get stronger.

Later that night the clock passed midnight, and the timer moved forward once again.

Your bloodlust grows

4 days until the next full moon

Gary was still suspended on Thursday, so he missed a big event at school.

"All right, everyone, so today we have a surprise transfer. I want you to please welcome your new fellow student," the teacher announced before the first class.

The door opened and a boy with bandaged arms walked through.

"Everyone, it's nice to meet you. My name's Innu."

CHAPTER 70

A BAD LIAR

When he woke up, Gary was still thinking about what he could do to get stronger. He only had four more days left until the full moon, and from what he had discovered, his ways to get stronger were very limited.

He could try to increase his stats naturally in the gym, though there were two problems with that approach. For one, his Strength and Endurance had grown, so he estimated that it would take time for them to grow, which was exactly what he lacked. Then there was also the issue of him still not having figured out how to increase his Dexterity.

Gary knew that it would be possible with the free stat point he would gain for reaching Level 5. He wasn't that far off, but he lacked a good source of Exp income. He could continue completing his Daily Quests, though those gave him a pittance in terms of Exp, and without any other source, it wouldn't even be enough to reach Level 5 until the full moon.

The only other way he knew how to receive Exp was by fighting opponents. If he was lucky, he might even trigger some sort of quest that would give him even more. Being suspended from school meant that he couldn't really start challenging the other fighting clubs, leaving him with one remaining choice.

Just as he had made up his mind to go out and look for some trouble, he received a text on his secret phone.

Heads up: the Underdogs have ordered the black color gang to retaliate against the red gang's advances into their territory. At the same time, they'll also be scouting the area for you. I know you're suspended, so keep your head low and stay off the streets for a while.

Well, that's just great. Gary sighed, looking at the message from Kai that had ruined his plans. Nevertheless, he was very thankful for it. It would be a disaster if he ended up in the midst of that.

With nothing better to do, Gary followed his normal routine, which included practicing his skills by gathering up his meat candy before going to the gym. As bleak as the day had started, he left the gym with a satisfied smile on his face.

Congratulations! Move, move, move, and keep moving. Catch everything and become the wind.
Dexterity +1

I guess all that hunting in the forest for squirrels and birds, as well as the sprinting on the treadmill, is really helping me out. Since this stat is the lowest, it should also be the easiest to improve, but it's also the one I need to work on the most as well. Billy was way faster than I was.

After that, there wasn't really much for Gary to do, and before he knew it, it was time for him to head to rugby practice. After changing, he saw Tom on the bench outside; not too far from him was someone he had seen quite recently.

Am I imagining things? Gary wondered, rubbing his eyes.

Strangely, both of them noticed him at the same time, waving him over. Tom and Innu then turned to each other, realizing that they were both calling the same person. Before the practice officially started, Gary ran over to them.

"What's going on? Why are you here?" Gary asked Innu.

"Huh, how come you already know the transfer student?" Tom

asked in surprised confusion. He was quite sure that his best friend had not once mentioned someone like Innu.

"Oh, me and Green Fa—"

Before Innu could spill the beans that they had met at an underground fighting match, Gary quickly placed his hand over his mouth.

"He's the . . . brother of . . . of one of Amy's friends!" Gary said, making it up on the fly. "Amy brings her friends over occasionally, and . . . well, you know where we live. And you know, she just brings her brother along for some reason!"

Gary honestly regretted his cover-up story the moment it left his mouth. Everything sounded like a convoluted lie. In hindsight, he should have just said that he had met him at the gym or something.

The whole charade told Innu that no one around Gary seemed to know what he was doing.

If he's planning to create a gang, then the people around him will naturally get involved. At some point, he'll have to either sever his ties with them . . . or bring them into the gang to protect them. I just hope he's prepared for one of those options.

"Oookay . . ." Tom replied, clearly not convinced. "Didn't you introduce yourself as an only child, though?"

"Well, she was my half sister. Do you remember what I said about my scumbag dad leaving us? Didn't really feel the need to go into too much detail about family stuff." Innu added some details, going along with the lie. "As the new guy, I was just happy to see a familiar face. I mean, look at him, not like you could forget that green hair. Anyway, I think you should go out to the field. From what I've been hearing, you're like a minor celebrity now. I hurt my ribs in an accident recently, so I can't practice today."

Gary was thankful that Innu had played along, especially since he seemed to have a far easier time coming up with stuff. While the team started their practice in earnest, Tom and Innu talked about Gary. The new student learned a lot about Gary, whereas Tom was completely convinced that Innu didn't know his best friend at all. For some reason, he felt relieved at the fact that he seemed to be the only one who knew about this entire werewolf situation.

During a small break, Gary decided that it would be a good time to talk with Innu, if only to clear up the confusion. He excused himself loudly, claiming that he would take a quick bathroom break while meeting Innu's eyes. A few moments after Gary had left, Innu followed him. Of course, Gary had waited outside, as it felt awkward to talk in the bathroom.

"What are you doing here? How did you even manage to transfer this quickly?" Gary asked.

"As of today, I'm a student of Westbridge, just like you. I have Kai to thank for that one." Innu grinned. "I told you that I would be talking to him yesterday, remember? He asked me to inform him if anything happened in the whole Billy situation, so I told him everything about yesterday, how he attacked me in school and how you were there to rescue us."

"The next moment, he offered to help me transfer over. Apparently, he was going to propose this when we got closer anyway, and this special situation was a perfect excuse to speed up the process. Who is Kai anyway, for him to be able to do this sort of stuff? It's clear that he isn't exactly your average student . . ."

That was actually a question Gary would have liked to have answered as well. All he knew about Kai was that he had money, lots of it, and that he wanted to create a gang to get out of the Underdogs; he just didn't know why he wanted to leave. Gary had never asked, despite all the help Kai had given him, but he didn't really care since he had a million problems of his own to solve.

"Yeah . . . he does have his connections; that's all I know." Gary shrugged and started running back to the rugby field.

Over the next few days, Gary continued to do what he did every day, and each night he got a countdown of the number of days to the next full moon.

There wasn't anything Gary could do about it.

There were no signs of Billy, and no news of more dead people either. Gary started training with Innu. Since Innu was still recovering, he could only instruct Gary on how to fight, and in his spare time, Gary practiced these moves again and again.

Then finally, something strange happened with only two days left until the next full moon. He was walking home, with Tom and Innu accompanying him part of the way, a requirement that Kai had set up.

When Tom split off to head home, Gary found himself in a familiar situation. A group of students surrounded him, and they all wore the Eton High uniform.

Gary started to laugh. Normally he would be annoyed, but today he welcomed the threat, because he could use the extra Exp. Meanwhile, Innu couldn't wait to pay back those who had hurt him before.

Unbeknownst to Gary, similar scenes were playing out elsewhere. He wasn't the only target of this surprise attack. At that moment, every regular member of the rugby club who was supposed to play had been targeted.

In another alleyway in the streets of Slough, Eton High had sent out extra students to attack a certain individual. He walked out of the alleyway into the sunlight, his hands bloody.

They attacked me again, Blake thought, spitting blood out of his mouth. *These guys are scum!*

In the alleyway, six students lay injured on the ground.

CHAPTER 71

A MAIN QUEST

Six guys from Eton High had suddenly surrounded Gary and Innu, and it was clear that they hadn't come for a simple talk. However, Gary had instantly noticed that something was different about this attack compared to the last one. These guys were nowhere near as bulky, and as it turned out, they were far worse in a fight.

They don't seem to belong to the rugby club. Are they just regular students at Eton High? Did I mess them up so badly that they're now scared of me? No, otherwise they wouldn't have attacked me a second time and only sent out these guys, Gary wondered as he looked at the students rolling in pain on the ground.

After the fight, Gary had realized how much he had improved. Innu's training had paid off, and his improvement in stats, although minimal, really showed during this fight. He was practically untouchable to anyone who had never fought before.

"Hey, what was that all about? Why the hell did you get in my way, only to punch those guys out yourself? Were your three too easy?" Innu complained. "Look, I know you've been improving, and you might want to show off, but there was no need to do that. If this had been a game, then what you just did would amount to kill-stealing."

"My bad, I was just trying to look out for you. I was worried that if you fought, it would be bad for your injury. I mean, we have that tag team match coming up soon; I can't allow my partner to get any more hurt on my watch, right?" Gary said, rubbing the back of his head. "Besides, if this had been a game, shouldn't you have let me finish off the last guys for my Hexa?"

If only you knew, Gary thought; he had gotten in Innu's way exactly to "kill-steal" his opponents. His system rewarded him with Exp only for those he himself knocked out. This was a rare opportunity, and he had to make the most of it, even if it meant that Innu might feel patronized.

With his increased Strength and Charging Heart, it was far easier than last time. He hadn't received a quest for it, yet beating the six students had still earned him 120 Exp. Combined with the Daily Quest he had been doing each day before practice, it was enough for him to finally get the level up he had been working toward.

Congratulations, you have now reached: Level 5
A stat point has been granted
95/628 Exp

Hmmm, I had kind of been hoping to get another skill that might help me in my fight against Billy. Oh well, good thing I at least got Claw Drain recently. Hey, system, mind explaining why I got 20 Exp for these guys while I got 25 Exp for their friends? Is it because they're weak, or because my level increased?

As usual, Gary got no response. His Werewolf System truly was a fickle mistress. However, after a few steps, he did receive a new message.

New Quest received
You have grown as a werewolf, and you're still not dead yet. That's a surprise!
Continue to grow and reach Level 10, where a new class awaits.
Objective: Reach Level 10
Quest reward: Select a class

A class? Now this is really starting to feel like a game. What even is a werewolf class? That doesn't even make sense. I already had so much trouble wrapping my head around the alpha thing.

Gary would just have to worry about it when he reached that level—that was, if he could survive the night of the full moon. He knew he had no chance of leveling up five levels by then. So he decided to focus on what he could do.

He needed to figure out where exactly he would be putting this stat point. Knowing that Billy was out there possibly waiting for him to attack, it didn't seem wise to save it up. Now that he knew for a fact that each of his three base stats could be increased through training and hunting targets, he decided to place the point into Energy or Health.

I guess Energy is more versatile. Ten more Health points won't really help me, but this way I can use it for Charging Heart or Claw Drain. Being able to replenish my Health seems better than having a bigger pool, and who knows how many more skills I will get in the future. If only I knew if Billy also has skills like me . . .

Your Energy has now increased to a maximum of 120

There was another reason why Gary had chosen Energy. The closer it got to the full moon, the faster his points were going down, even if he turned off the marks.

"Hey, who ordered you to attack us? Spill it!" Innu yelled at one of the students as he grabbed him by the collar. The injured guy was still barely conscious, unable to reply.

"Let's just leave them be. I don't think they're going to say anything, and if we stay here, we might attract the wrong kind of attention," Gary suggested; he was in a good mood after feeling himself grow a little bit stronger.

"You don't understand; I know these guys because I used to be with them! I know everyone who could put up a fight, but these guys are just mere scrubs. They wouldn't attack us without reason. I need to know if Eton High got a new leader after I transferred!" Innu kept shaking the guy but not getting any answer, so he grabbed another. Still no reaction. He gave Gary an annoyed look, to which Gary just shrugged.

That night, Gary went to sleep as he did every night, but when he woke up, he was greeted with the message he had been dreading for a long time.

Your bloodlust grows even further
1 day until the next full moon

CHAPTER 72

REPLACEMENT

Eton High had clubs just like every other school. A couple of students had joined the rugby club and changed everything in the school. Although it was Sunday, they had a special training to get ready for tomorrow's match against Westbridge.

Out on the field, there were two boys who stood in front of everyone rather than a teacher. They were tall and had slender frames; their hands were in their pockets. One had long red hair that was tied up in a ponytail; the other one looked almost identical, except for his short hair.

The long-haired one gave his team instructions like a coach would until some students came running to the field. It was obvious that none of them were part of the rugby club.

"Sren, Leng, we dealt with those guys just as you asked; only groups four and seven had problems," one of the students reported.

"That's good enough," Sren, the short-haired brother, replied with a yawn. "Since the rest of the groups completed this task, it will be an easy win for us. Tomorrow's going to be a cinch, as usual."

On Monday morning, Gary reread the message that he had been dreading for the longest time.

Your bloodlust grows even further

1 day until the next full moon

The full moon is nearly upon you. Every fiber of your being is waiting in anticipation!

Current bonus: All Stats +3

Damn it; I was hoping I actually wouldn't get stronger. The more power I borrow from the moon, the quicker my Energy goes down.

Gary's suspension was finally over, and he had prepared the apology letter for Steven and his family. Coincidentally, it was also the day of their big match. This was why he had woken up extra early.

Gary started to feel the effect of his bloodlust, but fortunately, catching a few rats was enough to satisfy his urge and his hunger for the next few hours. He estimated that it should be enough to get him by until lunch, though he would most likely go out again instead of eating in.

At school, Gary and Tom were among the first to arrive, and Tom couldn't help but be worried about his friend as he shared his plan.

"I know I can't stop you from playing, but I want you to at least promise to meet up with me afterward, okay? We need to sort out your personal problem. If we can't stop you from turning, at least we should try to hold you somewhere where you won't be able to hurt anybody. I've done a lot of research, and there are quite a few people that you might end up going for. The most likely candidates are me as your best friend, your family members, and even just the first person you might see, so we need to try to stop all of that."

Gary was pretty sure there was a good chance that he would go for someone else entirely. Since he hadn't bothered to try to get rid of the mark on Gil, he was the only hunting target left. Ever since he had seen what Gil had done to the old man the other day, Gary was coming around to the idea that if anyone were to die, he wouldn't feel too horrible if it was scum like him.

In a way, he wouldn't be doing it himself either. It would be his werewolf self, so he wouldn't even feel like he was the one that killed him.

"Last chance to change your mind. Are you sure you should be playing today, especially with the full moon around the corner?" Tom asked, not hoping for much.

"I keep telling you, I'm fine, man. Have you seen me attack anyone?"

"You haven't exactly been to school, so who knows what you've been up to?" Tom argued. "There are plenty of annoying people in school that you might attack, and it might be worse when you're out there on the rugby field. Fine . . . I'll stop nagging." Tom could see the look on Gary's face; he wasn't going to give up.

At lunch, the rugby team was given permission to skip their afternoon classes to go through some plans for the evening's match. The whole school was also invited to watch, mostly because Mr. Root had promised Principal Young results.

When the rugby club went out on the field, there was something quite noticeable right away. Gary could smell it as soon as he arrived.

I've smelled this before.

It was only when he saw the conditions of the others that he realized everyone was injured in some way.

Mr. Root was pacing backward and forward, biting his fingernails.

"How could this happen? You're telling me that they've actually gone so far as to attack all of you?"

Some students had gotten lucky, running away and making a break for it while their friends had taken a beating; others seemed to have been let off easily. They had still been injured but not to the point that they required medical attention. Still, it would take them a week or so to heal naturally.

"Hey, do you think what happened to us happened to all of them as well?" Innu asked.

Mr. Root then let out a big sigh, shaking his head.

"Goddammit, letting you out on the field will do nothing but add insult to injury. There's just one choice left. Benchwarmers, I'll need you all to fill in the positions of the regulars! Get ready, everyone, because we will be playing tonight!"

Tom was pointing at himself because it took him a moment to process what this meant.

"I'm going to get killed," Tom gulped.

"Don't worry." Gary placed his hand on his shoulder. "I'll protect you."

Although they were meant to be words of comfort, it just made Tom worry even more.

That evening, everyone had gotten into their uniforms. It would be an interesting match, to say the least. However, one student in particular felt a growing headache coming on.

9 hours left until the next full moon

CHAPTER 73

THE BIG GAME

Kai was walking up the stairs, looking at the black face of his gold-rimmed watch. He could see that he still had a few hours until the match. All Westbridge students had been invited to watch their school's rugby team compete against Eton High's, and for certain reasons, Kai wanted to get back before it started.

The reason Kai had to worry about time was that at this very moment, even though it was a school day, he was at a different school. What was more, he had just opened the door leading to the rooftop, where he found a lone figure.

"I was told you would be here," Kai said. "A smoker, eh? If you treasure your body, you should drop it. In a couple of years, you'll start to feel the difference. It's up to you; the gangs sure as hell will enjoy squeezing the money out of you."

The student took another puff from his cigarette before throwing it on the floor and stepping on it. He then turned around, looking directly at Kai while making sure his hair was still in perfect shape.

"People from other schools usually only come here because they want a fight," Austin said. "However, the last person I fought saved my ass, so I've decided to take it easy from now on. Since you haven't outright attacked me or challenged me, I take it you want something else from me?"

Hearing this, Kai smiled and threw out a business card. It cut through the air easily, and Austin caught it.

"A little green birdie told me about your fight against a certain school invader. Apparently, you actually managed to hurt that over-sized pig monster, which means you're strong," Kai said. "Let me ask you something. What do you plan to do once you graduate?

"You might feel on top of the world right now, being in charge of all these kids, but that will change once you get out. I looked into you, and judging from your current grades, you'll barely pass, meaning you'll struggle to find a good job, and your so-called friends who might stick with you these days, well, they'll have no reason to stay by your side.

"Your fighting skills are good . . . for the average teenager. If you plan to join a gang, you'll quickly learn that out there on the streets, where people fight every single day, the best-case scenario is that your skills might allow you to be a team leader. You might not be at the bottom of the barrel, but you'll be far from the top.

"However, if you want a better future, come to the address on that card in a couple of days. If nothing else, I can at least guarantee that you'll see something very interesting."

Austin looked at the address on the card. When he looked up, he could see that Kai was about to leave.

"That's it? You've come here to give me a lecture and a sales pitch?"

"Yup, but the lecture was on the house. Now, if you'll excuse me, I've got a game to watch," Kai replied without turning around, shutting the door behind him.

It was about time for the match to start.

All the players who would be fielded today were currently in the locker room, yet Blake, Gary, and Gil were the only regulars. The rest were those who had usually done nothing but warm the bench.

All of the benchwarmers were nervous since this was a last-minute change due to unforeseen circumstances.

"My bones are too fragile for this crap! If any of those guys tackle me, I'm going to be killed," Tom whined; his legs were actually shaking. "Shit, I was just in the hospital. If I go there again, my parents will probably make me drop out and start homeschooling me!"

"Just pass the ball to me every time you get it, all right? You can let me handle all that stuff," Gary said, trying to encourage his best friend.

Mr. Root looked at the players at his disposal and couldn't stop shaking his head. Today would possibly be his last day as Westbridge's coach. Knowing this, he placed his hands on the shoulders of his most promising players.

"Blake, Gary, I'll be counting on both of you. Get out there and win this for our school! If you manage to do that, I'll treat you to an all-you-can-eat buffet!" Mr. Root promised earnestly.

"You mean it, Coach? You'll pay for all of us?" A large but unathletic student asked with large eyes, suddenly having found some motivation to give it his best.

Mr. Root hesitated. *I actually meant just these two, but I guess that would be seen as favoritism . . . Oh, what the hell. These kids need some encouragement, and if it saves my job, it's a cheap price to pay!* "Sure!" he answered, giving them all a thumbs-up. "Now get out there and score some points to earn your meal!"

Outside, the stands were filling up. It was a home match for Westbridge, so Eton High was the one coming to their school. Their buses had arrived, and the supporters as well as the players started to come out and walk toward the field and the stands.

Nearly all of the Eton High supporters were students, and the Westbridge students noticed that they all looked a bit rough around the edges. Glances from the other side caused the students to look away quickly.

"Kill them! Make sure you break their legs!" Innu screamed from the stands, standing up at the very back. Everyone turned around, yet for some reason, Innu's words gave them the confidence to shout and cheer for their team.

"Hey, do you mind if I sit here?" a voice asked him suddenly. When Innu turned, he saw that a beauty had approached him, someone he recognized from his class.

"You're . . . Xin, right? You sure you wouldn't rather sit with the girls from our class?" he asked, getting all red-faced. Xin looked at the girls, who were surrounding and praising Tiffany.

"I've actually just transferred here myself, so I'm still a bit of a loner. If it's a problem or you're reserving that seat for someone else, I can just look for another."

Innu quickly shook his head and patted the seat next to him, clearing off the dust, then gestured for the girl to sit.

Not far off in the stands, some of the parents had also come to watch the match. Today the seats were emptier than usual. After all, most of the regulars weren't going to be playing today. Nevertheless, several mothers had turned up because there was a rumor that a certain someone would arrive.

As it turned out, that rumor was true. A tall, muscular, handsome man who looked to be in his early thirties had appeared. He had a neatly trimmed beard and short hair, giving him the appearance of a top-class actor.

Of course, this person wasn't oblivious to the stares, and he gave his fans a friendly wave.

"He is so dreamy!" Tiffany squealed.

"It looks like Blake gets his good looks from his dad," one of her drones added.

Finally, it was time for the teams to face each other. Blake and Gil led the Westbridge team, as they were the most senior members. The captain of the rugby club walked confidently, yet his partner seemed to be somewhat lost.

Facing them was the team from Eton High, led by the twins Sren and Leng. As they saw who they would be facing, everyone on their side broke out in laughter.

Although most of the Westbridge team looked scared, two players were more determined than ever. They reached the center of the field and started to practice; soon the game would start.

"Gary," Tom whispered, "don't try . . . too hard, okay?"

Gary gave Tom a thumbs-up. He looked into the crowd and saw Xin and Innu sitting next to each other, and the next moment he felt something burning inside him.

Sorry, Tom . . . I might have to try a little hard.

What Gary didn't know was that not too far away, watching the field from behind some trees, was a large teenage boy.

We don't have long . . . I'll be waiting for you . . . Billy thought, licking his lips.

CHAPTER 74

THE RUGBY MATCH (PART 1)

Before the match started, Gary wanted to check on a couple of things. For one, his growing headache just wouldn't go away. He tried his best to hide it, as he didn't want Tom to notice, else his best friend would just nag him even more and make it worse.

7 hours until the next full moon

This was the reason for his headache, and this wasn't even the first notification either. Five hours ago, a message had popped up informing him that it was twelve hours until the next full moon, and it had repeated every hour since. Just like the previous ones, he mentally closed it before he went to check on his Energy.

100/120 Energy

The reason his Energy levels were still so high was that he had enjoyed a big lunch. He had eaten a lot and was even stealing food from the other students. At the same time, as he walked around at school, he could always find some type of creature nearby.

He hated to admit it, but he was getting used to this scavenger lifestyle. Nevertheless, without really doing anything and even after toggling off his marks, he had consumed 20 Energy points.

It looks like after this game, I'll have to go hunting again before trying to sort out this werewolf crap.

Gary let out a big sigh as he got into his newly assigned position. Today, he was placed on the right wing, while Blake would be on the left wing. Even though he wasn't left-handed, the star player could play well in any position.

I should probably refrain from using Charging Heart for now. Let's see how I do with just my basic stats.

Initially, one of the benchwarmers had been selected to start the match by kicking the ball. However, he dropped it, and it hit the ground as he swung his leg and missed. To avoid further embarrassment, Mr. Root asked Blake to be the kicker. It was a good strong kick that made it to the other side, signaling the start of the game.

In rugby, the players naturally ran as a line together; the same was true for the other team. To score a point, a player had to run up to the long white try line to score. The main rules were that a player could only throw back the ball, a player could use their feet and hands on the ball, and other than that, players were free to tackle each other as they wished.

Gary immediately ran toward the player who caught the ball. The Eton High players were confident in their strength, especially when they saw a scrawny boy come toward them. Even if they got tackled, they intended to pass the ball to the next person before falling.

However, Gary got close and immediately dived down, hitting the ball carrier's legs. The surprised student fell down like a sack of potatoes. Part of his surprise was due to the unexpected tackle, but the other part was because of the strength of the player who tackled him.

When the student fell and dropped the ball, a boy with short red hair picked it up almost instantly. Sren ran forward, but Gary quickly recovered and went in for another tackle. As he dived, the new ball carrier quickly spun around, evading the attack.

"Too slow," Sren sneered, running forward. He used his agility and the protection of his teammates to avoid most of the Westbridge team. Blake was their last defense.

Another player ran across, trading paths with Sren. It only took a split second, and the redhead continued to run forward. Blake tackled him to the ground, but he no longer had the ball.

"You might be a good player, but you seem to be lacking in the brains department," Sren jeered.

The referee blew his whistle, signaling that Eton High had scored the first point of the match. As for the player who had scored, it was none other than Leng.

"Damn it!" Gary cursed, kicking the ground. He was most upset that he had let the other person get away. During the last two weeks, rugby had become more than a mere hobby for Gary. Thanks to the system, his performance had improved immensely, allowing him to play earnestly. He knew that he was basically cheating, but it just felt good to be recognized for once. Of course, being allowed to work off his frustration was a nice bonus.

The game restarted with Eton High kicking off. Alas, now that Westbridge was in possession of the ball, things only got worse. The passes were bad as it instantly became obvious that the players on the field lacked any actual practice.

Gary was having his own problems; whenever he saw that Gil was open, the only other decent player on their team, he refused to pass to him.

It didn't help that they were all scared of getting hit by the other team. They all got rid of the ball so fast that one might mistake them for playing hot potato instead of rugby. Tom was in the unfortunate situation that he got passed the ball, but Gary was too far away. Having hesitated for too long, Tom ended up getting hit before he could pass.

Eton High scored four times before Blake managed to finally score a single point, for which he had Gary and Gil to thank. Unlike in professional rugby, the high school didn't use multiple points per touchdown and just counted them as one for simplicity.

"Arghh!" Gary yelled. *I can't catch those two redheads. They're too fast and nimble. They get away every time, even with my current speed! I should be okay if I use it until the end of the game, right? I know halftime still hasn't been called,* Gary thought, trying to convince himself, unwilling to let his first rugby match end in a complete catastrophe. It would be one thing if the other team were simply better than theirs, but it just didn't sit well with him that they were losing because of Eton High's dirty tactics. To be honest, Gary wasn't sure if they could win even if they had all of their regulars; that was what was more annoying. Eton High was a good team, so why the need to resort to dirty tactics?

> *Skill activated: Charging Heart*
> *All stats have temporarily been doubled*
> *–10 Energy*
> *Dexterity 10 (+3)*

CHAPTER 75

THE RUGBY MATCH
(PART 2)

Gary had already been doing well in the game without having to use Charging Heart. This was mostly due to the power of the moon; otherwise, he would have still fallen slightly behind the athletic students, but now with Charging Heart active *and* the power of the moon, Gary was at his strongest.

Since Blake had luckily managed to score a point, it was time for Westbridge to kick off the ball again.

"Coach Root, let me do it." Gary raised his hand, asking for permission.

With how things were going, Mr. Root didn't really care. It was obvious that Eton High would put more people on Blake now, leaving virtually no chance for a comeback. Blake and Gil didn't voice any objections, so Mr. Root just allowed Gary to do as he wished.

Getting ready, Gary dropped the ball and booted it as hard as he could. He poured all of his frustration into kicking the ball and didn't hold back. The ball went high in the air, farther than any of Blake's kicks, and down so far that some people even thought it was going to hit the try line. In the end, it was a few meters short.

Sren had run all the way to the back, but even with his speed, he was unable to get back in time to catch it.

"Did you see that kick? I don't even think I've seen a kick like that in professional rugby games," one of the parents commented.

"Well, it's a smaller pitch, but that was definitely an impressive kick," another added.

Some of the Eton High players, and Blake too, had noticed that Gary's kick had no signs of proper technique; the ball shouldn't have gone that far. Meaning he had done it all with raw power.

Gary, I'm thankful that you're on our team, but the improvement you have had is abnormal . . . Just what did you do? Blake thought.

The game went on, and Blake surprisingly managed to snatch the ball from one of their players, but just as Mr. Root feared, the team had him surrounded. They knew there was no need to focus on the other players, and they were blocking his path from passing to Gil. Gary, seeing this, suddenly appeared out of nowhere.

"You can do it, right? Then go show them what you got!" Blake chucked the ball right through the gap toward Gary, and after catching the ball he was off like a rocket.

Gary just ran straight. He knew better than to try to use fancy footwork to evade the opposition. One of the Eton High players went for the tackle, but Gary just kept running. He was like a train on tracks, not stopping in the least. Once he got past the first two opponents, it was smooth sailing until he reached the try line to score a point.

"I did it! I scored a point!" Gary yelled out in triumph. He then looked over at the stands and enjoyed the feeling of being cheered on, especially since the one person he was looking out for was giving him a standing ovation.

"Did you see that?" Leng asked his brother. "Since when did Westbridge have someone like him? Was he holding back on us the entire time?"

"Of course I saw that," Sren answered in frustration. It was one thing to lose a point to the star player, but this was completely unexpected, and he didn't like it. "No idea what's gotten into that guy.

According to our intel, he was supposed to be a benchwarmer, just like the rest of them. Now it seems like he's their star player. Let's just put more people on him!"

The game continued, but that wasn't the only point Gary ended up scoring. With his sheer power, he was able to force his way through nearly each time. At one point, some of the players on Blake were also put on him. Using that opportunity, Gary passed the ball, allowing the real star player to score.

When the referee called for a break, the score was 7–4 for the home team. They had managed to score nearly double the other team's points, but there was still a problem. Despite Gary's boost, he was unable to catch up to either of the twins. What was more, his Energy had decreased sharply, which would make it risky to use Charging Heart again.

During the break, Tom approached Gary. "I'm guessing your sudden boost in performance is due to the moon. Do you feel any different? Any sudden . . . urges?" Tom asked carefully.

Gary smiled. "Just a healthy desire to win this match!"

Both teams went into position. Gary noticed that the twins wore evil smiles. In those few minutes, they had devised a strategy for how to deal with the annoying green head.

After the kick, Gary was in possession of the ball, yet five people had him surrounded. It was the required number of people to stop him without making it too easy for Blake to score. Already used to this, Gary had no choice but to pass the ball to the closest person: Tom.

They had done this a few times already, and his best friend would usually just pass it on to the next person, but as soon as the ball left Gary's fingertips, two redheaded players ran through.

Before he had any chance to react, they both crushed Tom, banging into him from either side; he fell to the ground in seconds, but that wasn't the end of it. Turning around, they both stepped on Tom's hand with their studded metal boots, piercing his palm.

"Why the fuck is it always me?" Tom screamed in pain.

In an instant, Gary leapt from where he was, landing right on top of Sren, pinning him to the ground.

"I'll kill you!"

CHAPTER 76

VISIONS

Moments before, up in the Westbridge stands, Xin noticed something strange in the stands across the field. One of the Eton High students had a handheld camera and was filming the entire match. Next to him was another student with a laptop who seemed completely focused on it and nothing else around him.

"Doesn't that look a bit strange? They've been filming since the start of the match," Xin said. She had a feeling that things weren't as they seemed.

"Is it?" Innu just shrugged it off. His attention was on the game, ever since Gary started bulldozing his way through the field. There was a certain excitement from the spectators each time he got the ball.

"Don't a lot of sports teams film their matches? It's not like anyone else will film such an amateur match. It makes it easy to replay important moments and learn from them so they can improve," Innu added as he looked up. "Although now that I say it, that doesn't sound like them. Come to think of it, if they were that diligent about getting better, then they should have had no need to attack all the regulars."

"They attacked you guys?" Xin yelped. "No wonder I barely recognize any of our players."

If it had only been the camera guy, she wouldn't have thought much of it, but the fact that the student next to him was also looking at his computer instead of focusing on the game struck her as suspicious.

Just then, a loud shout from a familiar voice grabbed her attention.

"I'll kill you!" Gary shouted, having pinned down one of the Eton High players.

It was seemingly out of nowhere, and so fast that neither team knew how to react. Gary had already pulled back his fist and thrown a punch. Sren moved his head to the side just in time, and Gary ended up hitting nothing but the ground beneath him, making it hard for anyone looking to know just how hard the punch was.

The first player from Eton High to react was Sren's brother Leng, but as their eyes met, Sren just shook his head, and his brother backed down while also looking back at the stands to make sure everything was okay.

"You slimy little snake!" Gary cursed as he pulled back his fist again, aiming at Sren's chest. However, by this time, his teammates had arrived, trying to stop him from doing something stupid, and grabbed his arms.

"Stop it, Gary! He wants you to hit him! If you attack him, they'll kick you off the pitch!" One of the students tried to reason with him as he held on to Gary's outstretched arm.

But Gary wasn't listening, and he looked at Sren, who gave him a satisfied smirk, making him want to punch him even more.

Four people were pulling Gary back, and yet it looked as if it still wasn't enough for them to pull him off until Blake came and pushed him off Sren from the front. Sren didn't thank him, and just tsked as he got up and walked away.

"What the hell are you doing? That guy hurt Tom! If you get in my w—"

"Stop!" Tom shouted, holding his hand. "I'm okay. They only pierced my skin a little; it just hurt a lot, that's all."

Although this might have been the case, that wasn't why Gary was angry; he could tell that what they had done was intentional.

They had hurt his friend again after Gary had talked about Tom being safe next to him.

With this thought in his head, Gary continued to charge forward, and his teammates tried to hold him back again, but with Gary's strength, he was just skidding them across the grass.

Still, Blake stood firmly in his way. Seeing this, his father stood up from the crowd.

"He must be worried about his son!" one of the mothers said.

"That boy is so vicious; where is his mother?" another asked.

In the stands not too far away, Kai was also watching the match with Marie.

"Is this what you expected?" Marie asked.

Kai smiled. "No, it's even better. He's exactly what we need. I've never seen someone get so angry over a friend being hurt like that . . . he's perfect."

"*Gary!*" Tom shouted, getting between him and Blake. "I'm fine!"

Tom held up his hand, showing that his wound wasn't a big deal; he could even still play. Seeing this, Gary finally seemed to settle down somewhat.

However, the referee looked to be in a troublesome spot, wondering just what to do. Mr. Root quickly went to him and placed his hands together as if he was begging.

"Now come on, there's no need to do anything. These are just hotheaded teens. Of course they're going to get aggressive in a fight like this. Besides, in the end, our player was the only one that actually got hurt," Mr. Root argued.

The referee glanced at the teacher; he understood why he was being this way. Westbridge's team was mostly amateurs, and the one that had gotten involved in the scuffle was one of their star players.

If he was taken out of the game, there would be no hope for Westbridge. He also was aware of Eton High's reputation, so he was sure their attack wasn't a coincidence.

It was only because of this that the referee decided to keep the game going with no consequences for either side.

Before the match resumed, Gary looked at Tom's hand.

"You seem to be getting hurt a lot these days. Are you sure you're okay, and it's not just the adrenaline?" Gary asked.

Tom lifted his hand again, showing Gary the wound.

"Look, it's only a flesh wound; it just ripped the skin a little, it will be fine—"

Suddenly, Gary grabbed Tom's hand and looked at it closely. At first Tom thought it was out of concern and that he just wanted a closer look, but then he noticed that Gary seemed almost obsessed.

"G-Gary? Hey, Gary!" Tom shouted, yet he was still holding on to Tom's hand.

At that moment, Gary was having visions . . . visions of biting down on Tom's hand. He let go and almost fell to the ground as he backed up.

"I . . . I-I've got to get out of this game, Tom . . . I have to leave now . . ." Gary mumbled, and that was when Tom noticed a significant change in Gary.

His eyes no longer looked human; they had gone slightly yellow and changed shape.

"Are you . . . changing? Right here, right now?" Tom helplessly looked around for a way for Gary to disappear.

CHAPTER 77

WOLF'S HOWL

The look in Tom's eyes said it all. Gary saw the way he had been staring at him. No matter what had happened so far, his best friend had never made a face quite like this before.

Stop it! Stop it! Why are you looking at me like that! Gary thought.

Tom wanted to reach out to Gary, but his body froze up. He didn't know what to do, as it was the first time he had seen his best friend change. Sure, Gary had told him what he was, but seeing it happen appeared to have awoken a primal instinct in him that made Tom want to run away.

Tom had seen many Altered change into their beast form, but Gary's case was clearly different. Shaking his head, he managed to get a grip on himself and started to look around to see if anyone else had noticed.

It was at that moment that Gary covered himself up, putting his head into his shirt.

Come on, Gary, calm down! Calm down! What's going on, system? I should still have time! The last notification was about the full moon being six hours away, so why am I changing now? Gary asked himself in a panic, still covering his head.

"Gary, it's going to be okay!"

He could hear Tom's voice, but he refused to look at him, afraid of what might happen.

"If you need to get out of here, then don't let us stop you. It's just a stupid high school rugby game anyway. Heck, it's the first one this season. Look, I want you to head over to the Cipen side of town, to a storage warehouse called Yellow Stack. There's a storage unit in my family's name. My parents use it to store some items from the experiments they run, but I managed to find out their passcode to it. Just in case, I placed a few things inside that should hopefully help with your . . . situation. If you feel like you can't control it, lock the door to stop you from going out. We'll get through this together . . . okay?"

Gary had carefully listened to Tom's entire speech. At the same time, he had done his best to breathe in and out deeply, further helping him calm his heart down. His Charging Heart skill had run out. Eventually, his heart rate lowered below 150 BPM, and slowly he came out from his shirt.

"Gary, your . . ."

From the look on Tom's face, Gary could tell that his appearance had gone back to default.

"Thank you, Tom. I-I f-feel better now. I-I believe I know what was causing the problem. I should be able to stay," Gary said hesitantly before quickly adding, "Just for a short while! I mean, Mr. Root practically begged the ref to let me stay, so I don't want to upset everyone now."

It had to be Charging Heart. Yeah, that must have been it. With how close it is to the full moon, my elevated heart rate must be messing with me. Tom's wound might have just triggered it. I swear, after this game, I'll head straight to that storage unit! Gary tried to calm himself as he inched back to his position.

The game was about to resume, though Tom wasn't sure if Gary had made the right decision since he had no idea how Gary felt. He only knew that getting close to his best friend wasn't advisable right now, not because he was scared of him, but because he was afraid that his wound might be the cause of Gary's change.

369

As the game resumed, the two teams continued as normal. Eton High had possession of the ball, and Leng was holding it tightly. He looked over his shoulder for a second to see where his brother was, yet in that brief moment the ball was snatched away from him by none other than Blake.

He ran past all the others, proving why he was the team captain and team ace. Sren, who was farther back, went in for the tackle, but with a jump, Blake narrowly avoided it and went on to score the try. Everyone from Westbridge started to cheer the star player's name. The girls' screams were especially deafening.

As the game continued, Gary became far more passive than in the first half, not that it stopped his team from passing him the ball. After all, that was what had gotten them the points so far. However, Gary's speed had dropped noticeably, and something had changed in him ever since the fight.

"You're slow, even slower than at the start," Leng jeered as he tackled Gary to the ground. Meanwhile, Sren picked up the loose ball and continued to run forward, but once again, Blake was ready, as if he had predicted Gary's fall.

He stopped their advance, and it was time for another turnaround. Alas, he alone could only do so much. Fortunately, they had managed to get a good lead in the first half. The game came to an end with a score of 9–9, making it a draw.

"We drew! We freaking did it!" Mr. Root cheered. *I get to keep my job, and I don't even need to treat anyone to dinner!*

Of course, it was all thanks to Blake, and the team started to toss him into the air, celebrating their draw as if they had won. Although Gary had done a lot for the team, it had been limited to the first half.

But Sren and Leng were acting strangely; it was as if they had lost.

"What is wrong with you all?" Sren shouted in anger, punching one of his own teammates, causing him to fall to the ground. The spectators could see this, but now that the game was over, they could do nothing about it. Neither Eton High's teachers nor the other player did anything about it, seemingly used to this sort of behavior.

"We knew that Blake was a good player. We knew if we played against them with him, it would be risky," Leng complained. "What we didn't expect was for *him* to be good as well."

Of course, Leng was referring to Gary, who seemed to be staring into space with his head full of his own thoughts. His headache was becoming worse, and a slight dull ring had appeared as well. He felt as if all the noises were being drowned out from the outside.

"That stupid git cost us a shit ton of money!" Sren cursed. He picked up the nearby rugby ball and threw it directly toward Gary. Those in the crowd watching gasped but could do nothing as it hit its designated target.

It was a clean hit, connecting with his head from the side, making Gary fall to the ground.

"Arghh, my head!" Gary yelled out, his hands on the grass, clutching at the mud.

"Is he seriously hurt or something? Rugby balls aren't that hard," Innu said, looking at his gang leader worriedly. He was furious and was ready to give Sren a taste of his own medicine, but he knew it was impossible to get to him. Not with his entire team behind him.

Tom didn't want to get close, afraid that the smell of blood would just make the situation worse.

"No, he's acting really strange. I don't think the rugby ball caused that. He looks to be in incredible pain, and . . . it looks like he's sweating," Xin pointed out. It was hard to see from her position.

The two of them weren't the only ones who had noticed this. Kai and Marie had both been keeping an eye on Gary as well. The action of the sore loser was way out of line, but Gary's reaction was also unnatural.

"Gary, get out of here!" Tom shouted from what he hoped was a safe distance. "You have to go home early, don't you? Your mom and sister are waiting for you."

This was a lie. As far as his family knew, he would be staying at Tom's tonight after the match so they wouldn't get suspicious, but he was just hoping his words would get through.

Ahh-wooo!!!

"Was that a . . . wolf howl?" the crowd wondered. It sounded so clear and clean; it was a sound they had only heard in movies, and they could tell it had come from the direction of the woods near the fields.

"A wolf? Here in our backwoods town? That's crazy." Innu nervously laughed it off but glanced toward the nearby woods.

When they turned around, though, Gary was no longer there.

CHAPTER 78

THE FULL MOON

It was only for a split second that Tom had taken his eyes off Gary to look in the direction that strange howl had come from. He looked everywhere on the field for his best friend, even asking some of the nearby players, but none of them had seen him disappear. Their focus had been on Blake and then on the wolf howl.

That definitely sounded like a wolf . . . Don't tell me that was the other werewolf? Was that howl meant to be some sort of challenge? . . . please be safe, Gary!

He wasn't the only one who was confused about Gary's sudden disappearance, though. Innu and Xin both had seen him get hit by the rugby ball, as well as Tom frantically searching for him. They both decided to head down from the stands and ask him what had happened.

Surprisingly, two more people were moving toward Tom from another area of the stands.

"Tom, you're Gary's friend, right? We saw him get hit by that scumbag, but now he's gone. Is he okay?" Xin was the first to speak. The girl's question was along the lines of what Kai himself had wanted to ask, so he decided to just listen. Innu, noticing that Kai had come down, felt a little awkward since he didn't know how to behave around him.

"You're also looking for Gary? Hang on a moment; what do you care anyway? I haven't heard you asking about him even once during his suspension, but now you're worried? You don't even know him that well, and you're just the new guy, and you two . . . holy shit, aren't you Kai Hemper, that rich kid from the year above us?" Tom realized who the newcomer was.

"The one and only." Kai let out a laugh at Tom's hilarious expression. "Would you kindly tell us where that green head is? We've become . . . acquaintances, and I have something for him."

Tom had a bad feeling about that. He had no clue how Gary had come to know all of these people or why they suddenly cared for him. For as long as Tom could remember, it had just been the two of them against the world.

I can't tell them about Gary, at least not today. No one can know about what he's going through right now. Otherwise, they might think he's the one that killed all of those . . .

"I don't know where Gary is. It's dark out; he probably went home!" Tom shouted as he started to run away from the others before turning around for a moment. "Don't go out after midnight tonight, especially you, Xin. Just stay home!"

The other four looked at each other, and they all had the same expression. It was clear that Tom did know something and was trying to hide it, even though they didn't know why.

"Well, should we follow him?" Marie asked.

"Depends. Does anyone have a better plan on how to find Greeny?" Kai asked, but none of them spoke up. Innu moved over to Kai and Marie to join them but noticed that Xin was following them.

"Hey, it's pretty dark, and you know how this town is. I mean, I'm happy to protect you and all, but I'm sure your parents are worried about you." Innu tried to gently tell Xin to go away without being too patronizing, yet still appearing strong.

"Don't worry, I can handle myself," Xin replied as she looked into the crowd of parents; a man in a suit was standing up. As long as he traveled with her, things would be fine. Kai didn't voice any objections, just shrugged; with that, the four of them decided to follow Tom's trail to see where he would go next, hoping that it would lead them to Gary.

Gary was covered in sweat as he sprinted toward the direction Tom had told him. He wasn't sweating because he was tired; he could feel his heart pounding in his chest. He was running through the streets, staying in crowded areas.

That howl, I'm sure that had to be from Billy! Has he somehow already transformed? If that's the case . . . he must be after me. Anyone who comes near me will be in danger, and it's the same for those close to me.

For now . . . with all these people around, I don't think he'll attack me . . . I hope. Gary gulped as he recalled how Billy had attacked Innu during the day in school, so who knew what he was planning to do. An hour had passed, yet Gary had neither encountered Billy nor felt his presence. However, he had finally made it to Yellow Stack.

Five hours, five more hours. He isn't around, is he? Gary wondered as he sniffed the air. He could only smell industry and faded scents. Turning the marks on, he needed a moment to find them, as they were quite faint.

Tom had picked a perfect hiding place. This area didn't seem to have many residences. Just factories with workers who would have already gone home. Unfortunately, Gary was still in his rugby uniform, which didn't have a hood, so he opted to enter from the roof instead of the front entrance, in case any people or cameras were there.

Fortunately, Gary had had a lot of practice sneaking around recently, and with his current stats, it was quite easy. There were plenty of ledges and pipes where he could pull himself up with his own body weight, which would have been impossible in the past.

One of the windows of the large warehouse had been left open at the top, and going through it, he found himself on some type of metal railing. He looked to see if anyone was inside and even sniffed the air, but the coast was clear.

I guess the storage units themselves are quite secure, so there's no need for a night guard.

Gary looked at his personal phone. Tom had sent him a text telling him it was storage unit 23 and that the passcode was Gary's birthday. He walked down the row of units until he saw a large yellow painted *23*.

I can't believe I'm going to spend the night, or maybe even the whole day here. He walked up to the container, and on the side of it was a little digital keypad. He entered the code, and the door slowly opened as the white ceiling lights were turned on.

Whoa, what the hell is this place? This looks more like an abandoned lab than a storage unit, Gary thought as he stepped inside. He could see strange machines; he didn't even know what they did, but they looked incredibly expensive.

There were also books upon books piled up in the room; from what he could see, most of them seemed to be about scientific theories and discoveries. He carefully walked through to the back room, which looked different. It was the only place that had been cleared out. There was a table, and on the table were a set of chains and a bag.

Gary closed the door behind him and locked it.

Wait, what happens if I transform? Will I be in control? If not, will my werewolf self know the code for how to get out? . . . Or maybe I'll become a primal beast who can't think straight? System, mind giving me a sneak peek or something?

Gary looked inside the plastic bag, and he couldn't help but laugh because at one point, he would have loved to receive such a thing, especially in February, but now it looked very unappealing. After all, it was practically poison to him right now.

The chain on the table was thick and heavy, and the table could be raised and had holes in it. It also had cuffs that, once shut, could only be opened by keys.

So I guess he wants me to strap myself in this thing, right? Should I do that now? . . . But I still have a few hours. Gary wasn't sure how much leeway he had, so he started to figure out the process of chaining himself up.

Where did Tom even buy all this stuff? Probably online. Oh god, I don't even want to think how much all of it cost . . . Thank you, Tom. I promise I'll pay you back . . . I just need to literally survive first, though . . .

Gary was finally set; the only thing left to do would be to lock the chains on his legs and arms. Tom messaged him, saying to text him after everything was over and he was back to his regular self. If he didn't hear from him, he would come to unlock him in twenty-four hours.

Gary placed his phones on another table to the side. He waited until the timer was down to its last hour. Since Billy hadn't appeared, he decided to lock both of the cuffs on his legs and then finally locked the ones on his hands. He waited and waited, but time seemed to be moving incredibly slow. His only company was the system, which was counting down to midnight.

All right, it doesn't look like Billy followed me. I just hope he can't sense where I am when I change, and I hope this will be able to hold me back.

Finally, the time had come.

The power of the moon is at its strongest and empowers you
Transformation has begun

CHAPTER 79

TRANSFORM

As soon as Gary saw those messages, he started to feel a change in his body. It began with his heartbeat. Someone seemed to have set the intensity to maximum. When he checked his status in the system, he saw that his heart rate was constantly rising, already having surpassed 200 BPM, with no signs of stopping.

It felt like his organs were trying their best to either burst through his chest or jump out of his mouth. With the increased oxygen flow inside his body, Gary was experiencing everything more vividly, from his feet all the way to the top of his head. He pulled on the chains from the pain, yet they did their job perfectly, preventing him from touching his head.

Unfortunately for Gary, though, the strange sensations didn't stop there. The next thing that he noticed was that his skin started to feel uncomfortable. He felt constricted, as if he had put on a shirt that was a few sizes too small. He wasn't sure if he was hallucinating, but he believed that he saw it start to fall off him.

"ARGHHH!" Gary screamed in pain, his throat on the verge of ripping, but he needed to do something to release the pressure that was building up. The veins on his arms and neck became visible. They had grown in size, looking like faint tubes about to burst from the pressure they were under. His muscles started to grow, and his skin started to fall off his body, replaced by dark black fur.

Someone, please make it stop! This pain, I can't take it anymore! Gary begged internally as he screamed out all his frustrations, aware that nobody was out there to hear or help him. It was becoming too much for him, and he was sure that he was losing his mind.

I have to stay focused! I have to stay conscious! He concentrated on the people he was trying to protect: his friends and family. Gary feared that something very bad would happen if his transformation overwhelmed him, and he wasn't sure that he would be able to live with himself if he hurt any of them.

Just when he believed himself able to tolerate the pain, his very bones started stretching. It was a hundred times worse than any growth spurt, and it affected all of them at once. At some point, they collectively cracked before they all began to regenerate on the spot, growing longer and more durable.

His face was itching all over as if a million tiny invisible bugs were crawling on it. His mouth, jaw, and nose seemed to shift around; his vision was changing. Gary didn't even register that his ears had also elongated, as his consciousness was slowly fading.

I'm sorry . . . was the last thing running through his mind.

The four teenagers had been diligently following Tom for a while now, ever since he left the locker room. He had led them to an area of Slough called Cipen. It was one of the more upmarket areas of the town—as nice as a Tier 3 place could get, at least. It was obvious that a lot of money had been put into this area, as there was a lot of nightlife despite how late it was getting. There were restaurants, bars, and even clubs.

It was an unusual sight in Slough, making Tom's presence more than strange. So far, it had looked like he had been walking around aimlessly. Kai had carefully made sure that they stayed a distance away from him, cautious that Tom wouldn't spot them, but as time went on, they noticed that he wasn't even paying attention to his surroundings, being far more concerned with his phone.

"Huh, so this is where all the bigwigs of Slough live? I don't even see any gangs here; that's a nice change," Innu commented.

"Of course, there are gangs here." Kai sneered at the other's naivety. "Otherwise, this place wouldn't be able to operate the way it is. In fact, this area is one of the more important places because of how much money it generates. You not seeing anyone just means that this particular area is protected by a gang nobody dares to mess with."

They were on a busy main street, and some of the adults were giving them funny looks, wondering what kids were doing here at this late hour. The only one who didn't look out of place among them was Kai. He even walked like the others.

He's right, but who is this guy to know so much? Xin thought.

As they continued to follow Tom, it honestly didn't feel like he was doing much, and the group would constantly check with each other to see if it was okay for them to be staying out this late. Tomorrow was another school day. Innu had no problem; he was free to do as he wished, similar to Kai and Marie.

However, Xin just had to check that a certain someone was still following them.

"Well, you guys surely have nothing better to do. It's almost midnight, and this is what you're doing?" Kai asked. "Well, I guess everyone has their special circumstances."

No one said anything, so they continued on their wild goose chase until their target decided to head out to the park. It was a shortcut that led to Yellow Stack and the warehouse side of Cipen.

Tom's plan was to stay here since it should be far enough away for Gary to notice him, yet still close enough that he could get to Yellow Stack if something happened.

Eventually, they all just watched Tom sitting down, staring at his phone. The group waited, hiding behind some trees a safe distance away.

They waited and waited until Marie got frustrated. "Ugh, this is getting annoying!" she called out. "Hey, Tom!"

Immediately he turned around, facepalming as he realized that he had been followed. Since Marie had revealed herself, the rest came out as well and headed toward him.

"We all have better things to do. Just tell us where the hell Gary went. Don't even try to bullshit us that you just came here for a walk. Cipen might be considered safe and all, but it's still incredibly dangerous!" The girl demanded an answer, impatiently tapping her foot.

Tom got up and started to panic, looking for a place to run off to, but suddenly all of them stopped in their tracks. Behind them, they saw two glowing eyes in the foliage.

They could hear someone breathing heavily, letting out a nasty, snarling noise.

"Look out!" Kai shouted as he sprinted to Tom, grabbing him by the wrist and pulling him forward. At that moment, two large claws destroyed the bench he had been sitting on just moments ago. Turning around, Tom saw what Kai had just saved him from.

The figure looked close to two and a half meters tall. It had bulging muscles and long claws and was covered in black fur, making it hard to see in the darkness. Its muzzle was large, and its razor-sharp teeth stuck out from its mouth.

"It's a . . . a . . . w-w-w-werewolf!" Tom managed to stutter out, his hands shaking. All of them froze in place, unsure what to do. Its glowing eyes were hypnotic, making them feel like prey in front of a large predator.

Fortunately, someone else ran in front of them all, waking them up from their stupor. It was the man in a suit who had followed behind them.

"Xin, get away!" the man yelled, turning his head. "I will deal with this Altered!"

The professional bodyguard was about to pull something out of his jacket . . . yet he never got the chance. The creature swiped once with his mighty arm. Before any of the teenagers could blink, the head of the man who had wanted to save them separated from his shoulders, flying past them into the park.

The next second, the body fell to the ground, releasing a torrent of blood.

All five of them knew that their lives were in danger . . . their chances of surviving this were slim to none.

CHAPTER 80

NIGHTMARE IN CIPEN PARK

There were a lot of dangers that everyone needed to look out for in a Tier 3 town like Slough. The teenagers were being cautious, yet they were all quite confident in their own skills, believing that no matter what they would face today, they would be able to deal with it.

However, that was limited to their own common sense. A werewolf had naturally not been something any of them had been prepared to ever see in their life, much less tonight. They had all slightly frozen in fear of the beast that had appeared in front of them. Before they could react, the enormous creature had killed a man in front of their very eyes without any effort whatsoever.

Tom became watery-eyed, and he could feel something warm soaking his trousers. Trickling down his leg.

Did I just . . . wet myself? . . . Werewolves have a sensitive nose . . . Let's hope this will make me unappetizing to eat . . .

However, the beast didn't attack them outright; instead, it started to dig into the dead person on the ground, ripping the corpse to pieces with its sharp teeth.

"Everyone, we need to get out of here now!" Kai instructed, and he didn't need to tell them twice. Xin noticed that Tom was still slightly frozen, so she grabbed him, dragging him alongside them.

Now that he was no longer looking at the beast, he started to run with the others.

"What was that? That thing didn't look like any Altered I ever saw!" Innu asked as he ran.

"Who knows, it might be the thing responsible for all those killings on the news!" Marie theorized.

The group was following Kai. Unfortunately, the park was large with big open fields. The impromptu group leader had a bad feeling that once the beast was done with its meal, it would follow them. At this late hour, the chances weren't great for them to find someone else in the park who might catch the werewolf's interest.

"Let's go through the trees. That will take us directly to the main street, with a lot of people. It seems hungry, so hopefully it will be distracted by all the adults that will make more of a meal than us," Kai suggested. The others agreed, if only because they had no better ideas and just wanted to get as far away from that thing as possible. Only Tom had a different thought running through his head.

That . . . must have been Gary! I bet he came right for me. One of those books mentioned that a werewolf would come after those that were closest to him as a human. So he either came for me . . . or Xin . . . or maybe even one of those people I don't know. This is probably the worst group to be with right now! Tom was panicking, but he didn't dare leave the others.

At the same time, Xin had tried to call someone during their escape. Until today she had thought that her trusted bodyguard would be able to stop any gangsters that were after their group, but when facing an Altered, only another Altered stood a chance.

Come on, Jayden, why aren't you picking up? I really need your help right now! Xin prayed sincerely, but there was no answer on the other end. She could only send him a text about her emergency, hoping that he would read it sooner rather than later.

The group entered the forest and began running through the trees, but that was when they noticed something up above. They heard a creature moving quickly, breaking large branches as it went from one tree to another.

Damn it! Why couldn't there be some large fat guy in the park today hoping to lose a few pounds? That would have made for a tastier target! Kai lamented their lack of luck. His plan was sound, yet he didn't know that the werewolf was after one of their group in particular. Before they could get out of the forest, the beast had dropped down, blocking their path.

Now they were practically in the middle of nowhere, with no one around to help them, but Marie had finally gotten through to someone on her phone.

"911, what's your emergency?" the operator asked.

"HELP, WE'RE IN CIPEN PARK AND THERE IS AN AL-TERED ATTACK!" Marie shouted, but before she could finish, someone grabbed her head from behind and pushed it down into the leaves. It was so sudden and hard that some dirt flew into her mouth. Xin's quick reflexes had saved her life.

The werewolf had leapt at Marie and her phone, seemingly understanding that it was a bad idea to allow her to finish the call. Luckily for the group, it not only missed its target but also crashed into one of the trees behind them.

Unfortunately, they all knew better than to hope that this would be enough to keep such a creature down. The werewolf stood up and started to look at them all, sniffing the air with its bloody muzzle.

"Gary!" Tom shouted with tears in his eyes. "Please . . . please don't attack us! Look at us; we're your friends! Part of you knows that, right? Please, you have to recognize my voice!"

The others believed that Tom had lost it and was now talking nonsense. How could this beast be Gary? Was he so far gone that he was hallucinating before his death? However, that name did elicit a reaction in the werewolf, and it stopped for a moment.

"Are you crazy? What part of him looks like that green head? This is a monster!" Innu shouted at Tom.

385

Hearing Innu's voice, the beast turned around to face him. The teenagers weren't sure if they were imagining it or not, but it almost looked like the beast was smiling, revealing its sharp teeth with pieces of flesh still stuck between them.

It's . . . going after Innu? Kai wondered. It dropped down on all fours before charging at Innu. The teenager tried backing up but found his back against a tree.

"Oh shit!" Innu was convinced that would be the end of him, and he regretted opening his mouth. As the beast was moving, though, two rocks came flying toward it, hitting it right in the face, with one rock nearly hitting its eye, causing it to close that eye slightly.

Innu did the only thing he could do and jumped to safety as he saw the beast flinch. He managed to roll on the ground underneath its side, causing the werewolf to crash into another tree, breaking part of its lower half, and a few seconds later, the tree toppled over.

"Why did you guys stay? You should have run!" Innu shouted, confused but thankful as he saw that Xin and Kai were the ones who had thrown the rocks. From the looks of it, they had gathered more and were ready to throw again.

"Just look at you. Once that thing was done with you, it would swallow you whole. A few seconds won't do us much good. If that thing is going to kill us all anyway, might as well try and put up a fight!" Kai explained, while Xin just nodded along.

"Fight? Kyle, have you gone completely mad? This isn't your average gang member! That thing killed a bodyguard in one blow! We'll be done if its claws so much as graze us!" Marie shouted.

"Gary!" Tom continued to sob. The werewolf, recovering from its daze, turned around, yet once again it focused on Innu.

"What the hell did I ever do to you? Do you have a craving for black meat?" Innu was ready to cry.

So it wasn't a coincidence. This thing really seems to have a grudge against Innu, Kai realized. Even in a situation like this, Kai's mind was busy trying to make the optimal decision, and right now, it was connecting the dots. *Hang on . . . a grudge against Innu . . . the news reports . . . sudden strength . . . It can't be, is that thing actually . . .*

The werewolf ran forward, and the group had to prepare for the worst.

"*GARY!*" Tom shouted once more at the top of his lungs, afraid his friend was going to kill someone in front of him.

Ahh-wooo!!!

Another howl resounded, and Tom felt a gust of air as a blur of fur rushed past him. The blurry black object leapt and slammed into the werewolf's side, sending the two figures toppling through the woods.

Soon both of them stood up, and the group couldn't believe their eyes.

"There are . . . two of them!" Xin cried out in despair.

CHAPTER 81

HELP THE WEREWOLF

The two werewolves stared at each other, then both slowly started to move up and down, each seemingly waiting for the other to make the first move. As the group of teenagers looked at the two creatures, they noticed some small differences between the two.

The most obvious one was their difference in stature. The one that had just arrived was about a head shorter than the first werewolf, and while it was also muscular, it seemed to be more lean compared to the other one, which was more buff. The color of their fur was also different; the bigger one was clearly black while the newer one was more brownish.

"Oh God, it's another one of those monsters!" Innu shouted as he looked at the creature that had saved him from certain death. He was grabbing his chest as his already fast heartbeat became even faster, making him start to worry about suffering a heart attack.

The larger of the two creatures turned to look at Innu, yet the smaller one used that opportunity to leap in, almost tackling the larger one by the waist. It pushed it a small distance away until the larger werewolf dug its claws into the other one's ribs.

The small werewolf screamed out in pain and let go, though the wounds in its side started healing at a visible speed. But before the smaller one could fully recover, the larger one dug its claws into the smaller one's chest and slightly lifted it up, then began running and slammed its body into a tree.

The brown werewolf screamed once more and snarled at the larger one, clearly struggling. Desperate, it used the tree to kick off from the larger one's chest with its powerful back legs, making its opponent let go.

"These two really don't seem like normal Altered," Kai said. "They seem more like two wild beasts fighting over their territory."

"Who the fuck cares what they are? This is our chance to get out of here! If we stay here, we'll just end up as the winner's meal, so let's go!" Marie said, then turned around and headed away from the fight. Innu followed right behind her; he'd come too close to death already, and he didn't feel lucky enough to survive a third near-death experience this evening.

Xin hesitated, but just when she was about to run off, she noticed that the one person who had been dragging them behind a lot lately was still staring at the fight.

"Tom, come on, we gotta get out of here! What are you waiting for?" Xin called out, grabbing his hand.

Meanwhile, Kai had continued paying attention to the fight between the two, deciding whether to run for it or help the smaller ones. Unfortunately, the werewolf whose identity he presumed to know not only was larger but had also proven to be faster and stronger.

The smaller werewolf was getting hurt far more often than its opponent. Although all their wounds were healing, with each blow one of the two parties was proving its dominance in this fight.

Just then, the larger werewolf picked up the other one by its legs and swung it into a tree, destroying the tree and greatly hurting its opponent.

Hearing the cries of the werewolf was hurting Tom internally.

I'm sure of it, that smaller werewolf . . . the reason it didn't attack us and went straight for the others . . . it's you, right, Gary? Tom thought. *You heard my cry and came to save us . . . and now . . . you're losing to the other omega. This must be the one you were talking about. I'm sorry, I'm so sorry for thinking that that was you, that you might have attacked us before.*

At that moment, Xin grabbed him.

"Look, we may not be friends, but there's no way I'm leaving you here to die!" Xin insisted, dragging Tom behind her, yet she felt him resist as he pulled back.

"We can't go now! That smaller werewolf saved us! We have to help him! Please, if we don't do anything, he might kill him!" Tom begged.

Seeing the look on the other teenagers' faces, he could tell that all of them thought he was mad for planning to help a monster. Even Innu, who had been saved by the smaller one, thought it had been a coincidence.

Still, though, Kai had noticed Tom's strange actions.

"He keeps calling them werewolves instead of Altered as if he's certain that that's what they are.

He also thought the big werewolf was Gary before . . . However, if my guess is right, that larger one should be . . . and now he wants us to save him . . . could it be that he mistook their identities?

Of course, there was no way for Kai to confirm his thoughts, and as much as this situation fascinated him, he treasured his life far more than satisfying his curiosity. Marie stopped waiting around and took off running; Kai soon followed, along with Innu, and that was when Xin started to drag Tom along with them. But Tom couldn't help but continue to look back.

"I'm sorry!" Tom shouted.

The group had run a little farther into the trees, yet they could still hear the fighting going on behind them. But then, though, they heard panting and the sound of growling getting louder.

Don't turn back, don't turn back! Innu told himself.

"It's chasing after us!" Xin shouted, forced to look back because she kept dragging Tom along, and she could see that the larger werewolf was behind them.

No . . . it's the other werewolf . . . does that mean Gary lost? Tom was worried about his best friend.

When the werewolf was close enough, it leapt toward the group, its claws reaching out toward Tom. It was about to touch him, but a few inches away from Tom's face, it came to an abrupt stop.

Opening one eye as he noticed that the pain he had expected never came, Tom saw that Gary had returned, just in time to save him from the other werewolf. His best friend was covered in wounds that did not seem to be healing, yet he was still putting up a fight.

Seeing that the larger werewolf was about to attack, Tom picked up a rock. However, before he could throw it at the werewolf, someone grabbed him by the wrist.

"Don't stop me, Xin! If you don't want to help him, that's fine, but I have to help him get rid of that other werewolf!" Tom shouted.

"Don't worry; you can leave that to us," an unrecognizable voice said.

Surprised, Tom saw that instead of the new girl, it was actually a large man holding his wrist. He wore in a trench coat, and not too far away from him was another person in a similar getup. The pair of them wore black masks covering their faces, hiding their identity.

Pulling off the trench coat, the man revealed a strange jagged black armor. It looked like the type one might find in a museum, showing off how their ancestors had once fought, yet this armor, despite the medieval look, had several weapons strapped to it.

The most noteworthy weapon was a strange sword that appeared to have been elaborately crafted.

The next action confused Tom, as the man took out what looked to be a baton. He pushed a button, and the weapon began to emit electricity.

"Are you . . . Altered Hunters?" Tom asked, unsure whether this was a good thing or a bad thing for his friend.

CHAPTER 82

THE MORE, THE MERRIER?

The two strange people whom Tom suspected to be Altered Hunters charged forward without hesitation. The others couldn't believe that people like this actually existed.

They had all heard about the Altered Hunters' existence through the news every now and then, but the stories about them didn't seem realistic. As an organization that seemed to be against the very existence of Altered, how were they able to match up against those superhuman people?

Right now, they were able to witness it for themselves . . . at least they would have been able to if it had been safe for them to stay. Altered Hunters were considered dangerous criminals on the same level as gangs, if not worse, which was why most of the group was still inclined to get out of there as soon as possible.

"We won't get a better chance than this; let's go!" Marie hurried them along, already running ahead, with Kai following closely behind her.

"Tom!" Xin shouted one more time. He looked at her, and for a brief moment it appeared as if he was going to follow her, but then he turned around and continued watching the fight. In his mind, Gary wasn't safe. In fact, his situation might have just gotten worse.

Having had enough of Tom's nonsense, Xin lifted her leg and swung it out, delivering a roundhouse kick right to his head. He fell to the ground, knocked out cold.

"What did you do that for?" Innu shouted in confusion, not having expected the girl to be this ruthless. Xin picked Tom up off the ground and dragged him over to Innu.

"I don't know what's wrong with him. First, he calls one of those beasts Gary, then he wants us to help one of them, and now it seems like he wanted to stay behind. He can hate me later if he wants to; right now, the important thing is to get to safety. Anyway, you said you were strong, right? Help me carry him; he isn't that heavy."

Innu wanted to decline, especially since there were literally monsters chasing them, but in the end, he felt like he couldn't say no to Xin. Fortunately, from the looks of things, the Altered Hunters seemed to be doing a good job facing the werewolves.

As they placed Tom on Innu's back, they heard a loud growl from behind, and to their surprise, both of the werewolves seemed to be ignoring each other as well as the Altered Hunters and were now staring at Innu.

"Why me again?" Innu cried out in despair as he ran as fast as he could with Tom on his back. The werewolves leapt into the air, yet the Altered Hunters were ready for them.

"I'll take on the bigger one; you can handle the small one, right?" the larger hunter asked his companion, who nodded. The two of them intercepted the beasts without any sign of fear, using their specially made batons. Each one hit the underside of the werewolves, electrifying them on the spot and causing them both to plummet down.

As soon as they landed, the werewolves both swiped at their respective attackers, yet the Altered Hunters proved to be skilled enough to avoid the fast claws. Slowly the two werewolves and Altered Hunters were getting farther and farther apart, though by this time, the teenagers had managed to run quite a distance away.

The large hunter was only slightly shorter than the black creature that he was facing. With the armor and weapons on him, it looked as if he would be able to put up a good fight.

"Are you sure you want to stay in your full form? You're just making it easier for me to fight you this way," the hunter said, taunting the beast. The next second, the werewolf got on all fours and leapt toward the hunter. With his electrified baton, the hunter hit the werewolf's ribs, yet the werewolf seemed to have expected it. Its sheer size, weight, and momentum allowed the large creature to push through despite the damage it had sustained.

The hunter shoved his forearm into the black-furred beast's mouth. When the werewolf closed its powerful jaws, it was stupefied, surprised that its teeth were unable to break through whatever armor the hunter was wearing.

"This is no ordinary armor!" the man shouted, and realizing that the baton did little against his foe, he put it away, pulling out the sword by his side. He swung it fast, and the werewolf was barely able to get away, but not before the weapon lightly scratched the outside of his chest.

Blood had been drawn, and the creature could smell burnt flesh. Looking at the sword, he realized that it was far from ordinary; the edge was lit up in a scorching red.

"I saw flesh between your teeth, and you have the stench of blood on you," the hunter said. "You Altered make me sick!"

Not too far away, the smaller hunter was facing off against the brown werewolf. Not only was it smaller than its fellow beast, but it seemed slower and less powerful, which was why he had been tasked with facing this one. Nevertheless, his training had taught him never to underestimate his enemy. One moment of carelessness could spell his demise.

The small hunter pulled out a second electrified baton and held one in each hand, carefully watching the werewolf. It had gotten on all fours and pushed off its powerful legs, taking a swipe at the young hunter.

He leaned back and narrowly avoided the blow, which was faster than he had imagined and nearly made him lose his balance. Still, he caught himself with his arms, arching his back, and went to kick the beast who had now jumped over him.

Seconds before his foot made contact with the beast, a small blade emerged from the top of his toes and pierced the brown werewolf right in the stomach. The creature howled in pain, and when it landed, it rolled about on the ground. Blood was dripping from the werewolf. Unlike the other one, this one's wounds seemed to be healing at a far slower rate.

When the werewolf's back was turned, the hunter could see that the hair on its head was slightly green. He was unsure how he had missed such a striking detail.

Reminds me of someone, the hunter thought, but as soon as the werewolf turned around and showed its giant teeth, he knew there was no time to think about unnecessary things.

The group had finally made it out of the forest and onto the main street. They all wanted to collapse right then and there, as the adrenaline that had helped them get this far had nearly been exhausted.

"We're finally safe." Marie fell to her knees on the pavement, yet two shadows soon cast over her.

"We received a report that an Altered had appeared in Cipen Park. Are you the ones who made the report?" When Marie looked up, she saw two figures displaying golden badges with the symbol of a white rose.

CHAPTER 83

A BIRD?

As expected, after the Altered Hunter had brought out his sword with the heated edge, the larger werewolf became far more cautious. It leapt onto one of the large trees and climbed halfway up, continuously growling at the hunter as if trying to intimidate him. However, what it was really doing was waiting for its wound to heal, which seemed to be taking longer than its other injuries. Even when the werewolf stopped bleeding, a burn mark remained on its chest.

This Altered's healing speed is faster than anything I have encountered before, the Altered Hunter noticed. *Its fighting style resembles that of a wild beast, making it very unpredictable. Still, it's far weaker and has fewer tricks up its sleeve than other Altered I've had to face.*

From the belt around his waist that was loaded with various items, the Altered Hunter pulled out a small dagger and threw it at the werewolf. The creature quickly dodged the attack, jumping to another tree and digging its claws in to keep it from falling. The Altered Hunter then pulled on something, and the small weapon returned from the tree; a green liquid coated its tip.

Should have known this Altered is incredibly agile as well. It seems to be learning as it fights. I only have three more poison daggers. If I can just hit it cleanly once, I should be able to bring it in without getting hurt. It might be able to tell us if it has any comrades.

The second the Altered Hunter thought this, the werewolf began doing something strange.

It started to jump from tree to tree, although the movements weren't too fast; with the moon being the only source of light, the beast's dark fur made it hard for the Altered Hunter to keep track of it. The forest gave the werewolf a serious advantage in this fight, giving it plenty of trees to use. As it sprang from one tree to the other, the Altered Hunter eventually lost track of it, unsure where it would attack from next, leaving him with only one thing to do.

Wait.

The Altered Hunter held on to his sword tightly, and before he knew it, the werewolf had pounced on him just like before. He swung his sword, aiming to inflict the beast with a devastating blow, but instead of flesh, he felt like he had hit solid metal. The Altered Hunter's arms shook from the great impact. His sword had connected with the werewolf's claws, yet they had extended to the point that they were as long as its hands.

Just what are those nails made of? Similar to the baton, the Altered Hunter's current weapon had a button that would make it sear. However, as if the werewolf had predicted this move, it suddenly pulled back one hand to take a large swipe, hitting the Altered Hunter in the chest and sending him flying a few meters through the air. He remained uninjured thanks to his strong armor, but he had to acknowledge that this fight was going to be way harder than he had initially anticipated.

If I had known it would be this tough, I would have notified the others . . . or at least brought a better weapon along. Who would have thought that the Altered in Slough would be so abnormal? Unfortunately, it was too late for regrets.

The first thing the Altered Hunter had done upon landing was to roll to the side, ready for the creature to follow up its attack, but when he looked up, he saw that the beast's attention was no longer on him. Its head was looking slightly upward, and it clenched its large teeth.

A few seconds later, the werewolf was jumping from tree to tree, going higher and higher until it reached the very top of the largest tree in the area. It jumped off, leaping through the air, swiping its claws at what was above them . . . yet it completely missed the mark as its intended targets flew to the side, making it fall down.

Up in the sky were two people, a man and a woman, each one flapping large feathered wings on their back to stay airborne.

"Oh great, it's them," the Altered Hunter mumbled under his breath.

"It looks like someone managed to arrive before us," Frank said to his colleague.

"Indeed, but I'm more interested in the Altered. It doesn't look like your usual type. Very aggressive . . . though apparently lacking in the brains department. We need to bring it in for questioning. I have a feeling that it's linked with the recent killings, including those at the construction site," Sadie replied.

The two of them dove down at great speed, and when they landed between the hunter and the werewolf, the leaves were chucked up in the air around them. Frank was facing the Altered Hunter, whereas Sadie was in front of the werewolf now.

"You are always interested in the more dangerous-looking ones," Frank commented.

"White Rose, why do you always have to get in our way?" the Altered Hunter asked in a bitter tone.

"Because not all Altered are bad, yet you Altered Hunters seem to ignore that fact," Frank answered. "This time, you might have had a valid reason, but we know that's not always the case. I'm afraid we will be bringing you in as well. It's a shame; you would make great members of White Rose if only you could let go of your stupid dogma."

The White Rose agent flapped his wings once more and dashed toward the Altered Hunter, who swung his sword. Frank tilted his body to the side so the sword would hit his powerful wings instead. Then with another flap, he pushed the Altered Hunter to the ground. The force of the attack was enough to break a normal person's arm, yet the Altered Hunters weren't regular people.

The White Rose agent threw out his fist; his hand had transformed into strange talons, grabbing the sword. Frank flapped his wings, gripping the sword tightly. No matter how hard the Altered Hunter pulled, he was unable to get his weapon free and soon found himself in the air.

However, this wasn't the first time the Altered Hunter had had to fight against White Rose. He had many more tricks up his sleeve, and he pulled out one of the daggers coated in green liquid.

Meanwhile, the female White Rose agent was in the middle of a battle with the suspected Altered killer, and she had an easier time than she imagined. From her wings she had pulled out several of her feathers and thrown them at the werewolf.

Idiotically, the werewolf didn't try to avoid them and just ran straight toward Sadie. When the feathers hit, the creature discovered that they were far more dangerous than he had believed. The feathers were as hard as iron arrows, piercing the werewolf's body and pushing it back slightly.

The werewolf quickly pulled them out, allowing the wounds to heal, and out of frustration it tried to throw the feathers back toward Sadie, but they floated to the ground just like normal feathers.

"This seems like it will be a very easy job," Sadie sneered.

CHAPTER 84

TURNING BACK

When Tom opened his eyes, he found himself looking at a bright white light.

"What happened? Where are we?" Tom asked, looking around to see Kai. "Where is Gary?"

"Who knows?" Innu shrugged. "We followed you hoping to find him, but instead, we nearly lost our lives. Do you have any idea how often I nearly died today?"

On further inspection, Tom realized that he and his schoolmates were in what looked like a police station. He could see several criminals coming in and out and people in uniform busy with work, despite the late hour.

Sitting next to him were Innu, Marie, and Xin. Innu looked quite pissed as he recalled his experience, but he seemed to know that blaming Tom wouldn't do anything. Marie was still recovering from her shock, and someone had given her some hot chocolate to calm her nerves. Xin seemed nervous as she looked down and fiddled with her hands, not making eye contact with anyone.

A little while later, Kai came out from one of the offices.

"Good news, everyone. We're free to go home, and the police are even nice enough to give us a lift since it's so late. Probably also to avoid meeting with whatever was in the park."

"Wait, so we don't all have to give reports on what happened?" Xin asked, looking relieved.

"I said I would handle it, didn't I? Unless you feel it's your civil duty to tell them another version of the same thing I just did, let's get going. I don't know about you, but I could use some rest. If we wake up and still remember what happened today, then we will know it wasn't a crazy dream," Kai answered.

The others were thankful they could finally go home; Tom was still worried, but he knew it would be suicide to enter the forest on his own. He didn't even know if Gary and the other omega wolf would still be out there.

Gary, please be safe.

"By the way, why was I asleep?" Tom asked. "And why does my head hurt?"

The others just looked at Xin with grins on their faces, letting her be the one to explain it.

In the forest, a distance away from the three adults, another fight was taking place. The young Altered Hunter had no idea what was going on with his partner, yet he lacked the time to worry about him, for he needed to concentrate on the opponent in front of him.

Once again, the brown werewolf swiped at the young Altered Hunter's head. He rolled to the side, causing the blow to miss and hit the tree instead. Large, deep claw marks were left behind, shredding a huge chunk of the tree.

It has great strength. If that thing hits me in the head, I'm done for. Still, the young Altered Hunter remained level-headed. At every opportunity that presented itself, he would hit the werewolf with his electrified batons, stunning it for a while as the electric power went to work.

Just how many hits can this Altered take? That much electricity should have been enough to knock an elephant out by now. Does it have some special kind of resistance, or is it just healing this fast? the young Altered Hunter wondered.

Whatever the case, I can tell that its movements are slowing down with each hit. If I keep hitting it with the electric batons, then I can change to the sword and finish it off. You will become my first ever Altered kill, allowing me to get on my way to my first star!

Nearly all of the werewolf's strikes were missing the Altered Hunter by the skin of its teeth, yet once in a while it managed to get one in. Unfortunately for the creature, its attacks weren't strong enough to pierce through the special Altered Hunter armor.

Nevertheless, each hit served as a grim reminder of the powerful strength of his foe. The Altered Hunter had no clue how long they had been fighting; it felt like a long time, and that was when he started to notice something.

It . . . is getting smaller! the Altered Hunter realized. Dodging another hit, he used both electrified batons at the same time to shock its back. The beast let out another scream, only this time, rather than a beast's growl, what came out resembled a normal human voice in agony.

I'm right! As the Altered is getting weaker, it must be reverting back!

Seeing how the werewolf was slowing down and reverting, the Altered Hunter believed this to be his chance. He was also worried that his partner had yet to appear. Either he was having a much harder time, or something unexpected had happened.

The movements of the brown werewolf were sluggish and slow by now, making it easier for the Altered Hunter to avoid its swing. Using both of the batons, he started to hit the beast on its arms, its chest, its legs, all over.

In front of the Altered Hunter's very eyes, the werewolf began to shrink to the point that the two of them were on the same eye level. The patch of green fur from the top of its head had also started to spread out until, finally, one could see human skin underneath.

I thought this might have been a real monster for a second, but now I know that there really is a human underneath this abomination. I can do this! The Altered Hunter steeled his resolve, charging in and swinging his baton toward the werewolf's face.

One baton hit its large muzzle, and its face flung to the side. The large teeth started to revert, and the same happened to the muzzle. The Altered Hunter didn't stop there; his other baton hit it from the other side as well, making the muzzle shrink even more.

Third time's the charm! the Altered Hunter thought, swinging both batons toward the head again and landing a successful hit against his target. He was starting to see a human face underneath it all, but at that moment, the werewolf let out a final desperate attack, its claw slicing the mask off the Altered Hunter.

With that, the creature fell to the ground, completely exhausted, fully reverting to its human form.

Shit, he broke my mask! . . . Well, it won't matter. He's going to die anyway, so who cares if he sees my face now. The Altered Hunter tried to calm himself down, making a mental note to bring a replacement mask on his next hunt.

It had been a tough fight, and in a way, the young Altered Hunter had been lucky that his target had already been injured and hurt from fighting the other werewolf before. If that had not been the case, the Altered Hunter wasn't sure if the outcome of their duel would have been the same.

Placing the batons away, he pulled out a short sword, holding it in one hand. He carefully used the weapon to turn the human body over, wishing to imprint the face of his first kill into his mind.

". . . G-Gary?"

CHAPTER 85

FRIEND OR ENEMY?

The young Altered Hunter almost fell over backward as he recognized the werewolf's face. The beast had reverted into human form, revealing a teenage boy's naked body covered with visible scratch and claw marks, injuries sustained in his fight against the other werewolf.

What do I do now? The young Altered Hunter was in a panic. He had never expected to actually know the Altered he had been ready to kill. Just to check whether his mind was playing tricks on him, making him mistake the other's identity just because of the green hair, he went to turn over his body one more time.

However, just then, the boy on the ground abruptly opened his eyes, his vision hazy and his body in pain. He felt weak and tired, but he suddenly found a familiar face in front of him.

"B-Blake!" Gary blurted out, still finding it hard to move.

Touching his face, the Altered Hunter remembered that the werewolf had destroyed his mask, the one item that was supposed to hide his identity.

He saw who I am! He knows I'm an Altered Hunter! I can't let him go now! He's an Altered in the first place, so . . . I just need to get rid of him.

Blake looked down at the short sword in his hand, yet he couldn't find the strength to tighten his grip around it. He had been ready to kill the Altered, but now he hesitated. It didn't help that Gary was no longer attacking him, looking defenseless and confused.

I . . . I can't . . . He's my classmate. I have no idea how he became such an abomination, but I know that he helped me. He even took a hit for me from those Eton High thugs.

"My head hurts like hell!" Gary said groggily as he slowly lifted his body. Feeling a little chilly, Gary noticed that he had no clothes on whatsoever, and he was slowly starting to realize that he was in the middle of an unfamiliar forest as well.

"Why am I here? What the hell happened? And why am I naked?" Gary bombarded the hesitating Blake with a barrage of questions as he picked up the largest leaf he could find to hide his nether regions.

"Huh? You mean, you don't remember? You don't remember how you got here or what just happened?" Blake almost shouted, swinging his short sword about. Looking at the illegal weapon in his hand, Gary finally noticed the strange clothing his classmate wore, as well as the batons at his waist.

He looks pretty much like a younger version of that other guy . . . wait . . . no . . . how can that be?

Gary was starting to put the pieces together. The last thing he remembered before he woke up was the system notifying him about his transformation starting and then experiencing a type of torture that he never wanted to relive again. He could guess that his werewolf self had headed for the woods . . .

"Wait, Blake, I don't care who you are! What about Tom, is he okay? Did I hurt him? Did I hurt anybody else?" Gary asked, grabbing Blake by the shoulders, letting the leaf fall down.

Blake could tell that Gary was genuinely concerned, but he didn't understand what was happening to his classmate. As an Altered, Gary should have been in full control of his actions, even if this was his first full-body transformation. It didn't make sense for him not to remember anything.

That's right; Tom was with those other guys . . . I have no clue where he is now, but I still need to decide what to do. Gary knows who I am and what I am, but he doesn't seem to care . . . but I can't really believe his word and let him go. The Altered Hunter hesitated.

"Tom and your other friends are just fine," Blake answered. "At least they were when I last saw them."

Gary let out a sigh of relief, although he wasn't sure who those "other friends" were. However, he had one surefire way to check where Tom was. At the moment, he was unable to see any of his markings, so he immediately opened up the system screen.

You are unable to sustain your werewolf form
10/120 Energy
While your Energy is extremely low, emergency/passive healing function is unavailable!
20/100 HP

His stats were at the lowest Gary had ever seen, but he found it interesting that the reason he had reverted to human form seemed to be that he had run out of Energy. If that was the case, then he might have just found a way to avoid turning during the next full moon. Of course, he would have to find a different way to deal with his bloodlust, and it would mean his fighting capabilities would be severely limited.

Marks: 2/5

Two out of five, that means . . . Tom and Gil are both still alive! I didn't kill anyone! But why the hell am I here, then? And how did I run into Blake? Now that Gary realized his best friend was at least still alive, and he had managed to get through a turning, he looked toward Blake.

"Hey . . . come on, Blake. I know we're not the closest of people, but you have to understand . . . I'm not an Altered, or at least not a regular one, so can you please let me go if I promise not to tell anyone? I mean, we're teammates, right? You remember me, and you did good on the field today . . ."

The naked teenager was slowly stepping back at this point, trying to figure out where to run or even what direction to run. Blake put the short sword away and lifted both hands.

"Gary, I'm not going to hurt you. I owe you for helping me out. It's just my family—"

A loud howl interrupted him, and they both looked in the direction where it had come from.

Blake knew this was neither the time nor the place for the two of them to talk.

"Gary, I don't have time to explain, but you have to get out of here!"

Gary was inclined to agree, but he didn't know where to go. Heck, he still wasn't sure where exactly he was.

Looking around, Blake realized Gary's problem.

"It doesn't matter, just run away from the noise! If the others find you, they won't let you live!" Blake pointed in the opposite direction.

"I won't forget this, Blake. Your secret's safe with me!" Gary picked up the leaf and started running.

Gripping his sword tightly, Blake dropped his head in disappointment. Not only had he failed in killing an Altered, he had gone so far as to actively help it escape, missing his chance of getting closer to obtaining his first star and becoming an official hunter.

If this ever got out . . .

CHAPTER 86

ESCAPE

The fight in the forest was continuing between Frank and the Altered Hunter. It seemed both of them had underestimated their opponent. After the black-furred wolf had been hit by the strange feathers, it didn't make it easy for Sadie to use them again.

The beast was now taking cover by running between the trees, making it hard for her to hit him. Still, once in a while an attack would land, but it didn't matter because the werewolf would just pull the feathers out, its body healing the damage.

That thing's healing speed is seriously annoying! Argh, why did we have to be near a forest? Even if I fly up, I can't use my full-strength attacks!

Suddenly the werewolf pounced on top of her. The White Rose agent covered her body, wrapping herself in her wings.

Its claws gripped her wings tightly, and she scrunched up her face in pain. Her wings were harder than normal steel, and it had been a while since she had felt pain like this. The woman started to flap them, hoping that the beast would let go, but it had already dug its claws into her, blood dripping from them.

"Frank, a little help would be nice!" Sadie shouted. She didn't feel like she was in trouble, but she knew that with her partner's help, it would be far easier to deal with this strange Altered.

"I'm not having it so easy myself, ya know!" Frank shouted back. He had already drawn his wings back into his body. During the fight, he had been hit by the seared sword a few times, and he still felt the pain. The weapon was a high-class one.

Right now, Frank was using his hands, which looked like talons. His fingers looked like they were glued together with a single large thick nail at the end. He and the large Altered Hunter exchanged several clashes as Frank moved out of the way; he was forced to block more than he had the chance to attack, but at least his claws were able to take the heat coming from the weapon.

"You're quite skilled!" Frank praised his opponent with a smile. "What are you, a three-star hunter? That's how you guys rank yourselves, right? What is someone like you doing in a place like Slough?"

However, the werewolf didn't bother to waste time talking. It merely struck the White Rose agent with the sword, knocking one of the clawed hands away, and barged into him, its shoulder pushing him down slightly. Frank was then ready to attack with his sword again before he had no choice but to jump back.

Three feathers lay on the ground where he had been only a second ago.

"You were supposed to be helping me, not the other way around!" Sadie complained, her legs now transformed as well, giving her the look of a bird-type Altered. Underneath her clawed leg, the black werewolf was struggling to get out. Both of its arms were locked in place by her feet.

"You Altered can't even see the foolishness that has been brought on due to your existence. We both know that this beast isn't the exception but the rule! Can you imagine the future if this spreads?" the Altered Hunter shouted. "If it weren't for us, those kids would have died today!"

The next second, Sadie felt an excruciating pain as she realized that the werewolf had twisted its head, showing that it was far more flexible than she had imagined, and had pierced her foot with its large teeth.

On reflex, she had opened her talons, allowing the beast to get free at the moment. It let out a howl before running off into the woods at a great speed, nearly out of their line of sight.

"Look at your incompetence! Because of your meddling, you let it get away, and now it will just continue to rampage!" the Altered Hunter shouted; he turned away from Frank and ran in the opposite direction from the werewolf.

"Who do we go after?" Frank asked.

"Get the damn werewolf!" Sadie shouted. "At least the Altered Hunter won't harm the public; that thing was like a wild beast!"

Eventually, running the way that Blake had pointed, Gary found himself on the open road. He decided to follow it, hoping to find his way somewhere, but he was too embarrassed to let anyone see him as he was, so he ran closer to the edge of the forest.

While doing so, he couldn't get the crazy thoughts and events of today out of his head.

What do I do now? I only have 10 Energy points, and with the full moon out, they won't last long, Gary asked himself, as if hoping his ever-silent Werewolf System would choose now to provide some guidance. Of course, he wasn't surprised when it didn't. *I don't even know what time it is. How long until the full moon is over? Do I have to wait until the sun is up or until a full day has passed?*

That howl from earlier must have been Billy. He's probably going through the same thing as me, but if he meets me now and I'm in this state, he'll finish me off in seconds. At the same time, if I eat something . . . if I recover my Energy, will I automatically turn back into a werewolf?

Can I even risk it? Blake didn't seem to be the only one out there. There's a chance I won't remember anything, and it will happen again . . .

Gary continued along the road, thinking more and more about what happened, and eventually snippets of his memory returned, of him fighting against a black-furred werewolf, and how he hadn't exactly done well.

It was then that a little squirrel appeared at the edge of the forest. His stomach growled in response.

One squirrel surely won't hurt . . . Maybe getting some Energy back will allow me to think more clearly . . . Gary tried to convince himself as the saliva dripped down his mouth. He started chasing after the critter, even as he ran out onto the road.

Seconds later he saw a bright light from the corner of his eye. Gary turned around and saw that the car would soon be upon him. He was ready to jump into the forest, but his legs weren't working as he wanted; he was still too weak.

Luckily, inches before it reached him, the car came to a screeching halt.

"Do you have a death wish, kid?" An annoyed voice came from inside the vehicle as the car door flew open. Someone had gotten out, but the light was too bright for him to make out who it was.

"What the— Why are you naked? What's with all those scratches? Just what the hell happened to you?" the person asked, the anger in his voice replaced with worry.

CHAPTER 87
KIND STRANGER?

As the stranger left his car, the first thing on Gary's mind was to turn and run away.

"No, get away from me! It's dangerous to stay near me! If I'm next to anyone, there's a chance that I could . . . that I could . . ." Gary's mind was spinning as he took a careful step back, heading toward the forest.

"Hey, stop! Where do you think you're going, kid? You can't stay out like that!" the stranger shouted, and he was quickly by Gary's side. It was at that moment that his Energy dropped even lower.

8/120 Energy

Gary almost fell to the ground out of exhaustion, yet the stranger managed to catch him and easily carried him to his car, where he placed him on the back seat. Gary's eyes were closed, and he had fallen into a light slumber.

The stranger got back in his car and drove along the road, looking around frantically through the forest for something. Eventually, just when he had been about to head into the forest himself, his phone vibrated, and he read the text he had just received.

"Argh, so you're telling me I came all the way out here for no reason? No, no, I should just be happy that she's safe. 'Don't tell Dad'? Does she really believe she can hide that fact from him?" he muttered to himself, letting out a big sigh.

The stranger's monologue seemed to awaken Gary a little bit. Opening his eyes, he found himself in the man's car. He wasn't sure what to think about that. What were the chances that the stranger had rescued him out of the kindness of his heart?

Unfortunately, there was little he could do about it. He still had the same problems as before. At the top of the list was the immense pain that originated from his stomach. It felt like someone was reaching in and pulling his insides.

However, for some reason, it didn't feel as bad as the last time he was low on Energy. Gary theorized that it might just be because he had experienced a painful transformation. Compared to that, this seemed like a walk in the park.

"You're in luck, streaker kid; my plans just fell through. So now I can deal with you." The man addressed him, apparently aware that he was conscious again. "What happened to you? Why do you have no clothes on? And what are you doing out so late?"

Gary was trying to get a look at his savior, but with the man's face looking at the road ahead, it was hard to make out anything but his eyes from the rearview mirror. Still, he did notice a few things. For one, the car they were in seemed to be a nice one. The quality of the seats, the space, and the logo on the steering wheel indicated that it was expensive, probably even an import.

Then there was the man himself; from the side, he could make out defined triceps muscles sticking out from a short-sleeve shirt. He wasn't exactly a large person, seemingly a few inches taller than Gary, but there was hardly any fat showing on his arm.

He's even more ripped than that coach at the gym. Who is this guy? Gary wondered.

"Come on, streaker boy, I need an answer. Right now, I'm still feeling generous, but if you don't want to spill the beans, I'll have to just drop you off at the police station." The stranger addressed him in an annoyed tone. Gary wasn't sure if he was the reason for the man's apparent bad mood or if it had to do with the plans that had fallen through.

"No, please, not the police!" Gary pleaded. He knew that they had his blood on record now. If he was taken in, they might be able to link him to all the other cases, something he needed to avoid at all costs, but what would he say?

"This is just . . . I . . . I'm being bullied at school. They called me out here today before they took all my clothes. I-I can't fight back . . . they have connections," Gary lied, trying to cry to add to his story, though nothing but sniffs came out.

He considered this to be quite the plausible story. Of course, that didn't explain all the scratches all over his body. Gary just hoped that this sob story was enough for the stranger to ignore the inconsistencies and not ask any more questions. Fortunately, the stranger did indeed seem to feel too bad to pry into things any further.

"My condolences. I guess you're lucky that I found you, then. So where exactly did you intend to go before I picked you up? Shall I drop you off at your house?" he asked.

With the shape Gary was in now, home was the last place he wanted to be. He honestly wanted nothing more than to be left alone until this torture was over, but he couldn't just ask the stranger to drop him off at the storage warehouse. Come to think of it, he dreaded the thought of what he had done to get out of there in the first place . . .

If I stay with him, there is a chance that I might attack him as well.

"No answer again, huh. Home trouble on top of school trouble? Look, I'll do you a favor just this once. I'm staying at a hotel at the moment, and the room is way bigger than what a normal person needs. There are plenty of extra beds. I'll let you stay there for the night if you want. Then in the morning, you can leave and do as you like, no questions asked, all right?" the stranger offered.

"Yes, sir!" Gary immediately agreed, a huge smile on his face. Perhaps there would be a way for him to leave once he was in the room or the stranger had gone to sleep. It was late, after all.

"Sir? Do I really look that old to you?" the stranger complained. *Damn it, why can't I help but be nice to people like him. Is it because it reminds me of my own situation?* The stranger scratched his head.

A short while later, the car stopped before a very nice-looking hotel at the far end of Cipen. It was one of the Slough's fancier areas, but the good thing was that it wasn't too far away from the Yellow Stack.

Now that they were out of the car, Gary had a better look at the guy in front of him, who was all of a sudden taking off his shirt, revealing his hard abs and everything underneath. The next second he threw the shirt to the kid.

"Cover yourself with that and stay behind me for now," the stranger ordered as they walked into the hotel. Gary did as he was told. Fortunately, the man was slightly larger than him, allowing him to stretch the shirt down to hide certain exposed parts of his body.

Now that he got a closer look at this Good Samaritan, he saw that the guy had a familiar face, but Gary just couldn't quite pinpoint where he had seen him before.

"Welcome back, Mr. Tiger. Would you like us to help with anything in your room?" A woman greeted him with respect.

Holy shit, that's it! He's Jayden Tiger! One of the top Altereds in our country! What is he doing in a shithole like Slough? Gary, being the Altered fighter fanatic that he was, instantly recognized him after hearing the last name.

Any other day of the week, he might be fanboying over the chance to not only meet but stay with one of his idols, but now he was only worried.

He was running from one tough situation to the next.

415

CHAPTER 88

SURVIVING THE NIGHT

Gary had to stop himself from hyperventilating due to excitement. His inner fanboy needed to be contained, yet he couldn't waste any more Energy than he already had. Still, there was one silver lining to meeting Jayden.

If Gary were to turn suddenly, he was convinced that the Altered superstar could suppress him in a fight. Unfortunately, he didn't know what would happen after that point, so he made up his mind to never find out.

The receptionist was baffled at the disheveled sight of Gary but didn't say anything as he followed the VIP to the elevator. Jayden hadn't lied about his room being more than one person realistically needed; however, he had failed to mention one very important detail.

He was staying in the *penthouse*!

The room alone was around five times the size of the apartment where Gary lived with his mother and sister. Through the glass windows, he could see the entire town of Slough. This was exactly the type of life Gary had dreamed about when he'd wished to become an Altered one day.

Alas, he couldn't really enjoy it right now.

Leaving behind a still-baffled teenager, Jayden had gone to one of the connecting rooms and returned with a new shirt on. The Altered superstar then threw over a pair of briefs, socks, trousers, and a jacket.

"This should let you go around town tomorrow without alarming the police. If you go down the hall, the showers are to the right. There's a toothbrush and everything in each room.

"It's late, and I have an early start tomorrow. Just keep the clothes, there's no need to return them. Leave whenever you wish, though don't be surprised if I'm already gone by the time you wake up," Jayden told him. "Help yourself to whatever's in the fridge."

Turning around, the Altered superstar was about to close the door to his room but stopped a few seconds later and opened it again.

"Look, I know times are tough in the world at the moment, but if you don't do something about it, then you might be stuck in this situation forever. The biggest influence on your life is you. Don't wait for something to happen; change and make it happen." Jayden made a fist and swung it out.

Gary understood the message: Jayden wanted him to stand up to his "bullies." He smiled and nodded, thinking that right now his problem wasn't fighting off bullies; it was trying to stop himself from killing and eating them.

When the door closed, Gary saw his best chance to leave. Quickly putting on the provided clothes, he turned around and was about to head out, but he suddenly stopped, considering his current situation.

Right now, he was at a place where there was nobody else around. The only person who actually *was* around should be strong enough to contain him. And in case Billy actually tried to attack him again, that person could actually protect him from the other werewolf.

His family still believed that he was at Tom's. The only thing worrying him was that he was unable to contact his best friend. After saving Tom's contact info on his phone, he had never bothered memorizing it. Unfortunately, he'd left his phone at the storage warehouse.

Not to mention, right now, he was still a threat to Tom.

An ornate clock above the TV told Gary that it was three a.m. The sun would rise in a couple more hours, so he decided to just wait it out. He sat on the large sofa to wait, and after a while his system sent him a notification.

4/120 Energy

What happens when my Energy hits 0? Will I even be able to move? Before Gary knew it, he found himself walking toward the fridge. Opening it, he was surprised to find it filled with all types of protein.

Steaks, chicken, lamb, and other animal meat, and, from the looks of it, all high-quality products. Saliva immediately started to dribble out of his mouth. He was sure that just half a pound of any of it would cost more than the rent for their small apartment.

This is what you would expect from a top-class Altered. Gary reached out, ready to grab the food, yet stopped inches away.

What if I can't control myself? No! I have to control myself. Gary picked up one of the raw steaks and, returning to the sofa, slowly and carefully took a small bite out of it. It was taking all of his will-power not to just swallow the whole thing in an instant. He had to grit his teeth and use his hands to hold himself back.

+2 Energy

I can do this! If I just eat a little at a time, stopping my Energy from going too high, it should be okay. When it gets low, I'll just take another bite. Yeah, I just need to hold myself back.

He continued battling with himself. More than once, he caught his body moving subconsciously. Gary had never experienced this type of mental torture before, but after what felt like an eternity, Gary could finally see it. There, through the large glass window, he saw the sun starting to rise while the moon was starting to disappear.

Sometime after that, he received new notifications.

You have successfully survived a full moon!
The blessing of the moon has passed
30 days until the next full moon

I did it! I did it! Gary jumped up, and the first thing he did was head straight for the fridge.

He had held back to prevent his Energy from recovering to the point that he would be able to transform again, worried that this transformation might last until the moon came up again, or worse, a few days, but judging by the system, it seemed like that wasn't going to be the case.

Jayden's alarm woke him up at six thirty a.m. As he walked out of his room, he was surprised to see that the kid was nowhere to be seen. He had expected to find him in one of the rooms, still sleeping soundly, but it seemed as if he might have disappeared after he had gone off to sleep.

However, Jayden's conscience was appeased. He had done a good deed and could only wish the boy the best from now on. He headed to the fridge to look for a snack, but when he opened it his jaw nearly dropped.

What the hell? I just had it filled yesterday! Did that frigging kid eat all of it? . . . No, that should be impossible. There was enough in there to last me a week. Did he steal it to try to make some cash or something? Argh, that doesn't matter; what am I supposed to eat now?

A little earlier, both White Rose agents had returned to the police station to file a report on the case, and they wanted to confirm something. One of the feathers they had picked up still had the blood of the black werewolf that had managed to flee.

Sadie wanted to make sure that the blood matched up with Billy's. This was her hunch, and Frank's as well. After filing their report, they left the interrogation room, still furious about failing to arrest the dangerous Altered. They had tried their best to find him from the air, but it was as if he had disappeared.

They were still in the police station when Roo Game, the young officer, came up to them with good news. "We found someone who claims to know Billy," he reported. "Since Billy is a dropout, it was hard to find anyone who knew him, but unexpectedly one of the suspects we brought in claimed he had seen him elsewhere.

"Apparently, the last time he saw him was at one of these underground fights. According to the suspect, they happen quite often in this town."

Sadie smiled. "An underground fighter, huh? There should be a few people who would have seen him and know him, then. Frank, looks like we'll be going undercover!"

As Sadie walked away, Frank noticed that she was limping; she had been injured in her Altered form. He thought that a wound like that would have been healed by now.

I hope that bite isn't infectious. Frank was worried.

CHAPTER 89

BEST FRIENDS

After replenishing his Energy by plundering the fridge, Gary decided to take some of the food along with him. With no better alternatives, he placed it in the coat pockets of his new jacket. Right now, he was in a rush, and there was a reason why he had left early.

He won't mind, right? I mean, the guy is an Altered superstar. Someone as rich as him can easily just replace all that food, and it's not like I'll see him ever again. Damn, if I had been in my right mind, I could have asked him for a signature! I bet that would have sold for a decent sum!

Around six a.m., Gary was sprinting toward the Yellow Stack building. He was hoping that he could grab his phone and check out what state he had left the room in. Perhaps it might give him an idea of what had happened after he had lost consciousness.

When he finally reached the Yellow Stack, though, he saw several black-and-white cars, which made him do a complete U-turn.

Damn, the police are here! Did something happen? Shit, did I trigger an alarm or something? What do I do now? Both of my phones were in there! And my clothes! I hope I don't get Tom in any kind of trouble. Gary started to panic. *Well, I was naked, so maybe I ripped all of my clothes off?*

In the end, he couldn't risk staying there. All he could do was head to school without his belongings. As for his school uniform, he had left it at school in his locker, since he'd left the rugby match yesterday in a hurry. He could only hope that after yesterday's match, Mr. Root wouldn't mind replacing his rugby uniform.

Running nonstop, Gary used the Charging Heart skill three times that morning: once to get Yellow Stack and two more times to reach his school. Fortunately, with the extra food he had consumed, his Energy was almost replenished.

Although the moon seemed to still be full, he had lost his additional stats, though it was a small price to pay for no longer losing his Energy as quickly.

My stats are now lower, though, and I can really feel it in my body. I need to improve them!

When he entered the school, almost nobody was there because it was so early. Gary had been running for an hour, which was quite impressive considering the distance. If anyone saw his accomplishments, they would have tried to recruit him for the track team.

The first thing Gary did was change into his school uniform from his locker. Anyone could see that his current clothes were too nice for someone like him. After that, all he could do was wait. Surprisingly, the first person who entered the classroom was none other than Tom.

Yes, he's here! The one person I could have hoped for. I don't know why he's early, but thank my lucky stars he's here!

He could see the marks again and knew they were getting closer, but he wasn't going to believe it until he saw them. What was even stranger was the first thing Tom did. He immediately ran up to Gary, giving him a big hug.

"You . . . you . . . *you're okay!* I'm so happy! I was so worried! I thought that you might have been hurt or stuck in that form forever!" Tom was crying, rubbing his face into Gary's shirt, covering it with tears and snot.

Gary had no clue what had happened. Before today, he would have pushed his best friend off, but after everything his friend had done to help him, it felt wrong of him to do that. Gary waited for Tom to finish letting his emotions out.

Still sobbing, Tom placed his backpack on the table and pulled out two phones as well as some ripped rugby clothing, handing them over to Gary.

"Wait, these are my things; how did you get them?" Gary asked. Tom looked incredibly tired.

What exactly happened to him? Gary thought.

"I went to Yellow Stack after leaving the police station. I thought that you wouldn't be there, since you were dealing with other things. I didn't know how I could help you, but I wanted to make sure that the person I saw was you.

"When I entered the Yellow Stack, the steel door had been ripped to shreds, the chains were completely broken, and there was something on the floor. I cleaned most of it up and grabbed your things before calling the police myself. I said there was a break-in, so there shouldn't be a problem there."

"Wait, what? I understand some of what you were talking about, but the other things make no sense. How did you know where I was or what I was doing?" Gary asked.

Tom went into the frightening details of the night before. How he had planned to wait nearby, how they had seen someone killed in front of their eyes, but most importantly, that Gary in his werewolf form had saved them.

All of that happened, yet I wasn't conscious for any of it . . . At least it didn't sound like I attacked the other guys . . . but why did I save them? Well, clearly that other werewolf had to have been Billy, Gary thought.

He had some theories, and they were all related to his system. From what it had told him, he should have been hunting those he'd marked with a Forced Bond, yet Gil didn't seem to have been there.

Since that hadn't happened, he could only imagine that his werewolf instincts had been trying to complete another quest: fighting the other omega wolf to see who would come out on top.

Lastly, there was also the Bond Mark that he had placed on Tom. Maybe Gary had protected Tom because of his mark, or there was a part of him that was still in his werewolf form somewhere, telling his werewolf self to protect those close to him?

This last one he thought was unlikely because Gary couldn't remember a thing; it was as if someone had taken over his body.

Maybe I can place more Bond Marks on people I really care for, like my mother and Amy. However, first I'll have to deal with a far bigger problem. Billy could still be alive, and if he comes out again . . .

"Anyway, thanks for helping us out, Gary. Now we have an entire month to solve this problem to prevent anything from going wrong next time. Just leave the whole mess about the storage unit to me; I'll find a way to explain things to my parents somehow. Looks like it wasn't much use anyway." Tom chuckled. "By the way, I was wondering, since when did you have two phones?"

CHAPTER 90

A GANG NAME

Gary didn't want to have secrets from Tom, especially after everything he had done to help him, but at the same time, he didn't want to drag his best friend into an even deeper mess. It wasn't fair of him, and it was likely that it could endanger his life as well as that of his family, more so than he already had done.

"Oh, this thing? My regular phone has been playing up a bit recently. You know about our financial situation, so I used some of the money I earned from that part-time job to get myself that brick for emergencies. You know how those old phones can never die, and the battery lasts forever." Gary smiled, still feeling hurt inside.

As for Tom, he didn't know how to feel. Gary had shared one of his biggest secrets with him, so why would he need to lie about a second phone?

"What about the police report? Did you say anything about me?" Gary asked, changing the subject.

"Actually, I wanted to ask you about that. The whole thing was strange. Do you know that rich upperclassman, Kai Hemper? He went ahead of all of us, but after he talked to them for a while, they all just let us go home. I thought he was just some rich kid, but just being rich shouldn't get you out of a situation like that. By the way, how do you know him?"

Scratching his head, Gary felt like he couldn't lie two times in a row; he was a bad liar in the first place, so he chose to stick mostly to the truth without revealing anything extra.

"He was actually the one who introduced me to that part-time job."

Things were starting to add up to Tom, but he still didn't know why Kai, who couldn't have known Gary for too long, was so interested in him that his entire group, which seemed to include that sudden transfer student Innu, had been willing to look for his best friend in the middle of the night.

A short while later, other students started to enter the classroom, unaware of the horrors Gary and Tom had lived through.

"Hey, Gary, you did a great job in the first half of yesterday's rugby match! I never knew you were that strong," one of his classmates congratulated him. "Oh, and Tom, how are you? I can't believe the referee didn't punish those bastards for stepping on your hand!"

Tom and Gary recognized him as one of the more popular kids of their year, meaning he was someone who would usually never associate with either one of them.

"A shame Gary didn't punch them out. Seriously, when you jumped those Eton High students, I was rooting for you; they would have deserved it. I'm still surprised you did that with their bad rep. I thought they were all going to jump you!" another one added.

The compliments didn't seem to stop, and after the day that Gary had had, it was a nice change. He thanked them all and just smiled back. The last ones to arrive were Xin and Innu, both resembling zombies. They were drained and dragging their feet along the floor.

"I guess they didn't get a good night's sleep, then." Gary gulped, feeling responsible.

Xin sat down in her seat and didn't look toward anyone. Gary wanted to go talk to her and apologize for getting her into such a mess, but it would have felt strange and given things away.

As for Innu, when he tried to talk to him, he didn't even let Gary utter a single word.

"You! I really don't want to talk to you . . ." Innu sat down in his chair and placed his backpack in front of him, proceeding to use it as a makeshift pillow. "Do you know what happened to us yesterday? Actually, scratch that, do you know what happened to *me*? I almost got killed like five times, and it was all because we went searching for you!

"Then, I have this psycho here, shouting your name all the time, trying to talk to some possessed Altered. Bad luck! That's all I have since I started following you!"

With that Innu just lay there. He knew it wasn't Gary's fault that this had happened, but he needed someone to blame all his frustrations on.

Lessons went on as normal, but as expected, Gary couldn't focus on his classes. Billy was his main worry. Even in his werewolf form, he couldn't beat the other werewolf. Gary had no idea how to beat Billy, especially since he had already killed and consumed humans, making him even stronger. The longer Gary waited, the worse his chances became.

Maybe the best option would be to get him before the full moon. Then I can worry about myself as well . . . but it means I have to be prepared . . . prepared to kill him.

A little while later, he felt his secret phone vibrate. Tom, who had been keeping an eye on Gary, took note of this. When it was finally time for lunch, Gary asked him if they could go and grab a bite to eat together.

"Sorry, I have to make a report to Mr. Root about the game. He said he wanted to talk to me about something," Gary lied again.

"Okay, I understand. I might just stay here and catch up on some sleep," Tom replied.

Watching carefully, Tom saw that Innu also looked at his phone, one that looked eerily similar to the brick model his best friend had, and went off in the same direction as Gary.

That phone and Kai, something is up with all of them. I wonder if this has something to do with how Gary was making money. Gary . . . I just hope you're not getting yourself in another mess.

Tom's guess was spot on. Gary had headed to the roof, where Kai and Marie were already waiting for him. A little while later, Innu joined them as well.

"It looks like everyone is here for our meeting," Kai said after Innu closed the door behind him. "We had quite an eventful evening yesterday, looking out for you, Gary. I'm sure your friend already caught you up on everything that happened.

"Anyway, regardless of this, tomorrow is the big day for you two; it's your first match, and it's also our debut as a gang. The reason I called you all here today was that I wanted us all to come up with a name, as members."

This came as a surprise to Gary. He had seen Marie interact with Kai that one time he had followed her, yet he had never thought that she would also be involved with this whole gang business.

"How about the Unbreakable Iron Group? Or I know, the Black Flames!" Innu suggested while pretending to wield the power of fire. Gary noticed that Innu had quite the childlike side to him . . . and that his naming sense was horrible, yet Gary didn't have any better suggestions himself, which was why he decided to keep quiet.

"After what happened yesterday, I actually felt inspired by those creatures. What do you all think about the Howlers?" Kai suggested, looking at Gary in particular.

"I like it," Marie said, while Innu shivered a little bit thinking about the howls he had heard from the Altered yesterday. However, he had to admit that it was a good name. A gang name should send fear into whoever heard it, though usually their own members should be exempt.

"I think it's good as well," Gary answered, really not having any better ideas.

After that, Kai reminded Gary and Innu to keep out of trouble until their fight before giving them the meeting place on the day of the match. He also advised them to stay inside as much as possible, because of recent events.

Since lunch was coming to an end, Gary headed back to his classroom, and as he was walking down the hallway he stopped dead in his tracks, and so did the other person opposite him.

"Blake."

"Damn it, I completely forgot about this."

CHAPTER 91

ALTERED HUNTER RANKS

Although Gary had survived the full moon, the number of things on his mind hadn't really lessened. For some reason, he had put this one in particular at the back of his mind. Perhaps because it had been the first thing he had been confronted with after reverting, or maybe it was because Blake being an Altered Hunter seemed as unbelievable as him being a werewolf.

Man, what is it with this school? Does it have some special attraction to strange people? I'm seriously starting to worry about running into vampires, dragons, and demons . . . Out of everyone, why did he have to be an Altered Hunter?

Planning to avoid the confrontation, Gary decided to do the easiest thing. He lifted his hand to wave at Blake . . . and then tried to walk right past him. However, as he did, a shadow was cast in front of him. Gary quickly moved to the other side, yet the shadow copied him. It was clear that the young Altered Hunter was blocking his way.

"Come on! You really want to do this, in school of all places? I can't get into any more trouble! I just came back after being suspended for an entire week! Look, I'm pretending that I never saw you, that everything was just a bad dream yesterday, so why can't you do the same?" Gary was screaming internally as he decided to go for a spin, trying to get past his schoolmate.

Right now, Gary was imagining himself on the field with the rugby ball in his hands, trying to get past one of the defenders. Unfortunately, Blake seemed to have predicted this and was already in the right position to catch him.

Shit. Can't things go my way for once?

Blake placed his hand on Gary's shoulder quite confidently and leaned in so no one else would hear.

"Look, I'm not too eager to have that conversation either, but we really need to talk about yesterday. Don't worry; I'm not planning to do anything else for you. Let's just head to the bench outside near the art building. I believe it's in both our interests to decide what to do next," Blake whispered before he patted Gary on the back and continued on his way.

Well, a talk doesn't sound too bad, but I haven't even had time to think about what to say! Damn it, Blake is a nice guy, right? I mean, he let me go yesterday in the woods. Surely he wouldn't lie to me to try to kill me now. We're in school with far too many potential witnesses. If he really wanted to kill me, he could have approached me outside of school.

Being relatively sure that it was safe, he decided to go with Blake. Nobody found it strange that they walked together. Although they hadn't won the match, everyone in school knew that Eton High had beaten up nearly all the regulars. Gary had only recently become one, and their teamwork had secured them a draw, making the two of them the superstars of the rugby club.

Alas, Gary was being reminded just how popular Blake actually was. Everyone went out of their way to greet him; a few girls even stopped him to give him gifts. Gary wasn't sure, but he wouldn't be surprised if some of those cookies had been baked early in the morning just for Blake.

On the other hand, only a few congratulated Gary here and there. It was obvious that he was being treated mostly as an afterthought when they noticed that he was with the real rugby star.

Damn it, would they all be thinking the same if they knew he was an Altered Hunter? This lifestyle, everything he's doing is fake . . . It was then that Gary realized the hypocrisy. Was what he was doing really any different?

Altered Hunters had a bad reputation. After all, becoming an Altered was something that everyone wished for. They were super-stars and instant celebrities, yet one crazy group of people had chosen to kill them for no apparent reason.

Or at least not a reason the general public could understand. If anyone did find out Blake was an Altered Hunter, he would probably be chased after for the rest of his life.

Eventually they reached a bench outside the art building, and he realized why Blake had picked this spot. No one was around, other than the students in their classrooms making art.

The two of them sat together for a while, neither one really sure how to start such a serious conversation.

Should I go first? Is he waiting for me to say something? Or should I just wait?

Just when Gary was about to speak, Blake started instead.

"My family . . . They have been Altered Hunters since seemingly forever. Altered have actually existed for much longer than you're led to believe. Just like us, they used to have a different name, but that's beside the point. It was only recently that Altered started to become more public about their existence.

"I don't know how someone like you managed to become an Altered. I actually chose to go to a no-name school in a Tier 3 town because I believed that it would allow me to separate my two lives. I never wanted to run into somebody I knew, but then I met you."

It made sense; although Blake hid the fact that he was an Altered Hunter, in the end, he was still a teenager like Gary. Gary knew how hard it was to kill someone you knew or someone you saw every day; the connection made it harder.

At a no-name school, it should have been impossible for anyone to afford to become an Altered or have the potential to be selected as one, apart from Blake himself, of course.

"I'm guessing it started when you got better at rugby. I didn't think much of it at the time, and I thought that it was actually fun to just forget about everything and try to compete for a change. You helped me forget about what I was . . ."

Damn it, the more I listen to him, the more I realize the two of us are alike. That's why I started to enjoy rugby a lot as well.

"And then you saved me, which is why I decided to do that favor for you the other day, but at the same time, Gary, this is a warning. There aren't many Altered in this town, which means that you will become one of our targets.

"How much do you know about Altered Hunters?" Blake asked.

"Not much, just what's on the news. I had no idea that you used that strange armor of yours," Gary replied honestly.

"We Altered Hunters have ranks," Blake explained. "These ranks are tattooed on our shoulders in the form of stars, and a lot of hunters are proud of them. The more stars, the stronger the Altered Hunter, and my father, who lives here with me in this town, is a three-star hunter."

"A three-star hunter? So what are you, and how do hunters even get these stars?" Gary asked.

It was the first question that made Blake pause for a moment.

"I don't have any stars on my shoulder yet. An Altered Hunter gets a star only if he manages to kill five Altered. Right now, I'm still an apprentice to my father, and you were actually supposed to be my first kill."

Now Gary understood why Blake's father was so dangerous. If he was a three-star Altered Hunter, it meant that he had already killed Altered in the double digits, beings that were superhuman with all sorts of different forms. He was experienced beyond belief.

"I guess I was lucky I ran into you then and not him." Gary chuckled nervously.

"That's my point, and it's why I came to talk with you. Since I'm in my apprenticeship phase, my father will accompany me until I earn my first star. We never expected to find two of you in Slough, making us split up. However, if I were you, I wouldn't go out anymore.

"The next time I'm with my father, and we spot you, I won't be able to stop him. If anything, I will have to help him," Blake admitted, and then he stood up and got ready to head back to class.

"Wait, Blake! The other were— the other Altered, did your father manage to catch him? Do you know where he is?" Gary asked.

Blake turned around; he didn't look pleased, which was a rare sight. "No, we didn't. Some White Rose agent got in his way, and according to him, he used the chance to escape once that other Altered fled. There's nothing in the news, so I guess they were unable to find that one afterward." He shrugged. "I'm sorry, I thought that the two of us might become good friends, but because of what I am and what you are, it might be best if we kept our distance outside of rugby."

Although Gary didn't know Blake too well, for some reason, his words stung. Maybe it was because he'd learned that the two of them could have been close, or maybe it was something else, but if Gary did meet Blake again, he didn't want to be his enemy. That was for sure.

"Shut up!" Gary shouted. "Don't go deciding that crap on your own! I'll kick your ass at rugby, and I'll kick your ass in fighting as well, but that's it! We can still talk in school; we can still laugh and have fun! You're still you, and I'm still me; nothing has changed! Who cares about who or what we are outside of school?"

Turning back around, Blake gave Gary a sad smile. "And that is why you're dangerous, Gary, because of your beliefs. I hope I won't ever have to pick between you or my father . . ."

ACKNOWLEDGMENTS

I wanted to leave a note to all my readers out there. As many of you know, I started my writing journey online producing webnovels. It quickly grew and became my full-time job. I never expected I would reach this point, and it's all because of those who supported me and continue to support me.

My family adapted to my full-time writing style. The sacrifices they all made were endless. I've lost count of the number of times I would take the laptop to holidays and special events, telling them I needed to write. I am thankful for how understanding they all were.

My father never forced me down any route and was happy to support me; he helped me when I was sick and needed to go to the hospital. My brother, who doesn't speak much in terms of words to me, was always there when I needed him most, and I know that if I were in trouble, he would be one of the first to act. In fact, the main character in this story, Gary, is named after my brother, who is very much my inspiration.

I hope that this book brings everyone who reads it even a small bit of enjoyment.

Thank you for supporting me,
Kawin Jack Sherwin / JKSManga

ABOUT THE AUTHOR

Kawin Jack Sherwin, AKA JKSmanga is an author from the United Kingdom. His works have sold 15 million copies worldwide and been featured on the *New York Times* Billboard. Several of his novels have also been adapted into comic books.

Originally starting as a scriptwriter for popular Japanese manga, Jack eventually took the plunge and wrote his own books, starting his run in the LitRPG genre. *My Werewolf System* is a book written by the author hoping to make werewolves look menacing rather than romantic.

His previous works include the My Dragon System and My Vampire System series, with many more to come.

Visit JKSManga online for updates and exclusive content:
Instagram.com/JKSManga
Facebook.com/JKSManga
Patreon.com/JKSManga

DISCOVER
STORIES UNBOUND

PodiumAudio.com

.

Printed in Great Britain
by Amazon